COMHAIRLE CHONTAE
LEABHARLANNA CHO:

SOMEWHERE IN BETWEEN

Ruth Gilligan grew up in the County Dublin suburb of Blackrock. She is currently reading English at Cambridge University and having a ball. Ruth has always been passionate about writing, and her other hobbies include music, drama, hockey and partying with her friends. She played Laura Halpin in the RTÉ soap *Fair City* for a number of years. *Somewhere in Between* is her second novel.

Also by Ruth Gilligan
Forget

RUTH GILLIGAN

Somewhere in Between

HODDER
HEADLINE
IRELAND

A CIP catalogue record for this title is available from the British Library.

ISBN 978 0340 92350 4

Typeset in Sabon MT by Hodder Headline Ireland
Printed and bound in Great Britain by Clays Ltd, St Ives plc

Hodder Headline Ireland's policy is to use papers that are natural, renewable and recyclable products and made from wood grown in sustainable forests. The logging and manufacturing processes are expected to conform to the environmental regulations of the country of origin.

Hodder Headline Ireland
8 Castlecourt Centre
Castleknock
Dublin 15
Ireland

A division of Hodder Headline
338 Euston Road, London NW1 3BH

www.hhireland.ie

To Mum,
for letting me go away,
but never letting go.

'TOMORROW'

Verse 1

Here we stand with tomorrow staring us in the face,
So take one last good look at this place.
'Cause we can try to hold hands, but it's not always easy,
We can make promises, but they may grow weary.
So just remember the lines on my face.

Chorus

I didn't think that it would be this hard,
To say the things I always knew would come.
I didn't think that it would be this hard,
But my bubble's burst, as I knew it would.
And it slipped through my fingers, yeah . . .

Verse 2

And there's people coming after, so who are we to
Stand in time, and say that we're not ready? Though I want to.
And we can take photos, but they don't taste,
And I can't say that I'm not a little scared.
But I'll leave the sad stuff up to you.

Chorus

Bridge

Here we stand with tomorrow staring us in the face,
So close your eyes,
And live in that bubble, one last time . . .

1

ALEX

Alex put down his pen. He was finished. Business Studies, the Leaving Cert, being locked up by his parents – it was all over. Life definitely began today, and he was finally completely free of school and all the restrictions that came with it. But rather than feeling the huge sense of relief others had expressed, or any sense of achievement, the only thought that filled his mind was how unbelievably drunk he was going to get that night.

As Alex sauntered out of the exam hall, his friend Barry casually enquired, "How did you find it?"

But Alex didn't care. Why would he bother wasting even the tiniest bit more energy thinking about anything to do with those exams? If truth were told, he'd found the paper impossible, probably because he hadn't done any preparation for it. But that didn't matter to him –

Alex had never been the academic type. In fact, he'd failed practically everything in his mocks and had always made it very clear that, in his eyes, apart from sport and socialising, school was a waste of time. So all that had concerned him over the course of the Leaving Cert was getting through it – until summer was finally upon him and freedom was his.

"Barry, fuck the exams – they're over. Let's go get wasted!" he announced with enthusiasm, chucking his schoolbag into the bin and swaggering out of his school for the very last time. Next stop – the pub!

*

Three more friends joined them and Barry ordered the pints. A relatively small amount were actually finished all their exams that day – some still had a week-and-a-half to wait before it was over. But Alex had chosen the subjects which would let him finish earliest, and he realised now that it was probably the best decision he'd ever made. The beer garden of their local was filling up, owing to the warmth of the afternoon sun. Two blondes were sipping WKD Blues in the corner and casting glances in Alex's direction. He was pretty sure he'd scored one of them before and mentally high-fived himself as she was definitely a looker.

"Walshy, do you know those birds?" One of the lads broke Alex's train of thought.

"Yeah, scored them both a while ago." Alex stretched the truth. "Anyway, fuck that, what's the plan for tonight?" Alex demanded, as they launched into a long discussion involving nightclubs, house parties and, most importantly, lots of alcohol.

Seven o'clock arrived out of nowhere and Alex, having knocked back his sixth pint, was hungry. He assumed his mother would have food ready for him and willingly accepted a lift home from Barry, despite his friend having had a similar number of drinks. Anyway, all that drink-driving lark was rubbish – they did it all the time and never had a problem. Blaring the music in Barry's Volkswagen Golf, Alex rolled down the windows and enjoyed the breeze as they zoomed down the dual carriageway. The speed, the alcohol, the constant remembering that he had finally finished the Leaving – Alex felt good. Life really had begun.

*

Alex's head hurt when he opened his eyes. He could hear a loud beeping and a faint buzz of conversation. He tried to sit up, but a sharp sting in his chest prevented him. What was going on? His whole being throbbed. Where was he? His view was slightly clouded as he stared up at an unfamiliar ceiling and his heart thumped loudly. He tried to make sense of it all as his mind tried to awaken itself as if from beneath a dark mist of the unknown. But then that unmistakable smell met his nose and it all became clear – he was in hospital. What the hell? He strained to remember how he'd got there, but all his mind could manage was a vague image of a red light, and the car not stopping and . . . Barry!

"*Psst* – Baz, wake up," he hissed up at the ceiling, assuming his friend nearby would hear.

"Oi, Barry, you muppet, you must have crashed the Golf." Alex laughed, seeing the funny side of the whole thing. But there was no reply. Unwillingly, he rolled his head slowly to the right, then to the left. No sign of Barry. Alex was confused. Just then a nurse walked in, and Alex started to realise how good this situation could be. But, seeing his eyes open, she ran away and came dashing back in again moments later, followed by a retinue of familiar faces. Alex's mum and sister, as well as Barry's parents, all looked panicked and, surrounding him, began to talk all at once.

11

"Oh my God, you're OK."

"Oh my God, what happened?"

"I can't believe you're awake."

"We were just getting coffee, I promise – we'd been with you all evening."

Alex wished they'd all shut up and, happily, as he opened his mouth to speak, an expectant hush fell upon the group.

"What time is it?" he asked.

Looking a little puzzled and slightly disappointed, his sister Chloe replied, "Just past ten."

Alex's heart sank – there went his chances of going out that night. What about celebrating? Now he'd be stuck in this smelly bed for the evening with this lot for company. The questions began again.

"Alex, dear, what happened?" His mother was close to tears.

"Mum, relax – I'm grand. We were just driving home from the pub and"

"Had Barry been drinking?" Barry's father interrupted, looking equally harrowed. Alex didn't know whether or not to lie, but since his head was too sore to think of anything other than the truth, he simply replied, "He'd had a couple, like. Sure we finished our bloody exams, for God's sake. Here, can I get some Panadol or something – my head's fucking killing me."

But rather than pandering to him as he'd assumed they would, Alex's spectators merely shook their heads, each one paler than the next, as Barry's mother began to sob.

Why were they all freaking out? He was grand – all he had was a slight headache and Barry was presumably fine as well, wherever he was. He doubted it had been like one of those crashes from the television – just a small knock.

"Barry hasn't woken up yet," Chloe whispered, while the adults all conversed in hushed tones at the end of the bed. Alex's head started to spin.

"Alex, what the hell – you could have died," Chloe continued, playing the mature one as usual. Although they were twins, Alex always felt that in serious situations she acted so much older than him. It was typical of her to make such a fuss.

"Chloe, please – I'm fine."

"Alex, you were in a car crash! You hit your head, Barry's still unconscious – how is that fine?"

"I told you – all I have is a headache. Baz will be back with us by morning. Please stop trying to freak me out."

"I'm not *trying* to do anything – I just don't get how you can be so calm!" Chloe spat. She stared at her brother with angry eyes, then softened again.

"Seriously though, Alex, you could have died. Imagine stressing for so long about the stupid Leaving and then killing yourself in a fucking drink-driving accident. Mum and Dad were petrified."

"Well it's a good thing I'm OK then, isn't it?" Alex tried to lighten the mood – he could see his sister was very stressed and she didn't deserve to be so worried over him. "Chloe, I'm fine. Let's just be thankful for that, yeah?" he assured her. She paused, and he realised just how tired she looked.

"Yeah, I guess. Just cross your fingers for Barry, yeah?" Chloe put her hand on Alex's shoulder in a rare moment of shared affection. It felt strange, yet appropriate. But Alex was too tired to reply and, as his eyes grew heavy again, he drifted off into a deep, welcome sleep. So this was what freedom felt like?

The next day, after rigorous tests conducted by some less-than-enticing nurses, Alex was deemed fit to return home, though he was given strict instructions to rest and avoid any sort of activity for at least two weeks. With the Leaving Cert Ball just over a week away, Alex was going to make it his aim to be fit enough to attend – like Cinderella, he definitely would go to the Ball! Unfortunately, Barry hadn't woken up yet. Part of Alex felt slightly anxious about this, but another part reckoned at least he wasn't dead, and he inwardly prayed it was just Barry being typically lazy about the whole thing. Word had spread about the accident and, as soon as he got home from the hospital, Alex was inundated with texts and phone calls, all eager to hear him recount the tale. There wasn't really much to tell, but nevertheless Alex was glad of all the contact. His friends seemed quite shocked at Barry's continued lack of consciousness, but Alex assured them that it all would be fine – it had to be, hadn't it?

The days that followed were a blur and Alex was strangely appreciative of the chance to switch off after all the build-up before the exams. Chloe was still studying away, as her Spanish exam was the coming Tuesday. Alex never understood how, or why, she worked so hard. She wasn't a genius by any stretch of the imagination, but around exam time, particularly this year, she'd been spending more and more time at her desk, endlessly cramming. It always surprised people, including Alex, how well she did in school – growing up, Chloe had had something of a reputation amongst her peers of being a "party girl" and had probably scored the vast majority of South Dublin at one point or another. Alex used to be embarrassed by this, particularly as he too tried to mingle amongst the same people, but luckily, more and more, Chloe had calmed down, even getting a steady boyfriend, and Alex was now definitely the sibling with the notches on his bedpost. Just as it should be.

*

The police needed Alex to make a statement about the crash, and for some reason this unnerved him greatly. He had avoided actually delving into his memory to try to ascertain what exactly had happened. Why did it matter? He was fine and Barry . . . Alex felt his chest tighten slightly. Every day that passed, he was sure it would be the one when the phone rang, bringing news of Barry's awakening. But the call never came. It had been less than a week, Alex conceded. But he couldn't talk to anyone about his worries, not wanting to admit them out loud, and still holding on very tightly to the certainty that soon, very soon, it would all be OK.

*

Friday evening arrived and Barry was still in a coma. It was the night of the Leaving Cert Ball and, despite everything, Alex was damned if he wasn't going to go. He knew it was rather late to discuss it with his parents and hoped that this would in fact work to his advantage. He felt fine. Well, maybe not fine exactly – his head still hurt – but he'd feel a lot worse if he missed out on the social event of the year to date, and had to stay within those same four walls for yet another night. Tuesday evening had been hell, as Chloe came home from her last exam brimming with glee. She and her friends were going out on the town and Alex had never been so jealous in his entire life.

His dad came home from work. It was time to make his plea.

"Dad?" He tried to sound casual.

"Yeah?" his father replied, sounding weary from his week's work.

"Look, I was just wondering . . . the Leaving Cert Ball's tonight, and, like . . . everyone's going and I really do feel OK . . ." he lied, desperate to convince.

"So what are you asking?" Mr Walsh cut to the chase, knowing where this was leading and not liking it one bit.

"Well, like, can I . . . can I go? Please?" Alex begged.

His dad paused, his brow wrinkled into a half-frown as his conscience deliberated with itself.

"Alex, to be honest, I'm not sure that's the best idea . . ."

"Dad, seriously, I feel grand," Alex interrupted, foreseeing his father's complaint.

"To be honest, Alex, it's not just your health I'm worried about," he explained, his brow looking increasingly furrowed.

"What?" Alex queried, confused.

"Well, son, I just think . . . it's only been a week . . ."

"Ten days," Alex corrected.

"OK, fine, ten days. But it's a bit soon, don't you think?"

"What . . . Dad, what are you getting at? If you're not talking about my health, what the hell are you talking about?"

Mr Walsh seemed intensely hassled as he grappled with his thoughts.

"Look, Alex, do you not just think . . . well . . . you've more important things to be thinking about than . . . than balls right now?"

"What do you mean?" Alex asked, confused.

"I mean, Alex . . . look, we need to talk – your mother and I have been meaning to sit you down . . . but you've been weak and recovering and we didn't know when was the best time, but . . ."

"Dad, just spit it out!" Alex's frustration was growing – all he cared about right now was getting out tonight.

"Alex, I'm talking about the small fact of the near-death experience you had last week – or, sorry, have you forgotten about it?" His father's voice was sarcastic, getting louder with every word.

"I'm sorry?"

"Well, in case you hadn't noticed, Alex, you and your friend were in a drink-driving accident that almost killed you both. Do you not think you need a bit of perspective before you go gallivanting out on the town again? I mean, for Christ's sake!" his Dad bellowed, looking thoroughly agitated. Alex knew that when his father used the Lord's name in vain, it had to be bad. Mr Walsh was taken aback by the strength of his own words, and took a deep breath to calm himself down.

"I'm sorry . . ." he said, his breath heavy as he met his son's eyes.

"Dad, please, can we not do this now? No matter what happened last week, I've still just finished my Leaving Cert. I still deserve to celebrate like all my friends, for God's sake. I've been cooped up here like a fucking prisoner – can I not have one night of fun at least?" Alex pleaded. He had never seen his father like this before, and what was even more worrying was that he had no clue why he was freaking out so much.

Mr Walsh had steadied himself once more, and now just looked completely sapped of energy, his suit and tie hanging limply on his weary frame.

"Just go," he muttered.

"What?"

"Go – go have fun. You're right – you do deserve it . . ."

"Dad, what's wrong?" Alex wondered, confused by his father's defeated tone.

"Nothing . . . look, just go enjoy yourself. We can talk about this some other time . . . Just have a good night, but for God's sake, don't overdo it, and don't do anything stupid." With that, he turned on his heels and headed to the kitchen, hunched over and looking older than ever.

Alex didn't know what to feel. Part of him felt thrilled with the unexpected turn of events, but another part was shocked at the pathetic reduction of his father he'd just witnessed. He seemed so upset. Something wasn't right.

*

An hour later Paddy Walsh returned his son's goodbye and heard the front door slam. Chloe too had gone out, and his wife was still not home, working late in the office as she so often did. He sat on the couch, half-listening to the news, but finding his mind preoccupied with other matters, as it had been ever since the accident. He still couldn't get his head around it, still couldn't believe that his son, whom he loved so very much, had taken such a risk – made such a foolish decision – and almost lost his life. He couldn't even begin to imagine what was going through Barry's father's head at that moment. He prayed for him every night, his heart aching as he compared his son's narrow escape to their son's fate. Yet all week he'd watched Alex, sitting in front of the TV day in, day out, and never once did he mention it. Never once did he seem slightly perturbed, regretful even, that he had been so stupid as to allow his friend to drive drunk, putting both their lives at risk. Maybe the reality just hadn't hit him – maybe Alex was still in shock. But although Paddy Walsh did not wish any sort of pain or anxiety upon his boy, this was something he needed to be bothered by – Alex needed to take a step back and realise just how very foolish, and lucky, he'd been.

*

The pre-Ball drinks were taking place in Alex's friend Andy's house, where Alex was being quizzed by an attentive group of girls about the sequence of events that had led to his friend's coma.

"So, was he covered in blood?"

"You must have been traumatised?"

"An experience like that must really change your life?"

The girls, as usual, were reading way too much into the whole thing, but Alex was never one to turn down female attention, especially when numerous pairs of made-up eyes were fixed sympathetically upon him.

"To be honest, I was just in shock. I think I still am. I'm worried about Baz, but at the same time, I know he'll pull through. He's so brave . . ." Alex poured out the soppiest stuff he could manage. The girls were lapping it up. It felt good. To his left, his friend was rolling a joint, crumbling the hash between his fingers and sprinkling it over the tobacco as if it was second nature to him. To most of the guys there, it almost was. Alex took another swig on his beer and, although his head still thumped, it was steadily growing lighter with each can. Jennifer, a girl with whom Alex and his friends had always hung out, and whom Alex had scored several times before, was looking particularly good. Her tight black dress hugged her slim, curvy frame, and Alex had a feeling that, tonight, history would be repeating itself. Again.

"Hey Jenny." He nodded as she walked by.

"Oh, it's the hero of the hour," Jenny replied brightly, though there was an undeniable edge to her voice. Alex knew he'd broken Jenny's heart more than once in the past, and thus she was always slightly wary of him. That said, they still got on well and he knew how to play her. So although it would take more effort than usual for Alex, the image of that dress and, more importantly, what was under it, was enough incentive to fuel his quest.

"Jen, aren't you glad I'm alive? I heard you were sick with worry – couldn't sleep a wink," Alex teased, noting a slight flicker in Jenny's piercing stare.

"It's hardly a joking matter, Alex. A lot of the guys are really cut up about it all. And anyway, you know I hate it when you call me Jen." She was trying hard to resist him, but he could feel her slowly being drawn in.

"Sorry," he said gently, "my head's still a bit all over the place from the crash. You look amazing by the way." He undressed her with his ice-blue eyes and she sat down beside him, knowing she shouldn't, but unable to stop herself.

Her friends stared as they witnessed the familiar sight of Jennifer being taken in again by Alex Walsh. But their stares were of two emotions – disappointment, as they'd spent so many nights wiping

Jenny's tears after Alex let her down for the millionth time. But also jealousy that such a hot boy, even higher on his pedestal now that he'd survived a near-death experience, was showing interest in her and not them. It wasn't fair.

Andy too was disappointed, having just come back outside with a drink for Jenny to find that his seat had been taken by his best friend. Some things would never change, he shrugged, deciding to down the drink himself in one go and get on with his night.

"Have you been in to see Barry yet?" Jenny asked tentatively.

"Seen him? Jen – he's asleep. Why would I go in to visit him?"

"They say they can still hear you, though, feel you there. It just seems so weird going out like this when he's so ill. His parents must be distraught." Jenny seemed so affected by Barry's state that Alex couldn't help but feel a little jealous. Why was everyone making such a fuss? Barry was fine – he was asleep – as soon as people started worrying it meant there was actually something seriously the matter. Barry would be fine! He just wished they wouldn't feel so bad that they were out celebrating their exams being over. Had they forgotten about the months of torture and nasty cramming they'd just endured? Luckily, Jenny noticed his agitation and knew she had to change the subject.

"Sorry, Alex, I know you must be really sensitive about it all. I shouldn't go on about it. Anyway, how did you find the exams?" she tried.

Alex wasn't entirely happy with the new topic of conversation either, but cracking open his next can and taking a long gulp, he realised that thanks to the exams, it had been over a month since his last 'proper' encounter with a girl. Thus if a couple of lines about some tough papers was going to secure him what he wanted, so be it. He was horny, and Jennifer would soon be his.

*

SOMEWHERE IN BETWEEN

They stumbled into taxis and stumbled back out when they'd reached the venue for the completely sold out Leaving Cert Ball. A huge queue stretched back from the main door, but luckily Alex was his school's rep for all such events and so was entitled to use the VIP entrance. He could bring one other person into the VIP area too and knew that Jenny had assumed she'd be his chosen companion for the night. But, realising he was starting to sober up, Alex grabbed Andy instead and informed him that there was some serious drinking to be done. Andy did not object.

The exclusive VIP area was very impressive and as Alex surveyed the plush couches, countless candles, and most of all large supply of good-looking females, he knew just how good the night would be. The lads headed to the bar, pausing only to greet a few girls they knew, who threw their arms around Alex and flirted outrageously with him. They had heard about the crash, but unable to waffle before he'd had at least three more drinks, Alex continued to the bar. He ordered two pints for himself and Andy, but the barmaid's reply was not what they had expected.

"Eh, boys, look behind you," she suggested. "It's all free."

Sure enough, across the room was a huge table completely covered in alcopops, there for the taking. Being a rep definitely had its perks! The boys headed over and, like kids in a candy shop, picked up two drinks each and knocked them back, the sweet liquid quenching their thirst and sugaring their excited taste buds. Downstairs, where the rest of the crowd was, the DJ interrupted one of the latest tunes to enquire, "Hey, did anyone here just finish their Leaving Ce-e-e-ert?"

The whole place erupted with screams and shouts of pure delight and relief. Alex felt every inch of him relax, and almost two thousand fellow sixth-years shared his glee.

"Hey you," a familiar voice called out from behind once the screaming had subsided. He turned around to the face he knew so well. On nights like this they often completely ignored one another,

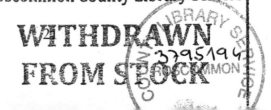

but tonight his sister was obviously under the influence, too.

"Hey, Chloe. So sweet there's free drink, isn't it?"

"Yeah, I know. I love being a rep! Pity the alcopops are minging, but whatever. How were your pre-drinks?"

"Pretty good. I thought your lot were going to pop down?" Chloe and Alex's friends sometimes hung out together.

"Yeah, we ended up going to this other guy's house. He had free champagne so that was the end of that!" Chloe hiccupped, sending her friend beside her into convulsions of laughter.

Chloe then announced that she was off to find her boyfriend, Sam, and instructed both Alex and Andy to have a "savage" night.

As she strutted away, swaying slightly, Andy couldn't help himself. "I know you're going to kill me, but your sister is looking so hot tonight."

Alex felt the usual twinge he always did when his friends reminded him of how highly they rated his sister. He wasn't protective of her; he just found it weird that anyone could even look at her in that way. Some of them had even scored her in the past, but his reaction had warned the whole group that, at least for the time being, Chloe Walsh was out of bounds.

The majority of the night passed in a blur, and Alex was in flying form. The car crash was an instant ticket to free drinks, and once the table of alcopops had emptied, Alex moved back downstairs to join the main crowd, where his hand was never devoid of a glass. Outside, the smoking area was completely packed, and Alex decided a cigarette was just what he wanted. He got one from a guy he used to play rugby with and then located his own friends, lighting up and pulling deeply on the cigarette. His gang cheered loudly when he arrived.

"Man, you are the only person I know who would be out drinking and smoking only a week after a fucking car accident," one of his friends said, clapping Alex on the back.

Alex merely smiled, feeling proud, as he joined in the usual messing and bantering with the guys. But suddenly he realised one or two of them weren't playing along – they were exchanging rueful glances which, had Alex not known better, he would have seen as unimpressed. Surely he was just seeing things, he laughed to himself – there was no reason for anyone to feel any sort of disdain towards him. He had done nothing wrong, had he?

His chest was still sore from the safety belt and as he rubbed it gently, swigging on his beer, he spotted a confused-looking Jenny, who was obviously looking for someone. Alex grinned to himself, knowing exactly who that someone was, and, walking up behind her, placed his hands around her waist. She jumped.

"Oh, Alex, it's you." She had obviously found what she'd been looking for, but did not seem best pleased. "Where have you been all night? It's nearly two. I've been looking . . ." Jenny didn't want to seem too desperate.

". . . for me? I was up in the VIP area for ages, and other than that I've just been getting mashed," Alex slurred, but seeing the anger in Jenny's eyes, decided to change his tack. "I've been looking for you for the last hour, though," he insisted and, surprisingly, it seemed as if she believed him.

"I'm really sorry – Danielle got totally drunk and has been throwing up in the toilet for ages. I had to stay with her, I'm sorry," Jenny pleaded.

Alex feigned hurt but then, unable to suppress himself any longer, as she just looked so sexy, grabbed her and kissed her. His mind was blurry and he had to concentrate to keep his balance, but as she pressed herself against him, desiring him as much as ever, he suddenly knew exactly what he wanted.

"Do you want to get out of here?" he suggested, hoping she'd ignore the chorus of "Walshy" that flowed from his friends, who had obviously seen their kiss.

"Alex, I don't know, is that such a good idea?"

"Of course it's a good idea. You look amazing tonight – what's the problem with me wanting you?" He played innocent, feeling something stir in his trousers as his body anticipated what was to come. Jenny looked away and then stared right into Alex's eyes, searching for something that Alex prayed she'd find.

"Jen, it's us – what could be so wrong about that?" Alex reassured her, knowing that, in fact, there were several answers to that question, but hoping she'd see past them.

Jenny took a step closer and, leaning into him, whispered, "My parents went away this evening. We can go back to mine. I'll just go grab my stuff."

Alex was elated. That had been easy! As Jenny headed to the cloakroom, he rejoined his friends, finished his cigarette and announced that he was leaving.

"But it's only half two – what the fuck?" one of the idiots who obviously hadn't caught on complained.

"I'm going back to Jenny's. Don't wait up." Alex gave a little wink to the group, turned on his heels and swaggered back inside. He realised the cheesiness of his parting comment but didn't care – he knew he was the envy of all his friends. The lads watched on: some in awe, some less so, but all, in one way or another, thinking of Barry. It wasn't right.

Alex's head felt light as he passed the crowded dance floor, noting only his sister and her boyfriend having yet another fight. "Oh well," he laughed to himself, joining the expectant Jenny and leading the way outside, feeling on top of the world.

*

Jenny seemed nervous as she unlocked her front door. Alex couldn't understand why – they'd done this many times before. And although he could tell she would have preferred to hang out and chat before they moved upstairs, he wanted her now. As soon as the door was closed he grabbed her, kissing her passionately, not caring that he probably tasted of smoke and alcohol. She melted into him and Alex ran his hands all over her, lifting her dress up to her waist and grinding against her as her back pressed against the door. They kissed and kissed until finally her hands began to undo his belt and Alex truly believed he could take it no more. He wanted to take her there and then but knew she'd never allow it, so instead he pulled away and suggested, as tenderly as he could manage, that they go upstairs. He led the way, knowing the familiar route to her room even through his drunken haze, and couldn't help but smile as they entered her pale-pink boudoir. It looked so girlie, so innocent, and yet it would only be a matter of minutes before she was moaning loudly, doing things to him that were far from innocent.

They undressed as quickly as possible, Alex's heart pumping loudly, yearning for everything that was to come. This was definitely the best way imaginable to celebrate his freedom – nothing mattered any more except the blinding pleasure which filled him as Jenny drove him wild. The Leaving Cert was over; he could do whatever he pleased. Life truly had begun.

2

CHLOE

Chloe watched as her brother stumbled past the dance floor looking very merry indeed. She had seen Jennifer passing that way only moments earlier and wondered were they headed for the same place. "Probably," she conceded, not wanting to imagine where exactly Jenny and her bother were off to. Chloe had sobered up significantly since the start of the night – she hadn't really had a choice, since here she was, at the side of the dance floor, wishing the ground would swallow her up and take her away from Sam. How had this happened? It was supposed to be the perfect night – their exams were over, they had only a week until Sam left for France on holidays and they had both agreed to make their time together amazing. But now they stood, in complete silence, not knowing what to say. All around them people danced to the pumping music, laughing and having fun, basking in their unfamiliar state of carefree joy. Nearby, a couple talked and kissed – the brown-haired girl looked up at her boy, her ringlets cascading down her back like a torrent of water, dazzling beneath the disco lights. They looked so happy, so in love. The boy took the girl's hand and spun her around like a dainty ballerina, their fingers intertwining together perfectly. Their smiles mirrored each other, as if nothing else mattered in the whole room but the pure joy that connected them both. Chloe was jealous.

Standing almost four feet from her, Sam had folded his arms and was also gazing around the room, his brow slightly tensed, obviously discontented. Bad moods didn't suit him. He was always the bright, happy one whom everyone loved – especially Chloe. Thus, whenever he was angry it was as if he was wearing something that didn't fit. He looked awkward, like a small boy wearing Daddy's shirt, swamped in a mood that would never convince.

They'd met earlier in the year at a French grind. There were only four people in the class, and since the other two girls had known each other, Sam and Chloe had had little choice but to talk to one another. Slowly a friendship had begun to form between them, and eventually something more. Sam wasn't like the other boys Chloe had usually gone for or been with. He wasn't tough or arrogant or worried about what people thought of him – he was just Sam. The guys Chloe hung around with, and particularly Alex, had taken a while to warm to him, finding his lack of inhibitions and disinterest in teenage politics so different from those in their circle. But as time passed, it became clear that Sam was just too nice not to be liked. Chloe had never been in love properly before Sam, but now she was completely smitten. Lately, however, between the stress of the exams and the looming inevitability of college and the future, cracks had begun to form in their seemingly unbreakable connection, and Chloe was scared by these more than she cared to admit.

"Chloe, please, this is stupid," Sam tried, finally ending the silence which had hung between them for almost five minutes now. She knew he was right. She could barely pinpoint what they were fighting about, though recently it seemed as if they didn't need a reason. But tonight was supposed to be fun. It was the first time they'd been out together in so long, and she'd been looking forward to it for weeks. He was right: this was stupid.

"I know it is. I just wish this didn't keep happening to us, that's all," Chloe sighed.

"So let's not let it. We've both been all over the place, studying and worrying and giving the Leaving our all. But it's over. It's all finished and we have the whole summer ahead of us. We have everything ahead of us. So let's start from now!" Sam really was amazing. Chloe knew he too was head over heels for her, and that was easily the best feeling in the world. She kissed him softly, slowly becoming that dainty ballerina who had been spun about in a flurry of joy. Sam was right. They had everything ahead of them. They'd be OK.

At half-past three the lights went up and the party was over. Chloe held Sam's hand tightly, as she had done from the moment they'd made up, and as they made for the cloakroom, a salty smell distracted the pair and changed their destination. Hot dogs! A queue had formed as tired, drunk, but delighted eyes sparkled at the sight of two Chinese ladies selling the freshly cooked food. This was too good to be true. Sam decided to go get their coats from the cloakroom while Chloe queued for the food. They separated with a kiss and Chloe was glad that things seemed back on track between them. She couldn't bear it any other way.

Slowly she edged her way up the line of hungry teenagers. The group of boys in front of her could barely stand and were slurring to one another in voices which Chloe could hardly comprehend.

"Do we have to go to that stupid house party . . .?"

"Come on, lads – there's going to be sooo many drugs . . ."

"I just want to get sick . . ."

"This hot dog's going to be fucking amazing . . ."

"High-five . . ."

Chloe couldn't help laughing as some of the most impressive sportsmen of the South Dublin rugby scene fell about the place. Their designer polo shirts with the collars up were stained with spilled drinks and other mysterious-looking marks, and she knew that they would definitely have sore heads in the morning. She'd been with one of them before, when they were younger, at their old regular disco. She really had changed since then. Every Friday she would dress up in a pretty top and jeans and her mother would drop her out to Donnybrook to go "dancing" with her friends. But as soon as she was in the door of the venue, she'd run, like the majority of other girls, straight to the toilets to put on a tiny piece of material that she hoped could masquerade as a skirt. Usually she'd been drinking beforehand. Usually she'd score at least a handful of boys in one night. Usually she'd get sick. Chloe couldn't help feeling slightly ashamed of her behaviour in "the good old days", but she'd had fun and that was what mattered. Most of all, she'd grown up so much since then, and now that she had Sam there would be no turning back.

As she neared the top of the queue, she began to feel strange. She watched one of the servers add greasy onions and a river of ketchup to someone's hot dog and wondered was it really worth it? During the exams, Chloe had felt that all she did was study and eat, so now that they were over, it was time to keep an eye on her diet. It was so hard – all night she'd looked around the room and seen skinny girl after skinny girl, surrounded by guys. None of them was in the queue. She knew she was still slim, but the extra study weight worried her and she vowed she'd get rid of it, and then some, by the end of the summer.

"One hot dog, please," Chloe ordered, her mind made up. She added her own onions, ketchup, mustard – the works. She wanted so badly to take a bite, but she couldn't. She waited for Sam to return with the coats and then presented him with his feast.

"Where's yours?" he enquired, taking his first mouthful.

"Eh, I already ate it."

"Really?" Sam managed, chewing appreciatively.

"Yeah, I skipped the queue so by the time you were finished getting the coats I had polished it off – it was just so yummy!" Chloe didn't like lying to Sam. But if she hadn't, she would have to explain her reasoning to him and he would never understand – he'd probably just launch into a spiel about how her figure was perfect and there was no need to take such measures. But there was a need. He had to say she looked perfect, but she knew otherwise. Just a few pounds less and she'd be happy. She was in control. It felt good.

*

The next morning, Chloe was awoken by the humming of her phone. She fumbled with it lazily until it displayed the message.

I'M OUTSIDE. 4GOT MY KEY – LET ME IN QUICK.

Chloe groaned, throwing her phone across her bed and cursing her brother for taking her away from her warm nest. She trundled down the stairs, making a vague attempt to stay quiet, as her parents were still asleep. Opening the front door, she said nothing, just glared at an apologetic Alex and turned on her heel.

"Thanks, Chloe—" Alex began, but she interrupted with an acknowledging grunt, not wanting to engage in any sort of conversation. She needed her bed.

Slipping between her sheets once more, Chloe replayed the previous night in her head. She and Sam had shared a taxi, finally finding one amidst the havoc which had ensued after the Ball. Fights were starting, and a flashing ambulance pulled up, obviously to cart off some poor girl who had had a few too many – the usual early morning scene. They'd eventually hailed their ride home and once the taxi had pulled up outside her house, Chloe had been sure that things were perfect once more between her and Sam. But was that enough? Why did they have to keep fighting? What was the point in always being perfect in the aftermath when the row before was so painful? Lying in her bed now, Chloe wrestled with her thoughts before realising that she definitely wasn't going back to sleep.

Standing up once more, her head gently spinning, Chloe went downstairs. The summer light poured into the kitchen, pale and dazzling at the same time. Wrenching open the fridge, the cool air gushing over her warm body, she closed her eyes in appreciation before taking the orange juice and pouring a large glass. She stepped out into the garden, her bare feet tickled by the grass and her eyes stinging slightly from the strengthening sun. The sky was unusually blue – as always, the weather had been brilliant during the exams, but Chloe prayed it would last just a bit longer, rewarding her for her patience all through June. A breeze blew, tickling the leaves of the apple tree. Chloe couldn't help but smile. The morning birds sang their beautiful tune as they hopped from branch to branch, chatting to one another like middle-aged women, eager to share, to know, to be heard. One washed itself in the birdbath, dipping its tiny head into the cold pool, fluttering its wings with glee and sending little splashes around it, like a small child learning to swim. Chloe loved summer. "Who doesn't?" she wondered. It was peace and warmth and happiness, and nothing was going to spoil her coming months. She had definitely earned it. Her stomach began to rumble, but she told herself to ignore it and took another gulp of orange juice. It was cold in her mouth and as she swallowed she could feel it chilling her insides. The fruity taste awakened her taste buds. See – she could have a satisfying breakfast without wolfing down a huge fry like her brother so often did. This losing weight thing was going to be easy, she assured herself happily, breathing in the fresh morning air and letting summer fill her. At last.

*

Chloe had always wanted to be an actress. As a child, like all her friends, she had aspired to glorious fantasies of the lives of movie stars. But as her peers slowly grew out of this, deciding such stars were simply meant to be watched and read about, Chloe remained eager to pursue her dream – be it on stage, television or the big screen. She attended drama classes once a week, but rarely admitted to anyone how seriously she took them. When she performed, she came alive. Immersing herself in another character, truly becoming someone else, was a skill she treasured and the thought of doing it as a career – being paid to practise her passion – was her dream. Her first choice in college was Drama in Trinity. Her first choice for a diploma was Drama in the Dublin Institute of Technology.

She had attended auditions for both and had been extremely nervous, knowing that how she presented herself on those single days would decide her fate. So she had given it her all and rehearsed constantly in the build-up. Both colleges had accepted her – pending her achieving sufficient Leaving Cert points, of course. But Trinity's ask was going to be much higher and Chloe doubted that she'd get in. But DIT would still give her the chance to practise the thing she loved and that, for her, would be enough. She hoped. During the exams, and even now, in the aftermath, as people spoke more and more of their hopes and aspirations for the coming year, the words "Trinity" and "UCD" rolled off the tongues of everyone she met. They were all going there.

But what about her? Of course, college was about moving out into the real world, but the thought of ending up in Drama in DIT, outside the bubble which she'd lived in for so long, was more daunting than she cared to admit. All her friends from different schools would now be united in this new world that, sadly, she wouldn't be a part of. And was her dream of studying drama enough to make it worth rejecting that world? Was she sacrificing too much? She pushed these thoughts to the back of her mind, compressing them so much it hurt, willing them to leave her alone and let her enjoy her summer.

*

"Morning!"

Hours later, Mrs Walsh awoke her daughter, who had been dozing on the couch. Even though she was only wearing a pale-pink T-shirt and shorts, Chloe's mum looked radiant. She always did. She was the sort of woman who could roll out of bed, dress herself in a black sack yet still look glamorous. Chloe admired her mother for this: the way she held herself, the way that even now – in what she had to admit was middle age – she possessed an elegant beauty. Mrs Walsh worked hard, a busy solicitor who was very much in demand, but still retained her soft complexion and a relaxed grace.

"Morning, Mum," Chloe managed, her head still fuzzy from her slumber.

"So, how was the Ball?" Mrs Walsh enquired brightly.

"Amazing. I'm wrecked, though. Is Alex up yet?"

"You must be joking! Still in a coma . . ." She trailed off, remembering that, since the accident, those were not words that could be used lightly. Briskly, she changed the subject.

"Did you take many photos? I'd love to see all the girls' dresses. Though your Dior number did look exquisite."

"Thanks, Mum." Chloe smiled. If her mother, the most fashionable lady she knew, said she'd looked good, then she definitely had.

"Where's Dad?" Chloe continued.

"Darling, it's a Saturday morning – where do you think he is?" Her mother was referring to the golf course. Chloe thought it was odd that she was not accompanying her husband as she so often did.

"I'd already agreed to do lunch with Sally, ages ago," Mrs Walsh said, noting her daughter's questioning eyes. "Pity – it's fabulous weather for a round. Oh well . . ." She headed back to the kitchen for a cappuccino and some organic muesli. Chloe vowed that when she was her mother's age, she too would eat healthily and try to maintain her figure. Though she didn't quite have one she'd like to maintain yet. She glared at her love handles, wishing they'd just disappear.

*

Sam's two-week trip to France edged closer every day. Naturally he was eager to spend as much time as possible with Chloe before he left. However, much as she knew she'd miss him, Chloe couldn't deny that she was beginning to feel smothered by her boyfriend's affections. Every day they had hung out or gone out or stayed in, and there were times when Chloe wished she could just crash in front of the telly, alone or with her girlfriends, or better still go for a run, and just have some time to herself. One night on the phone, she tried to make him understand.

"We'll definitely do something tomorrow evening, I was just thinking of going shopping with the girls tomorrow," she said lightly.

"But I'm leaving in three days, babe. I thought we could do something for the afternoon."

"Don't get me wrong, I want to see you too. But we've done something nearly every day since the Leaving finished – I just want to have some time with my friends, you know," Chloe explained.

"But you can have all the time in the world with them when I'm gone. I'll be in France soon and you guys can see each other morning, noon and night."

Chloe paused.

"Please, babe, we said we'd hang out tomorrow." Sam was becoming more insistent, and although Chloe knew this was just because of his love for her, it was becoming frustrating.

"Sam, it's one bloody afternoon. I just want time for me. From the moment the exams ended we've spent so much time together. Don't get me wrong – I love spending time with you. But I just want to be selfish for once and do my own thing."

"But why am I not part of that thing?" Sam enquired.

"You are! Sometimes! But not all the time. Just this once I want to do something else. It's not a crime!"

"You don't get it." Sam sighed.

"You're the one who doesn't get it." Chloe realised her voice was getting louder, but she couldn't help it. "You're only going for a couple of weeks. Stop being fucking selfish – I want to see my girls. So shoot me. Why are you being like this?" Chloe closed her eyes and willed herself to calm down. It wasn't that big a deal – so why was she getting so worked up? Her breathing was heavy and as the silence ached down the line, she prayed she hadn't gone too far.

"Fine," Sam finally whispered. "It's not about your friends. I just wanted to see you – that's all. Enjoy shopping."

"But we'll do something tomorrow evening, yeah?" Chloe asked brightly, trying to lift her boyfriend's scarily low tone.

"Yeah, maybe," Sam sighed. "Night, Chloe."

"Night. I love you."

"I love you too."

And he was gone. Chloe felt like kicking herself. Why had she done that? She wanted to see him tomorrow – of course she did. But shopping sounded like fun, too. She needed to get out of the house. She needed to control the confusion, the mixture of guilt and triumph, which ran through her. Changing quickly into shorts and a T-shirt, she left her house and began to run. Stars pierced the jet-black sky and the quiet streets seemed to welcome the heavy thud of Chloe's steps. She would run and run and run until it hurt, until she burned off as many calories as she could, until she could rid her mind of every last drop of guilt about Sam. The night would watch her struggle.

3

ALEX

Mrs Walsh plated up the roast chicken and baked potatoes before pouring herself another glass of wine. Alex was starving. Having been at the gym for most of the afternoon, he felt completely empty and was dying to tuck into this steaming feast. His father said Grace, as he always insisted on doing, and then it was time to eat. He barely chewed each mouthful before swallowing it appreciatively. His parents were chatting away to Chloe about her new job – filing for some big-shot company – but Alex was completely focused on his meal. Unfortunately, his father wasn't going to let him escape completely and asked the one question to which Alex was fast running out of answers.

"So, when are you going to get a job then, Alex?"

"I told you." Alex sighed, almost out of breath from his speed-eating. "Andy's dad is sorting me out." He leaned over and stole

Chloe's plate – as was the norm recently, she'd barely touched her food. Alex was just glad there was more for him.

"But, Alex, you've been saying that for a while. Is anything actually going to come from that?" Mrs Walsh continued to probe, sipping on her Sauvignon Blanc.

"Mum, I told you – the original plan was to work for Baz's dad, but it's not my fault he's a little preoccupied right now, is it?" Alex knew that would shut her up and planned on using the same excuse for the entire summer – there was no way he was getting a job. Despite their protestations, there was no doubt that his parents would keep him funded, so why would he bother even lifting a finger?

"How's Barry doing actually?" Chloe wondered.

"How would I know?" Alex wished people would stop asking him that. Every day that passed with Barry still unconscious, Alex felt himself grow increasingly worried. And he never worried. But what was going on? He'd walked out of the hospital the very next day, yet his best friend was still stuck in there, out cold. It scared him. Not that he'd ever admit it, but it did. So very much.

*

The next day, Alex and his father had arranged to play a round of golf. Although the sky was looking greyer than it had done in a while, Mr Walsh assured him that they'd be fine, and as the pair loaded up the Merc before setting off down to Wicklow, Johnny Cash blaring, Alex was in good form. He'd always admired his father: now a director of one of the country's top banks, he had the power and money Alex hoped to possess in his adulthood. Alex was unashamed to admit that they were close, as many of his friends and their fathers were too, and such afternoons as these, cruising down south to their favourite golf course, were quite common, giving the two men some quality time together away from the girls of the house.

Unfortunately, the clouds began to grow darker, filling the sky with a menacing blackness that showed no sign of easing up. Sure enough, the first drops of rain began to fall, and soon they picked up pace until they pounded like stones on the car roof.

"Not looking good is it, Son?" Mr Walsh finally conceded, even though they were past halfway in their journey.

Alex was disappointed, but brightened slightly as his father suggested pulling into the local hotel for some lunch.

They settled into a warm snug of the hotel bar and each ordered a drink. The waitress, a young girl with piercing green eyes, seemed to blush when handing Alex his and her slender fingers shook gently. The room was impressive, the walls covered with large hunting portraits, all browns and reds and rustic authenticity. The bubbles of Alex's Stella Artois danced upwards, and as he took his first mouthful, the sound of the lashing rain still audible outside, it felt good to be in the cosy indoors.

"So, I know you can't be completely honest when your mother's around, but how did the exams actually go?" Mr Walsh asked, with a look that assured his son that his answer would go no further.

Nonetheless, Alex was hesitant, not wanting to disappoint his father with the truth, but not wanting to lie either. He sighed.

"Ah, I don't know really. Some went OK, some really didn't. But to be honest, I still don't even know what I want to do next year," he admitted. "Like, Chloe has the drama thing, all the lads want to do law or engineering or whatever, but nothing seems to kind of . . . fit for me."

Alex's dad took a long swig of his shandy.

"To be honest, Alex, I was much the same when I was eighteen. It's very young to know exactly what you want from life–"

"But I do know," Alex interrupted.

"No, Alex," his father laughed, "money and a nice car don't exactly count as direction, I'm afraid! You have to work out how you want to actually get these things." His dad knew him so well.

"I guess I'll just see how my results go. Like, you know, I've mainly applied for business courses so hopefully one of them will pull through. Other than that I don't have a clue. If my results are shit, I'm fairly screwed, aren't I?" Alex realised for the first time he was actually a bit scared about the whole thing. And although he knew he could be somewhat open with his dad, he could feel himself beginning to clam up – the last thing he wanted was to let his father down.

"There are always private colleges. And you could repeat if it all goes terribly, you know? It will work out."

Alex stared out the window, not replying – the conversation was over. For in that moment it had hit him that it might well not work out. He'd been lazy – that was undeniable – but now school was over, and he was no longer the cool guy who didn't study; he was now the son who had nothing for his father to be proud of, and that hurt.

"Anyway, Alex, there's something else I want to talk to you about." Mr Walsh changed the subject, and Alex tuned back in, glad that they were finally going to discuss something new – anything would be better than the future.

"I was just wondering . . . you know your mother and I have been wanting to talk to you . . . but as I said before, I know you might find it hard to open up with both of us . . . Anyway . . . I just wanted to know how you're feeling about the whole . . . well, about the accident?"

"The accident?" Alex repeated, utterly surprised.

"Yes, Al – the accident. We've never fully discussed it."

"What is there to discuss? I'm fine now: my chest and neck have stopped hurting, I gave the police my statement – what else is there to talk about?"

Mr Walsh shook his head, growing more hassled with every moment that passed.

"I just want to know that you've taken a step back and really thought about it all," he explained, his eyes pleading with his son for something which Alex wasn't sure he could give him.

"What do you mean?"

"I mean . . . I mean, have you actually stopped for one minute to think about what a fucking idiot you were to get in that car . . . to let Barry drive after he'd been drinking?" Mr Walsh hissed, not wanting anyone nearby to hear, but his venom undeniable all the same.

"What?"

"Because I have this horrible feeling that the only thing you think about is the fact that you're OK, and that's what matters to you."

"Dad, keep your voice down, would you?"

"I'm serious here, Alex. Every day I watch you, and if I honestly thought I'd brought up a son who was coming out of this feeling absolutely no responsibility for his actions . . . well, I guess I'd feel I had . . . that I had failed you," he uttered, his voice no more than a whisper.

"Dad, what are you talking about? You haven't failed me." Alex still didn't understand where all this was coming from.

"Well then, promise me . . . promise me you'll just think about it. Not now, but when you're ready."

"Eh . . . OK . . . I promise."

"Thank you." Mr Walsh prayed his son had taken his advice on board. He didn't want to scare him – he didn't want to make him feel guilty. But he couldn't watch his own flesh and blood carry on the way he was, completely oblivious to the seriousness of the situation. It broke his heart.

Alex gazed once more out the window. The rain pelted down, showing no sign of ceasing, yet Alex couldn't bear to turn back and look at his dad. Drops bounced off the window pane, ricocheting at an awkward angle, so that the view was nothing but a wet blur – a watercolour painting gone wrong. Alex had lost his appetite. He wanted to go home.

*

Now that Chloe was working from nine to five each day, and with his parents at work as usual, Alex had the house to himself during the week. Generally he woke up about midday, played Pro Evolution Soccer on the PlayStation for a few hours, hit the gym and then went out with the lads. On one such night, in their usual spot in town, the drink was flowing and all were intent on getting very rowdy. Alex and Andy dropped yet another shot of Jägermeister into their glasses of Red Bull, cheered, and shouted "Jäger" before downing the artificial-tasting concoction.

"I fucking love Jäger Bombs!" Andy exclaimed, having swallowed his very quickly.

"Another?" Alex suggested, just about managing to slur the word out.

"Of course!" Andy replied. It was going to be a messy one.

After not one, but three more drinks the two boys decided to hit the dance floor, both thinking it would be a great idea to take off their tops and really let loose to the new Justin Timberlake track. Limbs flailing, Alex closed his eyes and gave it welly. Opening his eyes again, trying his hardest to focus, he spotted what he suspected was a group of good-looking girls and headed in their direction.

"Hey ladies," he announced on his arrival.

The females all turned to look at him, examining him from head to toe with a smile, and then continued to dance. Alex singled out the best-looking of the lot and shimmied in her direction, before placing his arms around her from behind and grinding in time with her. He could feel her slinky top sticking to his sweaty chest, but he didn't care – suddenly another feeling was brewing inside him.

"Fuck!" he exclaimed and stumbled as fast as he could off the dance floor, making it to the toilets just in time to feel the tidal wave of pungent vomit shoot from his mouth. Three times he wretched and filled the bowl with the variety of alcohol he had consumed that evening. Andy came in behind him.

"Aw man, how did that happen? You're usually a rock with your drink," he chided playfully. Alex didn't have the energy to reply, but merely flushed the toilet and made for the sink to rinse out his mouth.

"I was about to get stuck in and all," Alex spat angrily, disappointed by his display. "Let's get out of here," he commanded, his partying spirit all gone.

But even though he and Andy were leaving the club earlier than usual, it would have been a shame not to carry out their routine. Walking for almost twenty minutes south down Leeson Street, passing drunks and fights and fumbling couples, their familiar route eventually led them to their destination: Abrakebabra.

"Two chip butties, please," Alex ordered, letting Andy take a seat, as he too was starting to look a bit peaky. The hot baguettes arrived, bursting with mayonnaise-laden fries, the inviting steam spiralling upwards. With each bite, Alex felt more human, as a far more desirable taste replaced the rancid one in his mouth. Andy was swaying on his stool, chewing slowly, saying nothing, whilst bit by bit the diner began to fill up with people needing their post-night-out fix. One particularly rowdy gang stumbled in, cheering and chanting at the top of their voices. Alex was jealous – that was usually him and his friends; they were the noisy ones. So what had happened tonight? Why had he bottled so spectacularly? But before he could contemplate a reason, he was distracted by one of the leaders of the group, who had decided to drop his trousers and dance energetically in front of the appalled waitress. His friends encouraged him loudly, whooping and taking photos as he let it all hang loose, until a member of staff uttered the word "police" and, quick as lightning, the youth dashed out of the building, pausing only to rip one of the posters out of the window. Alex watched as he sped down the road, clambering to pull up his trousers whilst clutching his prized souvenir

– the torn image of a greasy doner kebab. Alex smiled, put in mind of a similar act he had once committed, but despite his amusement, it was time to leave. He grabbed Andy, wandered outside and hailed a taxi within seconds. They passed through the sleeping streets, zooming by the rugby pitch where Alex's school had played so many matches. Sometimes he had even been on the pitch himself, though the bar had been his more usual location. That same bar had played host to the teen disco Alex had frequented every Friday and Saturday night, all through his teenage years. Alex couldn't begin to count up the number of girls he'd scored in there, all as a result of that trusty line: "Eh . . . my friend over there was wondering if you'd meet me?" Worked every time! And though part of him cringed to think of his thickly gelled hair and awful chat-up attempts back then, the feeling of curious innocence, exploring the unknown world of discos and girls for the first time, felt like another lifetime ago. A split-second of nostalgia filled Alex, before he realised just how soppy he was being and returned to some manly conversation with the taxi driver, who was divulging some very interesting details about his recent trip to Amsterdam. Now that was dark and unknown.

*

A few days later, as he whiled away another afternoon on the computer, a heavy session of Championship Manager under way, Alex's phone buzzed. It was Jenny.

HEY STRANGER, TAWT WE WER GONA HANG OUT OVA D SUMMA? AINT SEEN U SINCE LEAVIN CERT BALL. WHER U BN? WANNA MEET UP? XX

Alex sighed; he knew exactly how the summer would pan out if indeed he did start meeting up with Jenny. But he also knew how much effort it would be to seek out an alternative, if not more than one, so for the moment he conceded that there was no good reason not to "hang out" with her, even if she had disrupted his computer game.

HEY BABE. JUS BN TAKIN IT EASY REALY — U NO URSELF, NEED 2 CHIL D
FUCK OUT AFTER D EXAMS. HEADN 2 SPAIN WIT D LADS IN A COUPL OF
WKS. U? X

Alex had almost forgotten about the trip. There hadn't been that
much talk of it, since he and the lads had been spending the past
couple of weeks being lazy by day and wasted by night. Thus they'd
never quite been in a fit enough state to iron out the details of their
holiday plans. But last time Alex had checked, he was going to be
spending two weeks in Andy's villa with a couple of the other boys
from school, getting a tan and partying it up.

However, some of the boys were being a bit weird towards Alex of
late – the odd sly comment about the accident and how quickly he'd
got over it. But the boys had no right to lecture him about any of that
– they didn't even understand. But Alex wasn't quite sure if he
understood either.

Jenny's speedy reply broke his trance.

TRYING TO FIND A JOB — NEED TO GET SOME MONEY 2GETHR 4 AYIA
NAPA. IM SO EXCITD 4 IT, ARNT U? XX

Ah yes, Alex smiled to himself; Ayia Napa! The real holiday, which
he certainly had not forgotten about. It was tradition for most school-
leavers to head abroad as soon as they'd received their Leaving Cert
results in mid-August, and in South Dublin, through a few enquiries
and a bit of networking, all the schools sought each year to ensure
they went to the same place. This year, Cyprus was the chosen
destination. Typically, there was much speculation in the media, and
of course amongst parents, as to how good an idea such trips were,
as they were generally perceived to be nothing but alcohol-fuelled
fortnights of sex, drugs and accidents. Frankly, Alex could not wait!

ARE U JOKN? ITS GONA B FUCKN INSANE! JUS OVA A MONTH AWAY —
JESUS IM GONA GET SO FUCKN OUT OF CONTROL. X

Alex felt himself begin to pump with adrenalin. Although Spain
with the lads was going to be good, too, nothing would ever compare

with Ayia Napa. The stories he'd heard from older years made him sure of this.

EH, COOL. . .NEWAY, LUNCH 2MORRO? MY TREAT? J XXX

Alex wished Jenny would just leave him alone to bask in the anticipation of those two weeks, but he was not one to turn down free food. She really was eager, wasn't she?

SOUNDS SAVAGE. IL PICK U UP @ 1. LETS GO SUMWHER NICE! X

Feeling content, Alex adjusted his boxers, leant back in his chair and spotted Chloe's *Lost* box-set on the shelf – his afternoon plans had been decided!

The next day, after grabbing his keys and shouting up to his mother that he was going job-hunting, Alex sped out of his driveway and towards Jenny's house. The early July heat spilled into the car as The Fratellis' album belted out, the volume and bass turned up suitably high. People had warned Alex that driving would probably feel strange since the accident, but as he pelted along, he was perfectly relaxed, with one hand on the wheel and the other texting Jenny, apologising for being late and telling her to be outside her door in ten minutes.

She was there, as instructed, looking far too made-up for the time of day, but Alex wasn't complaining – she was hot. She kissed him on the cheek as soon as she hopped into the car, said hello and began to chat, leading with, "Oh my God, does driving feel really strange since the accident?"

Alex rolled his eyes, but laughed, pulling away from her house with a rev so loud it made him smile. They were off.

"So how does The Gables in Foxrock sound?" Alex suggested, as its good food and somewhat pricey menu was just what he felt in the mood for. Jenny agreed, not batting an eyelid. Alex knew she was keen.

They got a table easily, and once the food was ordered, Alex decided it was probably time he started putting in a little effort. Moving his shades to the crown of his head, he leant back in his chair and allowed the summer sunlight to illuminate his chiselled face.

"So, any luck on the job hunt?" he asked.

"I think so, actually. I got an email this morning from this make-up place in town. My aunt's pretty high up there, so she put in a good word and they've offered me some work." Jenny seemed thrilled.

"Fair play. Good pay?"

"Yeah, it's all right. But it's really good experience and, like, you get a discount on all their products, which is, like, so cool!"

"Eh . . . great." Alex tried to appear enthusiastic, though the information was wasted on him.

"What about you, then? How are you going to pay for Spain and Ayia Napa? I'd say it'll cost a fortune," Jenny continued.

"Well, Mum and Dad have said they'll sort me out. They always said the sixth-year holiday would be my reward for working hard in my exams, and for all they know, I did."

"And when the results come out . . .?"

"Well, it'll be too late then, won't it? We're flying out to Cyprus two days later so they can't exactly cancel then, now can they?" Alex reasoned, reassuring himself.

"True . . . Do you reckon Barry will be awake for it?" Jenny asked quietly, not knowing whether to broach the topic or not.

"Barry, miss the sixth-year holiday? Somehow I doubt it!" Alex exclaimed, refusing to admit the doubts that were building. The only bad thing about lolling around the house all day, doing nothing, was it gave him time to think. And the more Alex thought, the less he liked what he was thinking. It had been almost three weeks. It wasn't right.

Luckily the food arrived, bringing a change in conversation, and, thankfully, a change in mood. Alex relished his steak, shovelling it in as Jenny daintily sipped her soup, trying at all times to look as elegant as possible. It was cute, he had to admit.

"So, how's Chloe?" Jenny enquired, though family was never an area of chat Alex generally explored on dates. He supposed Jenny was somewhat of an exception, since the girls were vaguely friends.

"Yeah, she's good. Working hard, I think – filing or some shit," he managed, between bites.

"I see her at the gym sometimes."

"Yeah, she joined straight after the exams. Bit strange if you ask me – she's never really been the fitness type. Then all of a sudden she's spending fucking loads of time 'working out'. Weird!" Alex concluded, his belly filling up and feeling very comfortable indeed. He examined Jenny, as she finished her soup – she looked amazing. Her dark hair was dead straight and caught the light as it framed her pretty face. Her dark-pink top made her look even more girlie, and Alex was reminded once more of why he liked her – there was just something about her which drew him to her. He'd been with prettier girls in the past, but nonetheless, he wanted her badly, and as she looked up at him from beneath her lashes, wondering why he was staring at her so intently, something inside him clicked. Something that had never clicked before. Alex didn't like it. He never fell for girls, and he certainly wasn't going to start now.

"Can we get out of here?" he suddenly announced. Jenny looked surprised, but realised that Alex was serious. She quickly paid the bill and left, trying to keep up with Alex, who strode briskly towards his car.

"Alex, are you OK?" Jenny enquired, "Do you want to come back to mine? I think my parents–"

"No, I'm going to head home, Jen," Alex interjected. Part of him was screaming at him for turning down the opportunity of a free house with Jenny. That situation meant only one thing, and there was no denying how much he was gagging for some action. But another part of him suddenly just wanted to be on his own. That click, the whole thing – he was confused, and the sooner he made it home, the better.

They sat in the car in silence all the way to Jenny's house. As the car pulled up outside her driveway, she hesitantly leaned in to give him a kiss. He responded, but pulled away soon after, thanking her for lunch and politely turning down her further offers of coming inside. She sighed, understandably at a loss, and shut the car door behind her, never once turning back as she strutted to her front door and let herself in.

"Fuck." Alex banged his head on the steering wheel, completely clueless as to why he'd just turned her down – what if he'd blown his chances with her for good? He kept his foot on the accelerator all the way home, not wanting to stop; not wanting to think. Just wanting to go quickly, to pass life out. To win.

At dinner that night, Alex's head was still all over the place, and his family weren't helping.

"So, how was your day, love? Any luck on the job-hunting?" his mother asked.

"Job-hunting? Ha! Alex was on a date today," Chloe teased.

"Fuck off, would you . . . Who told you that?" Alex was not in the mood.

"It's not what you know, Alex . . ."

"Shut up, seriously. We just went for lunch. It's none of your business," Alex snapped.

"Ooh, somebody's in a mood," Chloe retorted.

Silence fell upon the table until Mr Walsh finally attempted to break the tension.

"How was work, Chloe?"

"Good, actually – I really enjoyed it today. They're starting to give me some proper stuff to do."

Alex rolled his eyes, clearly unimpressed with his sister's showing-off.

"Oh piss off, Alex. Just because you don't have a job!" she spat.

"Why the fuck would I want one?" Alex snarled.

"Well, love, there is the slight issue of money," his mother interjected. "Where do you plan on getting that from?"

"Money?" Alex was confused. "Since when has money been an issue?"

"Since you've decided that not only do you want to go to Ayia-whatever-it's-called, but Spain as well." His dad's calm voice was nonetheless intimidating.

"But I thought . . ." Alex began to panic slightly.

"That we'd pay for it?" His father finished his sentence, putting down his cutlery, indicating that he meant business.

Alex feared what was coming next. He had so much respect for his father that he hated fighting with him, but if he could predict accurately what his dad was about to say, there was going to be no option but to object. Strongly.

"Alex, your mother and I just think it's a bit much – two holidays? Both for two weeks? Granted, we'd always said we'd pay for your sixth-year holiday, but Spain as well? If you're insisting on doing both, you're going to have to pay for at least one of them," Mr Walsh explained firmly.

"But, that's so bent! Were you planning on telling me this? I'm supposed to be leaving for Spain in just over a week – how'd you expect me to get the money at such short notice?" Alex's voice began to rise.

"Dear, you haven't even booked your flights. If you'd actually been serious about the whole thing, don't you think you would have organised things by now? I mean, how much do you honestly even want to go?" his mother joined in.

Looking into both his parents' eyes, searching in vain for some sign of weakness, Alex knew that he was defeated. Even worse was his sister's smug silence, which made him feel even more like an idiot. He left the table and climbed the stairs, two at a time, head pounding and heart racing. It was true – he hadn't even looked into planning anything, and he still had Ayia Napa, but on top of the day he'd just had, this was the last thing he needed. But why was he letting it all get to him? He'd awaited this summer and its prospects for so long now – the beginning of his adulthood, his freedom, his life. So how come lunch with a girl and a refusal by his parents were getting him down so much? It wasn't supposed to be like this. Things were supposed to be better now. Easier. He felt his eyes begin to moisten, but refused to give in. Alex Walsh didn't cry. He knew he was overreacting, but he couldn't help it. An intense feeling of unease had been brewing within him for weeks now, ever since the exams had ended. Ever since the accident. He lay on his bed and willed his erratic breathing to steady. His chest hurt and he fought with his panic until, slowly, his breath found a rhythm once more. Alex tried to make it regular – tried to instil into it the sort of order he thought his life had possessed. But suddenly, even that was in doubt. He needed to escape. But Alex knew it was more than a question of leaving his house – he could not shun his worries that easily. They would follow him around like a shadow. He needed to let it all out. To talk. But to whom? His parents? Chloe? Jenny? They wouldn't listen. And even if they would, he didn't want them to hear. He'd only be forced to listen to their advice, their analysis, their superiority. He didn't want to hear it. In fact, he didn't want to hear anything. He just wanted to talk.

As much as he hated admitting it, suddenly Alex knew where he should go – the place he'd been trying to pretend he wasn't obliged to visit. The root of all his distress and anxiety, the tiny niggling sense of guilt, gnawed at his soul, and he knew what he had to do.

*

"I'm here to see Barry Carter, please."

"It's quite late, you know – visiting hours are nearly finished."

"Please. I won't be long."

"OK then. Follow me."

Alex hadn't been in a hospital since the morning after the accident.

The artificially lit, spotless corridors seemed sterile and surreal as the speedy nurse led him onwards. They passed an old man, a patient, sitting on a corridor bench. He wore a harrowed expression, his wrinkles huddled together in every corner of his face. His frail hands were clasped as if in prayer, begging for help, health, mercy, freedom – anything he could get. He looked so alone as the world passed him by, ignorant to this shrinking being of past years, reaching his end. Alex tried to catch his eye, but to no avail – the man had given in to his solitude; his head remained bowed. He had given up.

"Here we are," the nurse announced.

"Thanks," Alex mumbled as she turned away. He wanted to ask her something, but didn't know if he could. He willed himself to try.

"Excuse me," he managed.

"Yes?" she replied, looking at him with those reassuring nurse's eyes.

"Eh . . . this is kind of weird . . . but . . . you know the way he's, like . . . sleeping . . . can he . . .?" Alex didn't know how to phrase his question without feeling like an idiot. Luckily the nurse understood.

"Yes, he can hear you. Despite Barry's coma, he will be able to hear you, or at least know that you're there. You should talk to him," she said kindly.

"Oh, right . . . eh, thanks." Alex wondered why he was suddenly feeling so uncomfortable. It was unlike him. Still, there was no denying his dry mouth or overwhelming desire to turn on his heels and head back to the car park. But his sense took control as he remembered why he was there and who was lying on the other side of that door.

Slowly he pushed it open, his hand shaking ever so slightly. The room was as he'd expected – clean, white, silent save for the beeps and whirrs of the machinery which encircled his friend. A bunch of yellow flowers sat in a vase on the table beside Barry's bed, their brightness trying its hardest to inject some positivity into the bleak image of the sleeping youth. Alex closed the door silently and made his way to the chair beside the bed. He was scared to make any noise as he sat down, trying to prevent his gaze from falling upon his friend, but eventually he gave in. Barry lay, stiffly, as if asleep. His chest rose and fell in time with the mechanical clicks and puffs of the apparatus, whilst various tubes and wires entangled into a medical mayhem, all united towards the single goal of making him better, of waking him up, of bringing him back. As Alex stared at his friend's lifeless form, he couldn't believe this was the same guy he'd grown up with, causing trouble, having fun. Alex always had in Barry a truly carefree soul that served as a constant reminder that seizing every moment was the only way to live.

But these past few weeks, Alex hadn't wanted to seize the moment. He wanted all his moments to just stop and give him a chance to catch up with himself, with life. Everything was changing, and he didn't like it. He wanted Barry to wake up. He wanted his parents to get off his back. He wanted to want nothing from Jenny but sex and fun. He wanted to get rid of the growing worry of his results and the newfound niggling question: "What will I do next?" He just wanted to be Alex Walsh. Was that so much to ask?

"Is that so much to fucking ask, man?" Alex boomed, startling himself by saying it aloud. He looked around, wondering would someone come in to tell him to shut up. He felt like such an idiot – he'd seen people in films chatting away to a loved one who was clearly out for the count and could no more hear what they were saying than they themselves could act. But now that he was here, he needed to talk, to make sense of it all. He felt as if he would explode otherwise. Taking a deep breath, bracing himself for what he was about to do, the first word forming on his lips, Alex made to speak, but another noise took its place. It was a knock at the door, and suddenly the friendly nurse reappeared, looking at him with those same warm eyes.

"I'm sorry, visiting hours are over," she informed him sympathetically.

Alex was shocked – he felt like he'd only just sat down. But a quick glance at his watch proved otherwise.

"Have I really been here twenty minutes?" he exclaimed in shock.

"Yes, you have. Sorry, I can't let you stay longer – hospital policy." She smiled.

"Yeah . . . no . . . it's grand. Thanks." Alex still couldn't come to terms with where exactly the time had gone. Never before had he sat and thought for that long. It was so unlike him. But then again, things were changing.

He drove home in silence – no blaring music so characteristic of his usual journeys. He needed some peace. He needed sleep. Bed came none too soon.

The next morning, things felt better. Alex slept in until midday, tottered downstairs in his boxers, made some toast and Nutella and settled into a football World Cup on Pro Evolution on the PlayStation. He realised what a fool he had been the previous night and that change was in fact good – if it meant no more school and lots more lazing around in the afternoon, then what was wrong with that? Also, it was still the summer – things were always different in the summer. And when it was time to start thinking about college or the future or all that stuff, he'd deal with it then. But for now, Alex Walsh was in a good place. All that emotional nonsense could leave him alone – life had begun, and he was going to take full advantage of it.

The afternoon passed by successfully, Alex managing to lead Ireland to the World Cup quarter-finals, pausing only to throw a pizza in the oven for lunch. The match was about to begin against a threatening-looking Argentina when the sound of a key in the front door made him stop. His mother? If she saw him still in his underwear at four o'clock in the afternoon, especially with the kitchen and living room in the state that they were, she'd flip. Luckily, it wasn't her. It was

Chloe. Alex returned to his game, not really in the mood for engaging in conversation with his sister. But then he realised that something didn't quite fit.

"Don't you finish work at five?" he asked over his shoulder, focused on Duff's spectacular run up the left wing, fingers twiddling with the controller, pushing the player on. Chloe didn't reply, but instead Alex could faintly hear another sound.

"Chloe, are you crying?" he asked bluntly, reluctantly pressing pause on what was about to be a sure-fire goal. Turning around to look at his sister, he wasn't quite prepared for what he saw. Chloe stood, in her shirt and skirt, her work attire, her face a red, puffy mess, streaming with tears. It seemed so odd to see someone in such formal clothes blubbering like a child, and Alex felt awkward, as he always did at moments like this. What was he supposed to do?

"Eh, what happened?" he tried, not knowing whether to get up and go to her or just leave her be. But the longer she stood there, in the same position, tears pouring down her into a heartbroken pool, he knew he had to do something.

"Come here," he said, and she finally started moving, joining him on the couch. Alex put his arm around her awkwardly – he'd never been into the whole affectionate sibling thing, and he and Chloe hadn't been getting on very well of late. But she instantly collapsed into him, her wails getting louder and louder, longing to be comforted, to be held. And so they sat, closer than any time Alex could ever remember, she encased in her sadness, he at a loss as to what was actually going on. Luckily, her sobs eventually began to subside.

"Chloe, what is wrong?" Alex finally enquired. She pulled away from where she had nestled into his shoulder and looked at him.

"It's Sam," she confessed. Alex had guessed as much – boyfriend troubles were generally the source of Chloe's tears.

"Have you guys broken up?" Alex suggested gingerly, not wanting her to break down again.

"No. No we haven't. He just rang me on my lunch break and we had a big fight and, it's not even that big a deal, I just got really upset and then back in work I was really sad and they noticed and told me to take the rest of the day off and I got really embarrassed and then I got the bus and I started crying again and . . . and . . ."

"Slow down, slow down." Alex tried to calm her, as her rant was building speed by the second.

"Sorry." She took a deep breath before continuing at a slower pace, "I'm just such a mess. Basically – you know the way he's in France at the moment – well, he rang to say that he's loving it so much that he's decided to stay an extra couple of weeks. Which is not a big deal, to be honest. I just . . . I just thought we'd spend more time together this summer. And why doesn't he think he'd love being back here with me, like we'd planned?" she demanded.

"Yeah, but Chloe, just relax. He'll be home in, like, two weeks. You'll see him then – I don't know why you're so upset." Alex struggled to sound as concerned as possible, but from where he was standing it just sounded like she was getting worked up over nothing.

"I know, I know. It's just, the fact that I got so upset kind of showed me that there's more to it than this. Like, suddenly all these cracks are starting to show in our relationship, and I just don't know what I want any more . . ." Chloe looked very close to tears again.

"Whoa, Chloe. Seriously, I think you're just majorly overreacting. Just wait and see what it's like when he gets home. Don't start reading into things before then. Chill out, yeah?" Alex thanked his lucky stars that he was not a woman – all this emotional turmoil over nothing seemed like far too much effort.

"Yeah, I guess." Chloe gave in, heaving an enormous, defeated sigh. "I think I'm going to go to the gym, clear my head," she announced, pulling herself up from the sofa. Alex watched her leave the room, unable to deny the pity he felt for her. Whatever was going on in his life, in his head, he never let himself get even close to a state like that. Chloe had been acting strangely recently, from what he'd noticed, but since she was always either at work or the gym, he didn't have much to go on. And even if he had, would he have been bothered? For right now there was virtual football to be played, and an Argentina to be destroyed. Happy days!

4

SAM

France smelled different from home. Sam loved the way the breathless nights melted into dragonfly days, while the unusual aroma of foreign herbs filled the air. The July heat was growing stronger, and Sam spent the majority of his days dipping in and out of the villa's private swimming pool. He had promised himself he would do at least a hundred lengths a day to try and stay in some sort of shape, but his visits to the pool mostly consisted of pleasant lolling in the cool water, where worries floated away and the view above was nothing but perfect sky.

Sam's father and his partner had booked the villa for a month, and Sam had originally planned to join them for a fortnight. But the sheer bliss of seclusion, up in the mountains of Nice, tucked away from the rest of the world, was too hard to leave behind. For the first time in a long time, Sam felt relaxed. The stress of the exams had really taken its toll on him, and Ireland offered no real escape. But here, no one knew his name. Sam could move as he pleased, and be who he wanted to be.

The extra weeks would also give him a greater opportunity to spend time with his father and Deirdre. Finally he was learning to love the woman his father had been seeing for quite a while. At first, Sam had been sceptical, naturally enough given the disastrous opinion he had of his mother's boyfriend. And since he only spent every second weekend in his dad's house, concentrated periods of time with Deirdre had never really been an option. But now that he had more time on his hands, he could find out more about this woman, since it seemed she was definitely going to be sticking around. But Sam was OK with this. He was more than OK – the way she made his father smile meant the world to him. He hadn't seen him that happy in a long time. Yet Sam couldn't deny a slight twinge of jealousy. He had once felt like that about Chloe. Sam remembered seeing her for the first time in his French grind, and though her name was infamous within the South Dublin social circle, she hadn't been at all like he'd expected. She'd been shyer, more polite and friendly than he'd thought she would be. And then slowly but surely, she'd let him in, and he her, and before he knew it Sam had fallen in love for the first time and it was perfect.

So what had changed? Why was he here, in the summer before he embarked on the next exciting phase of his life, having doubts? He was on the brink of adulthood, with only a few months before being plunged into the real world. Yet he was no longer completely certain that he and Chloe were going to make it in that world. He wasn't saying that they wouldn't – he still loved her with all his heart – he was just learning more and more these days not to take anything for granted, and he was becoming increasingly aware that he, Sam Gallagher, was growing up. And that meant only one thing: change.

Yesterday, he'd phoned her to tell her he'd changed his flight and wasn't coming home for another two weeks. He'd known she would be disappointed – if she missed him half as much as he did her, then that was a given. But he had thought that she would understand.

"Baby, I miss you so much, too. Like, you've no idea. It's just savage spending some time with Dad, and I really just need to chill out. It's so cool just being able to do nothing for the first time in, well, a year. You must understand?" he had pleaded.

"No, Sam. No, I do not understand. Because every day that I've been doing this stupid fucking job and working my ass off in the gym, I've literally been counting down the days till I'd see you. This is *our* summer. Next year is so unclear and scary and who knows where we'll both be at college and what we'll be doing. But for now we could have both been here, in Dublin, together. Isn't that what you want?" She had sounded both desperate and angry.

"Of course I want that. I want more than anything to spend time with my girlfriend – you must know that. But I'll be home soon. And we'll have all of August and September, and Ayia Napa – that's going to be amazing."

But she just didn't get it. If he could only convince her to stop reading into things so much and just accept that he was having fun, having some "him" time. He smiled, realising they'd had a similar conversation just before he'd gone away, only that time it had been him demanding to see more of her. But now he understood. It may have been selfish, but it felt good to be slightly selfish for once – there was so much going on in his head, so where better to sort through it all than beside a pool, in his favourite country, away from it all? Away from the South Dublin where everybody knows everybody's business, and you can't walk down the street without recognising so-and-so and knowing who the last person they scored was and where and when and what they were even bloody wearing! He loved Dublin, there was no denying that, but the politics and the very size of it made Sam feel almost claustrophobic at times. He needed a change of scenery. And though France was just what he needed now, he wasn't sure if it would be enough in the long run. He had applied to university in England and been accepted to a couple of very prestigious colleges in London. He'd told all his friends, Chloe, even his parents, that these were merely a back-up, in case he didn't get what he wanted in Ireland. But more and more, Sam found himself longing to go, to start again, to make new friends in a new bubble and leave behind the one he knew so well. Too well.

But that wouldn't have to mean the end of his relationship with Chloe. His doubts weren't really about her, just the world to which she belonged. If he could break away and still have her, still visit, still love her as much as he did now, then life would be perfect.

She was incredible – there was no denying that. Her past wasn't exactly spotless, he conceded, knowing just how many of the familiar South Dublin faces she'd got with over the years. But that was all in her youth – if you couldn't make mistakes and go wild in your teenage years, then when could you? But now she was his, and he never for a minute doubted her loyalty to him or her love. Because they clicked. They just clicked. And as long as she was willing to embrace whatever changes September brought, nothing would break that.

*

Later in the week, Sam's father decided they would drive to St Tropez for the evening – to have a stroll around, get some food and generally bask in its wealth and style. Having been only once before, when he was much younger, Sam was impressed. The port was stunning, the yachts like floating mansions, inhabited by the *crème de la crème* of society. Women with five-inch heels and five-inch poodles tottered along the street, trails of fashionable scents billowing behind them. Golden children giggled and played, even their joshing appearing chic, whilst painters displayed all kinds of art, hoping to catch the eye of at least one of the passing millionaires.

Dinnertime arrived, and the restaurants began to fill up, the electric buzz bringing to life even the simplest eatery. Deirdre found them a table, and Sam sat down and ordered a beer. Chloe would love it here, he thought to himself. The fashion and extravagance of everything would be right up her street, and he could picture her trying out some of her school French, in an effort to blag a tour around one of the stunning boats. Knowing her, she'd probably succeed! Despite the timidity Sam knew and loved within her, when she wanted to, she could put on such a front that no one was unsusceptible to her charms. No wonder she'd been such a success with the boys! Sam supposed it was part of her acting abilities, and if her drama classes had taught her one thing, it was how to ooze confidence at all the right moments. He decided to send her a text.

HEY BABY. JUS IN ST. TROP. TINKN OF U. HOPE WE'R OK - I REALY DO LOVE U U NO. MIS U XX

He prayed she'd reply.

"Well, now the drinks have arrived," Sam's father brought him back to reality, "I think it's time for a little toast." He raised his glass, and something about his coy smile told Sam that he had news. Potentially big news.

"Dad? Is there something you'd like to tell me?"

"Well . . ." His father was starting to blush. Sam knew what was coming, but allowed his dad to build up to it. He was excited.

"Deirdre and I have been together for over a year now. And this afternoon when we went for our walk . . . I decided . . . well, I decided before then, obviously . . . I mean, I've been thinking about it for . . ."

"Dad!" Sam exclaimed.

"Sorry, sorry. Well, yes . . . the thing is . . . I've asked Deirdre . . . well . . . I've asked her to marry me," he finally managed, before adding quickly, "Oh, and she's . . . well . . . she's said yes!"

His father waited for Sam to react, a glimmer of fear in his eyes.

But there was nothing Sam could do but smile and throw his arms around the enamoured pair, wishing them all the happiness in the world. In turn, they were both relieved and delighted, and Deirdre insisted on ordering champagne.

"When in St Tropez . . ." she joked, unable to contain her joy.

The meal was a triumph, all three of them united in looking forward to a future of happiness and love. Though Sam didn't know what the coming months would bring, he knew that, no matter what, he could truly rely on his father and Deirdre. Somehow, that made all his fear just disappear. He knew now that it would all be OK.

5

CHLOE

In St Stephen's Green Park, an old woman waddled slowly along the path, her only friend in the world by her side: a rust-coloured spaniel, panting and sniffing as it went. It paused, ears pricked, to take a closer look at the chattering ducks who glided across the pond, leaving ripples of conversation in the water as they went. On the banks, pigeons picked and twittered to one another, sharing secrets and searching for crumbs and surprises on the dirty ground. Outside the park gates, the city zoomed once more, racing time itself, but the haven of nature which the gates enclosed was the perfect place for the world to relax.

Chloe hated running in Stephen's Green at lunchtime – the chances of bumping into someone she knew were all too high, and the many pin-striped men, lazing on the grass, scoffing their Marks & Spencer's sandwiches, always stared at her sweating figure as she tried to wend her way through the afternoon crowds. But she didn't really have a choice: working in town, there were few options, and her brief hour for lunch would never allow her to make it to the gym and back. This would just have to do. Now that it was mid-July, the sun was always on full-power as Chloe ran, the blazing rays beating down and sapping her energy. It hurt. She had to stop. Bending over, her hands on her hips, a stitch stung her panting chest, stabbing with every breath. She drank from her water bottle and for a split-second wondered why on earth she put herself through this awful routine, day in, day out. But then she triumphantly recalled that, since the Leaving, she'd lost over half a stone and there was still another month until Ayia Napa. Thank goodness, she conceded, for there was no way she was getting into a bikini yet, that was for sure!

The pain subsided as she gulped her remaining water, and she decided it was time to head back to work. The remaining twenty minutes were just enough to shower and make herself look in some way respectable. They teased her in work about her running fetish. At first she'd insisted that she wasn't really into the whole exercise thing, it was more of a means to an end, but eventually she'd just given up and accepted the numerous athletic-related nicknames they'd endowed upon her, some wittier than others. They were a nice bunch – young, friendly and impressed with the way she'd been working. But there was no denying how boring the work itself was, and every day that passed just made Chloe more sure that acting was definitely the career for her, and she would give it her all if it meant avoiding a dead-end job like this.

That evening after work, they were all heading across to Café-en-Seine for "a few scoops" and invited Chloe to come along. As she'd only been there three weeks, she was reluctant to accept their offer, fearing she'd feel out of place. But since she'd turned them down more than once before, and didn't want to look rude, she nervously agreed to come along. The ornately decorated bar had always appealed to Chloe's taste, and she concluded that this couldn't be so bad, even if a tiny part of her felt guilty, having planned to go to the gym that evening.

"What can I get you, Chloe?" the guy that sat at the desk beside her asked brightly.

"Oh . . . em . . . a gin and slimline tonic, please, Joey," she replied gingerly.

"Grand so," Joey said, his thick Limerick accent never failing to put Chloe at ease. He was such a joker, and Chloe knew that as long as she stayed close to him for the evening, she wouldn't feel awkward. It was strange. All her friends thought she was the most confident girl in the whole world. But just recently, she had begun to feel increasingly self-conscious. Maybe she was just tired, she told herself, taking the drink from Joey and promising herself she'd perk up a bit. It was time to shine.

The evening passed by pleasantly enough – the lads from work messing and bantering as they always did, their suits and ties the only indication that they were anything other than bold schoolboys, as they skulled back the pints. Chloe wrapped herself in the moment and felt at ease at last, getting to know her colleagues better. But after a couple of hours, she realised she didn't want to make a big night of it, so she said her goodbyes and headed for the bus. As she watched the world pass her by from the top deck, she kept reaching for her phone to see if there were any messages. She'd been checking all evening in the bar, too, but still there were no texts. No Sam. She hadn't heard from him all day and it bothered her. Ever since he'd decided to stay on in France, she'd had an awful feeling that this was just the start of him pulling away. Which was weird, because only a few weeks ago she'd been impatient with him for smothering her.

But now she felt like she needed him more and more, and he just wasn't there. There were only so many text messages she could send, only so many times she could be the one to call him. It was up to him now, and he wasn't pulling through.

Someone had once told her that no two people in a teenage relationship love each other equally: there is always someone who likes the other more and hence can call the shots, whether they exercise this power or not. At the start of their relationship, it was evident that Sam liked Chloe more than she did him. He had texted her morning, noon and night and made no effort to hide his feelings, particularly once they got together and things started to get serious. But these past few weeks, Chloe sensed that a shift was taking place. Sam seemed so happy out in France, so determined to stay out there, away from everything and everyone, including her. And all of a sudden, she was the one who was yearning for his contact morning, noon and night.

Maybe it was just her imagination, she considered, given that her job and all the exercise were really taking their toll on Chloe of late. Her mother had even commented on how pale and washed-out she was appearing recently, putting her on a hefty course of vitamins and insisting she stop pushing herself so hard, particularly in the gym. Chloe was appreciative of her concern, but knew her tiredness was no cause for worry, as its only negative effect was this sudden quiver in her confidence, particularly when it came to Sam.

She got off the bus and embarked on the brisk walk home – a meagre replacement for the treadmill session she had scheduled for that night.

Alex and their dad were on the couch when Chloe arrived home, enthralled by some football match, believing that if they shouted loudly enough, the players would undoubtedly be able to hear their advice, valuable as it was.

"Hi." She attempted to make contact, but neither responded, too wrapped up in their own world.

There was no sign of Chloe's mother, save for the scribbled Post-it that clung to the plate of food on the kitchen table, indicating that it was Chloe's dinner. Chloe took one look at it and threw it in the bin. She wasn't hungry. Well, she was. But not really. She made herself a cup of green tea and headed into the other room to collapse in front of the television for her favourite programme, *America's Next Top Model*. The fashion, the glamour, the photo shoots and the sheer beauty of each contestant combined to form an hour of unmissable TV. That night, it delivered as always, Chloe's least favourite contestant being eliminated from the competition. "Rightly so," Chloe thought to herself, "look at the size of her," as the young girl made her emotional departure, her dreams crushed, her chances over, her heart broken.

*

That Friday brought a much-needed girls' night out for Chloe and her friends, and as Chloe dolled herself up in her friend Heather's bedroom, she vowed that she would have a brilliant night and try, just for a while, to stop thinking about Sam. The girls all looked fabulous, and after the usual photo frenzy, they turned up the music and started into their chosen drink of the night. Chloe sipped on the white wine her mother had given her and felt it going straight to her head. Not that she was complaining! She hadn't had a big night on the town in a while and was planning to paint it red. Once things were underway, Chloe announced that they were to play one of her favourite drinking games, where inhibitions went out the window and alcohol was consumed at pace.

"Anyone up for a game of 'Never Have I Ever'?" she called, only to be met with a chorus of giddy girls, delighted with her suggestion. With all the girls sitting in a circle, Chloe began the proceedings with her first confession.

"Never have I ever . . . had sex in my parents' bed," she proclaimed.

Everybody giggled, and the few girls who had unfortunately

committed this crime reluctantly stood up for all to see and took a hefty mouthful of their drink. So the game proceeded.

"Never have I ever . . . scored another girl."

"Never have I ever . . . given head in a toilet cubicle."

"Never have I ever . . . got sick in public."

Chloe was forced to own up to her actions on numerous occasions and soon could feel the alcohol having a definite effect on her.

"Here, ladies, can we please stop saying things that I've done? I'm going to be twisted before we even leave here!" Chloe made a plea to her friends. They all laughed, using the opportunity to slag their favourite girl.

"Maybe if you weren't such a slut . . ." one girl taunted, all in good humour, as the rest erupted into hysterics.

"Well, now that it's my turn," Heather interrupted, "I'll be nice and do one that you definitely won't have to stand up for."

Chloe was intrigued.

"Never have I ever . . ." Heather began, a glint in her eye, ". . . scored Alex Walsh!" The entire circle, save Chloe, exploded, standing up and knocking back their drinks, giggling and nudging one another, as Chloe hung her head in mock embarrassment.

"You all have shit taste," she informed them, laughing, as she realised that her glass was empty. Stumbling to the kitchen for a refill, she couldn't believe her eyes when she discovered her wine bottle was only half empty. She was plastered! Usually it took a lot more than that to have her on her ear. Granted she'd only had a small dinner, but still, that was embarrassing. She couldn't decide whether to have another glass to try and save face or whether to hold back, knowing she'd pretty much reached her limit. She compromised, pouring herself half a glass, and returned to the others, trying her best to walk in a straight line.

Soon after, the girls called for taxis and headed into town, each more tipsy than the next, all united in having a good time. Chloe had definitely had one too many, but was trying her hardest not to let it show. Leaning on Heather's shoulder for the duration of the drive, she thanked her lucky stars that she'd found such a great group of friends and vowed that, despite school being over, they would stay together, no matter what.

"I love my girls," she murmured, not meaning for the whole car to hear. But they did and adored the spectacle of their party girl blushing in her drunken state and hiccupping with coy embarrassment.

Leaving the taxi, Chloe tried her best to sober up. She strutted up to the bouncer of the nightclub, producing her ID with a smile and enjoying the realisation that he was checking her out. Confident Chloe was back, and the minute she stepped into the busy club, she vowed that tonight everyone would know it. She and Heather ordered a vodka and cranberry, and as she rooted around in her bag for some money, a deep voice to her left commanded her attention.

"Let me get that for you."

"Oh . . . thanks! Actually, no, wait . . . there's two of us . . . so you're grand . . . thanks, though," Chloe reluctantly declined.

"You seem like you'd be worth it." Her admirer wasn't giving up.

"Oh . . . well, I guess you'll just have to find that out then, won't you?" Chloe played his game and couldn't deny the tingles she felt as he raised his eyebrow, noting that she too was flirting. He handed the drinks to her and Heather, who made a speedy exit having spotted the boy she'd been lusting after for weeks, and Chloe felt her drunken butterflies dance inside her.

"I'm Steve," her admirer announced.

"Chloe," she replied, taking her time to fully survey him – he was well-dressed, in a black shirt and blazer, had short hair and melting eyes, which were staring right at her, almost into her. It felt good.

They talked, they laughed, and Chloe got drunker and drunker, as if that was possible. She discovered he was a third-year college student, and knowing she'd attracted a more mature guy just added to the flattery she felt. And he *was* more mature. The way he spoke, the way he held himself – Chloe felt herself being drawn in, and despite knowing somewhere at the back of her fuzzy mind that it was wrong, she couldn't stop it.

"Chloe, you have the most incredible body. Do you have any idea how unbelievably sexy you are?" Steve leant in and whispered into her ear the words which meant more to her than he could have known. He breathed heavily so that she could feel each slow exhalation tickling her neck, knowing his lips were only centimetres away from her warm, wanting skin.

"Steve, stop, I can't." She uttered the words, but the thumping music which blared from the dance floor muffled them. And she knew it would. Because she didn't want him to hear. She didn't want him to stop.

*

The following morning, Chloe felt dead. Worse than dead. Even death would be better than the throbbing agony of her head and the sandpaper tongue that sat in her groaning mouth. She hadn't had a hang-over this bad since – in fact, she'd never had one this bad in her entire life. How had she got so drunk? Or more importantly, how had she got home? The night was an unfamiliar blur, and the last thing Chloe could actually remember was . . .

Suddenly it hit her. Steve. She froze with shock, literally unable to move, to roll over and see whether someone was lying beside her. Whether *he* was lying beside her. Slowly she turned her head, fearing the worst, her heart thumping in time with the drum in her head. But there was no one there. No sleeping man, not even a scribbled goodbye note – nothing. She sighed the sigh she would always remember, so that if ever she found herself getting into a situation like that again, she could recall that moment of sheer relief and remind herself how scary it was to come so close to such a big mistake.

But what if she'd kissed him? Just because he wasn't snuggling up to her in bed didn't mean she was completely innocent. She needed answers. She needed them now. Panicking, Chloe managed to ignore the fact that every inch of her ached and rummaged around her room desperately for her phone. "Come on, come on," she shrieked, willing it to appear, possibilities forming in her mind that were too painful to think about.

"Looking for something?" Alex enquired from the doorway, holding up the very thing Chloe had been seeking. The look on her face obviously answered his question. He tossed the phone to her and turned to go, adding, "Oh, and you owe me for last night."

"What?" Chloe finally managed.

"Last night. Having to take you home at one in the morning wasn't exactly how I'd planned on ending my evening."

"You were there?" Chloe was confused. Alex looked at his sister to see if she was serious or not, but noted from the strange fear in her eyes that indeed she was.

"Man, you really were wasted. Yes, I was there – not for long, though, thanks to you. I had been in the club for a while and was strolling to the bar when I saw you chatting to some sleazy fucker who was seriously trying it on. I was just going to leave you to it – hey, your mistakes aren't my concern. But then he, like, leant into you and said something, and you like swayed and basically fell off your chair. Looked like a nasty fall, actually – are you OK?"

Chloe couldn't believe her ears.

"Go on!" she urged.

"Well, that was it really. I picked you up off the floor – I reckon the bloke thought I was your boyfriend, 'cause he fucked off fairly sharpish. So I looked around for Heather or one of the girls to get them to take you home, couldn't see them and was about to just feck you in a taxi on your own, but Andy told me not to be a dickhead, so he and I escorted you back here, had a few cans and a joint downstairs and that was the end of that."

Chloe was in shock. She'd caused a scene. Falling off her chair in front of an entire nightclub was not something she'd factored into her big girls' night. But it could have been worse. It could have been a lot worse.

"Well . . . thanks a million, Alex . . . seriously–" she began, piecing it all together slowly.

"Yeah, whatever. You owe me, remember," he interrupted and sauntered out of her bedroom.

"Oh, and ring Heather for God's sake, would you? You left your phone downstairs last night and she's been ringing all morning. I told her to fuck off so, yeah, you'd better give her a shout," Alex finished, shutting the door behind him and leaving Chloe alone once more to digest the information with which she'd just been hit. Her head started hurting again, but this was no time for moaning. She'd been lucky. Very lucky. And despite her normal reluctance to accept that her brother was anything other than completely wrong, she conceded that this time he was right – she did owe him. Big style.

*

"You don't think he, like, spiked your drink or anything, do you?" Heather suggested later that afternoon, having called around to check up on Chloe and get some answers as to where she had disappeared to last night.

"Honestly, Heather, I wish I could say I'd been spiked, but in all honesty I know I wasn't. I was so drunk. Like, so drunk," Chloe admitted with a sigh, still disappointed in herself.

"But, like, no offence, but you didn't even have that much. You used to be well able to handle your drink – now you're a complete lightweight."

"Yeah, I know. It's weird, isn't it? I don't know what's gotten into me," Chloe agreed, at a loss.

"Well, maybe if you started eating something . . ." Heather began.
"What?"

"Well, you've clearly lost weight, Chloe, we've all noticed. It's obviously affected your alcohol tolerance," Heather declared.

"So I've lost a few pounds. There's still plenty of soakage left on me – look at the size of me, for God's sake!" Chloe exclaimed, flabbergasted.

"Oh come on, you've a great figure–"

"Shut up, would you?" Chloe said, more firmly than she'd intended to. The last thing she wanted was a fight.

"Sorry," she added sincerely, hoping her friend hadn't taken offence. Heather smiled, but still the room was silent, the discomfort undeniable.

"Anyway . . . are you going to tell Sam?" Heather finally changed the subject.

"Tell him what exactly?" Chloe was once more on edge. After all, what was there to tell? But before she let herself get riled up again, she conceded that she too had been toying with this question.

She hadn't done anything. But she had wanted to. Or had she? Surely that had just been the alcohol taking over, making her feel things that weren't real. But the sensation of feeling wanted, feeling desirable – feeling like Sam used to make her feel – was something she craved these days, and last night, drunk or not, Steve had made her feel it, and it scared her.

Soon after, Heather left. Chloe eventually plodded downstairs, wholeheartedly relieved that her parents were playing golf all day, so she wouldn't have to face their cheery weekend ways. However, Andy was still with Alex, noisily battling it out on the PlayStation but nonetheless capable of shouting loudly as Chloe entered, ruthlessly slagging her for the previous night's performance. She would have told them to shut up, but she knew she deserved it. She'd been a mess; and despite feeling utterly wretched, she knew how she had to spend the rest of the day. She needed to regain control.

"I'm going to the gym," she informed the lads, though the information fell on deaf ears.

So off Chloe set, into the late afternoon sunshine, the cool breeze refreshing her. A good work-out session would sort her out. The sweat and the pain would make her pay and would draw out the nasty remains of the whole affair. She felt better already. She would be OK. She would fix herself.

*

The next day was Sunday. As usual, as Mr Walsh headed off to Mass he called out to the rest of his family, checking whether anyone wanted to join him. Usually he received no response. Sometimes, a "no" or two were faintly audible. He would then sigh and smile, reassuring them all that he'd say a prayer for them, and then he'd leave the house, alone, on his one-man pilgrimage. A devout Catholic, he never missed his weekly church session, often attending during the week too. It gave him peace. It gave him hope. And more and more recently, these were the things which Chloe sought. She decided to break the tradition.

"I'll come, Dad," she replied to his unexpectant question. He was shocked, but the grin which formed on his glowing face showed just how pleased he was with his daughter's change of heart.

They reached Donnybrook Church in no time, taking their places on the wooden pews and settling into the spiritual silence of their surroundings. Chloe felt out of place. She hadn't been here since she was a kid – except on Christmas Eve, when every family in the area rolled out for the celebration. But the stillness was oddly comforting, and Chloe set about sorting through the clutter in her mind. For the entire forty minutes, she zoned in and out of what the priest was saying, focusing more on the things which pulled at her attention, begging to be acknowledged, maybe even to be prayed for.

She asked God for forgiveness for Friday night's antics, praying that it would not happen again. She thought of Sam and asked that things get better between them, hoping that she was just overreacting. She prayed to lose more weight. She thought and prayed and hoped and asked, and suddenly it was time for Holy Communion, and then it was over and Chloe was on her way home, feeling more clear and more sure of what was going on in her head.

"I'm really glad I went," she informed her dad, not about to tell him that it hadn't exactly been a religious epiphany for her, but that she was undoubtedly appreciative of the time-out. During the Leaving Cert, Chloe had imagined this entire summer would be a time-out, considering the stresses and strains she'd been under because of the exams. But it didn't seem to be working out that way, for now that the school subjects had been emptied from her mind, so much else had rushed in to fill it, troubling her no matter where she went. Except that church. For now she was more relaxed and, as soon as she got in the door, she decided to build on this new sensation; she picked up the phone and dialled the number she'd been telling herself not to all week.

"Bonjour," Sam's polished French accent answered the call. At once, Chloe felt her stomach lurch, her love for him tingling inside her as she began to speak.

"Hey, baby. It's me."

"Oh, hey, wow, didn't know you were calling today." Sam sounded surprised, but pleasantly, Chloe hoped.

"Neither did I, really," she admitted. "So how're you?"

"Good, thanks. Think we're going to the beach today which will be savage. Tan's coming on pretty nicely, I won't lie." Sam sounded very pleased with himself. They continued talking about their respective weeks; their lack of contact meant neither knew what the other had really been up to. Chloe found herself laughing and smiling and generally remembering exactly why she loved Sam so much. But at the same time, the pleasure she got from their conversation only reminded her of the fact that he wasn't there, with her, and how badly she wished he was.

"I miss you," she admitted gently.

"I miss you too," Sam said.

"No, but seriously, I don't think you get it. I just . . . I really miss you. Like, I never thought it would be this hard. I know before you went I seemed kind of distant, like I didn't want you around so much, but I realise now what an idiot I was being, and I'm so scared I've, like, pushed you away or something," she gushed, feeling her voice begin to crack.

"What? Where's all this coming from?" Sam seemed more than a little surprised.

"Well, like, when you decided to stay on–"

"I thought we'd sorted that," Sam cut in firmly.

"Yeah, OK, fine – we had. But, like, then I thought I'd hear from you at least a little bit more. I get, like, a text a day, and I'm just feeling really weird at the moment, and I need you so much right now . . ." Chloe realised her emotions were getting out of control, as she longed to show him just how much she yearned to have him back.

"Chloe, please. Relax. I'm not pulling away from you – honestly. I'm just having fun and chilling out and soon I'll be home and it'll all be OK." Sam was far cooler than she, and it worried her.

"But what if it's not? What if this is only the start of us drifting apart? I don't feel that you want me anymore. I don't feel needed, Sam. And I need you so badly right now – do you know how scary that is?" Chloe begged, the first tear freed from her welling eyes, flowing downwards in a lonely stream.

The line was silent. Her heart thumped.

"Chloe, I love you. I really do – trust me. And of course I need you.

Just give it a week and we'll be back together and it will all be perfect . . . please?"

"OK," she conceded, hoping with all her heart that he meant it. But why wouldn't he? He'd always been true to his word, so why should she doubt it all of a sudden?

"But, babe, why are you feeling strange at the moment? Is something up?" Sam's voice was concerned.

"No, not really. Just not as happy right now as I want to be. Stressed and stuff." She tried to explain, barely knowing the answer to the question herself.

"Stressed about what, though?" Sam continued, his voice full of sympathy.

"I don't really know," Chloe admitted. "I just am. Thinking too much as usual – you know me!" She laughed, trying to lift her spirits. Sam laughed too, and once more the line was quiet, both unsure what to say next.

"Lunch!" Alex called up the stairs.

"Oh, did you hear that?" Chloe asked, disappointed that the moment had been interrupted.

"Yeah, it's cool. I think we're leaving for the beach now anyway," Sam replied.

Chloe really didn't want to let him go. She wanted to talk to him all day – to curl up and hear his voice and know that nothing else mattered but their love. But it was time to say goodbye.

"I'll be home on Saturday," Sam said.

"Cool. But I'll talk to you before then, yeah?"

"Yeah, cool. Love you."

"Love you too, Sam. So much," she concluded, putting down the phone and silently wishing it would all be OK, for it was the only outcome she could deal with.

Sunday lunch was served, and as the roast beef and Yorkshire puddings steamed on her plate, Chloe felt sick.

"Mum, I'm not really hungry," she tried, but a raised eyebrow from her mother showed that that excuse wasn't going to work.

"I'm not cooking dinner, pet, so this is it," Mrs Walsh insisted.

"But, Mum, Yorkshire puddings are, like, so fattening," Chloe pleaded. Alex laughed.

"One's not going to kill you, now is it, love, so eat up," her mother finished, smiling but her tone signifying that she meant it.

Chloe rolled her eyes, but her mum was obviously not letting this one go.

"Chloe, I mean it. Whatever's going on, it has to stop, OK? You need to eat, for goodness sake," Mrs Walsh snapped, an undeniable urgency in her words. She paused for a moment, regaining her composure before turning to her husband to ask about his week ahead.

Chloe slowly made her way through the plate of food, each bite just tasting of fat, filling her stomach with loathsome guilt. If Sam did mean all those things he'd said, he'd want to come home to a skinny girlfriend, not a whale. But every time she made to put down her cutlery and indicate that she was finished, her mother's stern gaze would fall upon her, commanding her to continue eating. Afraid to cross her, Chloe did as was desired and swallowed every disgusting morsel.

Finally the meal was over and, as she cleared the plates, Chloe's stomach felt huge, bloating hideously beneath her T-shirt. Alex was once more in front of the TV, whilst her parents finished their wine at the table. She had to do something. She felt ill. Slipping out of the kitchen, she quickly tiptoed upstairs to the bathroom, shutting the door behind her. She didn't quite know what she was doing, but had a vague idea as to how it would all work. Kneeling before the toilet bowl, Chloe closed her eyes, convincing herself this was the right thing to do. Her mind raced. She didn't need Sam. She didn't need to feel needed. The only thing she needed was to be her own boss, and if her mother was going to try and take that away by forcing her to eat that fattening filth, then she had another think coming.

Taking a deep breath, Chloe raised her index and middle fingers, and jammed them into her mouth. Nothing. She tried again, further back this time, but once she showed any sign of wretching, instinct moved her hand back out. Come on! she willed herself, eyes beginning to water. If she couldn't even manage this, how could she ever regain control of her world? Do it! she snarled inwardly, daring her body to succeed. Once more, she forced her fingers to the back of her throat, further and further down her neck until it hurt, and the wretching began again. Athough she could feel something instinctively willing her to stop, she kept her fingers there, jabbing and jabbing until the vomit came and she puked her lunch straight into the toilet bowl. It kept coming and coming, and when it stopped, she forced it to come some more. She was sweating and crying and the taste was revolting, but she was doing it. And that was all that mattered.

Finally, when there was nothing left inside her, she flushed the loo, scraping back the wet hair from her face and shaking as she stood up. Placing a hand on either side of the sink, she stared into the mirror. She looked wretched. If only they could see her now, she imagined – the party girl revealed. But no one had done this to her but herself, and that felt good. Sam could have his skinny girlfriend, but never ever would he have the kind of power that she'd just shown she had over her own self. Her breathing was heavy. She was tired, but proud. So very proud.

6

ALEX

Two weeks after his strange performance with Jenny, having been ignored by her on every night out since, Alex realised that he had to do something. But the fact that he wanted to worried him slightly, and he felt the same fear he had felt that day after lunch, knowing what was going on but not wanting to admit it – he was falling. It wasn't love – not even close. Alex laughed at the idea. But it was definitely want, a level of which he'd never experienced before. He'd tried to make it go away – scoring other girls, even getting very lucky with one lady the previous week. But despite the undeniable physical pleasure he'd experienced, the next morning that was it. He hadn't wanted any more. He had just wanted to leave. Undeniably, it had been like that on many occasions with Jenny, too: Alex slipping away the next day. But now he couldn't help feeling that next time, if there was a next time, he would stay. He would happily lie in Jenny's bed all morning, maybe go for breakfast – just hang out. He felt like such a girl admitting it, but if there was any chance of him getting that, then it was worth a shot. Jenny was worth a shot.

He had contemplated texting her, but it was far too easy for her to ignore that, and he'd only get stressed out checking for a reply. Instead, Alex decided to ring her.

"Hello?" she answered curiously, not recognising the number that was calling her.

"Hey, Jen. It's me." Alex tried to sound bright but casual.

"Oh." Jenny appeared genuinely surprised. Neither of them spoke, both parties unsure what the other wanted. Alex took control.

"Jen, look. I was just ringing to say I'm sorry for the other day. I don't really know why I was like that–"

"Or why you haven't contacted me since," Jenny added, her voice undeniably bitter.

"Yeah . . . well . . . that too. But look, I've finally realised I was being a twat. And I really want to see you again," Alex tried, not liking the eagerness of his tone, but unable to hide it nonetheless. Silence fell once more. He willed Jenny to speak.

"So why the sudden change of heart? I've seen you enough times since then – why didn't you say all of this to me before? Gagging for a fuck, are you?" she spat.

"Jen, come on. It's not like that. I know it's hard to believe because . . . well . . . it's me. I mean, I don't even know why I like you . . . Well, no, that came out wrong . . . of course I know . . . but, like, I actually properly like you . . . Fuck, why am I telling you all of this . . ." Alex wanted to stop, already imagining Jenny and her friends having a good laugh about this – the heartless player pouring out his emotions. It was embarrassing, but for some reason, he just kept going.

"I mean, there have been other girls – of course there have – but there's just something about you . . . and I just keep coming back . . . and I'm starting to realise that maybe there's a reason for that . . . like,

I don't know . . . maybe I do actually feel something, like . . . real . . ."

Alex wished she would say something to interrupt his incessant babbling. Finally, she did.

"Look, Alex. Part of me is thinking, 'no fucking way'. I've been down this road far too many times, and every time I promise myself it will be the last. No more Alex Walsh! I just can't keep doing it to myself."

Alex's pride was wounded. Was that it? Had she made her decision?

"But then there's another part of me that has never heard you talk like this before. So maybe, just maybe, you mean it this time," she concluded.

Alex could tell that, despite her wariness, she was intrigued, and slowly his confidence began to build.

"Babes, let me take you out for dinner. My treat. We'll go for food, have some wine, actually spend some time together – just see how it feels. Then you can decide what you want to do next . . ." Alex knew he was close to success. He no longer felt like a fool – he was on top again, and Jenny was going to be his.

"OK, just dinner," Jenny said.

"Yeah, just dinner. For now . . ." Alex added, unable to resist stating the obvious, hoping she wouldn't notice. Luckily she was too busy thinking where they could go.

"Actually, no, you choose," she suggested brightly, her voice so much more cheerful than only minutes before.

So the phone call had been a success, and as Alex said goodbye, promising to pick her up the following evening at seven, his ego beamed contentedly. "Too easy," he smirked, wishing there had been someone there to high-five him, commending that charm of his which worked every single time.

*

"Dad, I need a few lids for dinner – I'm going out," Alex announced the next night, putting on his coat, realising, as usual, that he was late.

"Ahem." His father coughed expectantly.

"Oh, sorry . . . please," Alex added sweetly.

"How much?" his father sighed, too tired to object.

"Well, I don't want to be stingy, so give me sixty and I'll give you the change," Alex lied.

"Yeah right!" His father saw right through him. Alex laughed.

"No, seriously though, we're going to Café Bar Deli. It would be such a mare if I was left short."

"Ooh, do I detect nerves, Alex Walsh? This wouldn't happen to be a date now, would it?" his dad teased.

Alex could feel himself blushing – a rare occurrence. Playfully, he punched his dad's arm, telling him to hurry up as he was late already.

"Picking her up, are we? God, we must be keen!" his father continued, handing his son a fifty with a wink.

"Thanks, Dad. See you later." Alex grabbed his keys and made to go.

"No drinking if you're driving," his father called after him, as all fathers would have. But Mr Walsh continued to be more cautious than ever since the accident. Such a tragedy, he sighed. He still found himself lying awake in bed at night, praying for Barry and his parents – unable to fully comprehend the reality of all that had happened. Alex seemed brighter, that was for sure, and at least he'd been in to visit Barry in the hospital. But Paddy Walsh just hoped that his son had taken his advice and really paused to take it all in. Life was so hard sometimes, he thought, but all they could do was be eternally thankful that Alex was OK and hope that soon Barry would be too.

*

As Alex zoomed over to Jenny's, he built himself up, feeling strangely nervous but also excited, surprised that a mere date was having such an effect on him. Unable to control himself, he grinned, just picturing what the lads would say if they could see him now. Thankfully, they were all far away, gone to Spain, unaware of their friend's recent antics. Alex thanked his lucky stars, knowing the slagging that would have surely ensued if he'd revealed that he, Alex Walsh, was taking Jenny on a dinner date. Jenny – the girl he'd always known was there for the taking; his back-up; his Plan B. Well, that was a bit harsh he conceded, especially as she came out of her front door and walked to the car looking far hotter than a Plan B ever should. She was gorgeous. She wore a little black dress and a silver cardigan and her jewellery, lip gloss and newly washed hair all dazzled beneath the streetlight. She sat into the passenger seat, leaning over to kiss Alex on the cheek. He was slightly speechless as he returned the kiss, smelling the dark, musky scent that surrounded her. She stared into his eyes and he into hers. He felt something tingle in his trousers. He wanted her.

"Shall we go? I'm starving," Jenny announced with a wry grin, pulling away from his gaze, evidently keen to play hard to get tonight. Alex was more than ready for the chase.

"You look hot," he complimented as they cruised down the Stillorgan dual carriageway. Jenny batted her eyelids and smiled appreciatively, and Alex recognised the nervousness and excitement which danced in her eyes.

They reached Ranelagh and luckily found a parking space. Alex stepped out of the car and ran round to open Jenny's door. He'd decided if he really wanted this – if he really wanted her – then a little bit of chivalry would help his cause no end.

"Wow, pulling out all the stops, aren't we?" she laughed, linking his arm and embarking on the brief walk to the restaurant.

Their table was ready for them. Alex pulled out Jenny's chair for her to sit down before taking his own seat and examining the menu.

"Someone's being quite the charmer tonight, then," Jenny

commented, evidently intrigued by Alex's new approach. Alex simply smiled in reply, changing the subject but still playing all his cards right.

"Do you want wine?" he enquired.

"Oh . . . well, are you drinking? Hardly if you're driving . . . well, I suppose you could have one . . . so yes please, then . . . if that's OK, like?" Jenny was flustered despite her attempted cool façade. Quickly she regained her composure, gazing at the menu pensively until the waiter arrived to take their order.

"I'm fucking starved," Alex declared as the waiter left, momentarily forgetting his polite persona. Luckily Jenny giggled in response, relaxing into her seat and fixing her eyes on him once more. She stared and stared, but showed no sign of speaking.

"What are you looking at?" Alex finally felt compelled to ask.

"Nothing," Jenny lied.

"Come on . . ."

"OK . . . I'm looking at you." She paused. "I'm happy," she admitted.

"Oh yeah?" Alex smirked, leaning into the table, daring her to say more.

"Yeah. It's just this – you and me . . . on a dinner date . . . Who'd have thought it?" She grinned, her sultry voice drawing him in.

"So does that mean you've forgiven me?" Alex took her hand in his, hoping the slate was cleaned.

"Maybe . . ." she replied, leaning further forward, giving Alex a clear view of her cleavage and causing him to try very hard not to suggest just leaving the restaurant there and then and going back to hers. Somehow, he managed, knowing he hadn't earned quite enough brownie points for that. Yet.

The wine arrived and, soon after, the food. It looked and smelled incredible, and thankfully the taste didn't disappoint. Alex wolfed down each course, constantly topping up Jenny's glass, just to keep her in high spirits. He only had two glasses, bearing in mind what his dad had said, but trying not to let his thoughts wander to Barry. Not now.

*

85

Their main course was cleared away, and both of them sighed with contentment, eager for a break before dessert (though Alex wasn't sure if Jenny had the same thing in mind for their last course as he did). But suddenly he felt something soft on his left foot, rubbing it ever so gently and rising slowly up his calf. Maybe she was on his wavelength after all! He looked her in the eye, wondering exactly what she was thinking as she took another sip of wine, allowing her tongue to touch the glass, making Alex wish it was somewhere else. He glanced at the wine bottle – practically empty, which meant his chances were severely increased and thus leaving him unable to resist asking, "So, do you want dessert, or will we just get out of here . . .?"

Jenny looked at him, and for one split-second he was convinced he'd pushed his luck too far. He held his breath in fear. But then he saw something else which made his heart leap once more, as hormones began to race inside him.

"Let's go," Jenny proclaimed, never once letting her gaze falter, as if sealing Alex into a deal that, this time, he wasn't allowed to break. But he didn't want to. He was going to have Jenny, and tomorrow morning he would still be there – because that was what he wanted. She was what he wanted.

They sat in silence as he drove to her street, the darkness finally taking over from the sunny day, kissing the world goodnight. Alex parked outside Jenny's house, turning off the engine so that only a charged silence filled the car, both hating the gap between them, wanting so very much more. But fate was having none of it, and just when Alex thought all his birthdays had come at once, Jenny's face fell, and he knew that something was wrong.

"What is it, babe?" he enquired timidly, fearing the worst.

"It's my parents," Jenny tipsily admitted, confusing Alex.

"What?"

"My parents, Alex . . . their car . . . it's home . . . they're home," she announced, clearly disappointed, as Alex's stomach plummeted.

"Fuck," he cursed, banging his fist on the wheel, his mind racing for a way to sort out this mess. He knew his family were all at home too. They had nowhere to go. But he had to do it – he had to have sex with Jenny. Right now. Desperate for a solution, he had only a vague idea that he doubted would work. But he was willing to give it a go.

"I want you so badly, Jen." He turned to her, his voice lower, showing her that their lust was mutual. She stared at him, not knowing what to do, clearly searching for a plan, just as Alex had. But leaning in, Alex kissed her, making all her other thoughts just disappear in an instant. He kissed her and kissed her, tasting her soft lips, which still vaguely awakened of white wine. He didn't care, wanting every inch of her there and then and kissing her with such passion that she would surely know it.

Gently, he placed his hand on her face, holding it softly in a brief moment of tenderness, before it started to slide downwards through her hair, down her neck, past her breast and then to her waist, pausing slightly just to tease, to make her see how much she craved it. Finally, Alex allowed his hand to continue, gently feeling the outline of her thong as it moved passed the end of her dress to her bare leg. Still Jenny's tongue seduced his, not wanting to stop, as his hand moved back up along her leg, though this time inside her dress, moving at so slow a pace Jenny thought she would explode with tingles. She wanted to press against him, to feel his body upon hers, but the awkwardness of the car meant the seats kept them uncomfortably apart. Nevertheless, Alex's fingers continued tiptoeing lightly, finding rest between Jenny's thighs, and she groaned loudly, unable to resist any longer.

"Alex, I want you," she breathed, eyes still closed, leaning her head back so that he could kiss her neck.

"Jenny, I have to have you," he replied, feathering her bronzed skin with longing caresses.

"Me too," she whispered in ecstasy, so Alex knew at last that his idea might, against all the odds, be put into action.

"We could do it here, you know," he suggested, praying she would agree. Jenny pulled away, breathing heavily and fixing her eyes upon his.

"What?"

"Here – we could just do it here," Alex repeated, his chest heaving with desire.

"I don't know . . ." she began.

"It's fine. No one's going to walk by – it's late. Plus the windows are fogged up enough as it is." Alex gave a nervous laugh, wishing he had had a better excuse. He could see that Jenny knew it was a bad idea, that she was afraid and shy and that her instinct was screaming at her to say no. But lust, and wine, and the reality of Alex Walsh finally actually wanting her was too exquisite a cocktail to ignore.

"What if my parents come out?"

"They won't," he reassured. "I promise."

And although they both knew he could never promise such a thing, for some reason it was enough, and as Jenny climbed into the back seat, Alex felt his hormones bubble with anticipation. It had worked.

He joined her in the back of the car, where the lack of space wasn't exactly ideal. She straddled him, pressing her groin to his whilst fumbling with his belt, as Alex began to kiss her once more. Slowly he removed her underwear, unable to keep his hands to himself, his mind going numb with uncontrollable pleasure. He throbbed with lust as they became more and more caught up in the moment.

"Do you have a condom?" she mumbled between kisses, lost in the bliss of it all.

"No, do you?" he replied quickly, not wanting to stop. But suddenly Jenny pulled away, bringing reality back.

"Alex, I'm not on the pill," she said.

His heart stopped. What could he say? Having come this far, there was no chance something so trivial was going to stand in his way.

"Jen, it'll be fine," he assured, moving in to kiss her once more. But she dodged his lips.

"Alex, I don't know. Is it worth the risk?" she deliberated, sounding more sober than she had done all night.

"Of course it is," he said, kissing her deeply and pressing her to him, before pulling only the tiniest bit away, so that their lips still lightly touched. "It'll be fine, Jen . . . trust me," he whispered sincerely, feeling a momentary hesitation in her before her body took over her mind and she kissed him so intensely that he was completely blown away. "This is it," he thought. "This is fucking it."

*

In the days which followed, Alex's spirits were sky high. His parents noticed, even Chloe noticed, that there was an undeniable spring in his step. It was strange, because he'd had sex with Jenny so many times before, but whether it was the kinky location or just the satisfaction of having her back, Alex was happy. Not that they were going out – he certainly didn't want to go down that road just before Ayia Napa, and indeed college. Alex loved being a free bird. But there was still a certain amount of security that Jenny gave him, which felt good. Plus, his head had definitely grown since Wednesday night, and he wasn't going to keep his escapades to himself.

HEY MAN. FUCKD JENNY IN D BAK OF MY CAR, OUTSIDE HER GAFF. HIGH 5! U MAY HAV BN IN SPAIN, BT DON TINK I DIDN HAV FUN W/O U! C U 2MO!

A similar text had been sent to the majority of the lads, all leading to general congratulatory messages, promising they owed him a drink the following day, when they returned to Ireland. The only one who hadn't replied was Andy. Alex wondered if there was anything significant in this lack of response but decided quickly that he was being ridiculous – why on earth would Andy have a problem with such an impressive conquest? Alex was really looking forward to seeing him. Although only some of his gang had gone away, Alex had still felt that things in Dublin were much quieter, mainly because the majority of people he usually saw out and about were all away too, securing an undercoat of tan before their journey to Ayia Napa. But also his friends who hadn't graced Marbella with their presence hadn't really been in touch. A few of the boys seemed to be acting strangely towards him since . . . well, since the accident. Alex was puzzled. Still, his close lads would be home tomorrow and the coming weekend was the first of August, and a bank holiday, which only meant one thing – Brittas Bay!

A number of Alex's friends, along with a barrage of people from the South Dublin circles, owned holiday homes down in sunny Brittas. South of Dublin along the coast, the white beaches and community atmosphere made it a haven for affluent families, who whiled away the time there all summer. Then every August bank-holiday weekend, the world and his drinking posse would head down, crashing on various floors and couches, for three days of drinking, socialising and the usual networking. As always, Alex would be sleeping in Andy's mobile home and was looking forward to it immensely, glad that all his group would be reunited, as well as being silently conscious of the fact that Jenny also had a place down there – and surely her parents couldn't be in it all the time!

But despite there being only a day until his crew arrived home, something else was on Alex's mind – a journey that he'd been putting off for a while now. Perhaps it was the effect of his good mood, or perhaps it was the many memories that filled him with thoughts of Barry and his crazy antics in Brittas in the past that now compelled Alex to visit him. This time he'd say something. This time he wouldn't be so scared.

Driving to the hospital, he couldn't believe that it was six weeks since the crash. Six weeks. But still nothing. Still no Barry. "No news is good news," Alex tried to convince himself, rolling down the window to allow the last breaths of July to gush in. Quite bluntly, at least his friend hadn't died. At least he was still in the same state, rather than having gone downhill. Alex sighed, stuck at traffic lights, gazing up at the birds who danced and chattered – comparing holiday stories, no doubt. Alex stared into space, mesmerised by the charms of summer, his favourite temptress.

A horn beeped. The light had turned green. Drivers were impatient.

Alex gave the car behind him the finger before whizzing off, furious that they'd spoiled his moment of pure detachment, losing himself in the sweet heat of nothingness before the future called him on.

Barry lay as he had done the last time: motionless save for the steady rise and fall of his chest reassuring any onlookers that, despite first appearances, he was in fact alive. Alex took a seat, feeling a little more at ease than last time, having got this far before. Staring at his friend's face, the cuts and bruises almost completely healed, Alex found his confidence sapped once more, unable to believe that there he was, living it up in his summer of freedom, while his friend lay there in some empty limbo.

But he willed himself to be positive, trying to draw on the joy that had filled him over the past few days, desperate not to lose such a feeling.

"Hey, man," he said, feeling awkward and ridiculous but convincing himself that this was the right thing to do.

"How are you?" Alex shook his head, perfectly able to see the bleak response to that mindless question. He continued briskly.

"So, let me see, do I have any news for you?" he pondered, shunning the feeling of stupidity which tried to creep in.

"Well, me and Jenny have been getting on really well. Went on, like, a proper dinner date earlier in the week, which was surprisingly cool. She's actually a really nice girl. I mean, I always knew that. But still, recently things have kind of changed. Like, I'm not just interested in fucking her – don't get me wrong, though, that's still amazing. But I think I, like, properly like her." Alex found himself hoping that Barry couldn't actually hear him, as he blushed despite himself.

"I don't, like, love her or anything. I don't even want to go out with her – we're about to go to Ayia Napa, for fuck's sake. Plus, nobody wants to be tied down heading into college . . ." he trailed off again, having accidentally introduced a topic he had been trying to forget about of late. It couldn't hurt to vent, though, as he was undoubtedly on a roll, and, surprisingly, it felt good.

"Yeah, so . . . college. What the fuck, like? What do I even want to do? What did I even apply for? I haven't a clue. I just want this summer to continue forever, like – no responsibilities, no worries . . . Well, OK, let's be fair, I have been worrying. Which is really weird for me. But, I mean, all I've been worried about is, like, shit to do with next year. So if I knew that I didn't have to face into all of that shite, then I could finally chill the fuck out, like, properly," Alex reasoned, his thoughts and emotions finally released from the box into which they'd been compressed by denial, pride and fear.

"But, like, that's all well and good if we all, like, just dossed around next year – it'd be savage. But then all the lads are kind of feeling the UCD buzz, and I just don't like the thought of us all turning into college poofs, you know. Why can't we just stay like this? It's sweet." Alex winced at his inappropriate concluding remark.

"Well, obviously it isn't sweet for you. But, like, you'll be awake again by the Napa, won't you? I'm supposed to be sharing a room with you, so you'd better not screw me over." He laughed, willing his friend to respond.

But nothing. Not a twitch, not a blink, not a single change to that beep and that click and that incessant reminder that Barry wasn't really there. He was just part of a machine now, waiting to come out of it. If he ever came out of it. But they'd both been in the same car. It was an injustice that more and more was starting to plague Alex. At first he'd just felt lucky, but soon that feeling had turned to a burning, unanswerable question: why him? Why had he been the lucky one?

"I don't get it, man." He found himself beginning to speak. "I mean, you were never exactly an angel yourself, but at least you had a bit more going for you than me. Like, next year – you had it all worked out – you wanted to do that engineering thing. And you would have got it, man. You still will get it . . ." Alex trailed off, trying to avoid any negativity.

"And this weekend, it's Brittas weekend – I can't fucking wait. But, like, every year it was always you, me and Andy having a ball together, knowing there was only a month of summer left. The barbecues, the beach, McDaniel's – the best pub in the world – I don't know if I can do it. I don't know if I can just go down there and pretend that nothing's changed. Because it has. So much has fucking changed." Alex poured out his thoughts, not knowing why he was getting so emotional considering the cheerful mood he'd been in earlier. Still the heart monitor beeped. Still the machines clicked.

"I'm sorry, man," he continued quietly, still conscious that if anyone saw him he'd feel completely stupid. "I don't want to be a big moan. Things are actually savage at the moment . . . Just coming here has an awful knack of putting things into perspective," he conceded with a sigh, knowing how true it was.

Alex checked his watch – he'd been there an hour. It was time to go.

"Listen, I better head. I'll see you, buddy. Will think of you in Brittas, yeah? But if you, like, change your mind or whatever, just give me a call." He laughed, a bittersweet attempt at humour, knowing that was the one thing that would make him truly happy.

The hospital corridor smelled the same as always. Things never changed in this place, Alex decided, as if his friend were caught in a trap of time; in a world that couldn't take that all-important step forward, the same step into the future which Alex dreaded to take himself. Life was complicated, he concluded, returning to the car, as a young girl skipped past him, clutching a bunch of pink roses for whoever she was visiting, her twinkling eyes and radiant smile so innocent in the face of the towering building housing sickness and death in its every corner. If only she knew, Alex sighed. If only she knew.

*

The drive to Brittas was full of banter, Alex thoroughly enjoying having his boys back in town. He sat in the passenger seat of Andy's car, a can of beer in one hand and an iPod in the other, shuffling around for a suitably rowdy song. It was only two o'clock on a Saturday afternoon, yet already the party had started, and since on previous years they had headed down on the Friday, they were now trying to make up for lost time. Two of their other friends, Luke and Kyle, sat in the back seat, both getting equally psyched up for the weekend ahead, knowing from past experience that it was going to be a blast.

Once they reached the supermarket, Andy parked the car and they began the challenge of buying as much alcohol as cheaply as possible. Since Andy's parents were already down in the mobile home, Alex knew that he'd be treated to home-cooked food all weekend and was looking forward to taking full advantage of Andy's mum's incredible culinary skills.

They loaded up the car with their dodgy brands of beer and vodka and hit the road again, almost able to taste the sea air as they neared their destination, each of them more filled with anticipation and excitement than the next. Finally they arrived, making Andy's dad come and get them with the special car pass necessary for the residents to get in, so as to keep out the millions of visitors who swarmed upon their holiday park this weekend every year. Luke and Kyle made their way to Kyle's mobile home, promising to meet up with the other two later, whilst Alex helped Andy unpack the car and to fit their minimal luggage and maximum alcohol load into Andy's tiny room.

Andy's parents were delighted to see Alex, as was their other son, Max, who was only two years younger than his brother and whom Alex rated very highly.

"Hey, faggot," Alex greeted him.

"Fuck off, Walshy, who invited you anyway?" Max teased, though unable to hide his grin. Alex grabbed him and wrestled him to the floor, taking a few punches as their ritual beating began.

"You two will never change, will you?" Andy shook his head in amusement, the novelty of such horseplay having long worn off between him and his brother.

"You boys must be starving," Andy's mum announced, arriving on the terrace without as much as a blink of an eye, as Alex and Max rolled around in a mock brawl.

"Yeah, I'm famished," Andy confirmed.

"Me too, Mrs Jennings," Alex managed, grabbing Max in a headlock before punching him some more.

"Right, well I'll make some sandwiches, shall I, and then you guys can go for a wander – see which of your friends are around." Mrs Jennings set off back to their little kitchen to prepare an afternoon feast for them all.

Stuffed, Alex and Andy just about managed to roll out of their seats and amble lazily down towards the beach for a nice siesta. The strand stretched out for over a mile, the pale sand smooth beneath their toes, while just behind the beach the tall dunes loomed, a mini desert save for the spiked grasses which carpeted much of the ground, dancing excitedly in the sea breeze. The water itself was a pale blue. The swell was gentle, as the weather proved perfect as always this weekend, a warmth in the air so lovely that the Irish Sea was almost bearable to swim in. The air tasted of summer, while the shouts of children echoed along the beach, chasing and building sandcastles, tiny emperors themselves, proud of their creations.

"Alex, Andy," a familiar voice called out, spotting the boys. A group of girls they knew waved in their direction and the lads strolled over to say hello. The girls wore brightly coloured bikinis, and their bodies shone with a mixture of sweat and suntan lotion, the smell of which surrounded them, summer's signature aroma. Alex and Andy sat down beside them on the sand, chatting about each of their summers and then all united in excitement for Ayia Napa. After a while, though, promising to see them that night in McDaniel's pub, the boys decided to keep making their way up the beach, knowing many more of their friends were around somewhere.

They spotted the lads from their school eventually, some playing in the sea whilst others sipped cans on the sand, preparing for the night ahead. Andy went for a splash, but Alex decided to chill out on dry land, crack open a beer and soak up the weakening afternoon sunshine.

"Have you seen Jenny and that lot around," he tried to enquire casually. Unfortunately, a chorus of whooping ensued, teasing their friend for his curiosity.

"No, sorry! But we have seen your sister. You should see her in a bikini, man – I'd definitely give her one . . . again!" Kyle teased brashly, and the boys exploded into louder laughter.

"You prick." Alex smirked, knowing that it was probably better to just keep quiet. They always had the trump card on him, though he'd forgotten Chloe was actually coming down too.

"Aha, speak of the devil," Luke called out, the boys all turning their heads to spot Walshy's sister, cheering and calling her over. Alex wished they would just stop. Unfortunately, she came over with her best friend

Heather in tow, both scantily clad like most women on the beach.

"We were just talking about you," one of the lads said cheekily. Chloe shot a glare in Alex's direction.

"What? Don't look at me," Alex said, putting his hands up in a display of his innocence. His sister turned back to the other boys, who, Alex noticed, were hanging on her every word. Then the lads who had been in the water appeared, all shiny wet, dripping from their salty bath.

"Oh, hey, Chloe, Heather," Andy greeted them, ever the charmer.

"Hey," they both replied.

"Here, listen, I'm having people over to mine tonight for a session before we hit McDaniel's. You girls are welcome to come along if you want," he said.

"Cool, thanks," Chloe accepted, her voice low and a glint in her eye that confused Alex. "See you guys then," she said, strutting away with Heather by her side, their steps in time with one another. The boys all watched them go, hypnotised by their swaying bottoms. Unusually, Alex also found himself fixed on the image of the departing girls. He couldn't figure it out, but something didn't fit. He'd always thought Heather had had a good body, but now, walking beside his sister, she looked huge. Suddenly Alex realised that Heather had the same cracking figure as always – she wasn't the one who had changed: it was Chloe. Alex knew she'd been spending a lot of time in the gym, and she hadn't exactly been eating everything in sight, but he'd never actually noticed a change in her appearance. Until now. He didn't want to dwell on it – frankly, she could look however she wanted as long as she was happy – and returned to subtly scouring the beach for the one body he did want to see – Jenny's.

Unfortunately, she was nowhere to be seen, and there was no way Alex was going to go looking for her properly – the lads would rip into him. Instead, he decided to send her a text, inviting her to Andy's little get-together that evening, hoping she had come down as planned.

HEY BABE. U IN BRITTAS? DIDN C U AROUND. JUS 2SAY, ANDYS HAVN PPL
OVA B4 MCDANIELS SO U+UR GIRLS SHUD CUM ALONG. TWUD B NICE 2
C U. XX

Within minutes he had a reply.

YEA, WE JUS ARRIVD - SOZ,TRAFFIC WOZ SHIT. COOLNESS, C U@ANDYS
DEN. CANT W8, XX

Alex grinned, trying to hide it from his friends, unwilling to give
them any more ammunition than they already had.

"Dude, it's half-past six. Dinner's at seven. We better head back
up," Andy informed him, rolling up his towel and putting his flip-
flops back on. So off they plodded back to the holiday park, wishing
the others goodbye as they all headed their separate ways, agreeing to
reconvene in Andy's at nine.

"Eh, I hope you don't mind, man, but I invited Jenny and all them
if that's OK?" Alex murmured once it was only the two of them.

Andy surveyed his friend's face.

"You really like her, don't you?" Andy almost accused.

"No," Alex protested weakly.

"Dude, I'm not thick."

"Yeah, but it's so gay. I never like girls. Not, like . . . properly."

Neither of them spoke.

"She's a savage girl," Andy said quietly, staring at the ground.

Alex stopped and turned to his friend, looking at him in
confusion. There was something in Andy's tone that didn't make
sense. Disappointment? Jealousy? Alex couldn't pinpoint it.

"What's that supposed to mean?" he finally asked.

Andy stared back towards the beach, his eyes flitting across the foot-
printed sand. He answered with a sigh, "Nothing . . . it's just . . . nothing.
It seems like you do actually like her, and now ... well ... it seems like she
really likes you, so ..." He swallowed deeply. "Just go for it I guess."

Alex could have sworn that something still was not quite right, but
decided it was just his imagination.

"Thanks," he said sheepishly, not knowing where that moment of seriousness had just come from, but glad that it had. He couldn't help but think of Barry.

*

After dinner, people began to filter onto Andy's terrace, where the patio heaters kept the slight chill of the evening at bay and his iPod speakers blasted out The Kooks, making sure summer spirits were high. Alex was on the beer, easing himself into the long night ahead. Everyone was in flying form and it was just like old times, as Alex and all the boys from school sat around the patio table in noisy relaxation. Chloe and her friends arrived soon after, his sister ignoring the shower of wolf whistles by coming to talk to him, asking about his day.

"Savage, yeah. Andy's mum cooked us such a sexy dinner." He almost drooled, thinking of their tasty feast.

"Yeah, Heather's mum made us yummy stuff too," Chloe said.

"Pity you had about two bites," a passing Heather remarked, continuing inside with Andy to get a glass. Chloe's eyes fell to the ground. Alex felt awkward, not wanting to get involved in any girlie image rubbish. Luckily, Jenny and her friends arrived just in time. She was dressed casually, in tight jeans and a T-shirt, but still she looked good, if not a little tired. The boys all welcomed her, some winking and raising eyebrows in Alex's direction, making him have to work not to be embarrassed. But he was happy she'd come, and eventually she strolled over to say hello, kissing him on the lips, leaving him feeling as proud as punch.

The drink flowed, with various games being called upon to assist with the speedy consumption of their alcohol. Alex could feel his head grow lighter by the minute, deciding that his mission for the evening was to get Andy's little brother wasted too.

"Here, fuckface, have another shot with me," he called over. Max willingly agreed and joined Alex in downing the sambuca with relish.

"You coming to McDaniel's?" Alex slurred, already cruising past the tipsy phase.

"Of course," Max replied, glad to be invited by the coolest of his brother's friends.

"We'd better get going, actually," Alex added, stumbling slightly as he climbed onto one of the patio chairs.

"Hey, guys, it's, like, half-eleven . . . we should . . . we should, like, go!" he managed, rewarded with a chorus of cheers and what might have been a slight glare from Jenny, though he couldn't tell. He'd talk to her when he got to the pub, but for now, there was some serious drinking to be done, and he filled his pockets with cans to keep him going for the five-minute walk.

McDaniel's was jammers. It was the only place to go this weekend, so various ages of Southside teenagers filled its every corner, the designer clothes and posh accents blurring together, as Alex finally made it past the discerning eyes of the bouncers, trying his hardest to convince them that he hadn't had one too many. He, Andy and Max went straight to the bar, ordering 3 requilas – a potent mixture of Red Aftershock and tequila – and downing the sharp shots apace. After that, the night was somewhat a blur, as Alex flitted around, knowing practically every single person in the place, buying drinks, moving clumsily on the dance floor and generally having a ball.

The guys from school were all on similar form, and Alex arrived behind a group of them, throwing his arms around their shoulders and blasting out their school anthem at the top of his voice. Some joined in, others just grinned, but despite his drunkenness, Alex noticed one of them slipping away, shaking his head and sitting down beside some chesty brunette. Alex ceased his singing, allowing the others to continue whilst he strained his ears to hear what the deserter was saying.

". . . I just can't look at him the same way . . . Barry . . . so fucking arrogant . . ." was all Alex could grasp, piecing together the bits in between as his heart sank from its fuzzy high. It was so unfair. He wasn't arrogant – he was just getting on with his life, as Barry would have wanted him to, he assured himself. It was time for another round of shots.

The night continued. Last thing Alex could remember was slipping out the back with the lads for a joint and the vague image of a glaring Jenny . . .

"My head," Alex groaned the next morning.

"Ha ha, serves you right," Andy called up from the bunk below. "You were fucked."

"Weren't you?" Alex grunted through the intense pain.

"Of course. Everyone was!"

"What time did we get home?"

"About five – the banter on the beach afterwards was deadly," Andy recalled brightly, despite his throbbing head.

"The beach? Oh yeah, I remember that . . . well . . . not really," Alex admitted.

"Ha ha, you were hilarious, man. You and my brother were both wasted, and you started your usual beating-up shit on the beach! Some people thought you were having a real fight – it was fucking funny!" Andy laughed.

Alex was too weak to reply, though at least Andy had explained why his bed was full of sand. He could barely move he was so hungover and tried to fall back asleep once more. But twenty minutes later, the intense aroma of Mrs Jennings' fry wafted into the bedroom. If there was one thing in the world that would get the boys up, this was it. Somehow Alex found the strength to arise and go in search of greasy food. It was worth the effort.

*

The day that followed was an even lazier repeat of the previous one, with a trip to the beach, a massive dinner and a drinking session in Andy's leading them back once again to McDaniel's, though Alex had to take it slightly easier that night, his liver officially not talking to him. Instead, he was on the lookout for Jenny, who hadn't come to Andy's this time and who Alex suspected was less than impressed with him. Eventually he spotted her at the bar with her friend, Megan.

"Hey," he said as he approached the two.

"Oh, hey," Jenny replied, giving nothing away.

"Here, listen, I'm sorry about last night – I got completely mouldy, and was in no fit state to talk to you." Alex came out with his hands up, fearing another fight with Jenny could be on the horizon. Fortunately, he was wrong.

"It's grand, you guys were all such a mess. Do you want a drink?" she offered, catching him offguard but allowing his heart to settle once more as he willingly accepted the pint and led her to a table so that they could chat.

"So, did you hear about the campsite last night?" she asked.

"No?"

"Yeah, loads of people had set their tents up down in the dunes, and then last night, these knackers came down and completely trashed the place."

. "Fuck."

"Yeah, apparently it was really bad, like. I was talking to these girls earlier on the beach, and they were pretty upset, like – they even said one of the tents got set on fire."

"Jesus," Alex exclaimed, though doubting it could have been that bad. Still, he was thankful for his bed in the Jennings'.

Hours later, they were still locked in conversation, as their friends came and went, joining the couple but then leaving them in peace. One face, however, spoiled his calm, for through the swarms of teenagers, Alex spotted Phil, Barry's cousin. Ordinarily they would have nodded in acknowledgement, having chatted quite a few times. But not tonight. The look in Phil's eyes was in no way friendly, as his ice-cold stare pierced Alex. Who did Phil think he was? If anything, Phil should be making an effort to talk to him, since Phil's cousin was Alex's best friend and thus they shared a deep concern.

"Who's that?" Jenny asked, noticing his distraction.

"Oh, no one."

"Is that that guy Phil?" she persisted.

"Yeah," Alex admitted, wondering how she knew his name.

"Jesus, he is not your number-one fan, is he? Why the hell is he giving you such filthies?"

Alex sighed. He didn't want to be talking about this. He didn't want to be thinking about this. But there was nothing he could do except answer Jenny's inquisitive eyes.

"He's Barry's cousin, OK? Look, can we not talk about this?" Alex said sharply.

"Oh, right . . . eh, yeah, grand . . ." Jenny stuttered, taken aback by his harshness.

Alex willed himself to get back to the good mood he'd been in all evening. Now wasn't the time to be thinking about Barry or his family or any of that. He wished it would all just stop. He wished Phil would stop staring.

But Phil wasn't going to stop. How could he? There was Mister High-and-Mighty, sitting there without a care in the world, as if nothing had happened. Every time Phil saw him out, acting as cocky as always, he felt like screaming at him: screaming that it was disgusting to be behaving that way when Barry had been lying in a coma in hospital for over a month. It broke Phil's heart. He'd known Alex through Barry for years now, never actually liking him, as his immense ego and jack-the-lad attitude had always irritated Phil. He could never understand why Alex's friends looked up to him when obviously he was a complete and utter moron. But they did. And so did all the girls. Even Jenny – a girl Phil had always had a thing for – seemed completely sucked in by Alex's carefree approach to life, which appeared more to Phil like sheer ignorance. But even now, after an event which Phil had truly believed might have actually had an effect on him, Alex seemed as selfish as ever. He'd heard that Alex had been in to visit Barry a couple of times, but as Phil sat with his cousin four times a week, wishing he would wake up, he could feel nothing but hatred for that arrogant waste of space who had walked free from that crash. It wasn't fair. Phil knocked back his pint and headed outside to the smoking area, unable to bear the sight of Alex Walsh any longer. It was disgusting.

An hour later, and Alex was finally enjoying himself again, employing tequila to distract him from Phil's piercing gaze and the worries it had brewed up inside him, managing to get himself quite tipsy. But he couldn't deny that a lot of that had to do with the company, as Jenny made him relaxed as always, flirting and playing more than ever. The buzz of the pub cocooned them, but a twinkle in Jenny's eye showed she was about to come up with an even better idea.

"Let's go," she suddenly whispered, catching Alex off guard.

"Where?"

"I don't know . . . out of here . . ." Jenny tilted her head to the side, indicating exactly what she meant.

"Oh . . . right . . . well, are your parents home?" Alex caught her drift, impressed that she had been the one to suggest it.

"Yeah, I think so," she conceded. "We could just go for a walk on the beach."

"Oh." Alex's heart sank.

But Jenny took his hand and dragged him up from his seat, kissing him deeply.

"You know, there are other things we can do on the beach, too."

she whispered into his ear, her hand sliding downwards just to ensure he'd caught her drift. Alex had caught it all right, and once more thanked his lucky stars – it seemed he had unleashed a new side of Jenny, of which he definitely approved. They left the pub hand in hand, out into the mild night, where the constellations dazzled in the inky black sea, lighting the lovers' every step down to the beach, where passion took over and their silhouettes became one.

*

Driving home the following day, the boys all agreed that the weekend had more than lived up to billing, as they sipped on their remaining cans and waved Brittas goodbye. But now it was officially August – the month of Ayia Napa, but also the month of exam results. Time was marching on, Alex realised, thinking once more of Barry. The future was on its way.

7

CHLOE

As soon as she arrived back from Brittas, Chloe went straight to the gym for two hours, not pausing once until she finally went home in the early evening. Sam was coming home tomorrow and Chloe was doing as many last-minute preparations as possible, determined to start off on the right foot. It had been just over a month since they'd been together and Chloe had hated every moment, hated the doubt and uncertainty as her own self-esteem plummeted by the day.

She was still disappointed; she'd wanted to be wonderfully thin for his arrival, hoping to blow him away with her amazing body, to show him how she'd changed. But still she looked in the mirror and didn't see what she wanted to. Not even close to her desired size. It had felt disgusting walking on the beach in Brittas, her bikini revealing her overweight body, as she felt all eyes on her. She knew she was skinnier than many of her friends, but to Chloe's eye, she still had a long way to go, and she wasn't giving up until she got there.

It was Heather's birthday that evening, so the girls were meeting up in Milano in town for dinner – after the long weekend they'd all had in Brittas, they weren't up to clubbing. Chloe was close to texting Heather, saying that she was completely wrecked and couldn't make it, but her conscience got the better of her – she was her best friend, after all. But the truth was, Chloe wasn't wrecked – not especially. She just didn't feel like dinner, didn't feel like eating. So instead, she came up with a better plan.

"Why aren't you ordering anything?" Heather asked her, as they sat in the buzzing restaurant that night.

"Oh, did I not tell you? Mum cooked Alex and me a huge dinner when we got home from Brittas – apparently she'd missed us or some shit," Chloe lied nonchalantly.

"Oh." Chloe could have sworn she saw a sliver of doubt in her friend's dark-green eyes. It must have been her imagination.

"So, what did you get from your parents, then?" Chloe changed the subject, not wanting to dwell on her fibs.

"A Chanel bag, money for Ayia Napa, insurance on my mum's car, a Tiffany's necklace . . . "

"Bloody hell, you did nicely!"

"Yeah, I suppose. It's my last teenage birthday, though – they can afford to spoil me a bit." Heather smiled from ear to ear.

"A bit?" Chloe laughed, wishing her parents were more generous with their money. They certainly had enough, but had always maintained that they would never spend it extravagantly on the kids. That said, Alex never wanted for anything, and the fact that he hadn't bothered to get a job this summer meant there was a definite double standard. But Chloe knew that she was better off – spending her own money felt so much better than constantly blagging it off her parents. Not that she had a problem with that from time to time, of course.

"So are you excited about seeing Sam?" Heather chirped.

"You have no idea," Chloe said. "It feels like it's been forever."

"Yeah, you've seemed kind of down without him . . . if you don't mind me saying."

"Oh, really?" Chloe was surprised, knowing that it was probably true but unaware that her friends had noticed.

"Yeah, you just haven't seemed the same since . . . well . . . pretty much since the Leaving ended. You've just been really distant."

"Yeah, but everyone's a bit all over the place this summer – after this, none of us knows what will happen," Chloe reasoned.

"Yeah, but like, because next year's so uncertain and stuff, the rest of us have been, like, clinging to each other. Whereas you, you've just been kind of drifting away," Heather continued.

"But I've been working, and going to the gym, and, like, I've been out loads – it's not like I haven't seen you, Heather."

"But seeing you doesn't mean you're not distant . . ." Heather trailed off, lowering her head.

"What?"

Heather seemed reluctant to continue, but managed to eventually.

"It's just, all this is . . . it's like, not even mentioning . . . well . . . not to mention . . . your weight," she finally got the words out.

Chloe felt herself clamming up. What was Heather talking about? Her weight was her business, and anyway, how had she noticed? She certainly wasn't talking about this here, and with a stern look into her friend's eyes, she turned to the girl on the other side of her. The conversation was over. Heather could leave her alone – she knew nothing.

*

As soon as she woke, Chloe felt a prickling excitement tickle her body awake, knowing that later that day she would see him – she'd

108

see Sam. He would be tanned and smiling as always, and would no doubt be delighted to see her, as she wrapped her arms around him and kissed him and welcomed him home, urging him never to leave her again. Ever. Luckily his flight didn't land until two o'clock, giving Chloe just enough time to go for a run before coming home for a long, hot shower and beautifying herself to perfection. The piping water hissed down upon her naked body, washing her sweat away and making it fresh and new for Sam – for his eyes, for his touch, for his all. She wondered how the day would pan out – would they go for dinner that night? Would they get to be alone? Her heart raced with all the many possibilities, as she washed her hair and scrubbed her every inch, feeling more alive than she had done in ages. So much for Heather's nonsense about her being distant, she thought – she wasn't going to be distant with Sam, that was for sure. In fact, if she could have it her way, they would spend every moment of the next two weeks together before jetting off to Ayia Napa, hand in hand, just like she'd always dreamed. Like they'd always dreamed.

Stepping out of her steamy cocoon, Chloe caught a glimpse of herself in the mirror. She was still dissatisfied with what she saw, but fully aware that now was not the time to dwell on it – she'd put extra effort into her hair and make-up and hope that Sam would be in some way impressed with what he saw. She dried and straightened her blonde locks and made up her face with precision, making particular effort to lighten the dark shadows under her eyes. A flattering outfit and a layer of lipgloss finished the look as she set off on foot to the dual carriageway, where she took the bus out to the airport. Luckily, Sam's mother was unable to collect him, so Chloe got the first greeting all to herself. At arrivals, she waited impatiently, willing time to pass at double speed, just this once. Finally the monitor displayed that his flight had landed and, soon after, there he was.

Sam's eyes scanned the crowd for her face as he walked out, leading the way for his dad and Deirdre, until out of nowhere, Chloe threw herself upon him. Caught unaware, it took a few seconds to comprehend what was going on, but once he did, he held her close, smelling her hair as she pressed herself to him. She felt different, but he had no time to consider how, as her lips, her soft lips, pressed themselves to his, welcoming him back with all the love in the world. However, eventually Sam remembered his father and future stepmother were still in the vicinity, and he pulled away with rosy cheeks.

"What's wrong?" Chloe seemed offended.

"Oh, nothing, it's just–" Sam made to explain.

"He feels a bit bashful around us!" Deirdre finished his sentence with a chuckle, so that now it was Chloe who blushed.

"Sorry," she explained. "I'm just so glad to see him."

"Don't apologise, you silly goose. It was lovely of you to come out to meet him," Deirdre said.

"So, we're going to get a taxi home, and we're dropping Sam off at his mum's – I take it you're coming along?" Sam's dad gave her a way out of the momentary embarrassment.

"Yeah, thanks – that'd be great." Chloe beamed, remembering Sam's mother was at work – at least then she'd have him to herself.

Sam held her hand in the taxi, as Chloe babbled on about all the goings on he'd missed, unable to contain her excitement. Though as soon as they reached his house and collapsed on the couch, he begged her to breathe, for just a minute.

"Sorry," she said sheepishly. "I'm just over the moon that we're finally back together."

"Wow, you really are wired!" Sam laughed. "Just chill out a bit, yeah? Hyperactive girlfriend freaks me out!"

"OK." Chloe giggled, taking a deep breath and allowing the pair to refamiliarise themselves with the novelty of silence.

"I'm serious, though," Chloe said, much quieter than before. "You being away – it was so hard. I don't know why, it's just . . . it's such a time of change and I was a bit all over the place and–"

"Is that why you're so thin?" Sam interjected. Chloe was silent for the second time. Why did people keep trying to lead her down this road? How had he even noticed she'd lost weight – it hadn't even been much over a stone yet. Maybe Heather and the girls had been getting him on side too. Chloe forced herself not to overreact, playing it as cool as she could manage.

"I just got rid of the extra weight I'd put on during the Leaving, that's all. I thought you'd like it," she tried, though not letting Sam answer her question, as she moved in to kiss him, passionately, delighted to feel him responding. She leaned back, pulling him closer, until she was lying down on the couch with Sam on top of her, running his hands all over Chloe's new body as her heart pumped fiercely against her chest. As he undressed her, while she sucked in her stomach, shy at its size, he gazed down at her, lying there in her pink underwear, not knowing what to think. Realising his momentary uncertainty, Chloe grabbed him again and continued to kiss him, deeper than ever, drawing him in as she made up for so much lost time.

Afterwards, they lay there intertwined, saying nothing, but Chloe felt more content than she had done all summer. All doubts she'd had about their relationship were nowhere to be seen as she held him close, knowing that no matter what lay up ahead, they'd be OK.

"I love you," she whispered, stroking his chest gently, unable to stop smiling.

"I love you too," Sam replied.

It was all she needed. All she ever needed.

That night, not entirely as Chloe had planned, Sam's mother was cooking them all dinner, and as Chloe looked down at her huge plate of food, she knew what she had to do. She couldn't turn the meal down, already feeling less than comfortable in that house, as Sam's mum and her boyfriend had never put her at ease. Thus she had no choice but to eat a decent amount of the dinner and then politely excuse herself and get rid of it. She was not letting them force her to slip up. It was only two weeks until Ayia Napa; she needed to lose more weight and frankly that was all that mattered.

Returning to the kitchen, having washed out her mouth and cleaned her watering eyes as best she could, Chloe put on a cheerful face. She was afraid that Sam would cop on and so offered to help with the washing-up, avoiding his gaze all the while, praying he wouldn't notice a thing. Praying she wouldn't be found out.

Saying goodbye that night was sad, but Chloe felt spoilt, knowing she'd see Sam again tomorrow. It was wonderful.

"Call me in the morning and we'll sort something out, yeah?"

"Yeah, cool," he agreed, kissing her tenderly, fuzzing her mind again.

"It's so good to have you back," she reminded him warmly.

"It's good to be home, baby," Sam said. "Just mind yourself, yeah?" he added in an unusually concerned tone.

Chloe looked up at him, not knowing how to take his advice. "What do you mean?"

"Just look after yourself, like. I'm back now, so if you need to talk about anything, I'm here. I'm always here. You know that," he reassured her, holding her close before she said a final goodbye and, getting into her mother's car, sped away into the mothy twilight shadows.

*

Sam was worried. He didn't know what was up, but Chloe had

changed. Her body and her face were different but, more than that, she seemed more needy and yet more cagey too. He liked that she seemed more eager, as in the past he'd always felt the more involved of the two. Tonight she couldn't get enough of him, spending the entire evening wanting to touch him, to remind him how much she had missed him. It made him feel good, but it wasn't Chloe. Not that relationships weren't always changing – of course they were, he knew. But on top of all this dependency, he couldn't shake the feeling that, all night, Chloe was holding something back. Like she wasn't letting him all the way in. Especially after dinner, there was a strange look in her eyes – wild with panic yet full of strength – which Sam couldn't puzzle out. He hadn't had the chance to either, since she'd barely made eye contact with him – making her romantic promises, yet avoiding his gaze. It didn't make sense. Hence he'd told her to take care, hoping she knew better than he did what was on her mind and praying that, with his help, she'd sort it out and return to her old self. The Chloe he really knew and loved.

*

Having made herself sick at Sam's house, Chloe had a new safety net, knowing that if it came to it, she could do it in other people's houses too. It made things much easier, as she could now avoid the many questions her friends had started to badger her with and polish off as much food as they wanted to see her eat, until she stole away to the bathroom and fooled them all, regained control and kept on track. It was simple. It made sense. It felt right.

Thanks to this realisation, coupled with Sam's return home, life was good again for Chloe Walsh, and she felt better than ever, her worries expelled and her confidence flooding back. She shared her time between her girlfriends, Sam and the gym, a different part of her being stimulated and brought to life in each situation, helping her to

grow as a person in ways she'd never thought possible. For all the while, no matter how much fun she was having and how her relationships were developing, Chloe knew that she was in charge of herself, becoming who she wanted to be, both physically and emotionally. It felt right.

GIRLIE NITE 2NITE @ MINE. B DER! XOX HEATHER XOX

Chloe sighed, reading the text, knowing that she couldn't attend, but secretly aware that her alternative plans would be far better.

SOZ BABE, NO CAN DO - HANGN OUT W SAM 2NITE. HAV FUN BABE! LOVEYA XX

AW NO. CALL HIM+MOVE IT TIL 2MO - 2NITES D ONLY NITE WE'RE ALL FREE. PLEAS XOX, Heather responded soon after. Chloe didn't liked being bossed around, so she decided not to write back. However, fate was against her, as the phone rang that afternoon.

"Baby, it's me," Sam's voice greeted down the line, making Chloe's heart dance merrily.

"Hey, handsome," she responded chirpily.

"Listen, babe, I'm really sorry, but I'm going to have to take a rain-check on tonight – Mum and her boyfriend want me to go to this thing with them, and apparently I don't really have a choice," he explained.

Chloe was gutted.

"Aw no, baby, I was really looking forward to tonight. I even turned down a sleepover with the girls," she moaned, hoping to make him rethink his decision. It didn't work.

"Oh, wow, you should definitely go to that then," Sam said.

What was going on? Something didn't feel right. But she reminded herself, as she often had to, that Sam's cheerfulness was not something to be suspicious of, and she made him promise that if she went to her stupid girls' night, then the two of them would definitely hang out tomorrow. He agreed willingly, putting her more at ease, knowing they were only postponing their date by a few hours. It would still be perfect. It always was.

Sam put down the phone, unable to shake the feeling of guilt which filled his tense body. His mum wasn't making him go anywhere. It had all just been a cover-up so that Chloe would go to the girls' night. Heather had rung Sam earlier on, asking him to help, as she and the other girls had decided that tonight they were finally going to say something to Chloe about her eating, about the weird way she was acting – about everything. Sam was relieved that he hadn't been the only one who'd noticed and he thanked Heather, agreeing that he would do anything he could to help. He felt bad, but he knew, in the long run, it was for the best. For Chloe. He wanted her back.

*

Chloe walked up Heather's driveway, willing herself to cheer up and trying to convince herself that it would be fun. Of course it would be. Most of her friends were already there when she arrived, greeting her with the usual flurry of hugs and kisses. It was good to see them. Maybe this wouldn't be so bad after all, she conceded, joining them under the mass of duvets and sleeping bags, though avoiding the bowls of crisps and jellies which littered the room. They watched some old episodes of The OC, flicked around the music channels and generally had some immature fun, clinging onto their youth, all quietly conscious of the looming results. It was just over a week until that all-important day, so innocent messing was just what they needed and about all they could manage.

Tired out from a pillow fight, the girls collapsed once more onto the mound of blankets, breathing heavily and shrieking with delight, simple joy pumping through them as, just for a moment, nothing mattered. Chloe couldn't remember the last time she'd let go like that

RUTH GILLIGAN

and was finding the whole evening more relaxing than expected. She'd needed time out. However, her friends had something else in mind, she discovered, as Heather's voice penetrated the gleeful silence.

"Chloe, can we talk to you about something?" she began.

Chloe instantly froze, fearful of what was to come. "Eh . . . OK . . ." she replied tentatively.

"It's just, me and the girls have been talking and . . ." Heather began, as Chloe lay on her back, still out of breath, staring up at the ceiling, feeling all her expelled worries come flooding back as she closed up into herself.

". . . well, we're just worried about you," her friend continued.

"There's no need," Chloe insisted flatly. Why couldn't they just leave her alone? Why were they all so concerned with her business?

Heather said, "Babe, you've just got so thin recently. And it's kind of scary how quickly you've lost all the weight and we just . . ."

"I'm just getting rid of what I put on over the exams." Chloe repeated her trusty line for the millionth time.

"Yeah, but it's not like you were exactly fat beforehand, were you? You've always been skinny . . ." Heather's voice increased in urgency, trying to make her friend understand their concern.

"So that's why I wanted to lose my exam weight." Chloe's tone was deadpan, forcing herself to stay strong, to keep her emotions at bay.

"But you're tiny, Chloe. You're getting scarily thin. And it has been so quick," her friend Ella joined in.

Chloe remained silent. They wouldn't break her down. There was nothing wrong with her! Nothing at all.

"Look, babe . . ." Heather's voice was almost a whisper. "We wouldn't mind so much if you were just eating healthily and going to the gym a lot–"

"But that's all I am doing," Chloe declared, exasperated.

"Babe, we know it's more than that. Why do you think we're so

116

worried? You basically haven't been eating at all. And then when you do . . . I mean . . . it's hard to say . . . but . . . well . . . Ella says she heard you getting sick at her house the other day . . . and I . . . well . . . I'm pretty sure you did it at mine last week too . . ." Heather trailed off, as if ashamed of what she'd said.

Chloe was hurt. Who did they think they were, spying on her? It was none of their business! But she knew she had to do something, and she had to do it quickly. Inhaling deeply, she began, "OK, you're right. I have been a bit of a mess. But I promise, I'm fine now. It was just a stupid phase – like, I literally made myself sick only, like, three times . . ." She paused, as if finding it hard to confess. "But I know it's really stupid . . . I guess just the stress of the results coming up, and let's face it, we're all a bit nervous about the old sixth-year-holiday bikini bod . . ."

"Tell me about it," Ella agreed. "I can't believe the whole of South Dublin is going to see me in swimwear – it's so not cool."

But Heather wasn't buying Chloe's story. Chloe knew she had to push harder.

"There's all this stuff in the media about size zero and shit – I just got swept away in it all. But, trust me – I'm OK," she pleaded.

"Well, as long as you're sure . . ." Heather still didn't seem entirely convinced.

"Heather, honestly. I'm so glad you guys brought it up because I've been meaning to explain. Plus, things were weird with Sam while he was away and my head was just fucked up, but it's so good knowing I have you guys . . . I'm fine now . . . I promise." She smiled.

Heather merely smiled back. She wanted to believe Chloe. But something was still not quite right – and it hurt. It hurt that Chloe couldn't even tell her best friend the truth. Heather sighed.

Ella, however, had been thoroughly taken in. "Ha ha, thank God for that!" she exclaimed with glee.

"You muppet," Chloe teased, trying to lighten the mood even

more, hugging her friend and willing her guilt to go away. She had lied
– she wasn't a mess. And she certainly wasn't going to stop the way
she was progressing. Her mother had been making comments too
and Chloe had similarly covered up, thankful that her mum worked
such long hours, as it meant Chloe could fib about her meals and
general eating habits, which prevented Mrs Walsh from prying too
much. No one needed to know the truth. For now, they were happy
and Chloe was happy. That was what mattered.

But despite the untruths with which she'd filled her friends' heads,
one aspect of her spiel was indeed valid – the results. Every day,
Chloe felt the knot in her stomach grow, knowing that in only a
matter of days her future would be decided. She envied Sam's calm,
as he, and most other boys she knew, seemed unfazed by the coming
event. Drama in Trinity was the thing she longed for, but had she
done enough? Had her hard work paid off? She prayed that it had,
but forced herself to consider what would happen otherwise. Drama
in DIT? Again she felt that sense of unease at the thought of going
to a college where none of her friends would be. Some of the boys
had applied to DIT for business courses, but they would be on a
different campus, and Chloe feared that, ultimately, she could be all
by herself.

"What's up?" Sam asked one day, as they sat in his room, watching
TV, noticing that she was staring aimlessly out his window.
"Ah, just the usual . . . results." Chloe sighed.
"Aw, baby," Sam sympathised, putting his arm around her and
pulling her to him. "Just relax, babe. What's done is done, at this stage."
"But what if I don't get it? What if I don't get Trinity?" she pleaded.
"Well, then you go to DIT – it's no big deal," Sam reasoned.
"No big deal? But, like, I wouldn't have anyone with me. It'd be so
weird."

"Weird? It'd be brilliant!" Sam exclaimed.

"Brilliant? Are you taking the piss?"

"No. Come on, babe. College is about branching out, meeting new people, broadening your horizons. A fresh start . . ." Sam trailed off, realising just how badly he wanted these things. Chloe didn't seem to share his sentiments.

"Yeah, it's a new phase. But it's going to be so exciting us all being in college, the old gang all together. That's what it's about. That's what I want," she explained.

Sam fell silent.

"What?" she asked, noting an odd look in his eyes.

"It's just . . . it's just you and I . . . we're so . . . we're so different," Sam concluded.

"Really?" Chloe began to panic.

"No, no. Don't worry, babe. I don't mean it in a bad way. It's just . . . socially, I guess. You love the bubble . . ." he tried to explain.

"The bubble? What are you on about?"

"Yes, the bubble – South Dublin, the schools, the sixth-year holiday, then college – you love it."

"Of course I do. That's how it works," Chloe said.

"But what if I don't like it? What if I'm sick of it?"

"And are you?" Chloe asked.

"I don't know . . . I think so, Chloe. I mean, when I was in France, no one knew me. It was a complete change of scenery. It was new and different and I loved it." Sam tried to make her see.

"So what are you going to do about it? About college?" Chloe asked, her nerves beginning to shake.

"Well, I don't know – I haven't thought that far ahead yet. A lot depends on my results, obviously."

"I suppose."

"But there is something I have been thinking about . . ."

"What?"

119

"Well, it's . . . it's Ayia Napa . . . I've been meaning to tell you, but . . . while I was in France I was thinking about it . . . and I just . . . I just kind of decided that it was a lot of money for something I didn't really want to do. That's not my idea of a good holiday."

"So what are you saying?" Chloe feared the worst.

"Look, Chloe, please don't get mad. I know you're going to be annoyed or whatever but just please . . . try to understand . . ."

"Understand what?"

"I've pulled out." Sam finally uttered the words he'd been dreading to say. "I'm not coming – I got my money back, well, except my deposit, but whatever. So yeah . . . I'm not going to Ayia Napa . . . I'm sorry . . ."

Chloe was furious. What had he done? Ayia Napa – the holiday of a lifetime, the one they'd all been dying for for so very long. And he'd pulled out? She couldn't even begin to get her head around it.

"What . . . why . . . what am I supposed to do?" she finally begged.

"What? What do you mean? You go, of course!" Sam replied, totally at a loss as to why that was even a question.

"Oh, great, spend another two weeks without you! So much for us having a brilliant summer together – first you fuck off to France for a month and now you're abandoning our first holiday together." Chloe's voice began to strengthen.

"Ah, come on, Chloe. You're going with your school friends; I was going to go with mine. This isn't about you, for goodness sake." Sam also was starting to get annoyed.

"It's never about me, though, is it? You staying on in Nice wasn't about me. You planning your future outside the bubble isn't about me. Do you even fucking care about me?" Chloe shrieked.

Sam said nothing. He wasn't doing this. He wasn't getting into a screaming match with his girlfriend just because he had decided against two weeks of drunken South Dublin being moved to some dodgy part of Cyprus. Calmly, he told her as much.

"There's nothing more I can say, Chloe. It's not a big deal, it's just a personal choice, but, like, it has nothing to do with you, or us, or any of that. I just don't want to go. End of story." He sighed, weary from the tension in the air, pressing in on him, willing him to apologise. But he wasn't sorry. Chloe's face looked even thinner when she was upset. Her eyes seemed so tired and sad as she gazed once more out the window. The late afternoon light gushed in – a golden river of hope, illuminating the sad silhouettes of a fading couple, promising that all was not lost, just as the day itself was living on, radiant and beautiful.

"I'd better go." Chloe finally spoke, her voice as weak as the light in her eyes.

"Chloe, please . . ."

"What?" she snapped.

"Please, don't be like this," Sam pleaded.

"Be like what? Sam, this is just so typical of us – the minute we're actually on a roll, something comes along and ruins everything."

"Oh, come on, nothing has 'come along'. I honestly don't see why this has to be such a big deal." Sam was confused.

"Well, I guess that's just another difference between you and me then, isn't it?"

"Chloe, please!" Sam was close to shouting as his patience ran thin. But it seemed whatever he'd done had pushed his girlfriend over the edge and she began to cry. Hot, stale tears poured down her lonely face and she doubled over, melting like a burning candle, a pool of emptiness forming below. Tentatively, Sam began to rub her back, wondering from where all this woe was coming.

"Baby, what's up," he coaxed softly. But she was gone – her tears were erupting from somewhere deep within, as if they'd been trapped in her broken heart for weeks. She needed to cry. He needed to let her cry. They sat for ten minutes, Chloe curled up in a melancholic ball, while Sam sought, not to make her stop, but to help her let it out, to set it free. To set herself free.

*

Finally, Chloe felt her weeping subside. Finally, she could sit upright again. Finally, she could look at Sam again.

"I love you," she whispered, embracing him as tightly as she could, noticing his confused expression but too weak to tell him all she felt – that those tears had been the release of so much fear and pain that had been dammed up inside her all summer. All she wanted was to be held, and hold her he did. Chloe couldn't believe the state she was in – was this what she'd been reduced to? But she promised herself that this was just a momentary weakness, that tomorrow she'd be back on track. Tomorrow, she would be strong again. Stronger than ever.

8

JENNIFER

HEY SEXY. WE STIL ON 4 CINEMA L8R? ALEX XX

Jenny felt her insides dance, as they always did when such a text arrived. She replied promptly, assuring Alex that their date was still going ahead and that, as usual, he could pick her up. She hadn't been to the cinema in ages and was looking forward to yet another proper date with the boy for whom she cared so much. If anyone had told her at the start of the summer that she'd be feeling like this about Alex Walsh, she would have laughed. The thought of him ever taking a girl or a relationship seriously would have been impossible to believe. Yet here they were – practically a proper couple. Practically. He still hadn't asked her out, to make them officially boyfriend and girlfriend, and Jenny often wondered if it was just assumed that they were an item, an unspoken bond which they'd just eased into. Then again, she dared not jump to conclusions, taking things very slowly, knowing that this was the most involved Alex had ever been with a girl and not wanting to scare him away. The minute he did ask her, though, she would say yes, wanting more than anything to be his girlfriend, for all the world to see.

He'd certainly changed. Jenny never would have let herself fall for the old Alex – the cocky, heartless, horny idiot who used and abused her more times than she cared to admit. But this summer had definitely seen him maturing immensely, and whether it was a result of the accident, or the looming future, it suited him.

They went well together; that was undeniable. And every moment that they spent together made Jenny so happy. But not only did they click, she also found him ridiculously attractive – she'd had sex in his back seat, for goodness sake! she recalled, shocked yet proud of their dirty encounter that night, where inhibitions were completely disregarded as chemistry took over.

The next day hadn't been so wonderful, though, as Jenny began to realise the chance that they had taken. Having unprotected sex was something she had always promised herself she wouldn't do – it was too risky. And despite the fact that a number of her friends had done it and suffered no consequences, with every hour that had passed, Jenny had felt sicker and sicker with nerves. Imagine if she'd got pregnant. The summer before the start of her adult life, she would have thrown it all away.

At first she had been angry with Alex for suggesting such a reckless idea and letting her go ahead with it, knowing it was so out of character for her. But it did take two to tango, so Jenny couldn't start pointing the finger elsewhere for her mistake. However, once she had made it, she realised that it was time to deal with it. The tiny chance that she had made a life-altering error was enough to gnaw at her soul and force her to make it go away. She had to get the morning-after pill.

*

So, over a week ago, feeling as she did and knowing through friends the place to go in such a situation, Jenny had dialled the number with shaking fingers.

"Hello, Well Woman Centre, how can I help you?" a chirpy voice had answered the call.

"Oh . . . yeah . . . hi . . . eh . . . I was wondering if I could . . . if I could, like . . . make an appointment," she stuttered, her throat drying up.

"Right, well we've lots of spaces left next week – what day suits?"

"Oh . . . no . . . you see it's kind of a . . . like . . . it's an emergency," Jenny finally blurted out, hoping they'd understand.

"Oh, all right. Well why don't you pop into us this afternoon at about four? Someone will be able to see you then," the kind voice assured.

"Oh, right . . . yeah, that'd be great . . . thanks."

"And what's the name?"

"Oh . . . eh . . ." Jenny considered lying, but her anxious mind couldn't think of an alternative. "It's, eh . . . it's Jenny . . . just Jenny . . ." she murmured.

"OK then, Jenny. We'll see you at four," the kind voice promised.

She put down the phone, her breathing so heavy it hurt her chest. Step one was complete. Now she just had to go there. She sighed, wishing that that could have just been it – enough embarrassment for one day. But she had to follow through.

Later on, Jenny had got the bus into town, praying that she wouldn't bump into anyone, as if they'd figure out where she was going. They would have had every right to judge her, she admitted, given the vendetta she'd always had against girls who chanced getting pregnant. And some girls did – that was the scary thing. But what would she do? Would she consider getting an abortion? Would she have the baby? The scale of such decisions had made Jenny's head spin, her mind racing as the bus bumped along. Just imagine.

*

She had reached the clinic. Her footsteps seemed to echo through the reception area as she entered, head lowered. Briskly, she made her way to the desk, muttering, "It's Jenny . . . just Jenny – I rang earlier . . . I have . . . I mean, I made an appointment . . . well, sort of . . . it's kind of an emergency!"

Daring to meet the gaze of the woman to whom she spoke, Jenny saw a warmth in those eyes which, just for a second, made her relax.

"If you just take a seat, Jenny, the nurse will be free in a couple of minutes, OK?" the woman said kindly.

"Oh . . . right . . . eh, thanks," Jenny warbled, back to her agitated state.

"And you'll need to fill out this form, please," the receptionist added, handing her a clipboard. She sat down as instructed, daring to glance around her, curious as to who else would be there. But there were no scantily clad teenage girls or dodgy-looking characters lurking about as she had expected. Rather there were fairly normal-looking women, hoping to receive some fairly normal medical attention in what, Jenny had to admit, appeared to be a fairly normal establishment. Her tension loosened ever so slightly. She filled in the form in a daze, scribbling her details without a second thought, though reminding herself not to give her address, for fear they would send her any sort of literature that would lead to an awkward conversation with her parents. Just imagine if they knew she was here! And for what reason. The idea didn't bear thinking about. But Jenny forced herself to focus on the fact that, thus far, the whole event wasn't proving to be nearly as seedy as she'd feared, and once her name was called and she was led into a brightly lit room, where a charming nurse greeted her with a smile, Jenny heaved a great sigh of relief.

"So, Jenny, what can we do for you today?" the lady enquired.

Jenny took a deep breath. "Well, you see . . . I, eh, I had . . . unprotected sex last night . . . so . . . well . . . you know," she tried, her nerves returning swiftly as she uttered her crime.

But there were no gasps of shock, or glares of disapproval.

"Right, so you'd like the morning-after pill then? Do you need to be checked for any sexually transmitted diseases?" the nurse asked.

"Oh . . . no, no – I'm fine thanks," Jenny insisted, not even wanting to go down that road.

"OK, well, as long as you're sure – I assume you're aware of the risks . . ."

"Yes, no. I'm sure," Jenny affirmed, wanting desperately to just stick to the task at hand.

"Right, well, I need to know the exact time at which you had sex. Was it just once?" the nurse continued, her voice still lacking any of the judgement which Jenny had been both expecting and dreading.

"Well, yeah, it was just once . . . and I guess it was, like, I don't know . . . I think about half eleven," Jenny surmised, casting her mind back to the drunken blur that was that messy evening.

"Are you sure?"

"Yeah, no, I'm sure . . . half eleven . . . pretty much exactly," Jenny declared, the answer resounding decidedly within her.

This certainty built and built, as she listened to the nurse's instructions when she was handed two pills, taking in all that was being said yet somehow distracted by the growing relief which was consuming her. Soon she would be out of there and it would all be sorted. She had done it.

All the way home, Jenny could have sworn that people were staring at her, knowing where she'd been, knowing how close she'd come. Although she felt more relaxed now, she still couldn't stop thinking about it. She called Megan.

"Hey, babe, it's me. Listen, you up for doing something this evening? I'm in weird form – need to hang out," Jenny had asked.

"Sure, babe. What you got in mind?" Her friend had been happy to help.

Jenny had stayed on the bus all the way to Megan's house and had spent the evening eating Ben & Jerry's chocolate ice-cream and watching films, cheering herself up slowly but surely, knowing that at least now, thankfully, everything was sorted.

*

But what if it wasn't? Now, over a week later, a feeling of anxiety replaced the excitement about the cinema trip which had been dancing through her. She wondered if the pill had done the trick – it wasn't foolproof, according to the statistics, and she still hadn't got her period. Jenny tried to distract herself, choosing an outfit for her date that night, but secretly she was praying that everything was OK. The last thing she needed, only days before the most important exam results of her life, was to have the vague possibility niggling at her that maybe, just maybe, she was pregnant. She had to find out.

Leaving her house, Jenny walked as quickly as she could to the pharmacy, feeling the same sense of awkward bashfulness she had on entering the same building the day she bought her first tampons, then again later, her first condoms, and here she was, buying her first pregnancy test. What rites of passage this shop had seen! Ensuring she at no point made eye contact with the lady behind the counter, Jenny found and paid for the small white box, shoving it into her handbag and making her way home all in the same breath, believing if she paused, even for a second, she'd have to acknowledge what she was doing.

Locking herself into her blue-tiled bathroom, Jenny wanted to keep up the pace and get the whole thing over and done with as soon as possible. Ripping open the package, her eyes scoured the instructions, knowing roughly what she had to do. Staring at the white plastic stick, Jenny's mind was about to explode, panic swelling from within. She sat down on the toilet and peed on the stick, following each step, placing it on the counter and waiting. Just waiting. Hoping she knew the answer which it would bring. Hoping and waiting and feeling her heart race. Five minutes passed. She couldn't take it any more.

Holding her breath, barely wanting to look, Jenny did. Her eyes blurred, her mind went numb and her hands shook as she picked up that prophesying stick. It was OK. She was fine.

Jenny exploded with laughter – a reaction she'd never expected, but now that the convulsions consumed her, it felt good. She'd been such an idiot! Of course she wasn't pregnant – what a ridiculous notion! She'd always been cautious about things like this, but this time she'd taken it to a whole new level and was thrilled she hadn't told her friends, knowing that, deservedly, they would find her paranoia hilarious. Not to mind what would have happened had she ever mentioned it to Alex. He would have run a mile. So he wasn't perfect – she knew that. But right now, Jenny wanted to run all the way to his house, kiss him all over and forget about the whole mess. Clearly her body was just in anxiety mode, counting down to the results and searching for something else, anything else, to distract her troubled mind.

But despite the overwhelming relief which filled Jenny, the coming Wednesday wasn't going to just go away. However, unlike her previous obstacle, where all she wanted was for the test to come out negative, this time, she didn't know what she wanted, what outcome she desired. Jenny had never been sure what exactly she wanted to do in college. Even now, she wasn't sure – maybe sociology, maybe English – she wasn't certain. But her parents were. Both lawyers themselves, there had never been any question as to what Jenny would do; following in her parents' footsteps was clearly her destiny. But was it?

Jenny had done work experience in the Four Courts with her mum, and then again in her dad's solicitor's firm and, frankly, neither had done it for her. All the rules and regulations and formal language was not her scene at all and, ever since then, she'd known that she was never going to pursue that career path. But she couldn't bring herself to tell her parents. She'd put it off and put it off until suddenly she was filling out her CAO form and all her top choices were some form of law. Her parents were proud, she forced herself to smile and that was that. That was how it was going to be.

It was her own fault, really – if she wasn't such a coward, she would have said something by now. But at this stage, all she could do was pray that, somehow, it all worked out – that she didn't get enough points for law and, instead, ended up with one of the arts options further down her list; the options which her parents disregarded as mere back-ups, but which Jenny longed for more than anything. So while her friends all crossed their fingers and prayed for as many points as possible, Jenny lost sleep over the fact that lots of points would mean a future she didn't want and a degree that didn't appeal to her in the slightest.

"Baby, you'll be fine, I promise," Alex assured her for the millionth time, massaging her tense shoulders as they sat in her living room only two nights before the results.

"Why don't boys get stressed?" Jenny moaned, knowing that, despite his support, Alex couldn't quite comprehend her tension.

"Well, if it's that bad, I know something that will take your mind off it . . ." Alex suggested with a wry smile.

"Again?" Jenny squealed. "I told you, my parents will be home any minute."

"Well, there's always my car outside," Alex joked.

Jenny thumped him, giggling shyly as he brought up, yet again, that raunchy night.

Turning around, Jenny kissed him, tingling all over, wishing so badly that her parents weren't in fact coming home. For in that moment, not for the first time, she knew. She knew that she'd fallen in love with Alex Walsh. But she couldn't tell him. She just couldn't. He wouldn't say it back, she'd look like a fool and everything would be ruined. Maybe the day would come when he would utter those words that would change everything. But for now, Jenny just had to be content with what she had, and she kissed him even deeper than usual, to show him how much she cared. And she did care so very much. Perhaps too much.

9

ALEX

On Tuesday night, sitting in the pub with all the lads, the nerves had finally caught up with Alex. He sipped his pint, but wasn't even enjoying the taste – his stomach rolled up into a sickly ball, oozing dread.

"You look fucking pale, man," Andy observed, the first thing he'd said in over ten minutes, as his mind too was fixated on tomorrow.

Tomorrow. Alex couldn't believe that they had actually reached the day they'd all dreaded since the minute the exams finished – it was like a fleeting nightmare, so bad it surely couldn't become reality. But judging by the look on each of his companions' faces, it was coming all right and was not going to be welcomed with open arms.

"Fuck me, we look like someone's died," Alex joked. "Is anyone here actually in any way confident about tomorrow?"

The lack of response reassured Alex that they were all in the same boat. Well, to a certain extent. For Alex knew at the back of his mind that, despite his friends' fears, no one had come close to doing as little work as he had. And that was what had set him apart, what had made him cool. But where did that leave him now? Sure, it would be funny when tomorrow he opened his envelope and he and his friends counted up his meagre points. But at the back of everybody's mind, would there be that tinge of pity, knowing that Alex had hit a brick wall and was left with nothing but his reputation? Nothing at all.

"Still," Alex reasoned aloud. "At least tomorrow's going to be a good night."

"Yeah – whether we're celebrating or drowning our sorrows, I am getting completely smashed," Andy agreed.

"I'm going to be such a mess!" Alex reaffirmed, high-fiving his friend, and his spirits momentarily lifted, remembering that tomorrow wasn't only about grades – it was also going to be one giant party.

"Is everyone going to that beach-party thing?" one of the quieter guys enquired.

"Yeah, obviously. Did you get a ticket?" Andy asked him.

"Shit, no. When did you lot get them?" the poor guy asked, clearly having missed something.

"My 'rents are making me and Chloe go out for dinner with them beforehand," Alex moaned.

"Shit buzz," Andy agreed.

"Tell me about it. Don't worry, though – I'll be in the pub all afternoon so it should pass quickly, and then I'll try to bail on it as soon as possible," Alex promised.

"Cool, man. I take it your sister's coming to the beach party too?" Andy wondered.

"Yeah, why? Oh, Jesus, there she is – did you guys know she was coming?" Alex exclaimed, spotting Chloe and two of her friends walking in the door of the pub.

"I may have texted her . . ." Andy murmured, avoiding Alex's eyes and changing the subject as he greeted the girls. "Evening, ladies." His face lit up, evidently glad to see them. The girls settled in amongst the lads, all in good form but, like their male counterparts, their minds elsewhere.

"Hey," Chloe greeted her brother. "Hope you don't mind us coming down?"

"No, no, it's grand," he assured her. In recent years he'd been forced to accept the fact that his sister and her gang were friends with his, so he was used to her being around. Though he did find it odd that Andy had invited them along without mentioning it to him.

"So, Alex was telling us about your amazingly fun dinner tomorrow night," Andy said to Chloe.

"Yeah, it's so bent," she admitted.

"But you're coming to the beach party afterwards, yeah?" he continued. Although Alex was now chatting to Heather, he couldn't help but spot a twinkle in his friend's eye.

"Course I'm going," Chloe replied, batting her eyelids.

"Excellent. Well you'd better save me a dance," Andy whispered, so that no one, not even an eavesdropping Alex, could hear.

"Maybe I will . . ." Chloe coyly replied, holding Andy's gaze.

Alex couldn't help but join in.

"You guys talking about tomorrow night? Are Sam and all those guys going?" Alex mentioned Chloe's boyfriend on purpose, noting how quickly both Andy and his sister dropped their eyes at the mention of his name. It wasn't that Alex was a protective brother, but the thought of his best friend chatting up his sister was just one step too far – he'd lose respect for both of them.

"Yeah, he's coming." Chloe tried to sound enthusiastic.

"Savage," Alex affirmed, hoping Andy had got the picture, and returned to his conversation with Heather, who was looking particularly well this evening, despite her nerves.

But although Andy knew exactly what Alex was trying to do, he wasn't going to give up. Not anymore. All summer, Andy had found himself thinking about one girl. Every time he saw her, he couldn't take his eyes off her and, although he had assumed it was just a crush, time had passed and still he felt the same. He hadn't said anything to the guys, barely even admitting to himself how much he liked her, but the reality was, he did. Andy had really thought that the last few times Alex had let Jenny down he'd blown his chances with her once and for all. But apparently she was gone on him enough to give him yet another chance. This frustrated Andy more than anything. What did Alex have that he didn't? Why was he always in second place to his best friend? It wasn't fair. But suddenly, Andy was beginning to see a way that he could settle the score, maybe even get on top, and it was sitting right in front of him. It was perfect.

By eleven, they all decided to call it a night, the conversation lagging due to sheer preoccupation. Andy had the car and was more than happy to drive Alex and Chloe home, where they both quickly headed to bed, willing sleep to come but never quite succeeding.

Alex couldn't remember the last time he'd been so stressed about anything. But now that he'd started, he couldn't stop, as all the possibilities played out in his head. What if by some miracle he did do well? Did he actually want to go to college? Was it his scene? Mind you, from what he'd heard it was nothing but non-stop partying and insane drinking and that was definitely his scene. Who was he kidding? Of course he wanted to get in somewhere. Anywhere. But whether he would have the chance or not was another thing, and the uncertainty taunted him into a light slumber, where nightmares teased his weary soul

*

His eyes opened. He closed them again. But that split-second was enough to know that, yes, he was awake and, yes, the day had come. Checking his alarm clock, he saw that it was twenty past eight. The results were out at nine. There were forty minutes till he'd know. Forty minutes till everything changed.

Everything.

"Alex, Chloe – breakfast," his mother shouted up the stairs, having taken the morning off work for the occasion. "How could you expect me to concentrate when my only two children are going through that?" she had told people, justifying her morning at home.

Alex groaned. He didn't want to get up. But his mother did cook a mean fry, and there was no question of him going back to sleep now, so he peeled himself from his warm bed and headed downstairs, where his mum and sister busied around the kitchen in their dressing-gowns.

"Morning," he greeted them both. Instantly his mother stopped what she was doing, ran to him and gave him a big hug.

"Morning, darling," she whispered, squeezing him tightly, appearing even more nervous than Alex himself.

"Sit yourself down, love. I think we're all sorted," she instructed tenderly before serving him up a huge plate of bacon, eggs, sausages and all the trimmings. Chloe sat opposite him, looking like death, the bags under her eyes greying her whole complexion.

"You look wrecked," Alex said.

"Didn't sleep a wink," Chloe explained, sipping mindlessly on her orange-juice.

"What time are your results?" he asked.

"Not till ten. Mum's going to give me a lift down," Chloe replied.

"Are you sure you don't want me to take you to your school?" Mrs Walsh tried, wanting her son to let her be a part of his experience too, for she was certainly sharing in his nerves.

"No, Mum. Thanks. I'm just going to drive down myself. I don't want any fuss," Alex told her, trying not to hurt her feelings.

"OK, love. Just call me as soon as you get them," she made him promise.

"Me too," Chloe added.

"Yeah, yeah, grand. Don't hold your breath, though, girls." Alex sighed, wishing the fuss would stop, knowing it was only building up to a complete anticlimax. A disaster.

He finished his food, knocked back his orange juice and excused himself to go get dressed. Alex threw on a hoodie and some sweatpants, not caring what he looked like, and tried to steal out of the house as silently as possible. But his mother ensured she had the last word, giving him her clearly much-rehearsed pep-talk, as if it could make any difference now.

"Look, love, you know, whatever that envelope says, we're all very proud of you. Exams are only a small part of life, and if things don't work out as you wanted, it's not the end of the world. We can sort it – it will all be fine," she assured her son. "Just know that your father and I are so proud of you and we love you very much," she concluded, kissing his forehead.

Alex thanked her, wished his sister good luck and got into his car as quickly as he could manage. Proud? Of him? Guilt consumed him as he sped through the quiet streets, knowing that despite their lack of expectations, his parents were about to get a nasty shock. It was an awful feeling, knowing that he'd let them down, that after paying for such a fine education, their efforts were completely wasted on their son.

As he drove in to the school grounds, it felt weird to be back. The familiar twists and turns of the avenue brought him back to his schooldays – those days which he'd longed to be free from. But now, the innumerable uncertainties which filled his every day made Alex wonder was this really better? Was freedom all it was cracked up to be? Parking the car, he wasn't sure, but he had no time to draw a conclusion, for the future was knocking on his door, demanding to be let in.

*

Filing into the school hall, Alex's classmates greeted one another and wished each other luck but were nonetheless very subdued, just wanting to get the next ten minutes over with. Alex found Andy looking just as harrowed as he was. Time ticked by. Fear flowed like a disease through the room. The clock turned nine o'clock.

Their principal took the stage, instilling words of reassurance and advice into the fine young men who stood before him, until various teachers arrived with boxes of envelopes, all arranged in alphabetical order, and the moment had come. As soon as their headmaster's speech concluded, some boys practically ran to find their envelope, desperate to be put out of their misery. But their hustling and bustling frames only rooted Alex to the spot, as he realised he was no longer impatient to get it over with – he wanted to just stand there, one last time, in his school, free from worries. The worries of the real world.

"Will we open them together?" Andy suggested.

"Grand," Alex agreed, his mind numb as his body followed his friend. Already he could hear the curses and the cheers of the other boys and that grating sound of the ripping open of envelopes. The exposition of the future. It all became a cacophonic blur, as Alex, devoid of sensation, spotted the relevant box.

"Alex Walsh, please," he told the teacher, who searched the envelopes, located the correct one and handed it to him. His fate.

Andy found him once more and the two boys headed outside to open their envelopes in peace. Alex felt ill.

"Man, I don't think I can do this," he informed his friend.

"Come on. Don't be such a pussy." Alex realised that he was right – nothing ever scared Alex Walsh, and since when did he even care?

Tearing off the top of the envelope with anxious fingers, Alex pulled out the piece of paper that said it all. His eyes scoured down through his six subjects.

It wasn't good. He'd passed four. He'd failed two – biology and Irish. Which was bad news. The majority of universities in Ireland required applicants to at least pass ordinary-level Irish. But Alex had always hated the subject and, towards the end, had rarely attended the class, knowing that his teacher had pretty much given up on him and choosing rather to take a free period and chill out. Clearly the teacher had been right to give up. His other grades were as he'd expected, with geography taking the award for highest mark – a C3. This was bad. This was very bad.

"So, how did you do?" Andy tentatively questioned.

"Shit, as expected." Alex sighed, trying his hardest not to be down. He had no right to be disappointed – frankly, he'd got exactly what he'd deserved. He'd failed.

"You?" He finally returned the question, having forgotten about his friend's similar situation.

"Not too bad, actually. Kind of surprised to be honest. Might actually be OK." Andy was clearly chuffed with himself, but not wanting to boast in front of his obviously underwhelmed friend.

"Will we go find the others?" he suggested, noting that the moment was more than slightly awkward.

"Yeah, whatever," Alex said, shoving the piece of paper into his pocket and ambling towards his friends, all emotion washed clean from him, leaving him filled with nothingness. Total nothingness.

His phone rang. It was his mother. He cancelled her call, unable to bear her voice right now. Instead he composed a text which he sent to both his parents, and his sister, hoping it would be enough to shut them up for the afternoon.

DID SHIT. FAILD IRISH. TOLD U NOT 2 GET UR HOPES UP. C U @ DINNER.

He sent a similar one to Jenny, knowing he'd see her later but not wanting to talk to her about it now. Not yet. He turned off his phone. It was all over – not just the event itself, but also the vainglorious hopes of the school waster, finally learning that, no matter how much faith he had in his capacity to wing the exams, it didn't work like that. Work worked. But Alex hadn't, and now he had to face the consequences.

*

139

"What do you want to do now?" he asked Andy after almost an hour.

"Well, like, it's only ten. Still too early to go to the pub. I guess we could go back to mine, play a bit of PlayStation – usual," Andy suggested.

"Yeah, grand – let's just get out of here," Alex pleaded, the noisy buzz still driving him insane as students and teachers flitted about, asking how everyone did and rejoicing in their respective outcomes. Alex tried to stay as far removed from it as possible, not overly keen on sharing his disastrous results with other people – people who didn't care. What was more, he couldn't help but feel their eyes upon him, catching a brief glance and somehow knowing he was disappointed, and feeling pleased. Feeling that maybe that was what he deserved after the accident. Knowing that, had Barry been there opening his envelope, he would have done a million times better than Alex – that it would make so much more sense for Alex to be the one in hospital. He detested their glances and was close to screaming if he didn't get out of there. Now.

He drove back to Andy's with Luke and Kyle in the car too, both pleasantly surprised by their results.

"Man, are you OK? Like, are you proper fucked off?" Kyle asked Alex, unsure what was going through his friend's mind, since he was showing so little emotion.

"I did shit. I'm fucked. But whatever," Alex simplified it, ensuring he showed no sign of being affected by it all. He didn't want to think. He just wanted to get on with the rest of their day, and that was that.

For the following hours in Andy's, Alex beat them all at football, Formula One racing, wrestling, venting his building frustration on the console and dominating accordingly.

"Whoa, someone's on form," Andy commented.

"Just pissed off," Alex mumbled, scoring yet another cracking goal.

"I thought you said you weren't really bothered," Luke said.

"Of course I'm fucking bothered," Alex retorted, hating having to point out the obvious. "No spa is going to be happy with totally failing the fucking Leaving, you idiot."

"Hey, I was just asking," Luke said, surprised by the venom in his friend's voice.

"Sorry," Alex said. "It's only starting to hit me now. Like, I'll get over it. It's just a bit shite, you know?"

"Yeah, no worries," Luke said.

"Still, it's one o'clock, lads – definitely time for the pub," Andy. joined in, brightening the eyes of all present.

"So what the fuck are we waiting for?" Alex cheered, already feeling better. They grabbed their coats and left Andy's for the brief stroll to the watering hole, where celebration and consolation would be combined into an afternoon of bittersweet pints.

All day, Alex drifted in and out of various emotions – disappointment, anger and shame. The thought of Barry also danced in his mind – Alex wondered if his parents had gone online and got his results. He wondered how he'd done. Surely he'd got engineering, just like he'd always wanted – he'd put the work in and, despite trying to cover it up sometimes in front of the lads, Barry was undeniably clever. But for the most hideous of reasons, he hadn't been a part of the day – the day about which they'd all spent so long thinking, wondering what their fates would be. But no one could have imagined Barry's to be what it was. Alex sighed. What a horrible day. He had to make it better.

So as the day wore on, the more he drank, the more Alex lulled himself into blissful periods of nonchalance, where he genuinely didn't care about the results and pushed any thoughts of Barry to the back of his mind, rather forcing himself to grow excited and pumped up for the party ahead. Once six o'clock came, it was time he made a move, leaving himself an hour to get home, shower and get ready before their family dinner and the big night out.

As he arrived home, Alex realised that the drink had definitely had an effect on him, as the six steady pints made him fuzzy inside.

"Hey," Chloe greeted when he entered the sitting room. She had sent him a text to say she'd got four hundred and fifty points – an impressive score, but nowhere near enough for Drama in Trinity.

"Hey. Listen, well done, by the way. Sorry I didn't text you back – I only just turned my phone on again. I was kind of fucked off," Alex explained with uncharacteristic sincerity, the alcohol making him more concerned.

"Yeah, I don't know. I'm pleased, but I'm not thrilled, you know?"

"Fuck off – four fifty is unreal," Alex pointed out.

"But it's not enough, is it?"

"You'll get DIT. At least you'll get something . . ."

"Yeah, I guess. Anyway, how did your friends get on?" Chloe changed the subject, noting her brother's saddening eyes.

"The lads all did pretty well – were surprised, like. Two guys in my year got six hundred. What about yours?"

"Yeah, the girls were all generally delighted. Heather got five thirty – unreal. Means she has BESS in the bag. Oh, and Sam did incredibly too," Chloe said.

"Hmm," Alex managed, realising that everyone seemed to be happy. Or at least they had done well and would end up somewhere decent. He didn't have such a luxury.

"Anyway, we'd better get changed." Chloe broke his thought train once more. "It's only half an hour till we leave."

"Where are you drinking tonight before the party?" Alex asked.

"Don't know yet. You?"

"Kyle's, I think. You girls can come along if you want," he invited.

"Oh, thanks. I might do something with Sam, though – I was with him this afternoon so we said we'd try to pregame together."

"Cool, whatever. I'm going for a shower," Alex concluded, leaving the room.

"Alex!" His sister called him back, stopping him in his tracks.

"What?"

"It'll be OK, you know. Don't worry, yeah?"

"Yeah . . . eh . . . thanks," he stumbled, appreciating her concern but deciding once more that, for the evening ahead, he was just going to forget about it all and concentrate on what really mattered: getting wasted. It was the only thing keeping him going.

Dinner wasn't as bad as Alex had expected, as his parents took himself and Chloe to L'Ecrivain – a pricy but truly scrumptious French restaurant in town – where the alcohol flowed and Mr and Mrs Walsh toasted them both, congratulating them on finishing school and being proper adults at last. Alex raised his glass and cheered, downing yet another glass of white wine. However, his parents seemed keen to discuss the results in more detail, having not had the chance to talk to either of them properly, especially their son, who had turned off his phone since his disappointing revelation.

"Mum, please, not now – can we just leave it?" Alex pleaded, loathing the idea of such a conversation.

"But, Alex, you haven't even told us exactly what you got – we can't react because we don't even know what your results were." His mother was clearly hurt that she was being kept so in the dark.

"Trust me, you don't want to know."

"But, Alex . . ."

"Not tonight!" he snapped. His father threw him a warning glance and Alex knew he'd overstepped the line. But he didn't want to talk about it – he just wanted to focus on forgetting and having a good night. Luckily, his parents seemed to have got the picture, moving onto a new conversation as the food began to arrive.

The tiny portions were made up for by the number of courses, slowly and tastily filling Alex up, yet giving him plenty of time in between to top up his and his sister's glasses. They all relaxed into the evening and ended up making their way through a serious amount of wine.

"Can we get the taxi to drop me off at Kyle's?" Alex asked his drunk parents, suddenly noticing that it was nearly ten and thus time to get the show on the road.

"No problem," his father affirmed. "Do you want to go now?"

"Yeah."

"All right, I'll just get the bill. What about you, Chloe? Where are you off to?" Mr Walsh enquired, rooting in his pocket for his credit card.

"Well, I was supposed to be doing something with Sam's friends . . . "

"Fuck that – come to Kyle's," Alex interjected, finding the alcoholic blur of sibling banter unusually enjoyable.

"Well, yeah – I think all my friends have gone there anyway, so I may as well," she agreed, slurring slightly.

Off they set, hailing a taxi easily and flying out to Foxrock, stopping at Kyle's house for the twins to get out. Alex was in flying form and entered the house with chants and cheers, whilst the others greeted both Walshs with rapturous whooping, all clearly well under the influence at this stage too. They were all dressed in beach attire (Alex and Chloe had brought theirs along to change into) to be in keeping with the nightclub's theme. Summer lived on! Alex smiled as he observed them all, before availing of the free beer Kyle was supplying and settling in amongst his gang.

"You seem in better form," Andy pointed out.

"Ha ha, wouldn't be hard now, would it?" Alex said. "Fuck that shit anyway – it's time to party!" He high-fived his friend, signifying that he was definitely back to his old self.

"And just to say, your sister looks fucking sexy tonight," Andy added. Alex stopped, not in the mood for his friend's sleazy ways. His eyes warned as much but Andy still hald on to his newfound determination, adamant to put his plan into action. He didn't even think Chloe looked particularly sexy – more and more these days she was looking tired and withdrawn. But he was still going to pursue her, and to hopefully get some action at the end of it all.

By eleven, they all decided that it was time to hit the beach party, and to hit it in style. Alex went upstairs to change into his Bermuda shorts and lifeguard T-shirt, popping his sunglasses on his head and fixing his hair too. Pleased with the image the mirror offered, he felt his phone vibrate in his Hawaiian-print pocket.

HEY HANDSOME. HOPE UR IN BETA FORM. WE'V JUS ARRIVD @ D BEACH PARTY. CUM SOON? XOX JEN XOX

Alex realised that he hadn't thought about her all evening, but he was glad that she would be there on his arrival. Leaving Andy's bedroom, he met Chloe on the landing coming out of the bathroom, having changed into her skirt and bikini top.

"I feel so fat," she exclaimed as she saw her brother looking at her scantily clad torso.

"Chloe, shut up, you're tiny," Alex assured her, meaning it more than she knew.

"Fuck it, I'll probably hate all the photos in the morning, but right now I'm too drunk to care," she declared, stumbling down the stairs as Alex followed behind her, staring at her vertebrae, which poked out from beneath her skin. She really was thin.

"Taxi posse?" Andy half-asked half-told his best friend, as Alex downed his can and headed outside where the convoy of taxis they'd ordered waited, growing more and more impatient as the havoc intensified. Alex needed to go to the toilet, but was shoved into a taxi by the boys as they followed the many others towards the much, anticipated Results Night Party. Alex couldn't wait.

The queue outside seemed big but moved quickly, as everyone had pre-bought their tickets and so were just briskly checked for ID before being ushered into the tropically decorated venue, which surged with bodies, dancing and socialising in the two feet of sand which covered the entire floor. Alex went straight for the toilets, keeping his head low to avoid meeting anyone he knew, just until he had relieved himself. The boys' toilets, like the whole club, were crammed, and one drunken idiot was staggering about the place, getting in Alex's way and starting to get on his nerves.

"Here, move, would you?" Alex instructed, fit to burst if he didn't get to a urinal soon.

"Who the fuck are you?" the drunken culprit slurred, squaring up to him.

"Here, buddy, I just want to take a piss, all right?" Alex sidestepped him, not wanting any trouble, despite being unimpressed. But his enemy wasn't finished, and as Alex finally answered nature's call, announced, "Oh, look, everybody, it's Alex Walsh! Well, excuse me, Walshy – I forgot – you think you're some kind of . . . bigshot around here? Well, listen here . . . just be careful, yeah . . . because you can just fuck right off . . ."

Not impressed, Alex pushed past the rambling idiot, glancing only briefly at his face as he left the bathroom. And then it hit him. It had been Phil. Barry's cousin. Alex took a deep breath. He wasn't going to think about any of that stuff – not tonight. But Phil had been completely out of line, and Alex's anger began to boil. Who did he think he was talking to him like that? Why did he keep giving him so much attitude? Alex felt his rage surge forth, but reminded himself that he did not want to start his night by punching some idiot's lights out, and instead began to make his way through the crowds, searching for Jenny. He bumped into many people as he went, all dolled up in their brightest gear, grinning from ear to ear. The mini swimming pool was filled with splashing bodies, all having been convinced by alcohol that getting soaking wet was a great idea. Palm trees and parrots lurked in every corner, as Alex chatted to various punters, all seemingly delighted with the day's news and determined to have a good time. The words "Ayia Napa" hung on everyone's lips, as the first flights departed the following day, ferrying the initial batch of excited teens to their anticipated destination. Everyone was going. It was going to be immense.

Alex continued his search for Jenny but to no avail, being stopped every so often by people he knew, insisting on buying him shots. The more tequila which filled him, the harder it was to focus, making his quest even harder, on top of the growing number of relieved Leaving Certs who kept arriving en masse. Alex's head spun. The bass pumped from the dance floor, throbbing through him, focusing particularly on his stomach, where his self-made cocktail sloshed about, begging not to be added to. Andy found him at one stage, patting him on the back and saying something which Alex couldn't quite catch, his mind fuzzing up as the world became mush, blurring into a techni-coloured haze. He had to find Jenny.

Kyle grabbed his arm and pulled him to the bar, mumbling something about "snorkelling" and thrusting a Smirnoff Ice in Alex's direction. Alex did what he was told, unable to object, doubling the straw tightly against the rim of the bottle, opening his throat and allowing the whole drink to pour into him in seconds. For a minute he had an awful feeling that the drink would come back and haunt him, but somehow Alex forced himself to keep it down, not wanting his night to end yet. Not till he'd found Jenny. He took out his phone and stared at the screen but found it too difficult to focus, as three little screens danced in his vision, dizzying him even more. Alex tried to do one more lap of the club, bumping into people as he went, until suddenly, through the swarms of people, there she was.

"Jenny," he called out, gaining her attention and drawing her out of the conversation she was having with some guy. They looked cosier than Alex would have liked, and as he walked up to her, he recognised the man in question. Had he been in his school? Was he one of Sam's friends? He willed his eyes to focus, until suddenly it hit him.

"Hey, Phil. God, you just keep getting in my way tonight, don't you?" he declared, arriving beside them.

"What? Hey, Alex." Jenny was confused.

"I've been looking for you all fucking night," Alex informed her, clearly unimpressed.

"Me too. Plus I've rung you, like, four times," Jenny said sincerely. "But, anyway, you've found me now," she reminded him brightly, leaning in to kiss him. Alex pulled away.

"Don't want to interrupt anything," he growled, wondering how Jenny knew this idiot.

"Well, you are, Walshy," the third party interjected.

"Wait . . . no, you're not . . ." Jenny assured Alex.

"Good. Because frankly I've had enough of Phil pissing me off tonight," Alex replied quickly. "I actually wish he'd just fuck off, to be honest."

"Here, watch your mouth, Walshy. Just because I was getting comfortable with your girlfriend . . ."

"She's not my girlfriend," Alex contradicted, feeling his fists clench as rage towards this fool began to build inside him. Why was Phil doing this? What on earth did he have against Alex?

"Well, then you don't mind if I do this," Phil tested, putting his hands on Jenny's waist.

"What are you doing?" Jenny squealed.

"Get your fucking hands off her," Alex shouted, pushing Phil away from her, his blood beginning to boil.

"Don't fucking touch me," Phil bellowed, shoving Alex back.

"Look, man, I don't want a fucking fight." Alex tried to sound calm, reminding himself that he had finally found Jenny and would much rather be scoring her right now than breaking some plonker's nose.

"Oh, do you not?" Phil sing-songed. "Well, pity, because frankly I think you're a cunt, Walshy . . . an absolute, filthy cunt . . ." he murmured darkly. "In fact, you being such a cunt these days means I even considered fucking the brains out of your anorexic slut of a sister tonight, just to piss you off."

"Watch your fucking mouth," Alex threatened, inches from lashing out. How dare he talk to him like that. How dare he talk about Chloe like that. For the first time all night, Alex was thinking clearly, his every burning desire fixated on his loathing. "Don't say another fucking word," he warned.

"Or what?" Phil retorted. "Or you'll punch me? Or you'll call your friends over?" He squared up to Alex so that they were touching. "Or maybe you'll call Barry . . . oh no, wait – my mistake – my cousin's too busy fucking dying in hospital because of you . . ."

That was it. In that split-second, something inside Alex snapped and everything else in the world just disappeared. Only one thing mattered – only one single thing: he wanted to kill Phil. He punched him full force in the face, hearing a crack as his fist hit his nose. His knuckles stung, but he was only getting started. He punched Phil again, coming from under his chin and knocking Phil's head upwards, hearing a groan as he did so. Phil looked dazed.

"You piece of shit," Alex murmured, before ramming him backwards against one of the tall tables, which fell over on impact, sending Phil to the floor and, in turn, Alex too. There was screaming all around them, as people dived out of the way of the wrestling pair. Phil got in a few punches of his own, and Alex could feel hot blood gush into his mouth, but he just spat it in his opponent's face and kept on hitting him and hitting him, wishing him dead, wishing it was Phil on the hospital bed, not Barry. He could have sworn he heard Jenny's voice through the crowd, begging him to stop, and then Chloe's. But he wasn't going to stop – not until this guy took back what he'd said, not until he stopped trying to make him feel guilty.

"It wasn't my fucking fault," Alex boomed, his eyes watering as his fists kept pounding. And they would keep pounding until Phil learned that no one could speak to him like that about his best friend, or his sister, or touch his girl, or look him in the eye and call him a cunt. No one.

Suddenly Alex felt something grab him from behind, wrenching his right arm behind his back until it would go no further, and then wrenching it some more.

"Come with me, you little fucking toerag," the bouncer bellowed in his ear, dragging him roughly to the door, ensuring he smacked Alex's head off every wall they passed. They got outside, where a crowd of people stood back and gasped as the huge man threw this bloody mess onto the ground, kicking him in the stomach for good measure.

"If you ever come near this club again, you gobshite, I swear to God I will break both your fucking legs," the bouncer roared. "Now get off this property or I'll call the police, you scummy fuck."

Alex was winded. Every inch of him throbbed and blood poured into his eyes, making it impossible to see. He dragged himself up from the ground, wiping his face and noticing the many figures who stared at him in fear and disgust. But he had to go. He had to run. If Phil's friends had any sense, they'd be out here in seconds, seeking revenge. He had to get away.

Hobbling as fast as possible, he left the car park, looking over his shoulder as often as he could, dreading who would come after him. The main road was a risk – if any police saw him, they'd be sure to question him. As for a taxi, who would pick him up in this state? No one in their right mind would let him spill his blood all over their car. But he had to walk; he just kept walking. His mind ached. He was scared.

"Alex, Alex," a familiar voice called after him. He looked behind to see Jenny sprinting towards him. She reached him, out of breath, wincing as she saw his cut-up face.

"Are they coming?" Alex asked desperately, panic still racing through him.

"No. They came outside, but you'd gone. They were going to go after you, but Andy and the lads showed up and told them if they even went near you . . . oh, fuck that, look at the state of you," she exclaimed, utterly petrified.

"I just want to get out of here, Jenny. Please." He was still drunk but consumed with fear, wanting to be anywhere else but there.

"Come on, we'll get a taxi," Jenny suggested.

"Who would take me in this mess?"

"Here, I have tissues. Wipe your face and I'll try hail one. You can come back to mine," she instructed. Alex did as he was told, cleaning away as much blood as possible, as Jenny secured them a lift home. The taxi ride was a blur, as Alex dozed off, exhausted both physically and with relief. But he was safe now. He was going to be OK.

Once back in Jenny's, Alex's breathing finally steadied, his heart pumping at a more normal rate, allowing him to regain his calm. He sat in the kitchen as Jenny rooted through her cupboards for the first-aid box. Alex watched her as she took out the various antiseptics and creams, laying them out in a line on the counter before sitting down on another stool beside Alex.

"OK, this might sting," she warned, opening an antiseptic wipe and approaching Alex's face gingerly.

"Ah!" Alex winced, the sharp stab of pain worse than he expected.

"Hold still," Jenny snapped, her eyes focused. She wiped away his blood, cleaned his wounds – even his busted-up knuckles – and tenderly pieced him back together. Neither of them said anything, but for Alex, it was a special moment, her care for him displayed so genuinely, and he appreciated it more than she realised.

"Jen, why are you doing this?" He broke the silence at last.

"I was hardly going to leave you, was I?" she replied matter-of-factly, still concentrated on tending to him.

"Yeah, but I mean – it's only, like, one o'clock. Your night hadn't even nearly ended."

"Oh well." She shrugged, though her tone was firm.

"Look, I'm really sorry, Jen . . ."

"Don't."

"Why not?"

"Because . . . because I don't want to think about it, OK? Not tonight," Jenny explained. "I don't think you realise how scared I was."

"I know but–"

"No, Alex. You don't. I've never seen that side of you before . . . and I didn't like it." Her voice was harsh. She meant it.

"I know, Jen. I just . . . the stuff he was saying. Like, what the fuck? He was saying shit about you, and Chloe, and . . . and Barry . . ." He paused. "That's just not on."

Jenny didn't reply.

"I was just in a fouler. Like, the results really pissed me off . . ."

"So why didn't you just come and talk to me about it?"

"I couldn't find you, remember?" Alex realised how sober he now was.

"Yeah, because you were too busy getting wasted!" Jenny exclaimed, clearly frustrated.

Alex waited; his mind began to race again, now thinking of all the many implications of tonight's event.

"Ayia Napa," he suddenly whispered.

"What?"

"Ayia Napa. I'm going to be fucked. Phil and his faggot mates are going to be after me – I'll have to seriously watch my back . . . fuck!"

"Look, just don't think about that–"

"And what about my mum? How the hell am I going to explain the cuts on my face?"

"Alex, just shut up, would you!" Jenny finally exploded.

Alex was silent, completely taken aback by her outburst. "What?" he murmured.

"I said, shut up!" she reiterated, her voice still loud.

Alex looked at her, seeing the anger in her eyes and startled by its intensity.

"Jen, what's wrong . . .?"

"Nothing's wrong," she blurted, frustrated.

"Then why–"

"I'm pissed off because nothing's wrong. Alex, I just don't get how you can, like, completely miss the point."

"What do you mean?"

"I mean, of course Phil is going to hate you – his cousin's in hospital, for fuck's sake, and as far as he's concerned it's thanks to you."

"But it's not . . ."

"I know it's not. But come on, Alex. They were really close, you know – he was telling me–"

"Oh, when you guys were cosying up in the corner?" Alex interrupted, growing impatient.

"We were not cosying up – he was just talking to me about it."

"So what, you're on his side now?" Alex spat.

"I'm not on anyone's side. I was just saying–"

"Oh really? Because last time I checked you were on my side, so thanks a lot." He folded his arms like a sulking child, trying to figure out why Jenny was letting him down like this.

She tried to explain. "Look, Alex. I know Barry being in hospital isn't your fault – I never said it was and I've never thought that either–"

"Well, that's what it bloody looks like to me," he retorted, his brow wrinkled with disgust.

"Oh, piss off, would you," Jenny exclaimed. "This isn't even about the bloody accident. This is about you getting pissed off just because for once in my life I'm not fucking pandering to your every need. For once, I have my own opinion and you don't like it!"

Alex said nothing. He couldn't understand where all this was coming from – since when had Jenny felt like that? Of course she was allowed to have her own opinions – what made her think otherwise? His head began to hurt.

"Look, Jenny, I'm really sorry you feel like that." He apologised wearily, wanting it all to go away.

"No, look . . . I'm sorry. To be honest, I don't even feel like that . . . well, I do sometimes . . . but not really . . . ah, I'm just a bit drunk and a bit annoyed after today." She sighed, tiredness flooding over her.

Alex didn't know what to say or do. Should he give her a hug? Should he try and find out whether she really thought he was that controlling? Surely not.

"Let's just go upstairs. We're both knackered," Jenny suggested, standing up with a sigh and ambling out of the room.

"Oh, right. OK, well, yeah . . . let's go up," Alex agreed, assuming her parents weren't home, though for the first time in his life he had no other agenda. He just wanted to sleep, to wake up and for it to be the next day. For all this to have gone away.

He mounted the stairs slowly, undressed himself and slipped into Jenny's bed. Checking his phone, he noticed that it was off – he'd probably banged it in the scramble.

"Fuck, what if people have been trying to call me?" he said, worried.

"It's grand. While you were sleeping in the taxi, I rang Chloe and Andy – told them you were OK. Just relax," Jenny replied, still tense, taking off her clothes before joining Alex in the bed. But she didn't snuggle into him as usual, just rolled over without a word. Alex lay for a moment staring at the ceiling, wishing things were different.

"I'm sorry," he whispered in the darkness, meaning it from the bottom of his heart.

For a horrible second he thought Jenny wouldn't reply, but soon her voice flowed through the shadows.

"It's OK. Just . . . just remember I'm entitled to my opinion too, yeah?"

"Yeah," Alex affirmed.

"And just try and put yourself in Phil's shoes for a minute, yeah? It can't be easy."

"I know." He rolled towards her and placed a single arm around her curled-up frame. She took his hand in hers, her back still to him, but as she linked her fingers with his, Alex knew things were going to be OK. Falling asleep with Jenny in his arms – maybe it hadn't been such a bad night after all. And maybe the future wouldn't be so bad either if he had this. He thought of Phil, of Barry – of everything. But sleep caressed his soul and Alex gave in willingly, wanting nothing else.

10

CHLOE

Chloe's night had been going well, until she heard screaming from a nearby corner of the room, went to investigate and saw her brother and some guy tearing each other to shreds. Stunned at first, she was unable to move or speak, but as the urgency of the situation built, she found her voice and called out to them to stop. Alex was bleeding; they both were. It was awful. Chloe had never seen anything so vicious and was relieved when the bouncers showed up and sorted things out, though they had been more than rough with the boys too. Once Alex and his opponent had been chucked out, people began to get back to whatever they had been doing before the scrap. Yet suddenly a group of boys was running outside, closely followed by Andy and Alex's friends, so Chloe knew it wasn't over. She tried to go outside, to see what was happening, but security wouldn't let her leave, warning her that it was probably best she stayed inside. So she waited. She waited and waited until, finally, Andy reappeared.

"Oh my God, Andy, is he OK?" Chloe demanded.

"Yeah, he's grand. Jenny's gone after him so he'll be fine. We just had to take care of the other guys," Andy explained, sounding out of breath.

"Was there a fight outside?"

"Nearly. Lets just say that bastard Phil was trying to get his friends to go after Al, but we set them straight. They're back inside now and, trust me, they won't be going near him again," Andy assured, and Chloe believed him. She knew she could trust him, for if anyone had Alex's best interests at heart, it was Andy.

"Thanks a million, Andy," she exclaimed, throwing her arms around him, truly grateful for all he'd done.

"No worries," he replied, wrapping his arms around her too. Chloe realised that she didn't want to let go; relief flooded into her, expelling all her previous tension, as she buried her head into Andy's shoulder. It felt nice. She pulled away and realised he was staring straight into her eyes. She held his gaze, trying to gauge what he was thinking. For the second time recently, Chloe had an overwhelming feeling of being wanted, something she was experiencing less and less when she was with Sam.

She loved Sam. And she loved that he knew so much about her, that she could be herself around him. But right now it felt good that Andy didn't know her that well, relatively speaking, yet was staring into her, wanting her and making her want him too. Her heart throbbed. She held him tighter, feeling a connection that made her neck tingle as the tiny hairs stood up with electricity. She'd never thought of Andy in that way before, and if the truth were told, she thought he was extremely arrogant, just like her brother. But on the basest level, an animal magnetism surged between them which was devoid of emotion but thoroughly arousing.

"Shit." Andy suddenly broke the tension.

"What?" Chloe asked, disappointed that their moment had ended.

"My phone . . ." Andy explained, answering the call reluctantly. Chloe sighed, knowing it was probably for the best that they'd been pulled apart – who knew who was watching – yet secretly wishing they could have had a few more seconds, just so she could savour the intense sensation of chemistry, the like of which she had to admit she missed.

"That was Jenny," Andy informed her, turning around again having finished the call. "She's in a taxi with Alex, going back to hers. She says he's fine, just a bit shaken."

"Thank God," Chloe sighed, genuinely relieved.

"Yeah. Anyway, I told her I was with you so I'd let you know and she told me to make sure you weren't worried, 'cause he really is grand."

"Cool." Chloe was pleased with the news, but still mildly distracted by the fact that Andy was once more within inches of her, causing tingles to prick her warm skin.

"So, I guess that means I have to buy you a drink then," he explained, following Jenny's orders.

"Oh yeah?" Chloe replied with a coy smile, glad that he was sticking around.

"Well, unless you've any better suggestions for cheering you up . . .?" Andy teased, cocking his head and staring at Chloe once more, a half-smile creeping onto his lips.

"You have no idea . . ." Chloe said, wanting so badly to play along, but somehow finding the strength to admit that it would have been wrong – that she was attracted to him on all the wrong levels – and, sighing, turned and led the way to the bar.

They got a drink, which was just as well, since Chloe had been swiftly sobered up by her brother's antics and become more and more self-conscious about what she was wearing, covering her stomach

158

with one arm as the other held her vodka and cranberry. The longer she and Andy talked, the harder she found it. Despite his conversation being nothing out of the ordinary, he did look extremely hot in his beach gear. Chloe knew she had to stop spending her night with him, but she didn't want to. Then again, maybe she was reading too much into it – Andy was just being nice, looking after her because she'd been shaken by her brother's fight. Maybe she was making a fool of herself by engaging in the small amount of flirting her conscience was allowing. She was still tipsy after all.

"Listen, Andy, I'd better go find Sam," Chloe explained, hard as it was.

"Oh, OK," Andy replied, sounding let-down.

She thanked him once more for looking after her brother and headed off into the heaving throng of people, searching for her boyfriend, searching for the boy she loved. She did love him, after all. She loved him and wanted him and needed him. But did he feel the same? She didn't know anymore. And that was what scared her.

"Hey, baby!" Sam perkily welcomed her into the group in which he was talking. "How are you?"

"I'm OK," she tried, not sure exactly how she was at all.

"I heard about Alex. I tried to find you, but you were with Andy so I figured I'd just let you guys talk about the whole thing," he explained, his voice bright and sincere with no hint of jealousy or suspicion which, Chloe had to admit, he deserved to have. Chloe felt fear surge within her – maybe he just didn't care. Maybe this was just another instance of him pulling away. Her thoughts were going into overdrive, and she no longer wanted to be surrounded by drunken, gleeful teens – she wanted to be alone with Sam. To find in him again all the things she prayed hadn't gone. To put her mind at ease.

"Can we go home?" she asked, feeling exhausted.

"Oh, OK." Sam appeared surprised, but was willing to

accommodate his girlfriend, since she seemed out of sorts, probably thanks to the shock of her brother's trouble.

They said their goodbyes, got their coats and headed into the night air, where a line of taxis waited to ferry home the retiring celebrators. Deirdre had surprised Sam's dad with a trip down the country for a few days, so Sam had invited Chloe to stay tonight after the party. In the taxi, she willed herself to cheer up, to get back into the flying form she'd been in earlier on, knowing that if she wanted sparks with Sam, tonight was the perfect chance.

"Are you OK?" Sam asked once they'd paid the taxi and gone indoors, cosy in his sitting-room's warmth.

"Yeah, I'm fine, why?" Chloe asked.

"Nothing. You just seem a million miles away."

Chloe paused, deliberating whether to tell him or not, but conceding that, as always, Sam would listen, so it probably was for the best to talk, to open up.

"I'm just feeling kind of weird about us really," she admitted.

"Oh yeah?" Sam seemed surprised.

"Yeah . . . I mean . . . don't get me wrong . . . but sometimes I just feel like . . . like you don't want me. Like you don't need me. Like you have me, and we're comfortable, and that's that," she explained.

"Haven't we been through this before?" Sam sighed.

"Maybe . . . but I still feel like I like you more than you like me," Chloe reasoned.

"Oh, come on, Chloe. You know that's bullshit. I'm completely in love with you," Sam affirmed, though growing impatient.

"OK, I phrased that wrong . . . I mean, I know you love me . . . but you're just so happy to like . . . not see me all night or to just . . . I don't know . . . be comfortable," she repeated, becoming exasperated.

"Chloe, look. I was just kind of in my own little bubble tonight. I was so happy about the results, but it's also opened a load of

160

questions for me – what I'm going to do next and all that . . ." Sam trailed off. "And I did come looking for you after Alex's fight, but I honestly thought you and Andy would just like to be left to talk about it – I guessed he'd been involved and was calming you down," he continued.

"Hmm, I guess." Chloe gave in, knowing that, as usual, she was reading into things too much. But lately, that was what she did. Her confidence was diminishing, and she needed more and more to be assured of things which previously she would have taken as a given.

"Look, we have two days left until you go to Ayia Napa. Let's just have a ball, yeah?" Sam said. Chloe knew he was right. He was always right. She had to relax.

"Yeah, OK," she agreed.

Sam kissed her. She liked it. She kissed him back, softly at first, but then allowing her tongue to explore. Sam placed his hand on the back of her head, pulling her gently to him. The sparks began. But Chloe wanted more; she needed more. Still kissing him, harder and harder, Chloe took Sam's hand from behind her neck and slowly placed it between her legs, gasping as it arrived, feeling how she'd wanted to all night. Sam took the hint and, undoing her skirt, allowed his fingers to become the explorers. Chloe's mind went blank. She wanted Sam more than ever. She didn't want anyone else – no one else could possibly make her feel this good. Her confidence surged once more – the old Chloe came back to play as her senses went wild, pleasure filling her every inch. She led Sam upstairs, her heart thumping, and made love to him over and over, never wanting it to end. Never wanting him to leave. He was the one; the only one.

The next morning, Chloe stretched herself awake, nestling into the snug of blankets they'd created, as the morning glow licked into the room. Rolling over to her love, Chloe groaned appreciatively, happier and cosier than ever. But Sam wasn't there. She frowned, wondering why he'd left her, but, straining her ears, could hear footsteps coming up the stairs and Sam appeared once more, a fully laden tray in his hands, complete with a single white lily, fresh and new.

"Morning, sunshine," he greeted, placing the spread before her as Chloe sat up in bed, her eyes wide with delight.

"Sam, you legend," she cooed, inhaling the aroma of the hot croissant and streaky bacon as she sipped on the freshly squeezed orange juice.

"You're welcome," Sam answered, kissing her forehead before jumping back into bed.

"Where's yours?" she asked.

"Baby, I've been up for ages – I'm stuffed," he laughed.

"What time is it?" Chloe mumbled through her first mouthful of food.

"It's midday, Lazy Bones!"

"Holy shit," she exclaimed.

"Yeah, but it's not like we got the best night's sleep last night, is it . . .?" Sam said cheekily.

Chloe giggled, loving their intimacy. Loving it all. She chewed on her feast, her stomach receiving it all appreciatively. But as the bacon glistened on the plate, bringing back the guilt which had momentarily deserted her, Chloe froze.

"What's up?" Sam asked.

"Nothing," Chloe fibbed, pretending just to want some orange juice as her mind raced for a way out of this. A croissant – they were so fattening, for goodness sake, she chided herself, willing the panic not to show on her face.

"Oh, good. You know, it's so great to see you eating like this again – it's been a while . . ." Sam commented gingerly. But Chloe didn't care what he thought. What did he know? She still had half a plate of sinful food before her and there was no way he was making her eat it. She had to think.

"I'm feeling kind of hungover, actually," she lied.

"Really? The food will sort you out anyway."

"To be honest, it's not sitting too well."

"Oh?"

"Yeah, I might just leave the rest for later," she reasoned, hoping Sam wasn't onto her. She needed to distract him. "Mind you, it would probably help if someone took my mind off my hangover . . ." Chloe suggested, placing her tray on the floor and rolling back into Sam, kissing his face and drawing him to her.

"Again?" Sam exclaimed.

"Are you complaining?"

"Never . . ." he assured, pulling the duvet over both their heads and grabbing her to him once more. Chloe smiled as she kissed him – her plan had worked. Not only that, but it made her even happier to know that he did in fact want her, despite her previous fears. How wrong had she been? Plus, she might even burn a few calories this way!

*

Later that afternoon, having reluctantly gone home, Chloe was quizzed by her mum about the night before.

"So, was it a success then?" Mrs Walsh asked.

"Yeah, definitely. There were so many people there I knew – it was savage," Chloe enthused.

"And did Alex have a good one too?"

"Yeah, he seemed in great form. Stayed with one of the lads, I think . . ." Chloe covered for him, though unable to shun the bloody images of her brother's beaten face from her mind.

"Yeah, Andy's I think he said. Should be home soon, actually. He stays there a lot, doesn't he?" her mother said.

"Yeah, I guess . . ." Chloe agreed with a smile, noting to herself that she must warn Alex to use someone else's name in future when lying about the fact that he was sleeping in Jenny's.

"Ooh, that must be him now," Mrs Walsh announced, hearing the front door slam. Chloe's heart leapt. She wondered how her brother's face was looking today and if he had thought of a plausible excuse for the damage.

"Hi, darling," their mother greeted him, beaming. But Chloe watched as her face slowly changed into a grimace.

"Hi, Mum." Alex saluted. His face wasn't as bad as Chloe had expected, but clearly Mrs Walsh had noticed nonetheless.

"Alex, what happened?" she requested sternly.

"What?" Alex played innocent.

"Your face, Alex. What happened to your face?" his mum elaborated, taking no prisoners.

"Oh, yeah . . . ha ha . . . hedge-diving," Alex chortled.

"Hedge-diving?"

"Yeah. You know – you fuck yourself into a hedge and bounce back up: it's savage," he explained. Chloe had to admit she was impressed. This hobby was actually a regular occurrence amongst her brother and his friends, so it certainly worked as an alibi. However, their mum still wasn't convinced.

"What do you do? Dive in face-first?" she growled, not seeing the funny side.

"Well, like . . . not usually. We've done it lots of times before, like. I just must have picked the wrong fucking hedge," Alex laughed, playing it up as much as possible. Luckily, it was starting to work.

"Well, it serves you right then," his mother concluded, trying to conceal the small smile which tickled her lips.

Chloe sighed with relief, winking at her brother and thankful that he hadn't got into any more trouble – he'd had enough for the last twenty-four hours. It was good to have him home.

*

"So anyway, how are you feeling about yesterday in general – the results?" Mrs Walsh continued once Alex had left to have a shower, resisting his mother's invitation to sit down and have a similar chat. Chloe wished she'd made such a lucky escape.

"Oh, that . . ." Chloe sighed. "I'm OK, I guess."

"You know you did so well, dear. I meant what I said last night – your father and I are very proud–"

"Mmm . . ." Chloe interjected, not wanting to hear. She stared at the wall, feeling numb.

"What is it, dear?"

"It's just . . . oh, nothing."

"No, no, go on," her mum coaxed.

Chloe took a deep breath. "It's just . . . you and Dad being proud, I mean . . . it's just not . . . not enough," Chloe admitted.

"What do you mean?"

Chloe rolled her eyes. "I mean . . . I wanted to get into Trinity. Now I'm not going to. I'm disappointed – it's not that hard to follow." She felt somewhat annoyed that her mum didn't get it.

"OK, no need to be rude," her mother warned. "But you'll still get Drama in DIT, pet – it's the course, not the college, you should be thinking about."

"We all know that's bullshit," Chloe spat, her impatience growing.

"No it's not. You'll be doing the thing you love, the thing you've always wanted to do – what could be wrong with that?" Mrs Walsh soothed.

The quiet crept in.

"I'm just scared," Chloe finally admitted.

"Of course you are, pet – it's all going to be a big change. But it's exciting too; it's an adventure–"

"Stop! Please just stop!" Chloe shouted, interrupting her mother's speech and making her jump. "Please just stop telling me what I want and how my future should be and will be – it's not up to you. You don't get it. You don't know what I really want!" She felt her voice start to crack as a lump formed in her throat.

"Darling–"

"No, Mum. It's not fair. I just want to be part of the bubble. I want to stay with all my friends and all the people we know – Sam hates all that, but I don't. It's where I belong. And then Sam gets the points to go pretty much anywhere he wants – to stay in the bubble – but there's a look in his eye . . . I don't know, Mum . . . I think he might go away," Chloe reasoned.

"Is that what this is about?"

"No . . . well, maybe . . . I don't know . . ." Chloe tried. "It's all just such a mess."

"It's not supposed to be easy. It never is . . . I'm not trying to patronise you or belittle the way you're feeling," Mrs Walsh added, seeing her daughter about to make another attack. "But you'll soon realise that everyone's feeling the same way. I mean, look at Alex – he's not exactly flush with options now, is he?"

"Mum!" Chloe exclaimed, surprised to hear her talk about her own son in such a way.

"No, no, don't get me wrong – I'm not giving out. But he is going to have to think hard and make some serious decisions over the next while – just like you. It's not easy, pet – growing up never is."

"Don't I know it," Chloe muttered to herself, reluctantly realising that her mother was right. And despite Chloe's tendency to fly off the handle, she conceded that her mother was actually on her side. No matter what.

"Thanks, Mum," she ventured as she made to leave. "I think I'm going to go up and think about packing." Chloe had to keep reminding herself that in two days she was leaving the country.

"Chloe?" Her mum called her back, evidently not entirely finished with their conversation.

"Yeah?" Chloe answered, wondering what could possibly be left to say.

"Can you just sit down again a minute?"

"Oh . . . OK." Chloe was slightly suspicious of her mother's tone.

"I just wanted to talk to you about something else."

"What?"

"Well, I wanted to talk to you about . . . well . . . about your weight," Mrs Walsh explained slowly.

"Mum, please—"

"No, Chloe. Don't try and get out of this again, because I've been trying to have this conversation with you for a while now and—"

"Yeah, you and everybody else!" Chloe exclaimed, exasperated. She didn't want to go through this again – not now. She had enough to think about. Plus, she knew exactly how it would pan out – her mother would express her worries, Chloe would lie, they'd kiss and make up, end of story. But Chloe was too devoid of energy to go through the whole charade for what felt like the thousandth time. Unfortunately, her mum had other ideas.

"Well, do you ever wonder why everyone wants to have this talk with you? Do you never stop to think that maybe everyone's showing concern for a reason? Maybe because they're actually worried about you?"

"They've no reason to be worried." Chloe sighed.

"Really?" Mrs Walsh asked suspiciously, raising an eyebrow in disbelief.

"Really!" Chloe confirmed, her voice louder than anticipated. "I'm sorry, Mum, but I'm telling you – I've been eating healthily, going to the gym – it's no wonder I lost some weight. But I needed to lose it – that's all. So now I have and I'm happy. End of story."

"But, Chloe, you've been so distant and withdrawn too – like there's something you're not telling me."

"Mum, I've been bloody nervous about the results. And as I've just proven, with good cause. All my friends have been the same – we have had a reason, like," Chloe explained, half telling the truth and half pushing her mother away from the extent of the situation. She didn't need to know.

They stared at one another with silent tension. Slowly, Chloe watched her mother begin to give in.

"Well, I suppose it has been a stressful time . . . as long as you're sure you're OK now?" Her mum seemed to be coming round.

"Mum, I'm fine, trust me."

Mrs Walsh stared at her daughter, wanting to believe her, wanting to believe that she was OK. But it was becoming more difficult. Something was up. But if she started calling her daughter a liar then it was just going to make things worse and push her even further away. Maybe Chloe deserved the benefit of the doubt. "You promise?" Mrs Walsh finally spoke, looking her daughter in the eye and begging her to tell the truth.

Chloe hesitated. This wasn't going to be easy.

"I promise." In a way, she wasn't really lying – in her eyes she *was* fine; she was doing what she felt needed to be done, and if anyone else thought otherwise, then that was their problem.

"OK, well maybe try and get an early night," Mrs Walsh suggested. "You're exhausted, love."

"Yeah, I know," Chloe confessed, aimlessly leaving the room and mounting the stairs, noting just how weak her body was. It had been a demanding twenty-four hours, that was for sure – both physically and emotionally, as the tension of the build-up had been transformed into celebratory energy and now back into disappointment and fear. That conversation with her mum had been the last thing she needed. But it was over now, and she could get back to doing what she had to do. Growing up really was hard.

*

The following day was a mindless chore of washing and packing, as Chloe dithered over what exactly she would bring. It would be hot by day, but would the nights be cold? And did she want very dressy-up clothes or more casual, summery stuff? How many bikinis did she need? Flip-flops? The possibilities were endless and it enraged her even more to see Alex stroll into his bedroom and saunter out twenty minutes later, announcing that he was all packed and ready to go. How did he do it?

Still, the only thing which kept her going through the stressful preparations was the sheer excitement – she couldn't wait. All day, texts from her friends flooded in, reminding one another just how good the coming fortnight was going to be.

HEY GIRLS, WE'R GOIN 2 AYIA NAPA 2MO! WOOOOOOOOOOOO!! XX

BRING UR DANCIN SHOES LADIES! XOX

DONT 4GET SPARE UNDERWEAR ;)

With each text, Chloe found a new lease of life and slowly but surely the suitcase began to fill, outfits and spares being compiled into one multicoloured pile. However, one text caught Chloe off guard.

HEY BABE. ALL EXCITD? CANT FUCKN W8 2 C U IN A BIKINI AGAIN! C U @ D AIRPORT 2MO, ANDY X

Chloe read and re-read the various letters and symbols and tried to make sense of why he'd bothered to send it. Undeniably, whilst packing, the notion of Andy had popped into her head more than once, as Chloe thought back to the beach party and that brief moment they had shared. So what if there were more moments like that in Cyprus? She would never cheat on Sam. He was her rock, and as she was slowly starting to comprehend just how scary the coming months of her life were going to be, more than ever she needed that rock. She needed Sam. So there was no way she was going to throw that away over her brother's friend. She didn't even fancy Andy – not really. The connection they had was purely sexual. Plus, Andy was one of Alex's best friends, and since the other one was still unconscious in hospital, Chloe didn't want to go complicating

169

matters any further. So she'd have to avoid Andy: it was as simple as that. But part of her knew that it wouldn't be simple in the slightest, since her friends and Alex's friends were not only taking the same flight and staying in the same resort but had all been talking excitedly about the things they were going to do and how much fun they were going to have together. So she'd just have to be strong – but strong was not something which Chloe did well recently. It was not something which she did at all recently. She sighed. This was going to be tough.

As doubts ebbed and flowed within her, Chloe couldn't help but admit that things would be so much easier if Sam were coming. Not only that, it would have been perfect to have him there – to go on holidays and end the summer together like they'd always planned. Despite having been through that with him on numerous occasions, Chloe couldn't suppress the anger which bubbled inside her once more. Why had he pulled out? Why was he letting her down like this? The holiday where she both wanted and needed him more than ever, and he was leaving her on her own – it wasn't fair. What was more, Chloe still couldn't understand. Sam went on and on about "the bubble", "the South Dublin Circle" and all these other terms for the network which he seemed to find so suppressing and restrictive. But, as Chloe had admitted to her mother yesterday, it struck her more and more that if he was so intent on not going on holidays with these people, how was he going to enjoy going to college with them? If he didn't cop himself on and realise that he needed to stop generalising and start embracing the fun that was to be had in such an environment, he would never like it. Chloe knew that he'd applied to and been accepted into some colleges in England, but they were only a back-up if he didn't get what he wanted in Dublin. He'd got so many points that surely he had secured his very first choice. Surely all notions of going away would be forgotten about now. Wouldn't they?

*

Sam gazed up at his ceiling, the ornate plasterwork swirling high above him, out of reach. His room was bright, as the sunlight danced in every corner, illuminating even the darkest nook, reminding him that summer wasn't over. Yet. He'd been lying there for almost an hour, just thinking. Or trying not to think. He wasn't sure which. But it felt good to just laze on his bed and stare into nothingness.

This is it, Sam Gallagher, he pointed out. It's decision time. Having received a very prompt letter that morning from the London School of Economics informing him that thanks to his Leaving Cert results he was now officially being offered a place, Sam's mind was racing. He'd known it was coming – the moment he'd opened his results, he knew he'd done enough. But now that he had it in black and white – the paper so crisp and authoritative, the ink so precise and intimidating – he had to put his thinking cap on.

There was a knock on the door. His dad gingerly entered.

"You thinking?" he began, having just been informed of his son's dilemma.

"Yup." Sam sighed, wanting to tell his father and hoping he would have some advice or, better still, just make the decision for him.

"Your mother rang and filled me in – look, I'm sorry Deirdre and I were away while all this was going on . . ."

"Dad, it's fine. Honestly," Sam assured, not wanting his father to feel guilty. He was here now and that was what mattered. Maybe he could somehow alleviate the indecision which filled Sam's mind.

"I never realised you were so serious about going to England," his dad continued.

"Neither did I," Sam confided. "It's only recently I've been thinking about it loads, and then when I got my results . . . I just don't know what to do."

"Well, break it down simply, I guess," Mr Gallagher said, sitting down on the foot of his son's bed, melting into the mattress' springs. "What are the things that make you want to go?"

Sam took a deep breath, being as honest as possible.

"It'd be a fresh start . . . a change of scenery . . . bit of an adventure . . . new faces . . . plus the course sounds incredible . . ." he listed.

"OK. So now, the reasons for not going?" his dad coaxed.

"I don't know . . . it could be kind of scary . . . I'd miss you guys . . . Chloe . . ." he began, but then realised that he had nothing else.

"OK, well, let's look at this logically," his father rationalised. "Let me just say first off that in no way am I pushing you to do anything, and frankly I would really miss you if you went . . . but this isn't about me. It's about you. So, let's go through them. Missing us: you'll be home at holidays and London is not that far away – good old Ryanair will sort us out. I'd be more than happy to visit and sample the nightlife," he joked.

"Shut up, Dad," Sam laughed.

"Sorry. Anyway, yeah, so I think, much and all as we'd hate to have you gone and vice versa, I think Deirdre and I, and your mother, would manage. And so would you," he summarised.

So far, Sam agreed.

"Next, there's being scared. Samuel, you are probably the bravest person I know. And OK, OK, I'm not trying to take away from how hard it would be . . . at first. But think of all the things that you listed – an adventure, a fresh start – it'd be so exciting!" his father said triumphantly, his eyes lighting up with endless possibilities, infectious to behold. Sam nodded his head, finally feeling enthused about something.

"And then there's Chloe," his father reminded him. Sam's heart sank. His enthusiasm disappeared.

"Yeah . . .?" he wondered, hoping his dad would have a solution.

"Well, unfortunately, I can't help you on that one."

Sam felt defeated. The obstacle that kept getting in his way had left his father advice-less too. He was back to where he'd started.

"All I will say, though . . ." Mr Gallagher began, giving Sam a tiny shred of hope once more, ". . . is that, I know you love her, but . . . is she the one? Are you really going to spend the rest of your lives together? And even if the answer is yes, well then you'll both be willing to put in the effort and do the long-distance thing," he surmised. "If it is the real thing, it'll last no matter what. If it's not . . . then it'd be a shame to waste such an opportunity because of it."

Sam's father patted his leg before exiting the room, shutting the door behind him firmly, leaving a grave silence in the room, an emptiness longing to be filled. Sam returned to staring at the ceiling, replaying his father's words in his head. It was time to choose. He knew what he wanted.

*

Night-time was falling when Chloe finally closed the zip of her case, the sense of achievement overridden by her lack of energy. It had been hard work. She needed bed. She and Sam were going for breakfast the following morning, before they were forced to say goodbye and set off in their separate directions for the coming two weeks. Chloe was looking forward to seeing him, but dreaded that moment when they had to part. It seemed so much more significant than it actually was. But Chloe's heart could not be persuaded otherwise and had knotted itself into a thorny bush of anxiety, wishing that farewell would never come.

Changing for bed, Chloe stared at herself in the mirror. So this was it. This was the body the world was going to see on the beach. This was what she had worked so hard for. It wasn't bad, she confessed, knowing she'd lost almost a stone and a half and running her fingers over the various bones which protruded from her taut flesh. But it wasn't good either. It wasn't enough. She wished she had another week, reasoning that she would have happily eaten absolutely nothing and gone to the gym every day of the week. But it was too late. She had failed.

Sliding into her cosy nest, Chloe hated herself. She hated that she couldn't even manage a simple task – she had had all summer to get the body she wanted, the body she needed, but still she wasn't satisifed. Why hadn't she succeeded? Was she so weak that her control and her power were too pathetic to get what she desired? The girls in the magazines had got it. The skinny celebrities had got it. The newspapers were filled with articles about this "size zero" craze coming from America and polluting the minds of fragile teens. But Chloe doubted that she was a size zero. Well, she admitted, she was on her way. But that wasn't enough. Why had she been such a failure? Chloe tossed and turned in the flickering shadows, as angry tears were her only lullaby. A hateful sleep came at last, even darker than the night itself.

The alarm clock sounded. It was Saturday. It was Ayia Napa day. It was goodbye day. Chloe dressed in her chosen outfit, applying her make-up with extreme care – wanting to leave Sam with as good an image of her as possible, but also preparing for the mass of familiar faces who would greet her in the airport that afternoon. Alex was still in bed, so her mother gave her a lift to The Gables in Foxrock, where she was meeting Sam. He was there when she arrived. Chloe's heart throbbed as she walked to the table, but as Sam stood up to greet her, encasing her in his arms and kissing her tenderly, she knew she had to savour the next hour, to cling onto it for as long as possible so that all through her holiday she would remember all she felt for him in this moment. This was it.

"You look nice," Sam commented as Chloe sat down, relaxing her even further.

"Thanks," she replied, hoping he knew how much she meant it. But although Sam didn't think she looked well at all – her tiny frame seeming more shrunken than ever – now wasn't the time to think about that, he reminded himself, as he concentrated on the task at hand.

They ordered, Chloe opting for the porridge, assuring Sam that her stomach was not up for anything else. They talked and laughed, both of them cautious of mentioning the next fortnight as it became increasingly clear that, in many ways, it was going to be make or break. Chloe prayed that the former would occur, and as she relished Sam's company, feeling sparks and that click alive as always, she knew the odds were good. He looked so well and seemed so happy. Even happier than usual. She wondered why, but decided instead to just feed off his radiant positivity and strive to convince herself that worrying about this trip was a waste of time, for life was good and love – the best.

But as always, the clock was their enemy, as time decided that breakfast was over and Chloe felt that sense of dread return to her almost-empty stomach.

"I guess this is it," Sam summed up, having paid the bill and walked her outside into the glorious sunshine, where both their lifts were waiting.

"I'm going to miss you so much," Chloe began, tears already welling.

"I'll miss you too, babe. But promise me you'll have a ball," Sam urged, smiling as always.

"I promise," Chloe mumbled, her eyes completely wet by now.

"And promise me you'll look after yourself," Sam continued. She nodded, words stifled by her crackling sobs, which she tried to suppress but couldn't. She threw her arms around him, holding him close and smelling his smell for what felt like the very last time.

"You'll be back in two weeks," Sam reminded her, grinning. Chloe knew he thought she was overreacting. She knew she was too. But something within her, some sense of foreboding, told her that such dramatics were necessary. Chloe didn't care – all she could think of was this kiss, this last kiss, as Sam leaned in and their lips reunited, tasting farewell.

Sam pulled away. Chloe stared into his eyes.

"Bye," he finished sadly.

"Bye," she returned, rushing to the car with blurry vision, as woe morphed her sight, so that the world was greyer than ever. Her mother sped away as soon as Chloe closed the door – she didn't even have time to watch Sam disappear into the distance. He was gone. Her heart broke.

In the car once more, suitcases loaded and her father's goodbyes concluded, Chloe sat behind her brother as their mum drove them to the airport, where expectant friends awaited their arrival. The tears had stopped. But it was still hard. Chloe knew as soon as she sat down on the plane that excitement would take over, as the most anticipated holiday of her life commenced. Until then, she tried to smile, tried to think of other things. The world zoomed by the car as people busied themselves with everyday affairs, clinging to a dying August and begging Autumn to be patient, to give them just a little more time. Chloe sighed. The airport was near. The future was near. She had to take control. She had to smile.

11

ALEX

Having finally made his way to the top of the check-in queue, through security and onto the plane, Alex fastened his seatbelt and was ready to go – into the clouds and beyond. The aircraft was bursting with excited teenagers, babbling and settling into their seats for the five-hour flight, all "oh my Gods" and Abercrombie hoodies. Alex and Andy had brought a few cans onboard for the journey, so he decided to crack one open, making himself comfortable and starting his holiday exactly as he intended to continue it. Chloe and her girlfriends were at the other end of the plane, yet he could still hear their loud shrieks from where he sat, eyeing up the air-hostess and wondering what his odds were of joining the mile-high club with her.

"You so would!" Andy echoed his sentiments, examining every inch of the cabin crew as they gave their security talk.

"She could blow my whistle any day," Kyle added while the

lifejacket demonstration was underway. Alex high-fived him, but broke it gently to him that he hadn't a chance. Kyle sighed, but the boys made sure to keep his spirits up.

"Never mind, buddy – there'll be plenty more of that where we're going!" Andy reminded him, bracing himself as they took off, though quietly aware of the one girl he himself now had his eye on, as her brother sat to his left, sipping his beer and cheering as they cruised upwards. They were off.

After almost two hours, Alex was beginning to grow restless and so, as many others had, decided to go for a wander. Standing up, he realised his head was lighter than he'd thought but still continued to saunter down the aisle, stepping over crouched passengers who were visiting friends or making new ones, preparing for the coming weeks. Alex found Chloe and her gang and, squeezing in between Heather and Ella, nosed in on their conversation.

"We were just trying to decide who gets the camp bed, 'cause apparently the rooms for three only have two proper beds and one shitty one," Heather explained.

"Sure just throw Chloe on it," Alex suggested.

"Fuck off," his sister called from the row behind.

"It's grand," Alex continued, lowering his voice. "She's the only one who's not going to be getting any action, so you guys are entitled to the real mattresses." He nudged the girls suggestively as they blushed in agreement.

"Who's going to get the shite bed in your room?" Ella inquired.

"Well, we're in a room for four so hopefully we'll be grand. We'll probably stick Kyle on it, though, if it comes to it – not like he's going to be getting his bit, now is it?" Alex taunted.

"That's so harsh!" Heather remarked, giggling.

"So what, you're saying you'd do him?" Alex asked, raising an eyebrow.

178

"Well, no . . . but . . ." Heather tried.

"My point exactly!" Alex exclaimed.

So the journey continued with the banter interrupted only for the dodgy food they were served, which Alex ate numerous portions of since every girl in his vicinity was turning her nose up at the steaming mush. The boys continued to make their way through the cans, maintaining a steady level of tipsiness so that, before they knew it, they were in Cypriot airspace and ready to land. They had arrived!

Stepping off the plane, a wall of intense warmth greeted the tired but excited travellers, still smiling while they ambled across the tarmac towards the terminal, the sweet night air electric with their anticipation. Waiting for the cases to arrive, Alex and the boys joined the long queue at the airport alcohol shop, where they stocked up on vodka, which would hopefully last for them the first few nights. A number of the girls had clearly nipped into the toilets to top up their make-up, as suddenly they emerged once more, looking much fresher than when they'd left the plane, eager to impress at all times.

Baggage in tow, they were directed by a polite travel operator to the coaches which would deliver them to their respective hotels.

"Green Bungalows, please," Alex bellowed triumphantly and the uniformed lady pointed to bus number seven. So they entered the vehicle, disappointed that they had yet another leg of their journey to complete, but intent on remaining in high spirits, chatting excitedly about their plans for the night ahead.

"I reckon we just dump the suitcases and head straight out."

"No way – things don't kick off till much later over here."

"Plus I'm fucking starved."

"Yeah and I wouldn't mind a shower as well – I'm sweating like a pig here."

They brainstormed aloud whilst the lights outside their windows grew brighter and brighter, nearing their destination, until suddenly their guide, having introduced herself already, was booming down the microphone, "Green Bungalows. We have arrived at Green Bungalows." Whoops and cheers ensued and they bustled off the coach into a crowded, tiled reception. Alex could see the bar already. And beside that, the pool.

"Shotgun not signing us in!" he called out, the others following suit. As usual, Kyle was last to respond and so was put in charge of securing their room key whilst the lads made for the outdoor bar to order the first of many pints. To their left, people came and went – some dragging cases, searching for room numbers as they gazed around them, taking in their new surroundings. Others, who had arrived over the previous days, were dolled up and heading out for dinner, their sunburn already visible in the night air. The pool was lit beneath the palm trees, making it look so inviting, despite the large sign stating that anyone who ventured in after eight o'clock at night would be severely fined. Alex was tempted to push his luck, but decided he'd better get off to a good start with the staff here, since hopefully the coming fortnight would be messy enough as it was. He sipped his beer, unable to get over the heat given the late hour, but distracted by the numerous hot girls who were steadily flowing past him to their new bedrooms, which he hoped he would be frequenting at some point.

"We definitely chose the right place to stay, lads," he declared, despite the less than attractive white building which towered behind the pool. But Alex didn't care what his accommodation looked like, for it was what was inside that counted, he laughed, giving a firm thumbs-up to the residents and, better still, the twenty-four-hour bar.

"We're checked in." Kyle finally reappeared, holding key number forty-two and leading the way along the side of the pool, down some steps to their new pad. It was big enough – the first room a kitchen, with two beds down the end, and the bedroom next door with two more.

"Shotgun these beds," Alex and Andy declared simultaneously on entering the latter, throwing their bags onto the mattresses and showing no sign of budging.

"Bouncy enough, I see," Andy commented with a wink to his room-mate, who grinned knowingly in return.

As they took it in turns to use the shower, Andy suggested they go see where everyone else was residing. The other guys from their year filled the rest of their corridor, whilst most of the girls they knew were in another building, fussily unpacking and trying to instil some kind of order to their new abodes, which Alex knew would never last, especially if he had anything to do with it.

"We're meeting up with people in some bar called Senior Frogs later if you guys want to join us?" Heather invited.

"Sounds good," Andy swiftly replied.

"Yeah, but . . . I wouldn't mind grabbing some food first, though," Alex warned.

"Ha ha – apparently you ate about twenty plane dinners earlier, you mess," Chloe slagged. Alex was tempted to retort that she probably hadn't eaten a single morsel since they'd left Dublin, but he managed to restrain himself, not sure what he'd be meddling with. Not really wanting to know.

The boys ordered burgers and chips from the bar and set up camp in their room, cracking open their vodka stash. It was half-past eleven, so they decided to use the next hour to eat up, get drunk and then set out exploring, all eager to find out whether the Ayia Napa nightlife lived up to billing. They'd invited everyone round to room forty-two, and the mass of bodies made the already-warm room hard to bear. Alex had beads of sweat dripping down his forehead as he polished off his food, having to go outside afterwards in an effort to cool down, but forgetting that the climate here was such that the breathless night heat offered little respite from the clammy indoors.

It was beautiful, though. Alex leaned on the terrace railing, gazing up at a starry sky, mesmerised by the constellations and feeling a million miles from home, on the brink of the craziest trip of his life. His phone buzzed in his pocket.

HEYA. SO UV ARRIVD? MEET US IN SENIOR FROGS @ 12.30. JEN XX

Alex smiled, eager to christen the new bedroom, but wondering how exactly this holiday would pan out for Jenny and him. She had arrived yesterday and was only staying for a week, which left them just six days together. He hadn't seen her, though, since results night and was hoping things were going to be back to normal after their tiff. He was excited to see her – he couldn't deny that – and was looking forward to spending time with her. But he also couldn't deny that this wasn't exactly a place in which you wanted to be in a relationship. Of any description.

"God, it's smoky in there." Andy coughed, joining his friend outside.

"Hash?" Alex presumed.

"Yeah."

Alex said nothing, deciding to go in and have some, but his friend pulled him back outside with a comment which he certainly hadn't been expecting.

"Did you think about Baz today?" Andy asked quietly. Alex paused, rejoining his friend in leaning on the railing, staring up at the inky blanket of sky.

"How could I not?" he sighed eventually, glad that he wasn't the only one whose thoughts had been momentarily preoccupied.

"He would have loved it here, man," Andy conceded, his voice filled with something like regret.

"Yeah . . . well, why don't we take him here next summer? When he's OK again . . ." Alex suggested, willing his voice to sound cheery.

"Deal," Andy agreed.

Not another word was said, as both stared into the foreign

blackness. Though neither would ever admit it, each boy couldn't help but find himself thinking that forbidden thought that maybe, just maybe, Barry wasn't going to be OK. That maybe this was it. Alex needed a drink.

*

Stumbling out of the resort – Alex and Andy having decided that the only way to get past their momentary lull was to hit the vodka hard – the rowdy group headed up the hill, towards the infamous strip of nightclubs. A chirpy girl with big boobs and a twangy English accent spotted them coming and zoned in on their large party.

"Two-for-one cocktails and a free pass to Castle," she squawked. The boys stared blankly back at her, as if she had spoken in a foreign language.

"What?" Luke managed.

"Two-for-one cocktails and a free pass to Castle," she repeated, even more high-pitched this time.

The boys kept walking, feeling as if they were missing something, but after a few similar offers from other annoying people, they realised that she had been just one of hundreds of bar reps on The Strip, that, yes, she really had been offering them two cocktails for the price of one and that 'Castle' was the name of a nightclub. Sorted.

The Strip was unlike anything Alex had ever seen. Throngs of people surged in every direction. Half-naked girls with sweaty bodies, smoking and strutting on the highest of heels. Boys with rolling eyes pushing each other and shouting out unintelligible phrases. The locals wearing far more layers than the rest, wolf-whistling at any ladies they liked the look of. Heavy-set bouncers outside thumping clubs, their very eyes warning all who passed not to so much as consider messing with them, dangerous to behold. The flashing lights of these clubs, illuminating the sky above in a spectacle of neon, luring the drunken tourists their way. The thick smell of kebabs and fried meat, salty and enticing to anyone under the influence. The clubs themselves, each with a distinct theme, lavish and cartoon-like in their decor, as pirate ships, jungles and prehistoric worlds promised every sort of alcohol imaginable, with a free shot thrown in for good measure. The noise was intense – be it the overpowering melange of infectious beats or the sizzling buzz from the local tattoo parlour, preying on incapacitated customers. But through the unfamiliar novelty, something began to click, as the boys took a closer look. That joshing group of boys outside The Carwash Club – they'd played rugby against them over the years. Those girls holding back one of their poor friend's hair as she threw up – Alex had scored the majority of them. Suddenly the lads realised that all these people, these sweaty sweaty people, were friends of theirs. People that they knew. Or at least, that they knew to see. South Dublin truly had descended on Ayia Napa and, once the lads refocused their vision, it felt like home. Almost.

Senior Frogs was a small bar with glowing lighting, offering yard-long glasses of crushed ice and alcohol, which were to be drunk through penis-shaped straws. Sure enough, Chloe and her mates had met up with Jenny and hers and were all delighted to see the boys arrive. Alex made his way to the girl whom he'd been most looking forward to seeing and grinned from ear to ear as she kissed him softly, tasting the sweet Sex on the Beach on her lips and not wanting to pull away.

"Hello, stranger," she greeted.

"Missed me?" Alex teased, kissing her again, slipping in his tongue and giving her an extra incentive to answer the question carefully.

"Of course," Jenny assured, batting her eyelids and returning to take a sip from her suggestive straw. She was obviously tipsy, but Alex didn't care; things appeared to be completely back to normal between them and that was what mattered.

"So, how was yesterday?" Alex asked, curious as to how she'd spent her first day in Cyprus.

"Savage, yeah – just got a feel for the place. Found this joint, which is class, isn't it?" She cocked her head towards the giant frog figurine, the bar's logo.

"Seems good, yeah."

"And the place next door, you can get, like, an actual bucket of drink for a fiver – it's insane!" Jenny informed, laughing as Alex's eyes lit up at this information.

After an hour, the group moved on, giving in to the persistent reps and going to Castle, where the various towers and floors were packed with people, each room with a different style of music, though with one overriding theme throughout – alcohol-fuelled fun. Alex spent the night getting drunker and drunker, bumping into anyone and everyone he knew, but finding himself always back with Jenny, cheekily dragging her into dimly lit corners as he kissed and groped her passionately. His head was empty – nothing mattered. His limbs were free as he paused to thump rhythmically with the pulsing tunes, raving enthusiastically to each of the DJ's choices. He was wet with sweat as unknown masses of energy surged through him and kept him moving, always moving, through the night. Time became irrelevant. Each song melted into the next. Each shot melted into another. Money was no object. Life was intoxicating. Alex was free.

*

The next day, Alex didn't emerge from bed until two o'clock in the afternoon. He said goodbye to Jenny as she departed for her apartment, and he dragged himself up to the pool, where he collapsed on a lounger beneath the burning sun. Some of the boys

185

had already set up camp there, sweating the alcohol out of their system and groaning in pain.

"How're the heads this morning?" Alex ventured, but the boys merely grunted in response, keeping their eyes closed at all times and willing their throbbing aches to go away.

"What time did you get in at?" one of the boys managed.

"About six," Alex said. "But me and Jen didn't get to sleep till after eight . . ." he added, still managing to boost his ego despite his hangover, and the boys also briefly ignored their state to high-five and wink appreciatively at their friend.

Alex adjusted himself on his towel, sprawling out as his body sizzled, needing rest but finding little peace here, as giant speakers bellowed out dance music continuously, the repetitive beats like a headache themselves, echoing through the sweltering afternoon. Some boys decided to sample the all-day breakfast which was on offer, the plate of grease promising to soak up all the nastiness from the night before, but Alex's stomach, for once, was content in being empty, as he lolled the hours away.

Some of the female residents, posing at all times, sat on the water's edge, dipping their feet into the cool blue and swapping gossip from last night, their oversized shades displaying large designer logos – the perfect accessory to compliment their skimpy bikinis. Finally Alex could bear the intense rays no more and decided to plunge into the refreshing water, where his fellow teens splashed and played or floated away on brightly patterned lilos. It felt good to swim around and wash away the layer of sweat which filmed Alex's toned body. The water tasted slightly funny, but nothing could ever take away from its spectacular contrast to the outside air, a brief break from the burning day.

As Alex leaned on the pool's edge, chatting to the girls, he spotted Andy ambling into the resort, looking very much the worse for wear. He hadn't come home last night.

"Ooh, Casanova!" Alex shouted, alerting the rest of his friends to the arrival and they too teased their friend.

"Shut up, faggots, got more action than you anyway," Andy asserted, loving the attention.

"You look wrecked," Alex observed, noting the bags under his friends eyes. "Who was she?"

"Just some bird. Got talking to her in Castle and that was that," Andy summarised, crouching down on his hunkers to talk to his mate. "Fantastic tits," he added, just for effect.

But not content to let their friend get too cocky, Luke and Kyle spotted the wink from Alex as they walked over, seemingly to join their friends' chat, and on the count of three, they sent Andy flying into the water with a vigorous push. There was a loud splash, as the whole place turned to see who the unlucky victim had been, cheering as Andy's head re-emerged, grinning despite himself, accepting defeat. Alex cracked up, splashing his friend some more whilst Andy quickly rescued his phone and wallet from his pocket.

"Serves you right!" Alex laughed.

"Fuck off," Andy joked in return.

"Oh, by the way, you owe Kyle, like, ten pounds – we got the air conditioning for the two weeks 'cause that room was insanely hot," Alex informed.

"Grand," Andy agreed, not even thinking about complaining since their new home was indeed a furnace. "And we need to think about renting mopeds."

"Yeah, definitely. There's a rental place across the road so we'll get round to it at some stage," Alex replied, loving the pace here, loving the fact that there was no rush, no worries, no nothing. Just him, in that pool, under that magnificent sun. It was perfect.

That night, after drinking more vodka in their now slightly cooler room, the gang set off towards The Strip again, only this time they were easily persuaded into the pirate-themed bar, which promised that if they all bought a drink each, they would be rewarded with a litre of sambuca and a litre of tequila to share. The boys couldn't resist. Alex knocked back his vodka and Red Bull, before moving amongst his peers, pouring the liquors into their open mouths, drenching them with the free alcohol but keeping plenty for himself too. Soon the bottles ran dry and it was time to move on, and, since it was after one in the morning already, they decided it was time to go clubbing. Starsky's was the chosen venue tonight, and as the boys filtered into the packed building, where a variety of beats pulsed in all directions, they knew they'd found a good one.

All around the bar, girls danced on the counters, messing with their friends or wrapping themselves around the poles provided, giving the gents below a sizzling spectacle. But as Alex looked closer, he realised that these girls were not provided by the establishment, rather they were customers who were invited to take over the bar-tops and strut their stuff, and Alex actually recognised a number of the ladies doing their thing.

"See anything you like?" a husky voice spoke close to his ear.

Turning to face Jenny, Alex was indeed impressed with what he saw. Having been here two days, Jenny already was starting to bronze, her sexy glow revealed at every opportunity as her short skirt and tiny top left a generous amount of flesh on show, delighting Alex's eyes.

"You look hot," he announced as he surveyed her every inch. "Very hot indeed."

"Why thank you," she replied, her breath on his neck, making him tingle.

"Do you want a drink?" Alex offered, more liberal with his money here than he was at home, as not only was it a different currency, thus seeming like unending Monopoly money to him, but it was also his parents', so Jenny could have all the drinks she wanted as far as he was concerned.

"Yeah, please. But get me something in a bottle – apparently some girl got her drink spiked here last night – need to be careful," she warned, as Alex made to the bar, bought her a Smirnoff Ice and willingly received his thank-you kiss.

"So, did you get back OK this afternoon?" Alex asked, leaning on the bar but keeping Jenny close at all times.

"Yeah . . . got a bit of abuse from the girls when I got home, though . . ." Jenny admitted, looking up at him from beneath long eyelashes, fluttering flirtatiously.

"Oh yeah?" Alex smirked.

"Yeah . . . well . . . they were laughing that I didn't really waste any time, did I?" she continued.

"Well, we don't have much time to waste now, do we?" Alex pointed out, knowing that she only had five days left there and the holiday had barely begun.

"Yeah, I know. It sucks . . . how will you manage without me?" Jenny teased, throwing her head back as she laughed, the curve of her neck illuminated by the disco lights.

"I'm sure I'll manage," Alex teased back, though realising that it came out sounding slightly different from what he'd meant. Jenny looked at him, something amiss in her eyes. He knew what she was thinking – was he going to remain faithful on his second week, when she was gone. But faithful to what? Alex reminded himself. They weren't officially going out, plus, the last thing he needed in a place like this was restrictions. This trip was about freedom. But he knew Jenny would hate to know he'd slept with anyone else. He knew they were in deep enough for such feelings to be warranted. So he just wouldn't say anything. He would change the subject now, and let the following week sort itself out. What happened in Ayia Napa stayed in Ayia Napa; that was that.

*

After Starsky's, people had caught wind of a late-night club which was en route to Green Bungalows called Aqua. Walking hand in hand with Jenny, though still wholeheartedly involved in the chorus of rugby chants he and his mates were shouting out, Alex led the way into the nightclub, paying his way before descending the steps into the dark, slightly damp basement of a hotel, where even more loud music hypnotised the dance floor, all dancers well past tipsy by this stage, the time nearing five o'clock. Aqua was less full than the other clubs they'd been in so far, but the free drinks docket they'd acquired on paying in led them straight to the bar. And then Alex saw it.

"Holy shit, lads – check it out," he exclaimed, casting his eyes to the left as they all gazed upon the club's main attraction – water! Dark caves loomed over a dimly lit pool, as a waterfall in the centre cascaded down upon a kissing couple, who, like many others, had dared to venture in. The shadowy corners appeared the perfect location for naughtiness, whilst the centre stretch of water rippled invitingly, until one by one the boys gave in, eager to sample such a novelty. Having already removed and lost his T-shirt in Starsky's, Alex stripped off the rest of his clothing and waded into the warm pool with his friends.

"Imagine how much gross shit there is in this water," Kyle said, wincing as his mind considered the many possibilities of what lurked below.

Alex laughed, watching the kissing couple once more and wondering just how far people went in a place like this. Where was Jenny? he wondered, though chuckling as he realised by what train of thought the question had arrived. His kinky idea consumed him, until he felt a huge splash of warmth cover his body. It had been Andy. It was game on.

"You prick," Alex scoffed with a grin, sending water flying all over his friend and dunking him into the pool as they began to wrestle playfully in the lagoon. Alex's fuzzy head and bleary eyes were drenched as the horseplay continued, grabbing and punching and beating his friend in jest, their laughter reverberating off the low ceilings, as the kissing couple glared frustratedly, showing they were not impressed with their intimate moment being wrecked by such a display of immaturity. But frankly, Alex didn't care, glad that now he wasn't the only one not taking advantage of the potentially romantic situation. Then again he didn't really mind, having too much fun beating Andy up, and as Kyle and Luke joined in the playful scrap, he realised that maybe tonight Jenny would just have to wait, for acting the idiot with his closest friends was keeping him more than amused. "Mates before dates," he reminded himself, grabbing Kyle in a headlock and getting in some digs in his ribs. His mind was empty save for a youthful joy. Alex smiled. Life was easy. Life was good.

*

The next day, however, reality made a brief, biting comeback, as it was the day of the college offers. Some people were waiting for their parents to open the envelopes which would arrive at home and then calling them that afternoon to hear the dreaded news. Others were queuing up at the two computers in the Green Bungalows foyer, logging on to the Internet, armed with their passwords, to learn their fate – trying to hide their nerves in front of their peers. Chloe and her friends had decided to go in search of an Internet café, though Alex knew that, unless Drama in Trinity had come down significantly in points, his sister was not going to be a happy bunny. He, on the other hand, wasn't going to check. He had told his parents before he left to text him when the envelope arrived – warning them not to phone him for any reason. However, he knew what the news was going to be: he hadn't got any offers. It didn't feel very nice, but Alex was damned if he was going to let that bother him here – he had two weeks of complete freedom from it all and was going to embrace it with open arms.

Once they had all found out about their respective college news, the boys decided to finally get their act together and rent mopeds, taking them on their maiden voyage to the nearby beach. The white sand was covered in a variety of sun loungers, each area with different-coloured umbrellas, creating a patchwork quilt of lazing sprawl. As with everywhere in Ayia Napa, a pumping bass echoed along the shore, where numerous bars and restaurants attracted the throngs of people who had come to spend their days in coastal delight. The ocean was alive with various water sports and extreme entertainments, whilst in the distance the looming crane of the bungee-jump dunked and re-dunked adrenalin-seekers who, screaming, took the plunge into the warm, salty water, as twinkling blue as the flawless sky above. The lads made their way through the various tanning spots, before selecting their location, paying accordingly for their sunbeds and stretching out beneath their umbrellas, exposing their bodies to the vicious heat.

They had agreed not to talk about the offers, though all of the boys had seemed fairly content with their news – achieving the college places they'd been expecting. Similarly, Alex had received the text he'd been so certain was coming.

HEY DARLING. SO UR MAIL ARRIVD. NO OFFERS IM AFRAID. NOT 2 WORRY - WE CAN SORT IT OUT WHEN U GET HOME. OK? CALL US. LOVE U VERY MUCH. MUM XX

Alex switched off his phone. He didn't want to know.

"This is the life," Luke announced, rubbing suntan lotion onto his pale skin, praying he wouldn't burn.

"You know it, lads," Andy reiterated, picking up a handful of sand from beside where he lay and throwing it over Luke's sticky body.

"You fucker," Luke exclaimed, sitting up with a start, rubbing his chest vigorously in an effort to wipe away the itchy grains. Unfortunately, this just served to create a messy paste of sand and suncream, sending his friends into convulsions as they high-fived Andy's attack.

"I'm so hungover," Alex proclaimed through the laughter, remembering, as he pushed any college-related thoughts to the back of his head, that he was actually feeling very ill, almost shaking on his towel.

"Ha ha . . . well you were the one who suggested drinking more vodka when we got back to the room," Kyle pointed out.

"It seemed like a good idea at the time," Alex groaned, wishing Jenny was there to lavish some sympathy on his aching self.

"Famous last words, my friend," Andy said loudly, his iPod in one ear as he drifted in and out of the conversation.

"Anyone up for jet skis?" Luke wondered, reapplying his factor twenty, having had to wipe the first batch off.

"I'm not going with you, paleface," Andy chuckled in jest. Alex moaned even louder, feeling ill at the mention of activity.

"Maybe the girls will," Andy added, spotting a familiar group of slender bodies approaching, tensing his chest slightly as they arrived, hoping he was looking well.

"Hey guys," Chloe greeted and the rest of the girls followed suit, sitting on nearby loungers or upon the sizzling sand. The guys welcomed them and the groups conversed quickly about their respective college news before moving onto the much more appropriate topic of the previous night.

"We ended up in this club called Aqua," Andy recalled, moving his feet so that Chloe could fit her tiny self by where he lay.

"Doesn't that have a swimming pool?" Ella piped up.

"Oh, you know it!" Alex affirmed, thinking back to their juvenile messing with a grin. "Where did you girls go after Starsky's, then?"

"We just went back to Green Bungalows and stayed at the bar with some guys from Sam's year . . ." Chloe trailed off at the mention of her boyfriend's name. Not that anyone noticed. Except Andy. He watched her, her blonde hair wet from the sea, blowing gently back from her thin face. She was pretty, there was no denying that. But Andy was forced to notice that her body was less so, with awkward bones poking out, making it look as if she could snap in two at any moment.

"Oh my God, did you hear about the girl who got date-raped?" Heather said suddenly, breaking Andy's gaze. "Yeah, some girl from a school near us got her drink spiked last night in Starsky's, and I was chatting to friends of hers who I play hockey with earlier, and apparently she woke up this morning in some guy's apartment . . . couldn't remember a thing," Heather recounted, instilling drama into every word, relishing the gossip.

"Jesus," Luke said.

"Yeah, I know, it's awful, like. Imagine actually getting your drink spiked – who does that? I didn't think Rohypnol actually existed . . ." Heather finished.

"You muppet! But yeah, no wonder our parents got so freaked out about us coming out here," Ella conceded.

"Yeah, but all you need is a bit of common sense, like. It's not that hard – just keep an eye on your drink, don't be a tit," Alex reasoned.

"So what, you're saying it's her fault then?" Chloe spat at her brother, unimpressed.

"Of course not. But just, like, it's the same as home – have a bit of cop on and you'll be grand," he continued.

"Anyway . . ." Andy defused the momentary sibling tension. "I was talking to some lads in Green Bungalows who've been here since last week, and apparently one of the days we have to go to the waterpark."

"Aw, wow, that'd be savage," Heather enthused.

"Yeah, but apparently they said we should, like, take a night off so then we can go to the waterpark early the next day, 'cause, like, if you're going to pay into the place, you may as well get your money's worth," Kyle said.

"Shut up, you spa! We're in Ayia Napa – you can't take a night off!" Andy chided, moving his leg slightly so that it was just touching Chloe's lower back.

"Well, either way, we so have to go," Ella insisted, and the rest of the group chorused agreement.

Once that was decided, the group split into smaller conversations, gossiping even more as the nearby sea crashed musically, caressing the shoreline and tickling the toes of passers-by, the foam soaking into the drenched sand, fizzling out like the remains of an oceanic firework.

"Do you fancy an ice-cream?" Andy asked Chloe in a low voice, so that no one else would take him up on his offer. Although she may not have been as attractive as she used to be, the idea of getting with her had still fixed itself in his mind. He hoped Alex was watching.

"Not really, but I'll come along for the stroll," she said with a smile, standing up and stretching her body upwards, catching the attention of all the group.

Alex watched as his sister and his best friend ambled away, talking and pushing each other playfully. What was Andy doing? And more importantly, what was Chloe doing? That girl really was acting differently these days, and Alex couldn't help but long for her to change back – to see sense and be the way she used to.

*

Tuesday night, and the lads had caught wind of a bar which, for a set entry price, served all-you-can-drink alcohol until one in the morning, setting up its many customers for what could only be an eventful night out. Indeed, midway through their session in Coyote

Bar, the boys were all in flying form, tans starting to develop and thoroughly content with having got fully into the swing of their sixth-year holiday. Alex was making his way through the list of house cocktails, downing each one in a matter of minutes, stopping only to play pool with his friends. During one such break, Alex was beating Luke in magnificent style, but as he lined up his cue to pot yet another ball, he felt someone lean in close behind him.

"Look what the cat's dragged in," Andy muttered in his friend's ear, as they both cast their gaze towards the group of boys who had just strolled in.

"Fuck," Alex whispered, feeling his heart sink. It was Phil. Phil and his friends. This wasn't good.

"Have they spotted us?" Alex quietly asked his friend, despite Luke's impatient calls from the other side of the table.

"Yup."

"Shit."

"Just relax. They won't do anything. Not here . . . Just watch your back, yeah?" Andy advised, stepping away and returning to his drink, watching the newcomers whispering to one another, eyes all fixed on Alex as he narrowly missed potting his ball, cursing with more venom than such an instance warranted.

Even when the game was over, Alex triumphing over Luke convincingly despite his tension, he still couldn't relax into the evening. The intense sensation of six pairs of eyes following his every move was not one which left him feeling at all at ease. He wanted to leave.

"Hey, can we get out of here, man? Those fuckers are giving me daggers," he admitted to Andy.

"Don't mind them, man."

"I'm not really. But, like, let's just hit a club – it's nearly one anyway," he suggested, allowing his voice to show just a touch of desperation, indicating to his best friend that he was serious.

"Ok, buddy. Let's go," Andy willingly agreed, telling the rest of their group that they were heading to Carwash and that anyone who wasn't ready could follow on.

So Andy led the way as Alex and three others left the bar. Alex avoided the stares of Phil's group as they made for the door, not wanting any trouble yet surprised that it was bothering him so much. But it wasn't their threatening eyes which were getting to him; it was the reasons for their hatred. Of course, the mates were probably just eager to get revenge for their friend and give Alex a punch or two. But not Phil. There was so much more to it than that. He wanted revenge for what Alex had done to his cousin. But he hadn't actually *done* anything, Alex argued with himself as he so often did, begging the guilt to go away. He hadn't been driving. He hadn't crashed the car. He'd been through these thoughts a thousand times before, so why did he still feel that maybe, just maybe, Phil had a right to be angry? That, perhaps, there was a part of him that was to blame. Alex needed to stop thinking. He needed to get out into the air again and cop himself on and get back to having a good night. He was too weak for anything else. It hurt too much.

"Here, I'm sorry for being such a wuss," he admitted shyly to Andy.

"Look, man – don't worry about it. I was ready to go anyway."

Alex sighed, knowing his friend may have been just saying that to make him feel better, and knowing also that Andy didn't really understand what he'd been apologising for, oblivious to Alex's shameful train of thought. Then again, Andy was probably just eager to go to Carwash to see Chloe, so at least Alex could take solace in the fact that neither of them was being upfront. Either way, they were once again back on The Strip, weaving through the groups of familiar and unfamiliar faces, soaking up the contagious electricity. They arrived at The Carwash Club. Joining the queue, they watched an intoxicated girl attempt to take on the bouncer in a shouting match, before her friend eventually grabbed her, clamped her hand over her mouth and dragged her into the nightclub, telling her to shut up lest she be thrown out.

The club itself was in full swing once the boys got in, girls dancing on the counters, as seemed to be the norm in Ayia Napa, whilst music and cheap drink lulled Alex back into a more relaxed state. Sure enough, his sister and her girls were there too, so they joined them on the dance floor, Alex blissfully at ease, not caring who he was with so long as they were up for having fun – and doing lots of shots. Luckily, Heather and Ella were in the mood, and the three of them knocked back tequila after tequila, shaking their hips in between to the funky beats and generally having a ball.

The rest of Alex's schoolmates followed on from Coyote with news for Alex; Kyle and Luke pried him away from the bar to fill him in.

"They came up to us," both boys started excitedly.

"Who?" Alex wondered, hiccupping tequila.

"That gobshite Phil and his mates," Kyle elaborated.

"Oh . . . what did they say?"

"Just that you should watch your back."

"Oh–"

"So I pushed one of them," Luke informed quickly, eager to impress.

"And then I hit another – and his nose bled," Kyle continued, smirking as he hopped from foot to foot.

"But, like, some of the lads were telling us to stop because you, like, deserved to get beaten up. But we just kept going. And then we got thrown out!" Luke finished triumphantly, the two boys bursting with pride.

"Shit, and did they follow you?" Alex asked, worried that his friends had only made matters worse.

"Nope. And if they know what's good for them, they won't either . . ." Kyle declared, puffing out his chest and looking utterly pleased with himself. Alex was relieved but surprised. He'd never seen Kyle with so much confidence. And he'd certainly never heard of him punching someone. Alex pondered momentarily, only to be distracted again by Luke and Kyle howling, apparently like coyotes. Alex laughed at them, still confused about their bizarre behaviour but dragging them onto the dance floor nonetheless, rejoining the girls and losing himself in the night once more.

Stepping out of the club, the DJ having played his final tune, Alex was famished. He needed a kebab. He and Luke joined the queue for the fast-food joint just beside Carwash, edging ever closer to the counter, where, finally, a middle-aged lady in an over-sized T-shirt and glasses inquired politely, "What can I get you boys?"

"Two doner kebabs please – all the trimmings . . ." Alex announced, stumbling slightly as he dug the money from his pocket. Soon, their order arrived, steaming in its paper, the shavings of questionable meat sitting upon a bed of lettuce, wrapped in a pitta and drenched in a variety of sauces, making Alex's mouth water just to look at it. Devouring it in minutes, Alex had never tasted anything as good in his entire life. As he wiped the dripping sauce from his messy face, his lips tingling from the chilli dressing, he wanted another. Could he have focused on the handful of change which he produced from his pocket, he probably would have bought one, but exhaustion was now mixing in with his alcoholic hue, making Alex's eyes weary and his body lazy, content with the masterpiece of food which he'd just consumed. However, it wasn't time to go home, not while he was on such a buzz. So would they go to Aqua again? Would they go back to the twenty-four-hour bar and continue their session? Suddenly Alex knew where he wanted to be, where he'd find himself happier than anywhere else and for the least effort.

U AROUNND CAN I CCUM OVEIR 2 URSS? X

He managed to send the text to Jenny eventually, struggling to make out individual letters but hoping she'd catch the drift. Thankfully, within seconds, his phone buzzed with a reply, welcoming him back to Jenny's resort, hinting that, as intended, she was going to make him very happy indeed. Alex felt on top of the world, his head light and his spirits high.

"You going to finish that?" he asked Luke, pointing to the kebab he'd been staring at for the last five minutes. Alex took the lack of response as an offer, grabbing the barely touched delight and skipping off down The Strip feeling truly delighted with himself, as every step led him closer to Jenny's and every bite of kebab tingled in his mouth. The perfect combination.

*

Having swaggered home the next day, feeling very pleased with himself despite his throbbing hangover, Alex now lay by the pool chatting with Andy, willing his skin to bronze as his body soaked up the rays.

"So, hopefully Phil's bunch will have pissed off now," Alex concluded, referring to last night's antics.

"Yeah, well, it sounds like the boys gave them a good warning so I wouldn't be too worried if I were you," Andy agreed, sipping on his cocktail in an effort to make his body feel more human.

"Here, man, did you not think they were being a bit weird last night?" Alex continued, lowering his voice.

"What?"

"Luke and Kyle, when they came to Carwash – they seemed kind of . . . I don't know . . . different . . ." Alex explained. Andy looked at him, searching for something but realising that it wasn't there.

"They were on E," Andy informed him.

"Really?" Alex couldn't hide his surprise.

"Yeah, I think they did it the other night too – they were wired," Andy said, adjusting his shades.

"Oh, right," Alex murmured, slightly taken aback. Of course, he himself had dabbled with drugs on numerous occasions, but ecstasy? He'd never put Luke and Kyle down as the types to get involved in that sort of thing at all.

"I think they're idiots too," Andy announced casually, reading his friend's mind. "I mean, we're in Ayia Napa, it's fucking amazing as it is – who needs more than that?"

"Yeah, I suppose," Alex replied, not knowing what to think. He supposed he was curious, though the risks were undeniable.

"One bad pill and you're fucked, you know?" Andy continued, not moving a muscle as he concentrated on his tanning.

"Have you spoken to the lads about it?" Alex wondered.

"Not really, like, they know if we want some, we'll go to them. If we don't, we won't – simple as that."

"Right," Alex concluded.

"I did warn them, though, that they're not to keep any shit in our room. If that got found, we'd be so fucked," Andy added.

"Yeah, I'd kill them. Knowing this place, we'd get fined a fucking shitload – they're such scabby pricks," Alex affirmed, relaxing once more now that he had processed the new information. It didn't bother him – it was up to his friends what they got up to and, for now, he wasn't interested. Heaving a deep breath, Alex shut his eyes once more, zoning out into the poolside haven. But silence didn't last long.

"Here, man, can I ask you something?" Andy finally started to sound serious.

"Yeah . . ." Alex invited, being the one to play it cool this time as he remained flat on his back, welcoming the sun's sweet heat.

"It's just . . . it's Chloe," Andy finally said. "I like her."
"And?"

"And, I don't know . . . what do you think?" Andy asked, feigning sincerity. Alex sighed – he supposed he had to cut him some slack. He was his best friend after all.

"Well, to be honest, man, she has a boyfriend . . . like, that's kind of a problem for you as far as I'm concerned," Alex pointed out.

"Yeah, but . . . I really like her . . ." This was better than he had expected. Andy watched his friend squirm, deliberating what to say, in a rare occasion of a lack of confidence. Andy thought of Jenny – more and more his affections for her were fading as his plan consumed him. He was showing Alex that he had control too – that Alex wasn't the one with all the power – not anymore. And Andy knew that scoring Chloe would be the ultimate proof of this – bony body and all.

"Basically, what I'm asking is, would you have a problem if I went for it . . . like, really went for it?" Andy asked, spitting out the question he'd sought to ask all along, trying not to smile.

Alex thought. He did have a problem with it. He didn't know why, but he did. Then again, he couldn't really object. But if he wanted Andy to know who was in charge here, and that he needed to be careful, then Alex had to be honest.

"Look . . . I would find it weird. You're my best friend, she's my sister. It's not like I'm protective or whatever, it's just . . . I don't know . . ." Alex struggled to articulate his argument. "Mainly she's just so bloody fucked up at the moment, I don't want her, like, getting you involved too."

"What do you mean?" Andy said, caught off-guard – not expecting his friend to turn so serious, and feeling slightly guilty all of a sudden.

"Well, like . . . all summer . . . she's just been weird. I mean, her eating . . . her personality . . . something's up with her and I don't want to go there . . . and I don't want you going there either." Alex sipped his 7-Up.

Andy was silent, staring out to the pool where a group of crazies splashed and played. Alex sighed once more.

"Look, man, if you want, just go for it. I mean, I don't think your chances are too high, what with her having Sam and all . . . but like, I don't really give a shit . . . not really. So if you want, just see how you get on . . . but don't get your hopes up, yeah?" Alex concluded.

"Thanks, man," Andy answered softly, as he struggled to ignore all the complications Alex had just alerted him to.

Silence fell once more, and Andy found his mind drifting onto a more important issue, one that reminded him not to get caught up in his plotting too much, for at the end of the day, Alex was his best friend, and they were united more than ever now in one single worry.

"I was thinking about Barry again earlier," Andy continued, running with the serious line of conversation which was so rare for these two boys.

"Yeah?" Alex chirped, more interested in this than anything they'd discussed so far.

"Yeah, I mean . . . what if he doesn't wake up soon . . . what's he going to do about next year . . . like, college and stuff?" Andy vented.

Alex shook his head. "In fairness, Andy, what the fuck am I going to do? And I don't even have the excuse of being fucking unconscious," he spat, the stiff sensation of disappointment returning.

"What are you talking about, man? You'll be grand." Andy half-laughed, surprised by his friend's apparent concern.

"No, I won't," Alex retorted, wishing Andy would take him seriously. "I didn't get any fucking offers – I have nothing," he admitted, sharing the information he'd been hiding since his parents had texted him.

"Well, there're always private colleges, you know? You're Alex Walsh, for fuck's sake – you'll be sorted," Andy assured, unable to convince himself that his friend was being serious. Alex didn't worry about school. Alex didn't really worry at all. That was what made him Alex.

But Alex *was* worrying about school. Alex was worrying more and more lately. And Alex was starting to wonder what exactly was going to make him Alex from here on in. He was scared, but what was more, the awful reality was that, no matter how bleak the future was looking for him right now, nothing could be bleaker than the blackness which encased his friend day in, day out. Alex closed his eyes, wanting to block it all out. But even in Ayia Napa, where the sun always shone, he couldn't deny the niggling guilt which chipped away at his soul.

*

The next day, the boys lazed about on the beach, drinking and recovering from the night before, as they usually did these afternoons, truly embracing the Ayia Napa experience. The scene was as it always was – the whirring speedboats fusing with the continuous loop of pop music, the water alive with bathing figures, jumping and plunging below, ecstatic in their ocean activities. In the distance, as always, another being was flinging themselves from the bungee-jump crane, ricocheting up again with a barely audible scream once their heads tipped the waves. Alex was bored.

"Anyone up for the bungee jump?" he asked, feeling spontaneous.

"Eh . . . are you serious?" Kyle mumbled, having had a particularly heavy night the night before.

"Why not?" Alex retorted, the idea now consuming him as excitement pumped through his veins.

"I'll do it," Andy replied, casual as always.

"Anyone else?"

"Well, I was going to do it, like, definitely, before the end of the holiday . . . but I'm not sure about right now . . ." Luke said sheepishly.

"You snooze, you lose. Right, Andy, let's go," Alex announced, delighted with himself.

So the two of them mopeded round to the site, the other boys following behind, wanting to watch. The wind rushed against Alex's face as he sped along, adrenalin already beginning to sizzle through him, thwarting any possibility of nerves. He skidded to a stop in the bungee-jump car park, eager to get the show on the road. He paid the rather hefty fee, signing the release form and being lured in by the DVD, photo and T-shirt deal, deciding that if he was going to do it, he may as well do it properly. Plus, he couldn't wait to see the look on his mother's face when he showed her a clip of her son hurling himself into the abyss – it would be priceless. He joined the queue, with Andy right behind him, watching as each person in turn was tied up, taken up in the crane and brought to do the deed. Every time someone took that great leap of freedom, placing their whole lives in the hands of that chord, Alex felt his stomach lurch, but every time they came down safely once more, he knew he would be OK; he had to do it.

"Nervous?" Andy enquired.

"Nope, you?" Alex answered honestly, allowing his confidence to shine through.

"Yep!" Andy admitted with a nervous laugh, edgier than Alex had seen him for a long time.

The rest of their friends waited on spectators' benches, save for Luke and Kyle, whom Alex and Andy had chosen respectively to go up with them in the crane. Suddenly there was only one person ahead of him. Alex's heart started to thump. Maybe he was just a little bit nervous.

He watched as the crane levered up a small brunette and her supporting friend, until it stopped, seeming very high up. Alex gulped. The gate opened. The brunette shuffled herself forward. There was a pause. The voice of the instructor could be heard, "One . . . two . . . three . . ." Alex held his breath. She didn't jump. The instructor tried again, but to no avail. This girl wasn't budging. Alex felt for her.

"What a pussy," Andy mocked.

Eventually the crane lowered once more, the shaking girl ashamed to make such a return, nervous before the expectant crowd, her friend still reassuring her from behind. The crane stopped. The girl got out. It was Alex's turn.

Having had his legs tied up into an elaborate rope contraption, Alex bounced himself onto the crane platform, where Luke had been strapped against the railing, secure and going nowhere. The instructor introduced himself as Ben, hailing from Australia and full of fun. The gate shut. There was a whirr. Up they went.

"So, you nervous?" Ben asked brightly.

"Not really . . ." Alex tried, though becoming distracted as he looked down on the shrinking figures of Andy and Kyle staring up at him from below as he continued ever upwards.

Ben was babbling on in his sharp accent, words such as "safe" and "rush" and "incredible" being emphasised for effect. But Alex wasn't listening, for as they reached their peak height, he couldn't focus on anything except the breathtaking sight which spread out before him. He could see for miles. The deep blue water rolled into that glorious stretch of sand, where people became tiny dots of colour. Then nearby apartments rose upwards, reaching into the sky through the canopy of palm trees and lush Mediterranean foliage. Behind them, the mountainous landscape rolled both left and right, brown earth and green patches of growth patterned in all directions, like a child's drawing. Then there was nothing but sky. Alex watched as birds danced beneath the light of the sun, twisting this way and that, yet seeming level with him, as if he were flying too, or standing on one of the rare white clouds which fluffed the sky. What a sight.

Alex's mind was blank as he took it all in, oblivious to everything save for the overpowering freedom which consumed him as Ben instructed him to edge forwards, through the open gate, onto the tiny walkway. He was standing on air. Alex rushed with electricity. He was going to leap into that void and fly like those birds. He was going to do it. Ben counted. Alex didn't even hear the word "three", but he knew it was time. It was the time of his life. He jumped.

His wings outspread, he fell downwards, the air shooting past him on either side, as time ticked ever onwards. Yet he was still falling. It was never-ending. The sea below stared him in the face until, at last, he met it, his head dipping into the foaming water, washing away any worries which had ever consumed him. For now he was free. Nothing mattered except the mess of sky and sea and unintelligible horizons which blurred into one another as Alex bounced up and down, his head and his feet never knowing which was which as he tumbled through the intoxicating nothingness, screaming with delight. He was free as a bird. Alex Walsh was free.

"And then it fucks you up again so you don't know your arse from your elbow and it's all spinning and shit, and it's just . . . it's just amazing," he recounted to Jenny later that night in Bedrock – the Flintstones-themed bar.

"It sounds unreal," she said brightly, as Alex's eyes were alive with shimmering glee.

"Easily the best thing I've ever done, like . . . like, nothing compares – it was fucking out of this world," he announced for the millionth time since he'd jumped. He couldn't stop thinking about it – it had been too good to be true. He was still pumping with sheer adrenalin, his body shaking with tingles.

But he had to force his excitement away, just for tonight. For it was Jenny's last night, and she clearly wanted Alex's undivided attention, dreading the moment they would part. Alex tried to shut up. It was hard, but somehow he managed. The kissing helped.

"So, has it been all you expected?" he asked Jenny, inviting her to reflect on her crazy week, though quietly thanking his lucky stars that he'd chosen to stay a fortnight, unable to imagine leaving tomorrow.

"Yeah, it's been deadly," Jenny assured with a smile. "Messy at times, but absolutely brilliant."

"Yeah, actually, I meant to ask you – what's up with Megan? I said hi to her earlier, but she seems really bummed out," Alex pried.

"Oh . . . yeah . . . a perfect example of the messiness . . . she got really drunk last night and had sex with her ex." Jenny explained.

"OK . . ."

"What?"

"So why's she so upset?" Alex wondered, feeling as if he was missing the point.

"Why do you think, Alex? It was such a stupid thing to do – he clearly doesn't like her anymore. Plus . . . well . . . don't tell anyone, but . . . she's hasn't had sex since him," Jenny explained in hushed tones, obviously believing this to be truly controversial. Alex didn't quite agree.

"OK . . ." was all he could manage, not wanting to put down Jenny's best friend, but utterly confused as to why this was causing such a fuss. It was Ayia Napa after all – it wasn't the real world.

As he and Jenny passed the hours drinking and chatting, Alex felt a realisation slowly creep in – he was actually going to miss her. A lot. Their friends all headed off to Castle to club the night away, but instead Alex and Jenny decided to go back to hers. Holding her slender hand in his, Alex ignored the manic goings on which surrounded them, squeezing her soft fingers as the night enveloped the departing lovers, making their way home to spend the night together in Ayia Napa – in this parallel universe – one last time.

12

CHLOE

Week one blended into week two in a paradisiacal hue, the girls delighted that they didn't have to go home just yet, but unsure whether they could last a whole other week – their bodies tired, their livers exhausted, but their spirits so high that, somehow, it didn't matter. They would make it, and they would savour every minute. Chloe was pleased with how her tan was coming on, careful that she didn't burn, for she could never bear the shame of walking down The Strip, glowing like a tomato for all of Dublin to see. Instead, a dusting of freckles feathered her golden face, as her highlighted hair grew even lighter in the sun, pleasing her as she looked in the mirror. But it was still hard to look at the rest of her, to catch a glimpse of herself in one of her many bikinis, knowing that that was what they saw. Knowing that she could have done better. Eating was a problem here too, for despite being able to blame the dense heat and the even denser hangovers for a lack of desire for food during the day, every night all twelve girls in her group went out for a meal together, and Chloe found it hard to strike a balance between pleasing their onlooking eyes and not letting herself down.

"I'll have the Caesar salad please, dressing on the side," she ordered on one such evening, as the girls sat in the dimly lit Mexican restaurant – apparently the best place to eat in town.

"Jeez, one of these days you're going to turn into a bloody Caesar salad," Ella remarked after Chloe requested the same dish she'd had most nights since their arrival.

"What?" Chloe replied, unable to remember having asked Ella's opinion.

"In fairness, babe, we had to book this restaurant three days in advance it's so busy – are you sure you don't want to try the food?" Heather coaxed, attempting a different approach.

"I am trying the food," Chloe pointed out, hoping to sound more patient than she felt. "I really just feel like a Caesar salad," she insisted, taking a sip of her water and averting her eyes to stare at the colourful décor. The girls didn't say anything more, but Chloe could sense glances being exchanged. Her stomach rumbled. She willed it to be quiet. But it made her proud nonetheless. Quietly proud.

The next day, the girls got a taxi to the beach, all twelve of them squeezing into a people-carrier as the friendly Cypriot driver tried to make conversation with his crammed passengers. Nissi Beach was jammers as usual, the girls receiving their daily fill of cat-calls and wolf whistles as they moved through the various groups of men. They paid for their usual spot, rolling out their towels on the beds and lathering up for an afternoon of bronzing, giggling and gossiping. Chloe had started reading a book on arrival about an actress trying to make her big break in L.A., and was loving every page, but today she found her mind distracted.

"I can't believe my brother did the bungee jump," she exclaimed dozily, still zoned out, as she watched another lunatic take that leap of faith.

"I think it's so cool," Ella cooed. "I'd love to do it."

"You should," the other girls encouraged, laughing at the idea. Ella blushed, well aware that she would never undergo such an ordeal but allowing herself a brief moment of imagination, as she pictured herself up there, proving them all wrong.

"Anyone up for banana boats?" Heather suggested, restless on her lounger.

"No thanks," Chloe called back, having already experienced the inflatable mayhem that was banana boating a few days previously and lacking any desire to be flung into the sea again, the bruises still not having gone away entirely.

"I can't believe you got so battered last time," one of the girls remembered.

"Tell me about it – my right leg is still black and blue. I bruise like a peach!" Chloe laughed, though still slightly surprised at how easily her skin had reacted to the impact.

She closed her eyes, turning up her iPod and allowing it to drown out the voices of her friends. The therapeutic sound of the sea was just audible through Chloe's chosen track, the steady waves landing one after the other with a triumphant hiss, as if saying something Chloe couldn't quite catch. Whispering a secret for only her to hear. A secret she longed to know.

*

The next night, having had their daily siesta, the girls dragged themselves out of bed, into the shower and began to prepare for the evening ahead. Chloe dithered as usual over what to wear, the majority of things she'd brought proving too warm for the sweaty nights, leaving her with a small rotation of her skimpiest pieces.

"Do I look like a slut?" she asked her two room-mates, having finally selected an outfit of a short white skirt and a purple bikini top, complete with gold flip-flops and necklace.

"It's Ayia Napa," Ella reminded her nonchalantly, "everyone looks like a slut."

Heather didn't know how to respond, liking her friend's outfit, but not liking the scrawny body it exposed. Instead she decided to try another tactic to ease Chloe's concern.

"Look, get a few Bacardis down you and you won't even know what you're wearing," she suggested with a wink, lathering after-sun on her naked body as she sipped on her first drink of the night.

"Good point," Chloe noted, pouring herself a Bacardi and Diet Coke and indeed feeling her worries flow away.

A few more drinks and it was off back to Senior Frog's, where they were becoming regular customers, getting friendly with the good-looking, topless staff and receiving a variety of Senior Frog's merchandise for their custom, ordering yard-long drinks by the dozen. Chloe sipped hers appreciatively, the cold ice and sweet cocktail exactly what her body had been craving, licking her lips with satisfaction and pressing the glass against her neck, sending cool shivers through her.

"Lucky glass," a nearby male teased cheekily. Chloe turned to look. It was Andy.

"Oh, hello," she said, genuinely pleased to see him, and he kissed her cheek, doing the same to her friends as he joined their outdoor table. "When did you arrive?" Chloe asked.

"Just now – the lads are inside getting the drinks," he informed her, pulling up a chair right beside her so that they were ever so slightly separated from the rest.

"Good day?" she enquired, smiling, delighted he was so close.

"Yeah, me and your bro went water-skiing – it was insane."

"Oh my God, you guys are really trying everything, aren't you? You did the bungee too, didn't you?" she laughed.

"Yeah – fucking savage. Have I really not spoken to you since then?" Andy sounded disappointed.

"Not properly." Chloe smiled, taking another drink and allowing her tongue to peek out the tiniest bit, caressing the straw.

"Hmm . . ." Andy pondered, taking a deep breath. "Well, I've missed you."

"Oh yeah?"

"Yeah, of course," he insisted, nudging her playfully. Chloe felt those familiar hormones surge within her.

"So where are you guys going clubbing tonight then?" she asked, hoping the group would all stay together so that this mindless, sexual banter could continue.

"Don't know really – I'm easy," Andy replied.

"Oh yeah?" Chloe joked, cocking her head in mockery.

"Not like that . . . well . . ." Andy added coyly, smiling into her eyes.

"Your drink," a firm voice from behind announced, thrusting the yard into Andy's hand with a forceful jab.

"Hey, Alex," Chloe greeted her brother.

"Hey," he replied, not seeming eager to chat.

"Mum called me earlier. You still haven't phoned her!" she warned playfully.

"Well, I'm presuming you told her I was grand, so what's the big deal?" Alex retorted, colder than Chloe appreciated. But before her mind dwelled on her brother's apparent bad mood, it was already drawn into thinking about someone else who had called her earlier: Sam.

Chloe had been delighted to hear from him, loving the sound of his voice for the second time this trip, though giving him little time to talk as she had hurriedly tried to fill him in on all the many events of the holiday. She missed him. Though she never mentioned it to the girls, there wasn't a day that she didn't wish more than anything that he was there. Although she was liking the freedom of being able to flit between groups of old friends and new friends, feeling tied to no one, it was nonetheless difficult to watch her friends getting with other guys or going back to their rooms, whilst she curled up alone, her thoughts fixed on a boy so far away.

On the phone, he had told her that he missed her too, but as was typical of Sam, he didn't sound nearly as down as Chloe would have liked, seeming perfectly content without her. She had tried to make him jealous by going on about all the males she'd been spending her time with, but Sam didn't rise to the bait. Didn't he care? Chloe had felt a mixture of joy and worry after both their chats, not knowing what to make of them. Not knowing what to make of Sam, of their relationship. She needed to get home and find out. She needed him.

"Do you want another drink?" Andy's voice broke her reverie and snapped her back to the present moment.

"Oh, sorry . . . eh . . . yeah, go on, sure!" Chloe willed her mind to clear as she rejoined the world. She applied a layer of lipgloss, staring out at the numerous teens who passed in all directions along The Strip, some singing, some dancing, many stumbling, all smiling. Would Sam have liked it here? she wondered. For one thing, this "bubble" about which he never shut up was alive and well throughout the Ayia Napa streets, Chloe having bumped into more people she knew than she usually did in a club at home, hugging and kissing every long-lost acquaintance. This really wasn't Sam's scene. At all. So what about next year? Chloe hadn't dared to ask him about England whilst they'd been on the phone. Part of her feared the worst, whilst the other could never see him actually leaving – moving to another country all on his own. There was no way he'd go. Was there?

"You look hassled," Heather commented from the other side of the table, noting her friend's furrowed brow.

"Just thinking about Sam," Chloe admitted, knowing Heather would understand, to an extent.

"Miss him?"

"So much," Chloe replied, looking away and realising that maybe, just maybe, as she sat there outside that bar, in the humid Cypriot night, she was losing Sam. That he was slipping out of her reach – so far away and drifting even further. Her heart ached. She prayed she was wrong.

"Your yard," Andy announced, handing her the glass. "And I got us shots too." He grinned. Chloe tried to smile. Maybe tonight was a night for getting drunk. She needed to stop thinking.

"Thanks a million," she said to Andy, clinking their small glasses and downing the burning liquid. "Ugh . . . what the hell was that?" Chloe grimaced as her insides began to catch fire.

"Absinth. You looked as if you needed something strong," he explained with a wink. Chloe smirked, genuinely this time. For if anyone was going to lift her wavering spirits, it was this boy here, and so far, he was doing a pretty good job. A weight was lifted off her shoulders as the burning sensation passed. It was time to have a good night.

An hour and four drinks later, Chloe and Andy were still chatting excitedly, swapping crazy stories which they'd heard over their stay, gasping in shock at each new tale.

"This one guy got a bottle smashed in his face by some scumbag and had to get thirteen stitches," Andy swore, wide-eyed with exaggeration.

"Well, I heard about a guy who got stabbed by a bouncer." Chloe trumped his story excitedly.

"Yeah, right." Andy guffawed, noisily sipping the last of his latest yard.

"I'm telling you, that's what I heard," Chloe insisted, hiccupping twice.

"Off who?" Andy demanded, cocking an eyebrow in disbelief.

"Eh . . . hold on . . ." Chloe thought. "Ha ha, I actually can't remember . . ."

"See – liar," Andy teased, tickling her in punishment.

"Stop . . . I swear . . . stop . . ." she giggled, twisting and turning as his fingers sent her wriggling with delight, tickling her every inch, faster and faster. Chloe let out a huge squeal as he hit a particularly sensitive spot. They both stopped, startled by the high-pitched exclamation. Chloe looked around her. All their friends were staring right at them. Had she been sober, she would have blushed, but they could all get lost as far as Chloe was concerned – she was finally having a good time again, so they could shove their accusing eyes and suspicions and leave their friend to mess with whomever she pleased, loving every minute.

"Wow, I definitely just got a few filthies right there," Andy informed her in low tones, out of breath from their vigorous horseplay but smiling broadly nonetheless.

"Ah . . . well, as long as you don't plan on stabbing me," Chloe joked, trying to catch her breath.

"Well, wouldn't we have to get even closer than this if I'd any chance of doing that?" Andy said, leaning closer into her, still breathing heavily.

"Yeah . . ." Chloe agreed, liking where this was going.

"Well, give me the chance and I'll prove I wouldn't waste any time on hurting you if we were that close – I can think of far better things to do to you . . ." he whispered in her ear, rubbing his leg against hers. Chloe's heart sped up once more, feeling his every exhalation tingle her neck, willing him to kiss it, willing him to make the first move, so that even if she was forced to pull away, knowing her friends would see, at least she could feel that one kiss, those soft lips on her longing skin.

"Andy, we're going to Starsky's, come on," Alex's rough voice demanded, shattering the intensity of their connection, and Chloe pulled away from Andy instantly, as if caught in the act. They nearly had been, she reasoned, her pulse so vigorous her body ached.

"We'll follow on in a minute," Andy called out in return.

"Whatever – suit yourself," Alex threw back over his shoulder, rounding up the rest of the boys as they prepared to leave.

"What's up with him?" Chloe enquired, surprised by how gruff her brother was being, unable to remember the last time she'd seen him talk to his best friend in such a rude manner.

"Don't ask," Andy answered, shaking his head. "I think he's just hungover."

"Still? Eh, it's two in the morning – you'd think he'd be over it by now," Chloe pointed out, unconvinced.

"Yeah, but . . . well . . ." Andy suddenly seemed nervous, rubbing the back of his neck as he deliberated whether or not to continue. "I think it wasn't just the drink that got him last night," he explained, not giving too much away.

"What do you mean? Was he smoking hash?" Chloe asked, unfazed but wondering why Andy was making such a big deal.

"Not exactly . . ." he admitted.

"Oh," she said, her mind starting to conjure up possibilities through its drunken mist. "But it was drugs then, yeah?"

"Yeah . . ."

"Coke?" she tried.

"Nope."

"E?" she whispered.

Andy paused. His eyes answered her question, as suddenly Chloe stood up, toppling slightly with the speed of her rise but gathering herself together.

"That fucking idiot," she spat, making her way through the scattered chairs and walking with pace up The Strip, trying to catch up with her brother to give him a piece of her mind. She knew she was drunk, but what had he been thinking? Ecstasy? He'd never been big into drugs before, so what the hell did he think he was doing dabbling with something potentially fatal? He didn't have a clue. Spotting the back of his head as he marched along with his eager following of friends, Chloe paused before speeding to reach him, tapping him on the shoulder to make him turn around.

"What?" he answered her poke. The anger in his sister's face surprised him.

"What the hell is your problem?" Chloe shouted, catching him off-guard and his friends took a step back, startled by her vigour.

"What are you talking about?" Alex quizzed, embarrassed as passers-by glanced at the showdown.

"You know exactly what I'm talking about, Alex . . . ecstasy? I knew you were stupid, but this is a new low," she bellowed, clearly disgusted.

Alex rolled his eyes and sighed, indicating that he had been expecting something way more serious than that for the way she was carrying on. He turned away, about to continue on to Starsky's, in no way prepared to have this discussion now. Or ever, for that matter.

"Don't walk away from me," Chloe demanded, her face growing hot as she scrunched it up into an accusing frown.

"Look, it's none of your business," Alex growled, stepping close to her and staring fiercely into her eyes.

"Of course it's my business, Alex. You're my brother, for fuck's sake. What if . . ."

"Exactly – you're my sister, not my bloody mother," he pointed out, snarling with derision.

"But what would Mum say, Alex? One bad pill and that's it . . . You could have died," she reminded him, her voice starting to crack in desperation, the alcohol taking her from one extreme emotion to the next.

"Shut up, would you. I'm fucking grand," Alex shouted, wishing she would just disappear.

"No, Alex. I'm serious. Your friend is lying practically dead in hospital, and you're willing to just throw your life away for the sake of a quick buzz? That's not you, Alex. That's not you . . ." she finished, tears beginning to stream down her face. Perhaps she was overreacting, but she couldn't deny that she found the whole idea scary. Her brother taking ecstasy – it was insane.

Her brother, however, had fallen silent, staring at her with weakening eyes. The mention of Barry had hit a nerve and Chloe watched as the anger sapped from every pore. Neither spoke. The tension hung thickly.

"Chloe, I'm sorry . . . I couldn't find you . . . I didn't mean . . ." Andy had clearly been running around the place frantically in search of her. He stopped his speech as he took in the scene before him.

"Oh . . . you found him . . ." He sensed that a fight had taken place and noticed a curious mixture of hatred and sadness in his best friend's eyes, which slowly turned to fix upon him.

"I suppose it was you who told her, then?" Alex accused in a hushed, dark voice.

"Well, she kind of figured it out for–"

"Oh shut up. Don't give me that shit," Alex interjected firmly, the anger inside him brewing once more. But Andy wasn't going to take any of Alex's rage.

"Here, man. Don't even think about blaming me."

"And why not?"

"Why not? Because I haven't done anything wrong. If you want to take drugs, that's your choice, but you have to deal with the shit that comes with it. You can't have it both ways." Andy made his point loud and clear. Chloe looked at him, admiring what he'd said, but unsure whether her brother would agree.

"Whatever," Alex snarled, a hint of weakness showing through his tough façade, but he was determined to cover it up. "You're such a sell-out Andy – probably only told her to get in her pants," he surmised, turning away before adding, "Just piss off the pair of you."

Chloe watched as her brother strolled away, his friends looking blankly at one another, glancing at Andy too.

"Go with him – honestly, it's grand. I'll be up in a minute," Andy insisted, and the boys obeyed, following Alex but not knowing quite what they were going to do next.

"You OK?" Andy asked kindly looking at Chloe, who still gazed after her shaken sibling.

"Yeah, I'm fine. You can tell he knows we're right. He's just too stubborn to admit it," she said.

"Yeah . . . I don't think he'll be doing it again, if you ask me," Andy agreed, having also spotted the frailty in his friend as he conceded they were in fact right. "Will I take you home?" Andy asked, noting the tear-trails which ran down Chloe's tired face.

"No, it's OK," she replied. "I think I'll just find the girls. You go with Alex," she suggested, wanting so much to have him take her home, to hold her, to be held. But she had to be strong. Angry tears and alcohol would not break her down and cause her to give into temptation. She had to regain control.

"OK, well, if you're sure," Andy checked, his concern touching and his disappointment evident.

"I'm sure," Chloe forced herself to reply. "Thanks so much, though," she added, hoping he knew how much she meant it. She wanted to hug him, to say goodbye properly and release even some of the tension which bottled within her, but she couldn't trust herself. Not in the state she was in. Not with him. He walked slowly away, reluctantly leaving her behind, and her heart sank. But there was one group of people who would set her right. Without fail. Chloe took out her phone and sent the text which she knew would make her all right again. At least for a while.

HEY, WHER R U GIRLS? I DEFO NEED SUM SERIOUS DANCING RYT NOW. HAVOC ANY1? XX

Sighing, Chloe felt better already, a gentle breeze rushing along The Strip and bringing her to life once more as the tang of citrusy perfumes and sweet sweat infused the air, reminding her exactly where she was, so that worries ceased to exist and time became happy again.

Waking up after a successful girls' night out, Chloe's mouth was painfully dry, and a glance at her watch told her that it was still extremely early. So why was she awake?

"Hello, housekeeping!" the foreign voice roared from outside their front door. Chloe groaned. So did Ella – apparently she hadn't been the only one disturbed by this occurrence.

"Come in," Ella tried, her voice shaky, unable to even lift her head.

But housekeeping had got the message, bundling in cheerily, as the Cypriot maid set about her work – tidying the kitchen and throwing out the various empty bottles, as she hummed merrily to herself. Chloe snuggled back into her sheets, appreciative of the warmth, snoozing pleasantly.

"Maria, Maria," a voice down the corridor demanded. The girls' maid hollered back impatiently, unimpressed with being disturbed from her work as another member of the cleaning staff waddled in, babbling away in a language Chloe didn't understand. Thankfully, Maria was left alone again, mopping the floor, moving around the room whilst the three girls slumbered on, until the space was far more gleaming than it had been in a while.

"Thank you," Chloe attempted to call out, though her throat prevented anything verging on volume. Their door closed and complete silence descended once more, lulling Chloe into a dreamless sleep, gently leading her into the afternoon.

"What a sleep!" Heather yawned, stretching upwards just as three o'clock had come and gone. "Wow, our room actually looks half decent," she remarked.

"Yeah, the maids came this morning," Chloe informed her.

"Yeah, the Maria one is such a legend – can we keep her?" Ella joked, peeling herself from the sheets and trotting to the bathroom. "Fuck me, our shower's sparkling," she exclaimed.

Chloe laughed – the rooms were by no means perfect, barely even verging on average, but at moments like this she realised it didn't matter what their accommodation was like for, with only days to go, it had most certainly served its purpose.

"Pool?" Heather suggested, already stripped and ready to put on her bikini.

Chloe nodded in agreement, her hangover surprisingly bearable as she opened the curtains, allowing the startling sunlight to cascade in, twinkling off the newly mopped floor. Another day had begun.

The hours passed lazily by, the girls lolling and swapping stories and memories from their whirlwind of a night, with bar-top dancing and drunken kisses playing a key role in their adventures. Chloe stared at the brown butterfly on her ankle, remembering the group decision at five in the morning to get henna tattoos, as they charmed the artist into branding them all with the matching pretty creatures for as low a price as possible.

"Mine's smudged," Heather moaned, pointing at the blurred left wing of her design.

"Probably got ruined while you were grinding up against your ex," Ella teased with a wicked giggle.

"Shut up, you," Heather squeaked, blushing profusely beneath her sun cream, remembering the instance in question with a shameful shake of her thumping head. The girls all erupted into laughter, revelling in their friend's embarrassment, glad that her antics were being focused on, as they all had exploits from the night before which they were hoping to keep under wraps. As the afternoon progressed, though, it became clear that no one had a chance – no stone was left unturned, no scandal left unanalysed.

"What about Chloe and Andy, then?" Ella brought up, taking the heat off herself as the girls probed nosily, eager to know just how far she'd gone with the boy she'd befriended on the dance floor.

"Don't even think about changing the subject," Chloe warned giddily, though fearful as to exactly how serious her friend's suspicions were.

"No no, I'm a bit curious about this one too, actually," another girl piped up. "I saw you guys flirting – you know he likes you?"

Chloe froze, happily processing the last bit of information but unsure how to respond. She couldn't be honest with her friends – tell them that it was all just a sexual attraction but that nonetheless she enjoyed it. Instead, she led them in a different direction.

"He was just telling me about Alex doing E – I was really drunk and completely flew off the handle, had a huge go at Al," she explained.

"Oh wow, are you OK?" Ella enquired, feeling bad for her cheeky implication, not knowing why her friend had been so upset when she'd caught up with them last night.

Thankfully, the conversation was drawn to a halt as the voice they'd all grown to loathe – that of the resident barman – boomed down the microphone, announcing that Happy Hour was upon them and half-price cocktails were all theirs.

"So if it's a 'Screaming Orgasm' or a 'Barman's Willy' you're after, just come to the bar . . . one hour only, ladies and gentlemen . . ." he barked annoyingly. "You affluent shits," he added, forgetting that the microphone was still on – not that anyone had been left in the dark about his opinions on the South Dublin inhabitants, as he constantly reminded them just how much he detested them. The feeling was mutual.

"What a twat." Heather voiced all of their opinions, just loud enough so that he would hear it. "Anyway, I am so not up for cocktails, but I could totally do some chips – I'm famished."

"Good hustle," Ella agreed. "I haven't eaten anything all day – probably a good idea I give my tummy a go. Chloe?"

"Yeah, I will actually," Chloe replied, noting the look of surprise on her friends' face, but she wasn't doing it for them – she was just genuinely hungry, and one plate of chips wasn't going to ruin everything. Was it?

They ordered and paid for the snack, settling into the plastic chairs just as Luke and Kyle were strolling by, having availed of the cheap drink, both of them balancing three cocktails in each hand.

"Can we join you?" they asked, setting down their glasses and pulling up seats beside the girls. Both were in flying form, as usual, entertaining the girls with more crazy tales from last night in their typical lively fashion.

"You girls so should have come to Starsky's," Kyle complained.

"Don't think Alex would have been too happy with me showing up," Chloe said, pulling a face.

"Yeah, he was in a bit of a fouler last night all right. But he seems grand again this morning – from what I can gather he feels bad about having a go at you," Kyle said as the girls' food arrived. "He apologised to Andy and all . . . ooh, give us one of them," he exclaimed the minute the plates landed on the table, poaching a handful from Chloe's pile and chewing them appreciatively. She was glad that Andy and Alex had made up, but was now preoccupied with wishing Kyle had taken more, staring at her plate and wondering if this had been such a good idea. She began to make her way through the steaming fries, refraining from any ketchup or mayonnaise – trying desperately to thwart the guilt within her.

But it didn't work. Her plate was cleared, her stomach bloated and Chloe felt rotten. Why had she done that? If she was so hungry, why didn't she just have a salad, or some tzatsiki, or anything other than that greasy mess. Kyle had helped her out sufficiently, but despite that, panic sizzled through her. Unable to bear it any more, Chloe stood up, pushing her chair back to rush to the toilet, to undo her mistake.

"Where are you going, babe?" Heather stopped her, just when she thought she'd made her getaway.

"The loo," Chloe answered hurriedly, continuing her escape.

"Oh, I'm bursting to go too," Heather replied, standing up and joining her. Chloe was rooted to the spot. Her plan was ruined. She was defeated.

"Are you coming?" Heather wondered as her friend stood frozen. Chloe came to and plodded dejectedly to the toilets, realising that she'd blown it, that now she was going to pay for her mistake and that guilt would have to be her punishment. She had failed. She was weak. She hated herself.

Heather had known exactly where Chloe had been off to – it was obvious. It was obvious that Chloe had been lying, obvious that she was still losing weight and obvious that she didn't want to talk to Heather about any of it. Heather didn't know how much more of it she could take – she was supposed to be her best friend, for goodness sake, but these days, Chloe was a different person. Heather wished she'd just let her in and tell her what was going on. But Chloe persisted in pushing her further and further away and Heather wondered if there would soon come a point when she would just have to give up and admit that Chloe didn't want her help – that she didn't want her at all.

*

The following night, Wednesday night, was set to be a big one, as the two groups – the boys and the girls – decided to drink together in Coyote Bar before going dancing in Carwash, all hoping for a very late and a very messy one. Chloe had cheered up since her intense self-disgust the day before, all guilt now completely forgotten as her mind filled only with excitement for the night ahead, realising that life was short and their trip was drawing to a close, thus begging to be savoured.

"Somebody's making an extra effort tonight," Ella commented, watching Chloe apply her final layer of mascara, completing her perfect look.

"Well, we only have two full nights left here, girls – we need to make the most of them," she said, before pausing suddenly. "Shit – is it too much?"

"No, don't mind her . . ." Heather assured her, trying to see past the gaunt figure as Chloe glanced at her short shorts and backless top, wanting to expose her tan as much as possible, but not wanting to come off looking like a whore.

"Sure?" she pleaded, begging her room-mates to be honest.

"Sure!" they both insisted, lying but wanting her to feel happy nonetheless.

But it seemed that the outfit was going to work a treat, for as soon as Andy got her alone in the bar later on, he could not stop complimenting her.

"Chloe, I'm serious – you look unreal tonight," he whispered, making sure that nobody heard, but still eager that she get the point. For it was true – despite her being too thin, the amount of flesh exposed would make any boy's eyes pop out of his head. He knew then that if he was going to go for it – if he was really going to make his move – tonight was the night. The conquest would be all the more satisfactory if he took her home looking like that, leaving so very little to the imagination.

Chloe felt great as she knocked back the Coyote cocktails, her confidence stronger than it had been in ages, thriving on Andy's compliments and noting the many glances with which the other boys were rewarding her. As she and the girls grew tipsier, they realised that the bar was indeed intentionally designed like that of the film *Coyote Ugly*, with its wide bar and various poles, perfect for dancing upon. Chloe and Heather decided to give one such pole a try, wrapping their legs around it and spinning as best they could, falling about the place with laughter as their heads grew dizzier and dizzier. But for the first time in a while, Chloe really felt sexy, as the guys she knew so well looked up at her and were mesmerised by her flexible movements, Alex keeping his back to her at all times as he willed her to stop.

Eventually she and Heather dismounted, receiving a large applause from the lads and making their way to the bar for another drink.

"We're such sluts," Heather slurred softly.

"I know," Chloe tittered, high-fiving her friend and realising that tonight, maybe just for tonight, the old Chloe was back. She was going to embrace her with open arms, pretending to herself, even just for a few hours, that she was the confident girl she used to be. It felt so good.

Skipping to Carwash, the group were all on form, united in drunken glee having fully availed of the all-you-can-drink deal in Coyote and entering the club with broad grins and eager bodies. Chloe followed the rest to the dance floor, moving her body in time with Rhianna's signature tune, losing herself in the music. Her hips shook, she spun, she lowered herself to the ground, peeling herself back up slowly, enticingly, exquisitely. A pair of hands eased themselves onto her waist from behind and, without even looking, Chloe knew to whom they belonged. They pulled her back, so that her bum found the crotch of her new dance partner, slotting in as she dipped and grinded against it rhythmically, as they melted into one another. Chloe slipped her fingers in between those which squeezed her hips, holding them tightly, her hormones bubbling, sparks flying in all directions. Sweat trickled down her neck, the tiny beads tickling the upright hairs, tingling with anticipation.

Those firm, desiring hands turned her around, so that now she and Andy faced one another, interlocking their legs as they continued grinding, Chloe's mind going numb with lust, pressing herself against him, wanting him. Andy leaned in closer, breathing into her ear, showing her that he too was growing excited, their chemistry overpowering. Chloe reassured herself that they weren't doing anything wrong – they were just dancing. But she wanted more. She pulled back, looking into his eyes, gazing into that mutual burning desire. Andy moved in to kiss her, but she dodged his moist lips, unable to give in while their friends were all around them, potentially watching their every move.

"Not here," she breathed, groaning with temptation. But she didn't say "no". For no longer was it possible for her to rule out the idea entirely. It was beginning to consume her.

"Let's get out of here," Andy whispered, slipping his hands onto her bum, unable to control himself. Chloe's mind was ablaze – what should she do? She swore she wouldn't cheat, swore she would never do that to Sam. But she was drunk and she was horny and that intense feeling of being wanted, being needed – the very thing she craved these days – was now racing all over her body, demanding that she be selfish, demanding that she give in.

She didn't say a word, leading Andy away by the hand, through the throbbing club and out into the blissful air, keeping her head down all the way for fear that they would bump into someone, that they would have to stare reality in the face. For right now, she was gliding through a surreal world, where reason was corrupted by desire, and sensation was all that mattered.

"Hey guys," a familiar voice piped up, frightening the life out of Chloe as she jumped in shock.

"Hey, Ella," Andy managed, covering up Chloe's guilty surprise.

"Check it out – I just got my belly-button pierced," Ella boasted, seeming thrilled with herself and far too drunk and preoccupied to notice any strangeness between the wandering pair.

"Savage," Andy said. "Did it hurt?"

"Couldn't tell you! Where are the others?" Ella giggled.

"In Carwash – we're just going to get a kebab," Chloe finally spoke, praying Ella wouldn't invite herself along. Luckily she was much too intent on showing off her brand new body adornment, frolicking away towards the club and leaving Chloe and Andy alone again, their hearts racing as they reflected on their close call.

"Andy, I'm not sure about this," Chloe murmured, her head a mess of emotions.

"It's fine – just come back to mine. You don't have to do anything if you don't want to . . ." he assured, staring into her as her legs went weak once more, knowing that that wouldn't be the case. Because she wanted to. More than anything.

Sure enough, the minute they arrived back in Green Bungalows, and entered Andy's apartment, Chloe found the burning lust return, rippling through her and focusing in certain areas, whilst Andy led her to his messy bed. They were alone now. No one was watching; no one was judging. Andy pulled her to him, his gaze locked on hers, his manly arms encasing her. She wrapped her arms around his neck, her heart thumping so loudly she could have sworn he could hear it. For the second time that night, Andy leaned in to kiss her. This time, Chloe didn't dodge. His lips were so soft, timidly pressing into hers, taking things so slowly, Chloe thought she would burst. He was teasing her, making her want more. And it was working. She eased her body into his, kissing him harder, quicker, not knowing whether she was doing the right thing, not knowing whether she was doing the wrong thing – just knowing it felt good. So good. Andy stopped his games and began to respond, his tongue exploring, the passion building, as his hands ran down her back, smooth against her bare

skin, grabbing her to him. They kissed and kissed, Chloe not knowing how to stop, not wanting to know how. Andy's fingers fiddled with the ties of her top, loosening them until they pulled free, and he stepped away and allowed it to fall to the ground. So she stood, naked from the waist up, as Andy surveyed the sight before him. This was it – this was the moment of truth; this was make or break. Chloe thought of Sam, thought of their future, their past and her deep, deep love for him. This was wrong. This was so wrong. How had she found herself here? What was she thinking? But then Andy uttered the words that changed everything.

"Chloe, you have the most incredible body I have ever seen . . . I want you so badly," he lied. Her body wasn't incredible – it was childish and jagged and hideously thin. But Andy knew that if he wanted her – if he really wanted her to give into the thing which she knew was wrong – he would have to play on her insecurities and tell her all he knew she wanted to hear.

It worked. For Chloe finally felt that all her hard work – all her starving and puking and dieting – had paid off, as if it had all been building up for this exact moment. This was it.

She kissed him deeper than ever, easing herself down onto the bed and pulling him on top of her, his bare chest sweaty against hers. He kissed her neck as he removed her shorts, she in turn removing his as she arched her back, closing her eyes with pleasure. She wouldn't open them until they were finished, for nothing mattered except the incomparable perfection of that moment. Nothing mattered at all.

*

The sun rose. Chloe woke. Andy lay beside her, deep in sleep. She waited, not knowing what to do next. Eventually she lifted her head and saw that the other bed was empty. Thank God, she sighed, counting herself very lucky that her brother hadn't come home. But what if he had and had seen her snuggled into his friend, naked, and cleared off, horrified at what had happened? Chloe's head was viciously aching, but as the moments passed, how much of it was alcohol related and how much was purely the barrage of thoughts, battling it out in her cramping mind, was unclear. What had she done? She had to get out.

Easing herself from between the sheets, praying that Andy wouldn't stir, Chloe gathered her clothes, throwing them on quickly but trying to move as quietly as possible, remembering that Kyle and Luke slept next door and beginning to comprehend just how many implications her actions were going to have – her friends, her brother, not to mention Sam; she didn't even want to go there. Not now. Not until she got out of the danger zone and as far away from Andy as possible. Tiptoeing out of the bedroom and peering round the corner, Chloe was immensely grateful to see the snoring frames of Luke and Kyle, out for the count. She let herself out their front door, scurrying down the corridor behind the pool, mounting the steps two at a time, feeling her eyes well up as she sprinted to her room. Knocking on the door desperately, knowing that there was no way the girls would be up yet, she willed them to answer.

"Girls . . . open up," she pleaded, her whole body shaking as the first of many tears began to flow.

"OK, OK," an impatient voice from within replied, as the door finally opened, Heather's exhausted face frowning at her room mate. But as soon as she saw her best friend's tears, her eyes softened immediately, and she ushered her in, slamming the door behind her, hoping that Ella too would wake up.

"Baby, what's wrong?" Heather asked gently, leading her friend into the room and placing her down on the bed where she held her close, wondering what had made her so upset.

Chloe cried and cried, as hatred, anger, fear and regret surged forth, as she wished herself dead, loathing herself with every inch of her torn soul.

"Please, you know you can tell us, babe. Just let it out," Ella assured, having finally stirred to consciousness, startled by her friend's dramatics.

Chloe wanted to tell them, wanted to explain her heartbroken display, wanted to have them comfort her and tell her things were going to be OK. But things were never going to be OK again, and Chloe knew it. Shrugging her friends' comforting arms off her shoulders, she dragged herself under her quilt and shut herself away from the world. The world knew what she'd done – and, just for one last morning, she didn't want her friends to know. She wanted to keep them in blissful ignorance, still believing that their friend Chloe was a good person, a good person who loved her boyfriend and would never do anything to jeopardise that. Never. Somehow, she sobbed herself back to sleep.

The afternoon glow faded softly through the curtains once Chloe finally resurfaced, her tear-stained face coming for air from beneath the blankets, expecting to find herself alone in the room. But she wasn't. Heather and Ella sat conversing quietly on the other bed. On hearing her awaken, they stopped, turning to watch her unravel herself from the sheets and sit up straight, looking wretched.

"How're you feeling?" Ella broke the silence, her voice gentle and reassuring.

"Shit," Chloe admitted, though realising that, at least for now, she wasn't going to cry, for she had no tears left in her. She was spent.

"Do you want to talk about it?" Heather tried gingerly, not wanting to rush her friend, aware by now that this was big. Really big.

"Not really," she explained, noting her friends' disappointment. "But I suppose I have to tell you some time."

Chloe readjusted herself, crossing her legs and holding her head in her hands. She knew that once she uttered those words, once she told her friends the truth, everything would change. But she couldn't deny what she'd done, and if anyone was going to help her now, it was them.

"Take your time," Heather soothed, seeing her best friend's overwhelming distress.

Chloe kept her head bent, not wanting to look them in the eye. Swallowing slowly, she began.

"Last night . . . well . . . last night I was really drunk . . . really really drunk . . . not that I'm blaming the drink . . . because . . . well . . . I can't believe I'm telling you this . . . but . . . I knew exactly what I was doing . . . I mean . . ." Chloe stuttered, finding this tremendously difficult. The girls remained still, patient. Chloe continued.

"Basically . . . I'm not sure how to put this but . . . last night . . . I mean . . . last night I went back to Andy's and . . . well . . . we had sex," Chloe finally managed, whispering the last words, overcome with shame.

The girls gasped. No one spoke. A strange, alien awkwardness lurked as, for the first time in their entire friendship, they found themselves totally lost for words.

"Have you told–" Ella tried to find something sensible to say.

"No, of course I haven't told Sam . . . I only got back here this morning, and I've been in a heap since then – you've been watching me, for goodness sake–" Chloe grew agitated, but stopped herself almost as quickly as she had started.

"I'm sorry . . . I'm sorry . . . I shouldn't be taking it out on you," she said, hoping Ella wouldn't take offence.

"Don't worry," Ella assured. "But listen, you know you can talk to us about it, yeah? We're here for you, OK?"

"Yeah, babe. We're all yours," Heather added, her voice the first thing to make Chloe even vaguely smile all day.

"Thanks guys." Chloe sighed, releasing her head from her hands and sitting up once more. "Let's not talk about it now, though, yeah? I'm definitely not ready yet."

"Of course, take all the time in the world, baby," Heather replied.

Chloe lay down again. At least she had them on side. That was a start. A meagre glow of comfort in her gloomy world, where she feared the light would never shine again. Not properly. Not like it used to. And it was all her fault.

She spent the rest of the day moping about, reading her stupid book and feeling thoroughly cooped up but refusing the girls' offers to come down to the pool, dreading the thought of seeing him. Not that it was his fault, but for now, she couldn't bear any more reminders of what she'd done – her mind was vicious enough, stinging her over and over again with her sins.

The most painful sting arrived at nine o'clock when, after much insisting, the girls went for dinner without her, leaving her in her melancholic cell. Through the silence, a beep echoed; a foreboding beep, announcing the arrival of that sting, shrivelling her up into a ball of nothingness, where her heart was snapped in two and she had no one. Absolutely no one. And worst of all, no one to blame. Except herself.

HEY BABE. ONLY 2 DAYS 2 GO - CANT W8. LOVE U SO MUCH, S XX

Fresh tears were Chloe's only lullaby.

*

In the morning, she awoke once more, her phone displaying a new text, one which hurt just as badly, except that today was a new day and Chloe's last in Ayia Napa. Thus she was going to start and end the day with a smile if it was the last thing she did. For during the night, as she tossed and turned, some clarity had descended on her weary soul, as she realised that, however bad she felt now, however bad she felt here, the minute she got home she would really have to face the music. Right now, she had a day's respite before the scary reality which was Dublin, when life, her messed-up life, started again.

SOMEWHERE IN BETWEEN

HEY BABE. DIDN C U @ ALL YESTERDAY - HOPE UR OK. R NYT 2GETHA
WOZ AMAZN. XX

Chloe let her phone drop to the ground. She couldn't reply. Any
further contact with Andy would make things ten times worse, for
then it would be like they had a "thing". Whereas this way, it was just
one night, one drunken night. She couldn't let it grow to more than
that. If she had any hope of salvaging her life and her relationship, it
had to remain as that single mistake.

By the time her girls had woken, Chloe had had a shower, picked up
some fresh, hot pastries from the shop downstairs for her friends,
dressed herself in a bright, pretty outfit and was more than ready to
embrace her last day and make it as good as possible, so that maybe,
just maybe, she would look back on Ayia Napa fondly and remember
the craziest holiday of her life with a smile. Munching their croissants
appreciatively, the girls discussed their plans for the day.

"Well, we need to pack at some stage."

"Fuck that, Chloe's right – we need to have a really savage last
day."

"I've loads of money left."

"What time does our coach to the airport come at tonight?"

"Three. I think we should rent mopeds and go exploring like the
guys have been."

"Hmm . . . I'd rather get quad bikes – much safer."

"Yeah, but more expensive."

"You just said how much money you have left!"

So the girls deliberated and dithered, sipping on their orange juice
and finally coming to the conclusion that they would indeed rent
quad bikes and go to the cliffs the boys had told them about, where
the sheer jump into the sea had kept them occupied on many a day.

Ella, Heather and Chloe, with three of their other friends, went to
the rental place and discussed quad bikes with the owner, who

235

eventually hired them two quads to share, charging them through the roof. But the girls didn't care, for as they secured their helmets and zoomed off down the road, Heather driving with Ella and Chloe clinging on for dear life on one bike, they were free. Moving timidly at first, soon they got the hang of it, the Cypriot streets blurring past as the wind sang in their ears, rushing by in refreshing waves. They found their way to the cliffs, Cape Greco, remarkably easily, pulling up with a skid, dust flying all around them as they roared laughing, their spirit of adventure soaring.

But they weren't alone, and the sight of the boys, who clearly had had the same idea, slapped Chloe in the face with brute force.

"We can go if you want?" Ella suggested, picking Andy out amongst the gang and knowing that this wasn't going to be easy.

"No – it's our last day, I want to go cliff-jumping . . . I'm OK," Chloe assured her, closing her eyes, breathing in the sea air and building herself up. She had to be strong. She could do this.

The girls strolled over to the cliff edge, where the boys were gathered, taking it in turns to hurl themselves into the abyss, down into the inviting water below.

"Hey, ladies," Alex greeted, the rest of them following suit. Chloe could see out of the corner of her eye that Andy was trying to catch her gaze; she kept it well diverted, her heart echoing through her but her resolute strength keeping her there, pretending to be at ease, pretending to be happier than ever.

"So, are you going to jump?" Kyle asked jokingly.

"Of course," Chloe replied with a smirk. "You boys didn't think we came here just to watch you, now did you?"

A chorus of cheers and whoops emerged from the male camp, Kyle having been put right in his place and Walshy's sister seeming very cocky about the whole thing.

"Go on then – show us what you're made of," Andy coaxed. How dare he speak to her like that, Chloe thought to herself. How dare he speak to her at all. But at least he had given her even more fuel to prove them wrong, to prove him wrong. Stripping down to her bikini, slowly, somehow feeling as if she had to show Andy what he had had that one night and what he would never have again, then, walking calmly to the very end of the stony peak, Chloe peered down at the glorious waves below, where some of the boys treaded water and called up at her in encouragement and anticipation.

"Are there rocks?" she turned to ask her brother, wondering if he knew about Andy and her.

"No, you'll be grand. You'll definitely clear them, like. Just keep your legs straight when you're landing," he advised, his voice kind and sincere. For whatever reason that was, Chloe appreciated it.

She turned back to face out to the vast stretch of ocean, a kaleidoscope of the sun's reflection. The cheers from behind her and below faded away as her mind became clear. This jump was a jump of defiance, a jump to prove the world that Chloe Walsh was strong and that, even when weakness took over, she could still pick herself back up and face a challenge and have faith in herself to be better. It was only a jump, but for Chloe it meant so much more, and as she hurled herself off the edge, whizzing downwards before her body plunged into the salty cool, she had done it, and she was proud.

Quadding home, all three girls were wet, the other two having followed Chloe's lead eventually, but deliriously happy, as they celebrated their brave displays before the boys.

"You should have seen the look on Andy's face when you jumped," Ella shouted to make herself heard as they trundled along.

"Your brother looked pretty impressed too, I have to say," Heather added.

"It felt amazing," Chloe shrieked with delight, the adrenalin rush having served her guilty conscience well.

"Hey, is that a police car behind us?" Ella suddenly said.

"Fuck, it is," Heather confirmed. "And its lights are flashing."

The girls began to squeal, half in amusement and half in panicked incomprehension, wondering what was going on, as Heather tried to pull over on the dusty roadside.

The police car followed suit, a tall, uniformed man stepping out of the van and approaching the girls, who at this stage were totally confused. None of them knew what to do.

"Can we help you . . . eh . . . eh . . . officer?" Ella eventually piped up nervously. Suddenly the whole thing felt hilarious. Chloe had to try with all her might not to burst out laughing.

"You have three on your quad. You must pay fine," the man bellowed threateningly.

"What?" Heather questioned, not following, a smile creeping onto her lips too. Chloe wasn't sure she would last much longer. But the officer was serious.

"You have three on your quad. You must pay fine," he repeated, growling.

"But, we were told we were allowed to have three," Chloe informed him, her desire to giggle fading slightly as she wondered if this guy was more serious than her amusement had led her to believe.

"Who told you this?"

"The rental guy," Heather answered, anxiety creeping into her voice.

"Well, no – you must have two only. Now you pay very large fine," he insisted, showing no sign of budging.

The girls suddenly understood. What the hell? They pleaded with him, batting their eyelids, playing dumb and pointing out that they had no way of knowing that what the man in the rental shop had said was untrue. There was no way they could afford a fine. Panic spread between them all as they grew more and more desperate.

"I ring rental man," the policeman finally announced, giving the girls the benefit of the doubt. He dialled the number from the sticker on the front of their quad and stepped away from them as he pressed his phone to his ear. The girls held their breath, their eyes flitting between one another, wild with panic, trying to decipher what the policeman was saying down the phone.

Soon, he rejoined them.

"No, he says he do not tell you this. He say he tell you rules – not three persons."

The girls' hearts sank – they really had had it. They begged and begged but eventually gave up, furious with the lying rental man and feeling the victims of a hideous injustice.

But something in the policeman's eye gave them hope.

"OK, maybe I let you off just this once," he informed them.

The girls couldn't believe their ears, squealing a chorus of gratitude.

But he wasn't finished.

"Where do you go now?" he asked, his voice still heavy and commanding.

"We're just on our way home," Chloe replied sweetly, "to Green Bungalows."

"Well, one of you comes with me."

"But it's only round the corner . . ." Ella interjected.

"One must come with me . . . you come with me." He pointed at Ella, clearly punishing her for her interruption.

"Where . . . where are you taking me?" she mumbled, fearful of what would happen next.

"Just back to Green Bungalows," he replied, a hint of a smile breaking through his steely exterior, clearly amused by Ella's fright, as if she'd thought he was actually going to take her to prison.

Ella did as she was told, waving the girls goodbye and stepping into the police van, which pulled out and drove away towards their home. Chloe and Heather watched it disappear, pausing a moment before breaking their sides with laughter, tears literally streaming down their faces as they pictured their friend being delivered back to their resort by the policeman, her innocent face lost and confused. It was priceless. Chloe's stomach ached from her giggles, but the intense amusement which filled her was so welcome that she allowed it to take over. Just for a moment, just for one sweet, brief moment.

The girls whiled away the evening packing and getting ready for their departure. All were exhausted, their bodies weak from two weeks of burning the candle at both ends, living it up and partying like there was no tomorrow. But now tomorrow had come, and it was time to face the music and go home, back to the real world. Once the suitcases were zipped up and the rooms emptied, they headed to the bar for a couple of drinks, passing the few hours till three o'clock came, when the coach arrived to take them to the airport. The staff of Green Bungalows bade them goodbye, all delighted to see the back of the "affluent thugs" who had left their resort in a state of disarray. In turn, the departing residents longed for their double beds and the serious lack of cockroaches which home promised.

Some slept on the coach, most waited till the plane, whilst others chatted wearily to the person beside them, reminiscing on the past fortnight, unable to quite believe that it had all come to an end. But it had. And for Chloe, that was scary. Never once did she close her eyes from the moment they left Ayia Napa to the moment they landed on the Dublin tarmac, the grey September chill ready to greet them. Instead, her mind was beginning to process the many questions which would consume her for the coming days, and weeks, as she sought to put things right. To clean up her mess. Would she tell Sam? How could she not? How could she ever look him in the eye again and tell him she loved him, knowing what she'd done? But the intense fear of how he would react made her shiver, quivering beneath her newly tanned skin.

The rising sun tried to illuminate the gloom as the exhausted teens descended from the plane, infinitely more subdued than they had been on ascension, mere weeks ago. So much was different now, Chloe realised, placing her foot on solid ground and willing herself to be strong as the cold air pinched her skin, her tired eyes squinting in the raw light. It was time to go home now. It was time.

13

ALEX

In the lazy days after Ayia Napa, Alex barely left his house, catching up on some much-needed sleep and some even-more-needed TV and PlayStation. The boys came round most afternoons to join in his relaxation-fest, Chinese food and takeaway pizzas becoming their staple lunchtime diet. His sister skulked about the house in a strange mood – no doubt she was in bits having cheated on her boyfriend. Andy had filled Alex in the day after he'd been with Chloe, saying that he owed him that much to let him know, but evidently just eager to show off his conquest. Alex hadn't been overly bothered at the time, having got lucky himself that night and stayed in another girl's resort, but now that they were home, it felt slightly odd to have both his sister and his best friend under the same roof, knowing what they'd done. Chloe never entered the living room while the boys were there, particularly when Sam was around, as they locked themselves upstairs all afternoon. She obviously hadn't told him yet, and Alex didn't envy her mess. It all just proved the point that his no-strings-attached approach was the only way to go. It was simple and it worked.

But Alex had far more important things to be thinking about than his sibling's sex life, though the alternative wasn't much better, as night after night his parents reminded him that it was time to start putting his brain in gear about what he was going to do next.

"We know it's hard for you, love, but time is ticking, and if you're going to apply to a private college, then you really need to get going," his mother reminded him gingerly once again, not wanting to get him annoyed but concerned nonetheless that he get the ball rolling.

"If a gap year is what you want, that's OK too – you could get a job, do some travelling . . ." his father suggested.

"Yeah, but then what?" Alex pointed out. "Next year it would be time to reapply, and I'd still have shit points, I'd still have failed Irish and it'd all still be a disaster."

His parents said nothing, but both their faces said it all. They wanted so much for him, but knew he didn't even know what he wanted himself.

"You could always repeat." His mother carefully put out the idea which, up until now, had been avoided. Alex had hated school, thus the likelihood of him willingly going back was miniscule. Yet repeating was an option which Alex had found himself thinking about more and more. He would hate it, that was for sure. But the more he heard his friends talk about their new colleges and their new courses, the more he envied them. Maybe getting it a year late was better than never getting it at all. Private colleges were an option, but what did he want to do? Maybe a year back at the books would give him time to figure out what exactly it was he wanted to do in university – what he wanted to be. Plus, the phrase "back at the books" was hardly an appropriate one to describe Alex's track record, for he willingly admitted that he had never spent any time working. Perhaps for one year he could give it a try and, hopefully, reap the rewards. He knew he wasn't going to come out second-time round with enough points for medicine, or law, or anything even close. But anything would be better than the nothing he had now.

He discussed it over dinner one night with Jenny, who had taken him out to Little Caesar's for a meal, having not seen him since she'd left Ayia Napa. She herself was about to start Business and Legal Studies in UCD, a choice which she wasn't overly thrilled with but had settled for quietly, willing to give it a go and hoping that it all worked out.

"I don't think repeating would be too bad," she urged. "You could go to the Institute, like, and there would be loads of people you know there – it'd be almost like starting in college with all the familiar faces."

"Yeah, maybe," Alex said.

"What about Chloe? What's she going to do?"

"I don't really know – I've barely seen her, like, since we got home. She didn't get Drama in Trinity so she's trying to decide between Arts in UCD and Drama in DIT, or some shit like that," he managed.

"But isn't that an easy choice? I thought she'd always wanted to do drama?" Jenny asked.

"Yeah . . . I don't know . . . she reckons she won't know anyone if she goes to DIT in Rathmines . . . anyway . . ." Alex changed the subject, remembering that there was something else he'd wanted to discuss. "Listen, Jen, I want to ask you something," he began. Jenny sat up expectantly.

"I mean, I really should have asked you before now, but I kind of just assumed you'd say yes, but now I've left it really late and . . ." Jenny's eyes lit up. Alex suddenly realised what it was she thought he was asking. She was about to be disappointed.

"I was wondering would you come to the debs with me?" he asked quickly.

"Oh," she managed, surprised and underwhelmed. But quickly a smile curved her lips. It was definitely better than nothing. "I'd love to."

"It's, like, next week or something," Alex added, "so you'd better, like, get a dress or whatever . . . oh, and I think we're drinking in mine beforehand," he informed her, sounding much more matter-of-fact than Jenny felt, already dreaming of the kind of dress she was going to get and how perfect an evening they would have.

The Debutantes' Ball was a black-tie, end-of-school dinner and dance which every school had for its Leaving Cert graduates, and in Dublin, most of them had theirs in the winter months. But Alex's was taking place early, and he had finally begun to make the necessary preparations: the car was booked, he had just got a date, tomorrow he would nip down to the shops and rent his tux and all would be well. Typically, the evening was a lavish affair, and for Alex it would be the last time he and his entire year of boys were together. Thus, undoubtedly, havoc would ensue.

"So who else is drinking in yours beforehand?" Jenny asked, now getting excited about the event.

"The usual – me, Andy, Kyle and Luke. Plus our dates – we're sharing a limo," Alex informed her, glad that Kyle had been the one who was bullied into organising the stretch Hummer for the evening.

"And who are they all bringing?" Jenny asked, curious as to what girls would be accompanying her in rival ballgowns.

"Well, I don't know, really. Andy asked Chloe, but she said no. And God only knows about the other two!" he laughed, picturing his friends trying to actually be serious and invite someone.

"How come Chloe said no to Andy? Bit weird, isn't it?" Jenny said, able to think of a very long list of girls who would bend over backwards to be Andy's date.

"Don't ask me. I told you she's being weird at the moment . . ." For some reason Alex hadn't been telling people about his sister and Andy's escapades. Originally he had thought it would have been great to slag his friend about the whole thing, but over the past days, having seen how low his sister was Alex had decided, for once, not to stick his nose where it wasn't wanted.

"So, do you want to come to mine?" Jenny invited, changing the subject as she smiled at him in the candlelight glow. "I mean, it's not until late October, but I'll definitely want to bring you." She rubbed her foot against his under the table

"Oh, right . . . well . . . yeah, that'd be savage, thanks," Alex accepted, hoping to go to as many debs as possible in the coming months, and hoping to get as messy as possible at all of them too. Needless to say, he didn't tell Jenny as much.

The next day, as planned, Alex drove to Black Tie with his mother and selected his tux. However, since he was already going to two balls, and was definitely expecting an invite from one of Chloe's friends to hers, Mrs Walsh decided it would be better value to buy the tuxedo. Alex was chuffed, believing that he looked very dapper in the suit and bow-tie. He was actually starting to get excited about it all. His mother also reminded him to buy a corsage for Jenny.

"Twenty squids, are you taking the piss?" he exclaimed as he glanced at the price-tag, hoping his mum was going to shell out for it, as he certainly was not going to spend four drinks' worth of cash on a puny orchid. Luckily she did, making him promise in return that he would help set up their living room for the occasion.

The night arrived and Alex was true to his word, arranging dishes of crisps and nuts and lighting candles in the Walshs' fanciest room, having dolled himself up and feeling all ready to go. Chloe was in the kitchen taking mounds of sausage rolls out of the oven – she had been put in charge of serving the nibbles. Alex wondered what kind of creation Jenny would be donning but, having booked a room in the hotel for their private after-party, he knew that, however pretty or otherwise it was, it would eventually be coming off, a mere memory in a passionate finale.

The guests began to filter in – all four boys, their dates and their parents filling Alex's wonderfully prepared room and chatting excitedly. Mr Walsh was flitting between them, topping up empty glasses, whilst his wife took photo after photo, the flash like a strobe-light preparing the youths for the disco ahead.

"The boys all look lovely, don't they?" Kyle's mother commented as the gents lined up for yet another snapshot, nudging each other and messing while the parents urged them to be serious. The girls were set up for a similar portrait, and Alex watched them as he sipped on his fourth glass of champagne, feeling very pleased with himself. Jenny sparkled in her flowing purple dress as she grinned at the camera, looking truly stunning. She was easily the best-looking of the four girls. That said, Alex had watched his sister suss out Andy and his girl the minute they walked in, a mixture of jealousy and hurt on her perfectly made-up face. She clearly didn't want to speak to him which, given their close proximity for the next hour, could be difficult.

The wine and sausage rolls were consumed appreciatively, and a warm buzz began to grow in the room. Alex went upstairs to fix his hair, knowing their lift would be arriving soon and wanting to look his best for his departure, laughing at his own vanity but partaking in it nonetheless. He passed Chloe on the landing, looking far less happy than she had been presenting herself downstairs amongst the guests.

"You OK?" he asked kindly, mellowed from the champagne.

"Yeah, I'm grand . . . It's just hard, you know?" She knew her brother knew the deal, even though they'd never actually spoken about it.

"Well, just don't let it get to you, OK? We'll be leaving soon. You're doing good," he assured, sounding unusually sympathetic.

Chloe smiled, unsure where such kindness had come from but more appreciative of it than her brother could have possibly known.

Alex smiled in return, before continuing to his mirror where a final touch of Brylcreem would finish off his look.

Chloe made her way back downstairs, touched by her brother's words and knowing that he was right – she had to focus on not letting Andy's presence affect her. But from the moment he had walked into her house, her emotions had exploded, a mixed-bag of conflicting feelings. For one, she couldn't look at him without hating herself, without ruing that stupid night when she'd been such a fool. She still hadn't told Sam and knew that she was a coward, but she was too terrified as to how he would react. So she had spent the past week savouring their time together and allowing herself to live in the finite bliss of perfection which soon, very soon, she would have to destroy.

But aside from the wretched thoughts which stemmed from Andy being there tonight, she was also ashamed to admit to herself that he looked good tonight – very good. And nothing could deny the incredible connection they had had, albeit purely physical, on that forbidden night and many times before then. And despite herself, tonight was no different – there was just something about him. But she had to avoid it. She couldn't risk talking to him and what that might lead to. Not now. Not tonight.

Alex, however, had no restrictions for the night ahead as he bid the parents and his sister farewell. With only endless possibilities and two bottles of champagne in his suit pockets, he followed his friends out to the Hummer, eager to explore its plush interior as he held Jenny's hand, squeezing it tightly in affectionate excitement.

The vehicle didn't disappoint, with its huge white-leather interior pristine and luxurious as all eight of them piled in, conversing noisily. The hire company had provided a bottle of champagne and enough glasses to go around which, coupled with the extras the boys had taken from the house, meant that the journey was going to be a more than merry one. Alex popped the first cork out the window, while Andy put on one of the car's many dodgy CDs, blaring the music as the coloured lights flashed above them, reflecting off the mirrored ceiling into a techni-coloured spectacle. Their glasses filled, Luke took it upon himself to make the first of many toasts.

"To having a savage night . . . to getting out of control . . . oh . . . and to the lovely ladies who all look . . . well, let's be honest . . . who all look fucking sexy . . ." he bellowed, causing the rest of them to burst out laughing as they clinked glasses and knocked back yet another fizzy mouthful.

"Will you take the scenic route?" Alex called up to the driver, wanting to cruise around the streets for as long as possible in their impressive ride, for all the world to see. He wished he had brought some eggs to throw at the passers-by – the classiest act of hooliganism he ever would have committed. But he was happy as he was, throwing his arm around Jenny and closing his eyes as he slouched back into the comfy leather. This is the life, Alex thought. To celebrate, he leaned in and kissed Jenny's glossy lips, softly tasting their strawberry-flavoured sheen as they moistened into his.

"Mmm, I like . . ." he whispered with a cheeky grin, feeling a stir in his trousers as she giggled, looking cuter than ever.

"Eww, get a room," Andy shouted from the other end of the car.

"Already have one for later, buddy!" Alex joked back, making them laugh again as the vehicle sped on. The night was young but building up nicely as the car's tinted windows hid the partying group, nestled into their little corner of excess, never wanting to leave.

Pulling up to the school, the eight stepped out of their paradise and sauntered inside, where one hundred and fifty reunited schoolboys sipped cheap wine, caught up with one another and bantered with their old teachers, who stood back and watched the final product of their years of hard work and, above all, patience. Alex was thrilled to see all the lads, though it was strange to be back within school walls, remembering so much fun and so little work from the preceding six years. However, it all looked less impressive than it used to, for no longer did it represent the constraining world of rules and regulations; rather Alex had broken free from its control and was now an adult, devoid of such restrictions. Well, he reminded himself, unless he repeated.

Fetching a glass of wine for Jenny and himself, while she talked to some other girls in her year who had been brought along too, Alex spotted one of the old corridor supervisors – a young chap, who had always felt more like one of the lads than a figure of authority.

"Alright, Al," the teacher greeted.

"Well, look who it is. How the fuck are you?" Alex greeted, feeling full of the joys.

"Ah sure, you know yourself. This year's sixth years are all a pack of faggots in comparison to you guys, but I'll manage," he laughed, looking younger than ever.

"Well, now that we're officially finished, we can all go for those long-awaited pints with you and the other sound teachers," Alex reminded.

"Definitely. So tell me, what's next year bringing?"

"Ha ha, Sir, I thought you knew me better than that – I haven't a clue, obviously!" Alex joked.

"I should have guessed. Fuck it, I'm sure you'll be grand anyway. So which one's your date?"

"The one there in the purple," Alex pointed out.

"Nice one, man!" The teacher high-fived him. "Is she your bird?"

"Well . . . no . . . not, like, officially," Alex explained.

"Oh, I get you." He winked. "Well, would you look who it is – your partner in crime," he said, as Andy approached them.

"Hey, man," Andy greeted. "Jesus, you still look about ten!"

"Here, Al, we're all being ushered into the hall – speeches and shit, but Mr Kelly told me to make sure me and you were there."

"Weird," Alex remarked.

"Yeah, I know, but come on anyway."

So the boys made their way into the hall, grabbing their dates, and they found a spot to stand whilst the headmaster took the stage and called the congregation to order, looking as wrinkly and bitter as ever. He and Alex had never seen eye to eye, but again, now that Mr Kelly had been stripped of his authority over the ex-students before him, Alex saw him as nothing more than a shrivelled old man, feeble and weak.

"Well, boys, hello, hello. A bit of silence, please." He began the proceedings, his aged hands clasping the podium. "Right, chaps, well, here we all are, all together for the last time . . ." Alex's tipsy mind began to wander; he stared around at all the beautiful girls and, glancing at his watch, wondered just how much Mr Kelly was going to eat into his potential drinking time. He swayed slightly on the spot where he stood, but held Jenny's hand all along, liking the feel of her soft skin in his, looking forward to getting her alone later on tonight. But as his mind was just getting to the interesting bits of his daydream, there was a sharp dig in his ribs, as Andy nudged him back to life, tilting his head towards the stage, urging his friend to pay attention. Alex did as he was told, reluctantly, but suddenly tuned right back in to what was being said, realising its significance as his mind became clear.

"Today we want to take a brief moment to think of one of our students who cannot be with us this evening," Mr Kelly announced, his voice strong yet a trace of empathy creeping in. "Barry Carter was a member of this school for the whole six years, as well as the four he spent in our primary department. He played rugby, worked hard and was a very active member of school life, proving himself to be an extremely popular lad."

Alex felt his throat dry up. He hadn't been expecting this.

"As I'm sure most of you are aware," the old man continued, addressing a completely silent hall for the first time all evening, "Barry had an accident towards the end of June and has been in hospital ever since. We are told he is in a stable condition, but he has still not woken up. Thus it is our duty as his schoolmates, and indeed as his friends, to pray for Barry and to keep him in our thoughts," he said, bowing his head as he rubbed his brow, clearly troubled by the tragic tale.

"So let us all pray to God to bring him back to us, as he so truly deserves," he finished, closing his eyes as the boys followed suit, united in a solemn respite from their over-the-top evening, filling with guilt as they cast their minds to the friend they missed so much, wishing he was there and indeed praying that soon, very soon, he would be. Seconds crawled by, plummeting Alex into a darkness where Barry was out of reach and slipping further away. What was worse, he knew that so many people in the room were looking at him, somehow blaming him for this unforeseen tragedy. It hurt so very much.

"But, boys, don't let this sadness ruin your evening. You owe it to Barry to enjoy the evening which, unfortunately, he cannot be present for. So, let us all raise our glasses to the wonderful group of young men which stand here before me, as I wish you luck with your lives and your futures, whatever they may be. Enjoy your night," Mr Kelly triumphed, successfully cheering up his listeners, who had been unsure how the evening would unfold after such a reality check. But they knew that their old headmaster was right – they had to have fun and enjoy their last night together, if not for themselves, then for their absent friend. For Barry.

Back in the Hummer, the eight finished off their many bottles of champagne as they drove to Jury's Hotel, Ballsbridge, where dinner was to be served and dancing to commence. The meal was great, but it was the buzz which really made them all smile, as the steady hum of excited chat rippled through the carpeted room, its chandeliers dazzling down on the men of the hour. Once dessert was finished, the tables were pushed back and a live band tuned up to entertain the boys, starting with some fast numbers to kick-start the evening as the fun really began. Alex spun Jenny around on the dance floor, dipping her and twirling her so that she shrieked with delight, feeling every inch the princess she looked. Once the song ended, she was completely out of breath, excusing herself to go to the bathroom where no doubt she would frantically powder her nose and try to remove any signs of imperfection which would spoil her appearance. Alex, meanwhile, nipped off to the bar again, wrapping his arm around Luke as he went, announcing that they were going to do a shot of each flavour of Aftershock, and whoever was slowest to finish had to pay. Luke agreed happily, knowing that he could never beat Alex in a drinking game but deciding that if there was any night to give it a try, then this was it.

"Having a good one?" he asked, while the barman organised their order.

"It's amazing, yeah. You?" Alex replied.

"Oh yeah, savage. Did you hear about Tommy Flynn?" Luke asked, his eyes indicating that there was a story to be told.

"No, go on," Alex encouraged, always hungry for the latest gossip.

"Well, he completely KO'd about half an hour ago – had to be taken home – puked his ring so security threw him out," Luke recounted enthusiastically.

"No way? What a pussy! What about his date?" Alex wondered.

"Well, apparently, she was seen leaving with Greg Hunt, so I think it's his date who we need to feel sorry for," Luke continued, thrilled with his scandalous story as Alex hung on every word.

"Controversial," Alex exclaimed, missing the ins and outs of their schooldays, when someone was always doing something interesting to talk about in between, or indeed during, classes.

The Aftershocks arrived. The boys counted to three. Alex had all the shots demolished in seconds. Luke gladly admitted defeat, handing over the cash and patting his friend on the back.

"You've still got it, Walshy," he commented, wiping his mouth as the sickly barrage of flavours sugared in his mouth.

"Always will," Alex insisted with a wink, returning to the hall where he found a retouched Jenny, who had clearly been looking for him. Kissing her hello, Alex felt his head go lighter than ever, and she pulled away remarking, "Eww, what were you drinking while I was away?"

"Eh . . . nothing . . ." Alex lied cheekily, knowing that Jenny didn't believe him but not caring as he kissed her once more, sharing his taste and loving hers. So far, so good.

The night proceeded with a lot more dancing, a lot more drinking and an awful lot more craic, until suddenly it was four in the morning and the staff were bringing out trays of steaming breakfast rolls and jugs of orange juice to cap off the night and send the youths on their ways. Alex tucked into his tasty feast, his eyes closed as he listened to various conversations about where people were continuing on to – house parties and all-night bowling alleys appearing the favourite choices for after-party locations.

"I've been looking for you," Jenny announced as she wrapped her arms around Alex's waist, hugging him and thinking about where they were heading for their after-party.

"Don't squeeze too tight," Alex warned, the alcohol timidly sitting in his stomach. "Are you eating that?" he added, pointing to her roll. She shook her head and he gladly accepted it, devouring every fatty bite, licking his lips and feeling much better after his feed.

"So, are we going upstairs?" she whispered in his ear, trying to take his mind off food and direct it towards what was still to come.

"Oh right . . . yeah, I guess," Alex agreed, finding it hard to focus as he wished a few of the boys goodnight and stumbled out to the hotel reception. Somehow he managed to secure the key from the concierge, lead Jenny up to their swanky bedroom and collapse onto the bed with minimum delay, his drunken stupor leading him from one action to the next.

"Are you pissed?" Jenny asked, surveying Alex as he lay breathing deeply on the fancy quilt.

"No, no, I'm grand – just needed to lie down, that's all," Alex fibbed, his head spinning at a rate of knots as his body melted into the comfy mattress, wishing the dizziness would stop and wanting to cover up his drunkenness. Jenny kept trying to talk to him, sitting on the bed and touching him affectionately – clearly wanting something, anything. But Alex was growing more certain that he was about to puke, and had to focus all his energy on preventing such an outburst. The room was silent. Jenny was unimpressed. Alex knew he had to do something.

"Jen, I, eh . . . I want to ask you something," he began.

"Oh yeah?" she answered sitting down on the bed beside him.

"Yeah . . . I mean . . . I'm just a bit nervous about asking you . . . which is why I'm a bit weird right now . . . you know?" He tried his best to sound sincere, the whole room ebbing and flowing in a painful whirr.

"Hmm . . . OK, go on," Jenny replied, unconvinced.

"Whoa, chill out, babe . . . I mean . . . I just wanted to ask you if, like . . . you know . . . you wanted to go out with me? I mean, we've been unofficial for so long now that it just feels about time . . . yeah . . . you know . . ." he finished, hoping he didn't sound like too much of a mess, hoping his words would distract her from their slurred delivery. Luckily, his plan had worked.

"Oh my God, Alex . . . yes! I mean, I've been waiting for you to ask for so long now and . . . oh my God . . . this is so cool . . ." she exclaimed, babbling away while Alex felt his eyes grow heavy. He felt Jenny lie down beside him and snuggle into his back. He wished he had the energy to do, well, anything. But instead a delicious slumber stole him away, as his body gave in to sleep's promiscuous tease, loving every minute.

*

Bongos pounded in his ears. Nausea lurched in his stomach. Alex was unwell. Alex was awake. He had the filthiest of hangovers and dared not move a muscle for fear he would explode, every inch of him sensitive to even the slightest stir. What a night! He lay, still fully clothed, next to Jenny, who was just waking up.

"Morning, boyfriend," she groaned, stretching out before exhaling cosily, snuggling into him once more and falling back asleep.

Boyfriend? What was she talking about? Alex's sore head tried to comprehend, until one by one the pieces of the puzzle began to connect, painting a hazy picture of what had happened. He had asked her out. What had he gone and done that for? Alex would have shook his head in dismay had it not been such a risky procedure. But as he lay there, focusing only on his steady breathing, he thought, was it really that bad? He did like her after all. A lot. So maybe it wasn't such a bad thing that he'd finally taken the plunge and asked a girl out, that he was now going to be involved in what could be described as a relationship. Maybe even a serious one. His mind throbbed as such possibilities danced through it, sleep swiftly becoming an impossibility. Alex moaned. It was time to get up.

14

CHLOE

The more she thought about it, the more Chloe couldn't decide what she wanted. College was such a big step – it was going to occupy at least the following three years of her life – so it mattered. There was no doubt about that. Thus Chloe's mind was constantly working overtime, trying to make that all-important choice: Arts in UCD or Drama in DIT? The former would offer a haven of familiarity, where people she knew or half-knew would fill her every lecture. The latter the subject which all her life had consumed her, the only option she'd ever truly considered for her university years.

But it was so scary. She would be in a strange, new campus surrounded by strange, new people. She didn't like strange. And she didn't know how much she was in the mood for new. Everywhere she turned these days, she felt like things were changing, so why would she make the conscious decision to go where things would be very, very different?

More and more it looked as if her brother was going to repeat sixth year, to give it all another shot. Why couldn't she do that? Why couldn't she go back to school and try and get Drama in Trinity and not be stuck in this dilemma? But Chloe knew that, second time round, she might not get enough points for Trinity and, as her mother kept reminding her, she had Drama – she had it in her grasp – so why not just take it? Why not just go for it, like she had that day on the edge of the cliff, and jump into the unknown, take a risk and hopefully reap the rewards? Maybe she would. But for now, she had far more important things on her mind.

It was nearly two weeks since Ayia Napa, and still Chloe hadn't confessed – still hadn't looked Sam in the eye and told him the awful truth. What made it worse was that for the past fortnight they'd spent so much time together, just hanging out and catching up on the summer about which Chloe had always dreamed, when day eased into day as they found themselves encased in the constant glow of couply warmth. Each time she decided that today was the day she would finally come clean and suffer the consequences, Sam just looked better than ever or made her smile more than ever or, worst of all, told her he loved her. It was agony. Pure, self-inflicted agony. She loathed herself. She could take it no longer.

Up in her room, an early September afternoon huskily singing into every corner, Chloe and Sam sat on her bed. Sam was telling a hilarious story involving his friend and an ex getting themselves into a rather sticky situation.

"Just picture the look on his mother's face when she walked in!" Sam exclaimed, laughing heartily at his own punchline as he closed his eyes in amusement.

But Chloe didn't laugh. Instead she watched him in that tiny moment of pure delight, and it broke her. That was the exact instant when her heart finally snapped in two, as tears erupted from within her and rolled in fear down her tired face.

"What's wrong, babe? Was the joke that bad?" Sam teased, confused by his girlfriend's reaction.

But Chloe couldn't reply. Instead, those long-overdue tears of woe issued forth, gathering speed as her throat grew dry, realising that this was it. There was no turning back. Chloe was frightened.

"Baby, what's wrong?" Sam coaxed, as his girlfriend wilted like a dying flower before his very eyes.

But Chloe couldn't speak. Her voice refused to utter the words which would change everything, ruin everything. Minutes passed as Sam just waited, helpless, totally at a loss as to why his girlfriend just sat there crying, clutching her knees and looking utterly helpless.

Eventually, the sobs subsided. It was time.

"Sam, there's something I need to tell you . . ." she began, trying to sound calmer, as if she had floated away from herself and was merely looking down on a couple about to split up, watching on as their sorrow unfolded.

"While I was in Ayia Napa . . . I . . . well . . . look, before I tell you this, I just want you to know how much I love you and how much I regret it and hate myself and . . ." Chloe gushed, praying he could somehow keep all this in mind as he heard the terrible news. "You mean the world to me, Sam. You always will – no matter what happens, nothing can change that . . . I will do anything, anything in the world to make it up to you, if you just give me a chance . . . OK? I love you . . ." she begged, desperately trying to cling on to the love in his eyes, which was slowly fading. They sat in silence, poised on the brink of pure pain, not wanting to begin but knowing that time would soon give them that final push, sending them hurtling past the point of no return. Sam wasn't stupid. And Chloe watched as he began to guess the gist of what was coming, an ugly rage beginning to consume him.

"You cheated?" he assumed coldly.

The words sounded disgusting. Chloe nodded slowly, her world crumbling all around her.

"How many?"

"Just one . . .just once . . ." she insisted, the tension between them making it hard to breathe.

"Did you just score?" he continued.

Chloe shook her head. This was awful.

"You had sex?"

Chloe began to cry again. Sam's gaze fell. She watched as his eyes glazed over, his hands fiddling with nothing at all in an agitated twitch while his face twisted up, fighting the tears.

"Who was it? . . . Do I know him?" he murmured, unable to look at her, his lip quivering.

Chloe's mind raced. Should she tell him? Would it make things worse? But she soon reminded herself that nothing, absolutely nothing, could be worse than this. There could be no more lies. None at all.

"It was Andy . . ." she gasped, her sobs beginning again, knowing it was all over. The bitter truth had been set free and now she just had to sit and wait. She waited and waited, sobbing heavily, dreading what was to come. But Sam didn't speak. He said nothing. His eyes were still moist, but he didn't cry. He just sat there in silence, his fingers still fiddling, picking his nails or cracking his knuckles, the tiny sounds contrasting with Chloe's steady wailing, until both ceased, leaving only nothingness between the newly estranged pair.

"I think I'm going to go," Sam finally uttered, still not looking at her as he made to leave.

"Please, Sam . . . say something," Chloe pleaded.

"What do you want me to say, Chloe?" Sam spat, his eyes staring out the window to the peaceful, inviting world.

"I don't know . . . anything . . . I mean . . . are we broken up? Are we still together? I don't know . . ." she begged, wanting to go to him, wanting to touch him.

"What do you think?" he replied. "Look, I'm going . . ." he

reiterated, his emotionless voice even worse than his previous rage. For Chloe could take him hating her – she could understand if he was angry and bitter and filled with fiery loathing. But as he left her room, his face emotionless, as if he felt nothing – as if he didn't care – that was the sorest thing of all. Chloe rolled over and buried her face in her pillow. He was gone. Gone forever. She had pushed him away, no doubt, but nothing had prepared her for the emptiness which now swelled within her, as a petrifying reality made itself clear: she had no one. Chloe Walsh had no one. Her tears seeped into her pillowcase and she wished she could just disappear. Life was wretched – Chloe was wretched. But worst of all, she was alone, so very alone. And that scared her most of all.

All evening, and all through the next day, Chloe barely moved from that spot on her bed, whiling away the empty hours with thoughts about her break-up with Sam, the break-up of her world. She had tried calling him, tried texting him, but to no avail – Sam didn't want to talk to her, forcing Chloe to provide her own answers to the many questions which persisted in their relentless asking. How could he just sever all ties? She knew she was in the wrong, but could her one mistake erase the love he'd had for her so quickly? Maybe he'd been falling out of love with her as it was. Chloe's doubts from earlier in the summer added to her new concerns, wondering if Sam had even really loved her recently – his lack of urgency had been troubling her for months as she had tossed and turned with the notion that he didn't need her. Not like she needed him. What a fool she'd been.

"Darling, it's dinnertime," her mother called from outside her bedroom door, interrupting her solipsistic thoughts.

"I'm not hungry," Chloe shouted back, insistent.

"Honey, it's been over a day now – come on . . . Can I come in?"

There was a pause.

"I know about Sam," she said gently.

"What?" Chloe exclaimed in shock.

"He told us what happened as he was leaving yesterday – do you want to talk about it?" Mrs Walsh said, sounding genuinely concerned.

"What do you mean he told you?" Chloe asked, confused as to why he would do such a thing.

"Well, while he was leaving he told me that you two had broken up and that you were upset so I should look after you . . . but I was waiting for you to come to me," she explained.

Chloe sobbed once more. Why did he care? Why did he make it his business to see that she was looked after if he was prepared to leave her in a crumpled heap on her bed with so much left unsaid?

"I could bring your dinner up and we could have a chat about it?" Mrs Walsh continued, exploring every avenue to get to her daughter, to get her to let her in.

"Just go away . . . I'm not hungry," Chloe replied, the air of finality in her voice warning her mother to leave her alone. Reluctantly, she did so.

Chloe's tummy rumbled at the sound of the word "dinner". There it was – another aspect of her life that people would not leave her alone about. But now, the only thing she was sure of was that if she hadn't been eating much before, then she certainly wasn't going to eat anything now. The only thing she had left – the only thing she was sure of – was that she, Chloe Walsh, was going to get the perfect body if it was the last thing she did, for without that control, what did she have?

But Chloe remembered that her eating – her weight and the insatiable desire for control which accompanied it – had never pleased Sam. He'd tried to talk to her about it, commented on her figure and generally appeared unhappy with her newfound concerns. But that was part of who she was. And if Sam didn't like that, then he didn't like her. Not all of her. Chloe reasoned, in a rare moment of defiance, that if Sam was so unable to accept her for who she was, then maybe she was better off without him. She was flawed – wasn't everyone? And that night with Andy had been a mistake. So why couldn't Sam just forgive and forget and realise that, despite her imperfections, Chloe was still a good person? She was weak, but since when was that such a crime? Andy had appreciated her body, or at least he had told her how sexy he found it. So no wonder she'd succumbed to his charms – for he had wanted her. All of her.

For two days, Chloe played with such notions, until eventually she didn't know what she thought. Her body was too tired from a whole summer of pushing against the tide to fuel any determination she might have felt. The more time that passed, the more she allowed her fate to settle in. Her friends rang her and texted her, offering support if only she would take it. But Chloe wanted to be alone. She didn't need them. She didn't need anyone; because Chloe needed to get used to not having anyone.

However, Heather did remind her of something which otherwise would have passed Chloe by, leaving her in an awkward situation.

HEY BABE, HOW U DOIN? FEELN ANY BETA? JUS WANTD 2 REMIND U - DEBS IS IN 3 DAYS. I NO U PROB HAVNT 4GOTTEN, BT JUS IN CASE, U MYT WAN 2 SORT OUT WOT UR GONA DO BOUT A D8 ETC. I LOVE U BABE. CALL ME WEN U CAN. XX

The debs – of course! Chloe actually managed a small smile on receiving her friend's message, unable to comprehend that she had completely forgotten about the night which, for years now, she had been longing for. But what would she do? Presumably Sam didn't want to go with her any more. Right? But surely he wouldn't be so unkind as to leave her dateless three days before the night itself? Then again, she couldn't exactly point the finger at anyone about unkindness – she was the bad guy here. Whether she liked it or not. So, she would just have to send Sam yet another text, praying that, this time, he would reply, offering a simple, concrete answer so she could begin to think about her debs and maybe, just maybe, start to get excited about it.

HEY. ME AGAIN. LUK IM JUS CHECKN IF WE'R STIL ON 4 D DEBS. I COMPLETELY UNDERSTAND IF U DON WANA GO, JUS NEED 2 NO COZ ITS IN 3 DAYS. MIS U XX

Chloe dithered over whether to include the last remark but concluded that it was true – so true – so why shouldn't she say it? Now all she had to do was wait for a reply that might never come.

But bizarrely it did – in a most surprising way.

"Hello?" Chloe answered her phone timidly, startled by the appearance of Sam's name on her mobile screen.

"Hey . . . it's me . . ." he said quietly.

"I know," she sighed, her weary heart melting at the sound of his voice, feeling like forever since it last had. Chloe felt her hand shaking as it held the phone to her ear, wondering what was coming next. Fearing the worst.

"How're you?" he asked.

"Ah . . . OK," she admitted, too weak to pretend.

"Listen, I was just ringing about your text," Sam proceeded, and Chloe tried to figure out his tone of voice, unable to decide what emotion lay within it.

"Yeah . . .?"

"Yeah, well, I was thinking that, like . . . maybe . . . if you want to . . . we could still go to your debs together . . . I mean . . . if you want?" Sam suggested, his hesitation actually relaxing Chloe, as she realised she wasn't the only one finding this difficult.

"Yeah . . . I'd love to!" she exclaimed, both delighted and surprised with his decision.

"Cool . . . good . . . well, yea, that's sorted then," he said, trailing off into an awkward silence, as neither knew quite what to say. Moments passed.

"Why?" Chloe finally asked, feeling compelled to.

"Why what?" Sam wondered, confused.

"Why are you still coming with me? I mean, we've broken up, you haven't been answering my calls . . . so why do you suddenly want to come?" Chloe said frankly.

"Oh . . . right . . . well . . . I don't know, I guess I just figured . . . I don't know . . . one last night together . . ." Sam tried, though Chloe was still at a loss.

"OK . . ."

"Well," Sam continued, "I guess . . . look . . . I'm going to be honest . . . I've accepted my place in the London School of Economics. I leave next week. I guess . . . for old times' sake . . . I just thought it would be nice . . . a nice way to say goodbye . . ."

Chloe fell silent again. He was leaving? First he had left her as a boyfriend and now he was leaving the country? She couldn't hide her dismay.

"You're going? You dump me and then you decide to leave?" she said.

"Well . . . not exactly," Sam admitted sheepishly.

"What do you mean?" she asked, her heart beating briskly.

"I mean . . . look, I don't want you to get angry, but . . . I've been thinking about it for a while now . . . and then more and more, I guess, I've just kind of known that it's what I want to do – to go away," Sam explained.

Chloe was gobsmacked.

"So what, you make me feel like absolute shit for sleeping with Andy, but in reality all along you've been planning to move to England and leave me anyway?" she summarised, furious.

"No . . . it's not like that . . ." he insisted.

"Why were you so upset then? Surely my cheating on you just got you off the hook," Chloe spat venomously.

"I was upset because you made a fucking fool of me . . ." Sam reminded, sounding hurt. "But listen," he said, calming himself down. "My going away has nothing to do with you . . . I mean, I guess at first I just figured we'd be OK – that we were strong enough to survive it . . ." Sam paused. "But then I realised that things were starting to fade between us anyway . . . that maybe things were coming to an end . . . and then you told me about Andy . . . and . . . well . . . that was that," he finished, placing such a simple conclusion on it that Chloe could feel her blood boil. How could he say that? How could he say that their past two weeks together had been them "fading"? They were great, weren't they? There were cracks, sure, but every relationship had cracks. So what was he talking about? Her mind spun and spun until intense dizziness pounded in her head, begging to be let out. She wanted to scream, to make it go away, to vent it down the phone at Sam – Sam, who seemed so calm, so collected, so resolute.

But Chloe didn't want another fight. She didn't want to cry again. She'd sobbed her heart out for over two days now and she couldn't bear to start again. There was much to ask and much to say, but deep within her broken soul, Chloe knew that it wouldn't change anything. Nothing that either of them could say would change the fact that their relationship was over – and that was that.

"Are you still there?" Sam tried gingerly, unnerved by the silence at the other end.

"Yeah . . . I'm here," Chloe finally answered.

"OK . . . well, text me about drinking before the debs and stuff, yeah? Is there anything you want me to bring?" he offered kindly.

"No . . . no, you're grand . . . I'll text you," she replied, heaving a sigh of exhaustion.

"Right so . . . well, I'll talk to you soon then, yeah?"

"Yeah . . . bye, Sam . . ." Chloe managed.

"Bye . . ." he replied.

And then he was gone. Chloe stared at her phone, as if gazing at the remnants of their conversation. So there it was: they were still going to the debs together, but they were still broken up, and soon, Sam would be out of the country and out of her life. Chloe didn't know what to think. Maybe his going to London would make things easier for her – help her to get over him. But all that mattered now was that in three days' time, they would have one last night together. It wouldn't be the same, but it would be the closest thing Chloe was ever going to get. And she was going to savour every minute.

*

The night before her debs, having finally ventured out of her room for more than a few minutes, Chloe found herself alone in the living room with her mum, watching TV, as the boys had headed to the driving range to hit a few balls. Her mother had tried to make small talk – asking her whether she was excited about tomorrow night, who was wearing what – mindless questions which Chloe didn't have the energy to answer. She was still weak. It still hurt.

But all of a sudden, Mrs Walsh picked up the remote and turned off the programme in which both of them had been engrossed, leaving Chloe puzzled.

"What did you do that for?" she exclaimed. But her mother's eyes were still focused on the blank screen and an eerie vacancy spread over her face.

"Is everything OK, Mum?" Chloe finally asked, sensing that it probably wasn't if the atmosphere was anything to go by.

The silence closed in on them from all angles.

"Chloe, we need to talk," Mrs Walsh finally said.

"OK," Chloe replied.

"No," Mrs Walsh snapped. "We need to really talk . . . properly."

"Mum, what are you on about?"

"Don't give me that," her mother answered, raising her voice for the first time and giving Chloe a fright. "I'm sorry . . . I just . . . why won't you talk to me, Chloe?" she pleaded.

"Talk to you about what?" Chloe said.

"About anything . . . about you . . . about your life . . . about what's happened," her mother tried to clarify, searching deep into her daughter's eyes. "Chloe . . . I'm worried about you."

"I'm fine, Mum – I'm just upset about the break-up and stuff . . . and with college starting and all–"

"That's what I tried to tell myself," her mother interjected.

"What?"

"I tried to convince myself that things were bad with Sam and that you were finding all the changes at the moment hard," Mrs Walsh explained. "But I've got to stop pretending that this is just a recent thing . . ."

"What?"

"Oh come on, Chloe, help me here. All summer I've watched my beautiful daughter turn into this . . . this . . . broken young woman . . . and it breaks my heart," her mother admitted, her eyes starting to well up in a rare loss of composure.

Chloe didn't know what to say. She hated seeing her mother like this.

"I know you haven't been eating . . . I mean, your body's not well, darling . . . and your head – you're not yourself anymore . . . I know it . . ." the older woman said, tears beginning to stream.

Chloe found herself shaking, completely at a loss as to where all this was coming from. Sure, she was a little less confident, but her mum was making out like she was sick or something. She wished she would stop crying. But Mrs Walsh had much more to say.

"You've no idea how proud of you I was . . . I am . . . You worked so hard for the Leaving, then you got the job and paid for Ayia Napa, you're just about to start college . . . so I just . . . I just don't understand," her mother pleaded.

"Understand what?" Chloe wondered, though her voice too was starting to crack.

"Don't you know how wonderful you are?" her mother whispered, bitter tears stinging her face as she looked into her daughter's eyes.

"No," Chloe croaked, her throat now completely dry, barely able to utter the word.

"No?"

"No," Chloe repeated, feeling something swell inside her. "No, Mum – I don't know how wonderful I am. Because I'm not fucking wonderful, Mum . . . Everything I try to do, I fail, everything about me . . . I hate myself, Mum . . . so don't try and tell me I'm wonderful," Chloe sobbed, tears finally taking over as she felt her body start to crumble, giving way to the rush of woe which poured over her. "I lost Sam . . . I'm losing my friends . . . I make myself sick every time I eat dinner, Mum . . . I am not wonderful . . . I am not fucking wonderful," she shouted, her words echoing through the silent living room.

The women stared at one another, united in a moment of pure hurt, realising for the first time just how bad things were. Chloe knew in that moment that she had a choice: to bottle everything back up and walk away, to tell her mother to keep her nose out of her business, to go back to the excruciating routine of trying to be OK, of reassuring herself that she had things under control all by herself. Or she could give in to those kind eyes which she knew and loved so much and release the tidal wave of melancholic self-loathing which savaged at her soul every day. She could finally let someone try and help her to be OK again, help her to sort out this painful mess which she'd created all by herself and which she desperately longed to be free of.

They both waited, staring into one another in search of so much, needing the other more than ever. At last, Chloe spoke. She had made her choice.

"Mum, I just can't do it anymore . . . I don't know what's happened to me, but everything is wrong . . . I'm so scared . . . and I just feel so lonely . . . and I know it's my own fault because I keep shutting people out, because I thought I was strong enough – I thought I was in control . . . but I'm not . . . and I just can't take it anymore . . ." she wailed, surprising even herself with just how much pain was begging to be released. She cried and cried, going to her mother and curling up on her lap like she had done as a child, cocooning herself in her warmth and knowing that, if anyone could make it stop hurting, her mother could. Mrs Walsh stroked her daughter's head, rocking her slightly as she held her bundle of joy – this broken girl whom she had let slip so far away, but now vowed to help if it was the last thing she did.

Chloe shut her eyes, tears still dripping down her blotchy face, her chest throbbing from her powerful sobs which continued to break free – finally giving in to her mother's love, willing her, begging her, to make it stop hurting. Through her crying, she could make out her mother's reassuring voice, uttering things about help, and counsellors, and eating disorders, and insecurity – but Chloe didn't care; she didn't care how she was going to get out of all of this, just as long as she did. This was something she had to do. But unlike the many targets she had set herself of late, for the first time ever, she knew that she was actually going to reach this one, for she had the help of the woman she admired most in the world, and that, for Chloe, was the greatest comfort of all.

For hours they sat together, saying little but allowing their souls to come together – the protector holding the protected, wishing that she hadn't neglected her task for so long. The protected just letting the tears keep coming, flowing down her harrowed face until, finally, they stopped.

Mounting the stairs for bed, after a final kiss and hug from her mother, Chloe felt more exhausted then she ever had, her entire body drained of months of pain and woe, as her heart and soul collapsed within her. But somewhere deep beneath it all lay a tiny spark of hope, which promised Chloe that, despite the weary aches which filled her as she slumped into bed, things might be OK. That even though she wasn't there yet – not even close – from now on life was going to get better. The only way was up.

Shutting her eyes, Chloe couldn't help but muse on the fact that so much had changed in one summer - it had seen the steady decay of a happy girl, who was only now realising that it was time to put things back together. Rolling over, she sank into a blissful sleep.

*

Fixing the diamond hairpin into her blonde ringlets, Chloe stared at her reflection, surveying its every inch. Her pink dress, which her mother and she had purchased in Brown Thomas, was everything she'd ever wanted – elegant and simple, flowing to the ground, where the trail followed behind her, making her look like a movie star ready to receive her Oscar. Earlier that day she had got her hair done in Toni & Guy and her make-up at MAC, so she felt thoroughly glamorous as she applied the final touches to her outfit. Finishing off with a spray of perfume – the perfume Sam had once bought her – Chloe was ready; ready for what, she wasn't sure, but she was ready. The girls' school was providing drinks for them in the assembly hall at seven o'clock, so it had been decided to just meet there, after which buses would pick them up and take them on to the Pavilion in Leopardstown, where the rest of the evening's proceedings would take place. Chloe was excited, there was no doubt about that, but she also had a sense of the passing of time, as tonight was the night she'd dreamed about for so long – this was it: this was her debs. She remembered when they were small they would spend hours sitting there, asking each other, "If your debs was tomorrow, who would you bring?" Usually the answer would be the name of a latest crush or boyfriend or celebrity obsession, but now, it was the real thing, and she was bringing Sam, her ex. The title seemed not to fit, but Chloe was forced to concede that she'd have to get used to it. But not yet. Not until after tonight – their last goodbye.

Chloe was in a better place, slightly more at ease with things than she had been only days ago. However, that was no thanks to her friends, or friend, after Heather had sent her a rather unwelcome text yesterday.

HEY BABE - SO EXCITD4 2MO. LISTEN, STEVE RANG ME EARLIER 2 SAY HES REALY SIK, SO HE CANT CUM 2 D DEBS. SO I WOZ KINDA STUCK + I ASKD ANDY 2 B MY D8. HOPE U DON MIND, XOX

Chloe had been shocked, reading and re-reading the most insensitive message she could every remember receiving. Of course she minded. The night was going to be difficult enough as it was without her best friend stabbing her in the back and bringing the one person she and Sam definitely did not need to be near. Every time she would see him or see Sam looking at him, she would only feel worse again, constantly reminded that, yes, Sam was now her ex, and, yes, it was mostly because of that guy over there. She hadn't replied – not deigning to respond to such a heartless message which had completely altered her opinion of Heather, whom, up until now, she'd held in the highest regard. No doubt Heather would have made up an excuse about how Andy was the easiest option since they were friends and since Ella was already bringing Alex. But that wasn't good enough. Was Chloe overreacting? Probably, she conceded, but she slowly became aware of another part of the reason for such a reaction: she was jealous. It was an awful thing to say, and the emotion filled her with guilt, but now that she'd pinpointed it, she couldn't deny that it was true: she was jealous. Did she have the right to be? Perhaps not. But then again, she was a single girl now and, no matter the complete unsuitability of her confusing attraction to Andy, she couldn't deny that on some level she felt a connection to him. So how dare her best friend bring him as her date.

*

Meanwhile, Heather was hoping her friend would be feeling all these things. She knew bringing Andy wasn't very sympathetic, but her date had cried off, and maybe it was time that Chloe Walsh realised what it was like to have a friend who did whatever they pleased, without any consideration for people who cared about them. All summer, Chloe had looked Heather in the eye and lied, becoming this entirely new person. So was it any wonder Heather struggled to feel any sense of loyalty towards her? Sure, they had been best friends for years, but going on Chloe's recent performance, Heather owed her nothing. Chloe had left Heather in tears so many nights now, wondering what she'd done wrong – wondering why her best friend was pushing her away. It hurt so much and Heather had had enough. Andy was her friend and he was the perfect person to bring, as Alex was going too and the boys could hang out together. She knew Chloe wouldn't be impressed, but maybe this was what it would take for her to realise how much things had changed, and then maybe, just maybe, Chloe would want to put things right. Heather wanted that more than anything.

*

Of course, Chloe was going to have to avoid Andy for the evening – she owed that much to Sam. On top of that, she wanted to focus her evening on spending time with Sam, for what could be the last time for a very long while. She longed to dance with him, to have him hold her, maybe even kiss her. But she realised the latter would not be very sensible, and Sam was not the type to confuse an already messy situation. So it would just have to be a final, platonic acknowledgement of almost a year of their lives – her first love, her first real relationship. It was time to say goodbye.

*

As she opened the front door, Chloe's heart stopped, nervously greeting a very well-dressed Sam, welcoming him in and smiling brightly.

"You look gorgeous," he said, making her blush in anxious appreciation. "I got you this."

Sam produced a stunning white-lily corsage from behind his back, placing it onto her wrist and tying it on. Every time his skin touched hers, Chloe felt an electric tingle.

"It's beautiful," she said.

They stood in the doorway looking at one another, not knowing what to say – not knowing how to be. But it didn't feel weird. Somehow Chloe knew it was going to be OK.

When the time came, Sam took her by the arm and led her to the car where her parents and brother sat, ready to drive down to the school. She held his arm tightly, not wanting to let go, and held it again as they entered the Pavilion later on, when a lady from *Image* magazine stopped them and asked could she take a photo for their pages. Chloe gladly agreed, delighted to have been chosen and in some way happy that their photo – a single image of Sam and her – would be preserved in print, a final snapshot of an ended era. They posed, smiling, Sam's left arm pressing against the small of her back as his right gently rested across her thin stomach, looking ever the gentleman. He smelled good, as always, as his sparkling eyes glinted at the camera, awaiting the flash.

Once the photo was taken, the girl took their names. Seeing them written down like that reminded Chloe of the millions of times she had scribbled those exact words, surrounded by a big love-heart, on the back of her school copybooks and folders. All that seemed so long ago now – the innocent beginnings, where simple text messages developed into proper phone calls, before they finally met up and went on a real date. They had been shy at first, but had gradually eased into a growing bond which soon bloomed into love. If only they had known then, Chloe thought, how it would all end. If only.

The evening was a blur of wine and music and romance and nostalgia, as Chloe remembered the last time they'd been in that very place together: at the Leaving Cert Ball, all those months ago. They'd fought that night but had made up just as quickly, vowing to try harder not to find themselves arguing again. But just look at them now, Chloe smiled, as they finished their meal, chatting easily, with absolutely no sign of conflict.

The room looked beautiful, with its twinkling lights softly illuminating the dancing couples, spinning round and round so that the girls' dresses whirred into a coloured haze. Despite the size of the large room, a reassuring intimacy hung warmly in the air. The girls and their dates buzzed through the hall, catching up and saying a final farewell to their schooldays, where pony-tailed schoolgirls had blossomed into elegant women about to take the next step in the precarious journey that was life. Chloe had loved her school, but time moved on, and who was she to tell it to stop and wait? Still, it was scary to know that, all at once, her school-life, her relationship with Sam and, for the moment, her friendship with Heather had drawn to a conclusion, passing over to the part of her mind entitled "past" and opening up the "present" for a whole new set of experiences. But after the chat with her mother, she realised that now, tentatively, she would take the next step.

"Do you want to dance?" Sam asked gently as Chloe zoned back in, surprised by the offer but glad it had come.

"I'd love to," she replied, and they set off to the dance floor, which was steadily filling up as people finished their meals and went for a digestive bop. The DJ greeted them all in a typical smarmy voice, before putting on the latest number one, its infectious beats luring everyone's hips into motion as the party began to liven up. At first the girls felt strange bumping and grinding in their ballgowns, but alcohol and the resultant loss of inhibition soon saw them really let loose, feeling the flow of the music and letting their hair down.

Sam had never been the best dancer, but Chloe was still touched to have him there, making the effort and, most of all, making her smile as he moved in time with her, their bodies occasionally coming close, even touching, but then pulling away once more, remembering that things were different now, that all had changed. Track after track played on, the contagious rhythms eventually drawing everyone to the floor, united in an incomparable buzz where time was irrelevant and fun was everything. Chloe closed her eyes, savouring the worry-free bliss as her head moved this way and that, but on opening them again she saw the face which both intrigued and repelled her. Andy and Alex were throwing shapes, not far from her, looking drunk as usual, both smiling as they messed. At least he wasn't with Heather, Chloe thought, truly thankful that her brother seemed to be Andy's only companion – for the moment. She was careful not to let Sam notice that she was looking over his shoulder, fearful of how he might react, but still found it difficult to take her eyes off Andy. Out of nowhere, he turned and looked at her, staring straight into her eyes as if he had known she'd been watching him. Chloe wanted to look away, embarrassed, but something made her hold his gaze as he smiled his cheeky grin at her, the first eye contact they'd shared since their blissfully forbidden night. Chloe tingled, but she didn't smile in return. That wasn't what tonight was about, she reminded herself, turning back to Sam.

The music softened as the slow set began, couples pairing off into close contact as they swayed, holding each other, to the gentle melodies. Chloe looked at Sam, and he at her, and without a word they both stepped in, placing their arms around one another as they began to dance. She felt so safe beside him, as she always had, her fingers resting on his warm neck as they softly moved. So this was what goodbye felt like. She sighed, though happier now, as Sam held her close, his hands clasping her thin body for the very last time. Memories of their time together filled her as the song built to a crescendo – they had had happy times, that was certain. And maybe someday they would be friends and look back on it all fondly, knowing that love, while it had lasted, had been good.

The final chord played. The dance had ended. Sam pulled away.

"Thank you," he whispered.

Chloe knew what he meant. It was over.

15

SAM

Chloe's debs had definitely been a success, and Sam looked back on it with great fondness, knowing they'd had such a nice night together. But although it had left him feeling slightly sad that things had changed, he had nonetheless been reassured that things had worked out for the best. As he had danced with her, her bony frame pressing against his, he knew that he did love her. But he was no longer *in* love with her – and whether that was a product of her sleeping with Andy or just the steady ebbing of a finite romance, he didn't know. Undoubtedly he would always feel a connection to her – she had been his first love – but he was ready to move on.

He had seen her looking at Andy from time to time during the night, and he wondered if anything would happen between the two of them once he was gone to London. Sam admitted that he had no right to let such an eventuality bother him, but no matter how much the thought of breaking up with Chloe had been on his mind this summer, he could never fully forgive her for cheating on him. He had felt so hurt, so worthless – like such a fool. He had never understood cheating, concluding that if you found yourself wanting someone else so badly, then why didn't you just break up with the person you were with in the first place? It was too humiliating a thing to do to someone you apparently cared for, and despite the fact that he was getting over it, all evening he had still imagined Andy, and maybe even Alex, looking at him and knowing his girlfriend had wanted someone else. Had wanted more. And got it.

He hadn't been entirely surprised when Chloe had told him she'd cheated, though the details had been shocking. She had been acting so weirdly before Ayia Napa, begging for more and more proof of Sam's affections until he began to grow weary of her incessant demands. Would they have lasted if they'd been together when he moved? Sam didn't know, laughing that he had considered turning down the opportunity because of their relationship. He counted his lucky stars that he had made the right decision, knowing how furious he would have been right now if he'd stayed in Dublin because of Chloe. Maybe his leaving would make things easier for them – they wouldn't see each other on nights out, and he wouldn't have to watch something starting up between Andy, or anyone else, and her. Although he was almost over her, the tiny tinge of jealousy would always remain within him, knowing that, not so long ago, she had chosen Andy over him. Over their everything. But he would miss her when he left – that was for certain. He was going to miss everyone.

Going to university in England was not something Sam had considered at all when growing up, the thought rarely suggested or contemplated amongst his peers. Yet once it was mentioned to him by his guidance counsellor, he had begun to research it and found it an increasingly attractive idea, being lured by the courses, the colleges and, most of all, the freedom which England seemed to offer. So he had applied, like many others, as a back-up, hoping Britain would serve as a safety net if all fell through back home. But more and more Sam had found himself hoping for things to fall through – hoping that he would just miss out on the courses he wanted in Ireland and be forced to move away, to start again. All summer his mind had been preoccupied with the idea, longing for "new" and "fresh" and the exciting uncertainty which Dublin could never give him. He knew that if he stayed there, he would remain living at home, going to the same nightclubs with the same people, week in, week out. And it would be fun. But was that enough? Would that be a new phase in his world or just an extension of the previous one, as school melted into university in a seamless transition?

However, despite Sam's belief that he was doing the right thing, he was scared. With every leaflet his new college sent him or information he received, he found it increasingly difficult to convince himself that he wasn't going to be petrified. But he wasn't going to be the only one in that situation – there would be hundreds of first years in exactly the same boat, so there was no reason to feel too worried. Everyone kept warning him that the first week or so would indeed be hard, but then such discomforts would become a mere memory, about which he and his new friends would laugh, as they sat in the pub, having a ball. Sam hoped they were right. For despite all his protestations about wanting to step outside the box and leave the "Southside Bubble", the prospect of no bubble whatsoever was unnerving, knowing that when things were bad, or if things didn't go according to plan, there would be no familiar faces to turn to. The bubble had its advantages, but slowly Sam would create his own bubble, where the people he liked and the new places he had found would be encased, making him happier than ever before.

His remaining days in Ireland were spent packing his things, trying to stick to his meagre baggage allowance as best he could, whilst cutting as few corners as possible – not wanting to be without his familiar things when starting anew. His mother had washed and ironed all his clothes, and he piled them up into the case, leaving room for photos, shot glasses and a couple of posters with which he hoped to jazz up his student accommodation. His mum had also treated him to a couple of cookbooks and a notebook full of instructions about how to master such tasks as using a washing machine, ironing his clothes and other equally riveting activities which Sam was not looking forward to. For all that, being self-sufficient had a nice ring to it, of late he had become increasingly aware of just how easy he had it. The one thing he wouldn't miss about his Mum's house, though, was her partner, with whom Sam had never got on and who was undoubtedly delighted that he was leaving. Deirdre was another thing, though, as his father's fiancée seemed to be really dreading his departure and had insisted that she cook a huge goodbye meal for the three of them, just two nights before he went.

Sam finished collecting the things from his Dad's house which he wanted to take away with him, as the sweet smell of roast beef wafted up the stairs. Staring around his empty room, Sam felt a twinge of sadness pull at him from within, as he bid the four walls goodbye, a farewell to his childhood. A photo of Chloe and him sat on the shelf, left behind to be viewed by no one at all – the forgotten remains of the past. Picking it up, Sam smiled as he surveyed his own, younger face, grinning like the cat who had got the cream as he wrapped his arm around the vivacious blonde beside him, squeezing her tightly with affectionate pride. She too smirked brightly, the glint in her eye not recently to be found, as a much healthier, happier version of Chloe sparkled within the frame. She wasn't the same, that was for sure, and Sam found himself admitting that the Chloe he had broken up with only a week ago was not the Chloe he had asked out almost a year ago. Physically and emotionally, she had deteriorated, in Sam's opinion, as he had watched her lately struggle with insecurities he couldn't understand. Where had they come from? Chloe had always been the bubbly, outgoing one of the pair, stunning everyone with her constant energy and undeniable confidence. So what had happened? First, it had just been a passing comment here and there about the tiniest bit of extra exam weight, but before he knew it, Sam had watched her start to hate herself, eating little and smiling even less as she crumbled slowly before his eyes, dissatisfied with herself and trying desperately to "fix" the mess which she had become. But her insecurities hadn't seen her turn to him for help – rather she had curled up into herself and, in many ways, pushed him away as he struggled to figure out just what was going on. Was she anorexic? Perhaps. Was she messed up? Most definitely. And more than anything, Sam hoped that somehow she would sort herself out and find that inner happiness which seemed to have deserted her so completely, as her eyes faded into a matted grey, a mere shadow of their former glory which used to light up even the gloomiest soul with their infectious hope, just like in the photo.

"Dinner's ready," Deirdre called up, startling Sam and the picture frame fell from his hands. The glass shattered on landing, so that the happy pair were now distorted by the splintered fragments, the image spoilt and hard to make out. Sam smiled at the significance of the sight, not even going to pick it up, instead leaving it, broken, beyond repair.

Deirdre's meal was delicious, and she pulled out all the stops to give her future stepson the send-off he deserved.

"This is gorgeous," Sam complimented through a mouthful of beef and Yorkshire pudding, chewing every morsel appreciatively.

"I'll bet you'll miss meals like that," his dad teased, reading his mind.

"Never mind, he'll find himself a nice English lass to cook his food, won't you?" Deirdre defended with a wink.

"I bloody better – there's only so many tins of beans I'll be able to manage." Sam laughed.

"Speaking of women, have you spoken to Chloe since the debs?" his dad inquired, curious.

"No – sure it was only, like, three nights ago. I sent her a text to say thanks or whatever, but that was about it. We kind of said our goodbyes so I think I'll just leave it now," Sam replied, content with how it had all ended.

"You never told us how it went," Deirdre pried.

"It was good, yeah . . ." he answered truthfully.

"And?" she continued.

"And what?" Sam mocked her nosiness.

"And . . . I don't know – did you kiss her? Was it weird? Come on, Sam – I'm a girl, for goodness sake. 'Good' will not suffice," Deirdre explained with a giggle.

Sam laughed, admiring her honesty and gladly satisfying her curiosity.

"No, we didn't kiss. Yeah, it was a bit weird, but not really. It was nice, I guess . . . just kind of gave us both some closure . . ." he surmised, proceeding to wolf down his dinner, not wanting it to go cold.

"Well, fair play to you for going," she commended.

"She was a nice girl," his dad added, throwing in his opinion. "Possibly a bit complex at times . . . but nice all the same."

"Yeah, definitely. We'll probably stay friends – we'll see . . . don't worry, Deirdre, I'll keep you posted!" Sam joked, grinning at his future stepmum as he helped himself to another roast potato.

"So, are you nervous?" Mr Gallagher wondered.

"Of course he is – you're allowed be nervous," Deirdre said.

"Well good, because I'm bloody shitting a brick," Sam admitted, smiling despite the apprehension which bubbled inside him.

"Well, Christmas isn't too far away," his dad assured.

"I'll be back for my debs in November anyway," Sam reminded him.

"Ooh, I wonder if you'll bring Chloe?" Deirdre piped up excitedly.

"No way, you want to surprise them all with some English looker you've picked up," his dad chortled, sipping on his red wine.

Sam's mind wandered – he hadn't thought about his own debs; it wasn't for a while now. But despite its distance, somehow he couldn't imagine asking Chloe to be his date. It was too far, yet not far enough, after their split for it to seem right, for although they would have both moved on, maybe even found someone new, there would still only be a two-month break between them, leaving the tiny potential for the rekindling of a flame which, Sam was adamant, he wanted to leave extinguished.

If they were going to break up, they were going to stay broken up, he had always reasoned, knowing that, however hurt people got the first time round, the failure of a second try would only lead to further pain and the complete erasure of any chance of remaining friends. No, he would find himself "some English looker", as his dad so eloquently put it, and dance the night away with his new girl – starting the future as he meant to continue it.

"And then you'll have to come back for the wedding," his dad added, reminding him what they had been talking about, as he watched the engaged couple look at one another with the happiest of smiles, knowing that they were truly perfect for one another.

"Have you set a date yet?" Sam asked.

"No, not yet – probably around March," his father answered.

"I can't wait," Sam said.

"Neither can we," Deirdre cooed, brimming over with joy as the look of love dazzled in her eyes, warming Sam's heart.

It was time to go, and Sam was insisting that he walk back to his mum's house – the stroll would take him over half an hour, but he really did feel like the fresh air.

"But you have all your stuff," Deirdre objected.

"It's not that heavy, honestly – thanks, but I do just feel like an amble," Sam insisted.

"OK then." She gave in, though her eyes were sad as she realised this was goodbye.

"I'm going to miss you," she uttered, her voice low and honest.

"I'll miss you too," Sam reiterated. "Both of you."

Hugging his dad and Deirdre goodbye, Sam felt the knot of anticipation tighten within his stomach.

"You know no matter what happens, I am so proud of you," his father assured him, his final words somehow easing Sam's load as he bade them both farewell, setting off into the cool night.

Above him, clouds hid his homeland constellations, keeping in a vague memory of the day's warmth, as Sam strolled through the empty streets, dusky and hollow. He would miss Dublin, there was no doubt about that. The stone houses he passed held various families living their lives as he awaited a great change in his, their curtained windows like eyes staring down at the lone walker, his footsteps echoing in the street-lamp hue, which tasted of evening fumes and freshly cut grass. Autumn was slowly fainting into winter, as leaves kamikazed downwards, leaving the scratching branches which reached for the sky like haggard arms, desperate for some sun. Before Sam knew it, the lights would start and the advertisements begin, hailing in the commercial festivities, neon in the pitch-black sky. His dad was right – Christmas wasn't far off, and Sam would be back in Ireland, a whole term completed. How would he have changed? If at all? All summer he had been sensing a maturing occurring within him, as boy turned to man, stumbling as he went, as he let go of the past and grew into the future.

Sam picked up his pace, feeling the twilight nip at his ears and nose, which wanted to go indoors but seemed contented all the same outside, where Sam's shadow danced below, walking slowly into tomorrow – the great tomorrow – where nothing would remain the same.

16

ALEX

So it had been decided – Alex was going to repeat. He and his parents had finally come to the conclusion that he had little choice but to re-sit the Leaving Cert. But more than that, Alex had convinced himself that perhaps it was for the best to give it all another go – to actually do some work this time and maybe even see what making himself proud felt like. He was going to do this. Any of his friends whom he had told about his plans had simply cracked up laughing – finding the thought of Alex Walsh actually going back to school thoroughly ridiculous. But this only fuelled Alex even more, realising that he couldn't live his life any more to amuse his friends by playing the role of the token failure. The people he admired – his father, his friends, Jenny – all of their achievements contributed to who they were as they worked to get something, to get somewhere in life. So it didn't feel right that Alex looked back on the past six years and saw himself completely devoid of goals or motivations. He was going to give this a shot – to prove to everyone else that he could, but most of all to prove it to himself. That was what mattered.

However, steely determination was not the sole emotion which Alex was experiencing on the back of his recent decision, for there was no way he could deny that, in reality, he was annoyed – very annoyed. Why hadn't he just done all this the first time around? How had he become so blissfully ignorant to the fact that, all around him, his friends had been doing at least some work whilst he'd wasted his time. Now they would be going off to live college life, and he would remain a schoolboy – still part of an institution which he had always loathed. School and Alex had never exactly seen eye to eye, and the prospect of another year of early mornings, strict rules and irrelevant subjects in no way thrilled him. It wasn't going to be fun, that was for sure, but maybe for once in his life it was time that Alex did something which he didn't necessarily enjoy, but that he knew was the right thing to do.

He had had an interview with The Institute of Education on Leeson Street, as was required to secure a place in their repeat programme, and he had received a letter to say that he was in. Now it was only a matter of days till he started – till he went back to school. The phrase killed him, but he just had to grin and bear it – life was marching on and, for the first time in his teenage years, Alex had to march with it.

He was at least looking forward to going to school in town – lunchtimes would undoubtedly be more exciting, as he'd be able to meet up with all his friends and have a stroll down Grafton Street whenever he felt like it; plus, it would be such a change having girls in his classes, and he wondered just how much of a distraction he would find his female schoolmates. But Alex was under no illusion as to who would really be his friends by the end of the year – vowing that

287

nothing was going to change between him and the lads, as he would continue to go out with them as much as possible, even on weeknights, and remain a core entity to their continuous banter. He couldn't have it any other way, because there was no way Alex was going to let his decision to repeat sixth year affect his friendships, especially as his mates headed off to university. In fact, he was planning to take advantage as much as possible of their new lifestyle, hoping to attend freshers' weeks, college nights out and basically fit into the whole social scene as best he could.

Though he admitted to himself, reluctantly, that no matter how much he sought to be a part of the college social sphere, the reality would still remain that, for the moment, he was a schoolboy. The worst thing was, whether he tried to deny it or not, eventually there would come a point when he would have to accept this reality, otherwise his work ethic would remain non-existent and the whole year would be a complete waste of time. It was just so hard to hear Andy and the boys all chattering about what was to come, excitedly discussing their futures, now certain of what they were, while Alex still remained behind, eager to catch up but unfortunately unable to.

However, the more he listened to his friends, envying them and knowing that the best few years of their lives were about to commence, Alex resigned himself to the fact that such jealousy had to be honed in on, to provide him with the extra drive to get himself into a similar position – if he wanted it badly enough, then he could do it; he would do it. He also couldn't wait to see the look on his old teachers' faces when he came out the far end with a good Leaving Cert, went to college and proved them all wrong. For so long now, the entire staff of his old school had given up on him; they had ceased to comment on his lack of attendance, and even more severe lack of work, deciding that it wasn't worth their while any more. Alex hated this reality, but conceded that in ways they had been right: he had messed up; he had failed gloriously. But maybe if they'd just given him a chance – persisted in trying to make him see that he was throwing so much away – then maybe he would have pulled up his socks, albeit at the last minute, but at least he might have ended up with something. Well, this time he certainly would, he vowed, and he would rub it in those teachers' faces and show them that they had been wrong, so wrong. It wasn't like he was going to get straight As this time – he was enough of a realist to know that – but he was going to show them that he, Alex Walsh, could actually sit down and work for something. It wasn't going to be fun. But it would be so worth it.

So here he was, back to square one, longing to have advanced but reasoning that he had no one but himself to blame for his position and that no one but himself could drag him out of it. It was ironic too when he looked at his sister, who had started drama in DIT, because, unlike Alex, she was hating the fact that she had to advance, wanting to remain outside the big wide world for just a little while longer. She was scared. He was fed-up. Neither was content.

Outside his window, Alex watched the peeling grey clouds slump across an empty white sky, edging in on its nothingness and dimming the world below which gave in to the bleak September gloom. The trees huddled together, like fearful troops standing in line, set for battle against the vicious breeze. The birdbath was empty, the winged creatures preparing to depart for hotter climates and brighter skies. Mr Walsh's pitchfork stuck in the ground in the back corner, his work all finished as the evenings grew too icy to work, leaving the tool to become infected by time and rust into the uncut grass.

Alex took it all in – his familiar surroundings which, like his life, were going to remain familiar until next year's September gloom would creep in on a more mature man and find that even the menacing clouds could not dampen his spirits, for he would be leaving square one, leaping into square two and loving every minute of it. Of that Alex was sure.

*

"So when do you start?" Andy asked the next day, while the pair sat, as always, in front of the TV, hanging on Jeremy Clarkson's every word as a re-run of *Top Gear* dazzled before their eyes.

"Tomorrow," Alex replied, noting just how soon that sounded.

"Are you nervous?"

"Fuck no, why would I be?" Alex said defensively, though part of him couldn't help but tingle slightly with anxiety.

"I was kind of nervous starting in DIT," Andy admitted, having been nearly a week in college now and apparently loving it.

"Don't you have lectures today?" Alex teased.

"Probably – couldn't tell you. I've decided to kind of ease myself into this whole college lark," Andy explained with a smirk.

"Lucky for some," Alex said, knowing that it was very likely that he was going to end up working much harder than his friend this year.

"We have, like, a DIT night out next week for all the campuses, which will be savage," Andy informed.

"Cool."

"Yeah, you should come," he said, much to Alex's appreciation, but then added, "Do you know if your sister's going, actually?"

Alex rolled his eyes, fearing that Andy's splitting up of Chloe and Sam may not have made him feel bad – but rather might have given him cause for hope as he continued to pursue Chloe.

"You don't actually like her do you?" Alex asked, trying to gauge how much, if any, emotional attachment his friend had to his sister, but trying his hardest not to let it bother him.

"Ah . . . I'll see how it goes," Andy said.

"Yeah, right – you just like the challenge," Alex corrected, smiling.

"Maybe . . . but she was savage in bed . . ." Andy teased, knowing it would get a rise out of his best friend, his plan having been completed.

Sure enough, Alex was suitably appalled by the remark, dragging his eyes away from the television to smack Andy over the head, punching his left shoulder until he got a dead arm. Andy cracked up laughing as he took the beatings, knowing that he was in no position to fight back, just relishing his success in getting a rise out of his friend.

"Fuck you," Alex muttered, grinning. He returned to watching the TV, noting that if this was what the next few months were going to be like – literally, the same as always – then maybe it really was all going to be OK.

HEY BABY. HOW U FEELN BOUT 2MO? TRUST ME - UL B GRAND. WANA MEET UP DIS WKEND? LUV YA XX

Jenny's text arrived soon after Andy left, giving Alex even more support but putting him in mind of another potential worry. The closer he got to Jenny, the more he wondered if next year would take its toll on them. She was now in UCD with all the studs of South Dublin, going to lectures with them, doing lunch and generally getting to know them as more than faces from the nightclubs. So when they took a shine to her, and expressed an interest, and she politely replied that she had a boyfriend, and they asked what college he was in, Alex didn't feel very reassured by the thought of her answering, "Oh, he's actually still in school." It didn't have the ring to it which Alex wanted to scare away male admirers from his girlfriend. He liked her – he liked her a lot – but besides that, he wasn't going to be humiliated by losing her to some college jock just because he had been a little bit slower than most in getting his act together.

That said, there was always the niggling possibility that had Alex gone to the Institute single, then he could have properly taken advantage of going to school with girls, becoming the school stud he'd always imagined himself to be and seeing what it was like to score a girl in the back row of class when the teacher wasn't looking. Alex laughed – he had definitely been watching too many of Chloe's chick-flicks, giving him cheesy notions of what mixed-school life was going to be. Plus, if he was completely honest with himself, he was quite chuffed with how things were going with Jenny. It was strange, because asking her out had been a drunken mistake, one which he had very much regretted in the morning. But the more he thought about it, and the more he realised that having Jenny as his girlfriend was actually kind of cool, Alex felt rather pleased with himself.

But even better, Jenny was completely smitten with him, and in times of uncertainty like this, she was unfailing in her support and reassurance, building Alex up and making him feel that maybe he would be all right. More than all right. She would never cheat on him, deep down he knew that – no matter how much the college guys tried it on – so it felt good to have something concrete, something definite, in such a period of confusion. Because whether he had decided to repeat, to go to a private college or even to become a chimney sweep, Alex had known that either way he would still have had Jenny, and that was a feeling which he had never experienced before and was really growing to like.

Originally the thought of falling in love had never crossed Alex's mind – it wasn't on his list of priorities. But recently he wondered if there was a chance that he was falling, properly, for Jenny. And he knew that he would continue to fall, and maybe even land. Such a possibility was scary, but then again, something to look forward to amidst everything else. Alex smiled. Things were going to work out just fine.

With Andy gone, Alex had the house to himself, his parents still at work and Chloe presumably out with friends. But as he sat in front of the TV, the evening light beginning to fade and his stomach beginning to rumble, the doorbell rang. Alex considered not answering it – the couch feeling awfully comfortable in that moment. But somehow he found the strength to drag himself up and plod to the front door, though the face he revealed on the other side shocked him to the core.

"Are your parents home?" Barry's father slurred, pushing past Alex, the whiff of alcohol flooding into the hallway.

"Eh, no," Alex answered, thoroughly unnerved.

"Good."

Alex didn't know what was going on, but the look in his friend's father's eye told him something was not right, and Alex couldn't help but be afraid.

"Can I . . . help you?" Alex tried, whilst Mr Carter bumbled around the hall, looking at the photographs on the walls, squinting his bloodshot eyes to examine each one. He didn't answer. Alex felt anxiety creep up from his toes. His mind was blank.

"Mr Carter, look, I don't know . . ."

"Don't you Mr Carter me!"

"I'm . . . I'm sorry,." Alex stuttered, his heart pumping faster and faster. What was going on? Was he going to hit him? Nothing made sense. Time ticked by.

"Do you know what day it is?" Barry's dad finally broke the dense silence, his words stumbling every so slightly over one another.

"Sorry?"

"I said, do you know what day it is today?" the older man repeated, his voice even louder than before.

"No . . . no I don't, actually . . ." Alex answered, knowing full well what day of the week it was, but sensing that that wasn't exactly what Mr Carter was getting at. The silence pressed ever inwards. Alex was petrified, the whole moment feeling like a bizarre nightmare which he yearned to end.

"Today," Barry's dad continued, turning to face Alex for the very first time, as he stared straight into his frightened eyes, "today is Barry's birthday."

Alex's heart sank. It all became clear. He cursed himself for having forgotten as his mind rushed with a thousand thoughts. He made to speak, but the older man wasn't finished.

"Today is my son's nineteenth birthday, and do you know where he is? He's lying on a hospital bed, with his eyes closed . . . practically fucking dead," Mr Carter spat through bitter lips.

"His mother and I went to see him earlier. We brought balloons and some cards . . . She even made me sing fucking 'Happy Birthday' . . . Do you know how that felt?" he bellowed, the anger surging once more, making Alex jump as he cowered before this breaking man.

"I felt like a fucking idiot . . . I was singing 'Happy Birthday' to a boy that couldn't even hear me . . . and not just any boy . . ." he paused, ". . . my boy."

Alex watched Mr Carter's bulky frame collapse under the weight of woe as he slumped against the wall, tears welling up in his drooping eyes. Alex wanted to go to him, to tell him that things were going to be OK. But he couldn't.

"Why was it him?" Mr Carter mumbled, his voice cracking with every word. "Why are you OK, and he's . . . he's not? It doesn't make sense . . ." He held his face in his hands as the sobs began.

That's when it hit Alex. In that moment, he realised that things weren't OK. His friend was lying in a coma, and he was sitting there, perfectly fine, watching the sorry tears of the saddest man he'd ever seen. It wasn't fair. Barry's dad cried and cried. Alex was in shock, rooted to the spot as a tidal wave of guilt swept into his every pore. He looked back over his summer – those incredible months which, now he realised, had been a complete lie. It snapped his soul in two to think of all those drunken nights and fun-filled days he'd spent, living life as if nothing mattered. Every time someone had mentioned the accident, he'd had a drink. Every time his father had begged with him, pleaded with him to just try and have the tiniest bit of perspective, he'd rolled his eyes and shoved reality to the back of his head. How had he let it come this far? It was as if someone had slapped him in the face, as he stood numb, watching the agony of the man before him. That should be his agony. Alex cursed himself: he should be hurting more than anyone – he'd been there, he'd let Barry start that car and, worst of all, he'd continued life like nothing had happened. Alex closed his eyes. It was time to wake up to reality. At last, he had to let the truth break free, and he hated himself for it.

The stillness was eerie, as the two grown men stood united in pain. Time moved onwards.

"I should probably go," Barry's dad finally whispered. His voice startled Alex, who had been a million miles away.

"Oh . . . oh right. Well, let me . . . let me drive you home," Alex offered, coming to and realising that that was the least he could do, given the circumstances.

"No . . . no, I'd rather walk. Need to sober up before I go home, I think," Mr Carter said with an almost-smile, wiping his tears away with embarrassed awkwardness.

"Look, Mr Carter, I'm really sor–"

"Don't," the man interjected swiftly, closing his eyes to the younger boy's words. "I know."

Not another word passed between the men, both with so much to say, but both knowing that saying it was not going to change anything. For Barry's dad, Alex would always be the boy who'd got lucky and whom he couldn't help but blame, in some way, for his son's tragic position. For Alex, Mr Carter would always serve as a reminder of that awful day, when he had let Barry get into the car and turn the key and crash into his horrible fate. Neither was happy, but somehow they both felt a tiny bit better after their impromptu encounter, hoping that the next time they met would be for happier reasons.

Alex watched as his friend's dad left, looking older than he'd ever seen him as he ambled clumsily into the moth-eaten darkness, where lamplights breathed into their misty surroundings. Alex closed the door, his heart still racing as he returned to the couch. Everything had changed. That moment had altered him more than anything – more than the crash, more than finishing school. For for the first time in his life, everything clicked, and Alex found himself sitting there, looking into his soul and loathing what he saw. His eyes welled up. How had it come to this? How had he lived nearly nineteen years, and most of all those past three months, with a disfigured heart and a warped sense of perspective. He was the luckiest boy on the planet to have survived that crash, yet never once all summer had he felt thankful that he was walking around as arrogant as always in his carefree life. Somehow he had managed to come out of it all with a set of amazing friends, a girlfriend and a family who loved him. And he didn't deserve any of it.

Alex sat for hours, crying, paying the penance which he'd somehow avoided. He couldn't remember the last time he'd cried, but was grateful at least that he still could – somehow, he could still feel and was finally allowing himself to. He mulled over it all in a state of disbelief, as the image of Barry's crumbling father filled his mind. Only this time, he wasn't going to have a shot of tequila to make it all stop. This time he wasn't going to go and have sex with Jenny to distract him. This time he was going to sit there and beat himself up from the inside, until he fully came to terms with the person he had become and realised that he needed to change. Everything needed to change. It wasn't going to be easy. But it was time.

*

"So, a toast . . . to Alex," Mr Walsh announced that night at the dinner table, raising his glass in a grand gesture to celebrate his son's impending fresh start at school the following morning. His wife and daughter followed suit.

"To Alex," they echoed brightly, clinking glasses with each other and with Alex as he blushed slightly, pleased with the display but knowing he didn't deserve it. He hadn't told his parents about what had happened earlier, deciding that he had to stop relying on other people and take ownership of his actions and their consequences, however painful they may be. He sipped his Coke and wiped up the remains of his lasagne with a hunk of crusty bread, still warm from the oven.

"So, are you all set?" his mother asked, arranging her knife and fork on her plate, indicating that she was finished.

"Eh . . . I guess," Alex replied, taking a second to remind himself she was talking about school.

"So, do you need money for lunch? And what about a lift in in the morning?" she offered.

"No, I'll be fine," he replied softly.

His mother smiled as she and Chloe began to clear away the plates, leaving the two men to talk.

"Well, I know we keep telling you this, but I am actually really proud of your decision – it can't be easy choosing to repeat," his father commended, looking his son straight in the eye, assuring him of his sincerity.

"Thanks, Dad," Alex answered, genuinely grateful. How his father could still be proud of him, Alex didn't know, but the fact that he was was incredible.

"Plus, I think the extra year will do you good, to be honest," Mr Walsh continued. "I mean, it'll help you have a proper think about what you want to do, which in turn will help you work a bit harder this time, because at least you'll have something to aim for."

"Yeah," Alex agreed, seeing sense in his dad's argument, but his mind was still somewhere else – school seemed a million miles from the revelation which that afternoon had brought about. Tomorrow was a fresh start in more ways than one, as Alex was going to have to start changing himself, as well as his work ethic. His father was definitely right – the year would surely do him good.

"And maybe," his dad continued, leaning in and lowering his voice so that the women wouldn't hear, "you might think about toning things down – just a little."

"What do you mean?" Alex asked, confused.

"Well . . . just the drinking and the fighting and the–"

"Dad, I don't . . ."

"Ssh, it's OK – I'm not giving out. I was your age once, remember, and, trust me, I was all about burning the candles at both ends too. Just be careful, yeah? In light of everything that's gone on, just . . . just mind yourself," his father advised sincerely, his tone soft but firm, hoping his son would take heed of what he was saying.

"Right, anyone for ice-cream?" Mrs Walsh called out, enjoying their family dinner and wanting it to last for as long as possible. She fetched the tubs of Ben & Jerry's, scooping the sweet dessert into bowls for each of them. Alex took his first bite of cooling sweetness, refreshing after his hot feast. To his left, his father sat, relaxed, leaning back in his chair with his hands behind his head, still wearing his classy business suit from the day's dealings, but his face a reminder that, despite the pinstriped exterior, he would always be a family man at heart, as he stared around, pleased as punch with them all. Alex vowed that he was going to make him proud. At last.

To Alex's right, his mother munched her ice-cream, treating herself after cooking such a hearty meal, her face still flushed from the evening's preparations, yet her pearl earrings and cropped hair maintaining the image of a successful woman, glamorous to the last. She had done some modelling in her day, Alex knew, and always held herself in the most elegant manner, whether she was going out for dinner or emptying the dishwasher, creating an aura of calm wherever she went.

On the other side of the table, Chloe stared into space, picking at her ice-cream with mindless monotony, as her mind seemed a thousand miles away. Alex wondered what was going on in her head. She seemed a bit brighter these days, as if something was finally going right after the mess this summer had been for her. He didn't understand exactly what had gone on but, as usual, didn't want to go there, knowing that something darker lurked within her which he wouldn't dare uncover. But at least she was breaking free. Alex hoped that she, like him, had had her epiphany and snapped out of her temporary lull.

"Right, tea? Coffee? Any takers?" Mr Walsh offered, getting up from the table with a lazy groan, easing out of his comfortable stretch. Alex was about to accept, but suddenly realised it was time he did the thing that had been on his mind all evening. As he had sat there amongst his family, the night before he restarted school – a moment he would hopefully look back on as a milestone – there was just one more person he needed to see.

"I'm going to go to the hospital – I'll be back in a while," Alex announced, startling his mother as he stood up briskly and left the room. "Thanks for dinner," he called over his shoulder before slamming the front door, stepping out into the blustery night.

Alex drove away, travelling in silence, thankful that he had only had one glass of wine and noting the irony of such a thought.

He reached the hospital in no time, stiffening against the fierce gusts as he got out of his car, and pushed into the warm indoors. Mounting the stairs, Alex followed his route to Barry's room, entering silently as he always did, not wanting to disturb the never-ending stillness which blanketed his friend's body and its surroundings. The room was different than usual, the birthday balloons and multicoloured cards appearing thoroughly out of place in the shadowy dusk. However, Barry looked much the same as last time, despite his hair being a bit longer, flopping messily on his crisp, white pillow. Alex realised ashamedly that he really hadn't been here in a while; indeed, the past couple of months had been a hive of activity – which had found him in this room much fewer times than he cared to admit. Still, Alex could go nearly a month without visiting, and yet come back and find his friend here, just as he had left him. Time really was moving on, and Barry really wasn't getting any better. Alex sat beside his sleeping body, watching him breathe, watching Barry live in the most minimal sense of the word, and an overwhelming sadness consumed him.

It had been over three months now and Alex feared that those three months had only resulted in Barry's slipping further and further away. When would it be too late? When would he have slipped too far for anyone or anything to pull him back? Alex held his head in his hands, fearing the worst.

But no, he chided himself, he couldn't think like that. Things in his world had somehow started to piece themselves together, and who was he to give up on a friend so desperately in need? The doctors had mentioned nothing about deterioration, Barry didn't look any worse, so maybe he just needed someone to help him – to be the one to pull him back. Alex willingly accepted the task, still aware that, in many people's eyes, he was the one who had caused all this. He knew that he had lost friends and respect over this. So now, it was time to regain that respect by bringing Barry back. It was the very least he could do, he sighed.

"Hey, Baz, it's me . . . Al," he began brightly, taking off his jacket as he settled into the chair.

"Listen, before I start, I'm really sorry I haven't come by in a while – like, I know it's no excuse, but things have been just so manic and I . . . oh, I don't know . . ." he bumbled, feeling a surreal sense of not having the right to be there. He had to keep going, to earn that right.

"Look man, before I start . . . your dad called round today . . . Shit, happy birthday, actually . . . I can't believe I forgot. I mean, I always forget birthdays, but this one's kind of different, you know? I should have fucking remembered," he chided himself, ashamed in so many ways.

"But yeah, your dad called round . . . I haven't told anyone about it . . . I don't think I will. But it suddenly made me think, like . . . like, harder than I ever bloody have . . ." he trailed off, finding this difficult.

"I guess . . . I guess what I'm trying to say, man, is . . . I'm sorry. I'm just . . . I'm sorry," Alex repeated, relishing the only words he should have said from day one. It still hurt, but it felt good to finally give in and own up to the entire mess. He wasn't solely to blame, he knew that, but for the way he'd been acting ever since he may as well have been. So now, it was time to start picking up the pieces.

"I really am sorry. But all I can say is that I'm here now. And that's how things are going to be from now on, OK?" he assured, promising both his friend and himself.

He allowed the silence to settle, imagining that the wind had changed or the tides had turned – a moment when things were going to take a different direction as Alex moved slowly from being a boy in denial, to being a man.

"So yeah, let me see what news I have for you," he began, settling himself in for the night and searching once more for that hope which had recently begun to glow within him, wanting to pass it on.

"Ayia Napa was unreal . . . like, so crazy. I mean, I spent a lot of time with Jenny – you remember Jenny? And then I did the bungee jump . . . and then Andy slept with my sister, which kind of pissed me off, but whatever . . . and we went out, like, every night and didn't get in till, like, seven and just . . . oh my God, it was insane," Alex recounted, memories of that crazy fortnight flooding from him.

"And then we had the debs . . . shit, did you hear, actually – Mr Kelly made this, like, speech about you and told everyone to, like, pray and shit that you got better, which is cool 'cause he's a seriously religious prick so I reckon it'll work, don't you? Anyway, yeah . . . I brought Jenny, and then I went to Chloe's debs with Ella . . . Did I tell you me and Jen are going out now?" he added, liking the sound of those words as he said them aloud.

"Yeah, I asked her out at the debs when I was completely trollied . . .

but I'm actually kind of glad I did 'cause, like . . . I don't know . . . I really like her . . ." Alex admitted sheepishly, knowing his friend couldn't react, but just imagining how he would if he were awake – mocking Alex's newfound sincerity on the topic of relationships, one which he'd never taken seriously in his entire life.

"So yeah, we're going out and shit, which is cool . . . and I think Andy's going to keep trying it on with my sister – she broke up with her boyfriend – which kind of bothers me . . . but fuck it, I can't really say anything, now can I?" Alex conceded, knowing full well that were Barry with them, he would definitely have given out to Andy for such a conquest.

"And then . . . so . . . oh yeah – big news – I start in the Institute tomorrow . . . which will be really strange, but, whatever – I didn't get any college offers 'cause . . . well . . . as you might have guessed I totally ballsed up the Leaving . . . so yeah, just look at it this way – I'm taking a year to repeat it so that when you wake up we can start college together! Ha ha, that'll be savage . . ." Alex exclaimed, the thought having never occurred to him before, but it delighted him, knowing they were going to have so much fun together next year.

"And Andy's in DIT, as is my sister, but in a different campus . . . and Luke and Kyle are in UCD and so is Jenny . . . and then a few of the lads are going to Trinity for Engineering, but they haven't started yet . . . That's what you wanted to do, isn't it? I mean, what you're going to do, like . . ." Alex corrected himself swiftly.

So he continued, pouring out his heart, and his gossip stash, to Barry, feeling like old friends just catching up, despite the fact that only one of them was talking. But, for the first time, Alex was sure that Barry could hear him and the infectious positivity which he found oozing from him as he talked about his own life, and how things were all starting to work out for him, was undoubtedly seeping into his unconscious friend. Alex sat for hours – the nurse having obviously forgotten to come and tell him that visiting time was well and truly over. He talked of the past, the summer, the future, spending quality time with the friend he'd been neglecting, in so many ways, for too long now. He faded in and out of different emotions – finding himself almost out of breath after extended rants about various people, but then sitting in an excruciating silence, the reality of Barry's circumstances never quite leaving him alone. Shame was never far away either. It forced Alex to look at a self which he didn't want to see. But that's when he would start talking again, for as long as he was sitting there beside the person he'd been ignoring all this time, doing what he should have been all along, then maybe he was beginning to do the right thing. It was only a start, but at least it was something.

At last he checked his watch and realised that it was practically midnight. He exhaled deeply, steadying his heart rate as his body slumped into a comfy heap. Barry's monitors continued to beep. Silence stuffed the room once more. But Alex knew that something had changed, that despite the hint of fear which filled him every time he looked at his friend's sleeping frame, somehow things were going to get better now, and maybe even soon Barry would wake up. He said goodbye, wishing his friend a happy birthday one last time and vowing that he would visit again soon. But this time, he meant it. For if things were going to change – if Alex was going to change – then he needed to start getting his priorities straight. Despite how unimpressed he was with himself, Alex couldn't hide from the fact that, unjust as it was, things were starting to go really well for him. This summer hadn't been perfect, but somehow he had made it out the far end much more aware of things and thus, in the long run, much better off. He had his cross to bear, but that's what life is all about, he decided, putting his coat back on. Alex took one final look at his mate, smiling, as the future called him on.

Outside, a cold night mist licked into every pore, dampening the world in a shivering haze. But Alex didn't care. He had done it – he had made it through the toughest times and finally woken up to what needed to be done. His car pulled away and swerved out of the hospital car park, revving excitedly as Alex said goodbye, feeling the rush of speed as he zoomed down the dual carriageway. But Alex slowed down ever so slightly, knowing better. Growing up was hard, he conceded. But for Alex, at last, life had begun. Truly begun.

17

CHLOE

So Chloe had done it – she had stepped out of the bubble, at least a little, into her drama degree and had lasted over a week now, timidly edging into her new life, like a child dipping their toes in the water, testing the temperature before plunging into the splashy blue. There would be no plunging for Chloe, but so far things hadn't been as bad as she'd expected, as she allowed herself to admit that the course, and the people, were actually quite cool. She found the acting difficult, though, as her recent lack of confidence made her so much more conscious of herself as she performed tasks in front of her small class, lacking the faith in her abilities which she used to have. But the teachers had managed to put her at ease, and already she felt as if she had made progress, remembering just how much she loved acting and appreciating the praise which she received as a result of it. There were seven girls and five boys in her class, and Chloe had been a bit dubious about them on the first couple of days, particularly since a lot of them seemed to be performing from the moment they had walked in the door. But thankfully they had calmed down a bit and thus had allowed the quieter members of the group to begin to crawl out of their shells, placing the twelve on more of a level playing field, which Chloe much preferred.

So maybe she hadn't made the wrong choice after all – though as her girlfriends regaled her with tales from UCD and Trinity, listing off all the childhood sweethearts and infamous names with which they were now mingling, Chloe couldn't help but feel jealous, not recognising any of her fellow drama students, not even recognising the names of the schools some of them had gone to.

But in a way, that was a good thing too. Ever since her breakdown, and the simple perfection that had been her last night with Sam, Chloe was determined to start afresh. These people were a completely new group, and for that, she was silently grateful. Their country accents and banter made her smile, their friendly ways made her relaxed and suddenly the "Southside Bubble" didn't seem like the only option. Especially since she didn't exactly know what was going on with her old friends anyway – she was still speaking to Heather, but the fact that she was completely oblivious to just how upset Chloe had been about her bringing Andy to the debs still shocked Chloe. Did she honestly not see the problem with what she had done? And what was more, did she not notice that Chloe had been slightly off with her and that the pair hadn't talked much at all since the night of the debs? Presumably she would say that she was just too immersed in college life, but that was no excuse, Chloe reminded herself, adamant that no one was finding this period of transition as difficult as she was, having no familiar faces greeting her from day to day. But Chloe told herself to focus on the positives, as she began to learn that these new people didn't have to know the stuff about her she didn't want them to. They would never comment on her losing weight, for they had never known her any other size. They would never ask her about Sam, or their break-up, or Andy, because she didn't have to mention them – she didn't have to tell them, so they would never know. This anonymity reminded her of something to which Sam had once referred, making Chloe smile as she wondered how he was enjoying his new surroundings, as his adventure unfolded. She had contemplated texting him, just to see how he was getting on, but had decided that maybe it was too soon – maybe they both needed more time to get used to the idea of all ties being severed before they started trying to piece together a friendship which, Chloe sincerely hoped, would last.

Sometimes she still couldn't believe that they had broken up – it seemed odd after so long that he was not a part of her life at all. And in ways, it had all happened so quickly – one minute they had been together, and the next they were completely finished and he was living in a different country. Chloe sighed, still feeling mixed emotions about the whole thing, still wondering what would have happened had she not cheated on him. Sam had said that their split had been coming for a while – that their relationship had been fading – but if they hadn't had something concrete as the reason for the end, then would they just have continued as they were? Would they have given a long-distance relationship a shot? Chloe's mind wandered as she lay on her bed, weary from another day's monologues, her energy sapped from an entire afternoon of pretending to be other people, pretending to care what they said and felt and did. It had been fun, but each character had taken a little bit out of Chloe, leaving her ultimately drained of all remains of herself, tired and hungry. The former could be easily solved, as her feather duvet snuggled beneath her, drawing her in. The latter wasn't so easy. She knew things had to change – her mother was looking into counsellors for her to see – but for now, Chloe was just focusing on accepting that she had a problem and, most of all, that she needed to fix it.

She needed to start going to the gym again – to keep fit; but to stop relying on her old ways to keep her from putting on weight wasn't going to be easy. Still, she knew she had to do it, and she knew her mother would be there every step of the way. So she was moving on, doing herself proud. But properly proud this time – and that was the best bit of all.

*

Wednesday night meant going-out night, yet as Chloe dolled herself up for the evening ahead, straightening her hair on autopilot, her mind was somewhere else. Today in class they had been reading dialogues, and she and one of the boys, Hugh, had been given a rather romantic scene from a modern play to do. Chloe got on really well with Hugh and enjoyed preparing with him, as he kept her laughing all morning. She noted that he had amazing blue eyes too. Chloe also really liked the piece they were doing and was looking forward to acting it out, so that when the time came to perform in front of the whole group, she was eager to do it well, really throwing herself into the tenderness of the moment. The scene progressed, Hugh looking into her eyes with soft passion as he read the lines with sweet sincerity. In turn, Chloe fed off his emotion, finding herself completely transported by the script and she became lost in its power and intensity. They were nearly finished. The audience were silent and wide-eyed, enthralled by the magnificent performance as the bittersweet climax arrived unexpectedly.

"I just don't love you any more," Hugh whispered through the stillness, and Chloe heard their fellow classmates gasp. But as she stared at him, knowing what her next line was and preparing to say it, there was suddenly something in his eyes, something about the way he'd denounced his love for her – for her character – that made Chloe's mind screech to a halt. Images of Sam flooded in on top of

308

her, until she became entrapped by memories, desperate to be free. Sam didn't love her any more. He had said he still cared, but the look in Hugh's eyes right now, as he stood by his line, was exactly the look which Sam had worn at the debs, a mixture of tenderness and pity – the ultimate pathos.

Chloe felt tears erupting and she fled from the room, petrified that she was about to break down in front of a group of relative strangers. She made for the bathroom but knew they would follow her there, feeling too ashamed to let them see her like this. So instead she had left the building and run out onto the streets, lowering her head as she faded into the steady flow of passers-by. She walked and walked, calming herself down, perplexed by what had just come over her and feeling like such an idiot. Why had the memory of Sam had such a profound effect on her?

Now, finishing her hair, Chloe couldn't figure it out, blaming tiredness in general for her behaviour – she still wasn't strong, that much she knew. Some of her classmates had texted her to see if she was OK, and although she had tried to cover it up, insisting she was fine, Chloe now prayed she wouldn't bump into any of the drama crew that night in town when she went out, fearing that even the least bit of tipsiness would send her into a longwinded spiel about exactly why she had reacted as she did to the scene – sparing them absolutely no details about her recent break-up. It wouldn't be pretty.

Still, as she sat in a taxi with Ella and Heather, cruising into town after a few warm-up drinks, Chloe found herself more chilled out again. She was wearing a new purple top over her denim miniskirt, her fake-tanned legs shivering as she stepped out of the cab, the winter arriving in a gust along the footpath with biting severity. The club had a large queue outside it, and the glamorously clad young adults huddled close to one another, yearning to be inside, free from the crisp bite of September's farewell. The girls joined the line, saying little as they moved their way up it – too cold to talk as they cursed the elements for sobering them up.

Finally they were indoors, the low lighting, pumping beats and musky heat bombarding them as they checked their coats into the cloakroom and went to the bar, ordering drinks in the hope of restoring their former tipsiness as quickly as possible. The club was hopping, surging with trendy bodies who meeted and greeted one another and the steamy atmosphere was caressed with air-kisses. Knocking back her Smirnoff Ice, Chloe's eyes scanned the crowd, searching for familiar faces – not wanting to spend her whole evening with an unapologetic Heather, who was still annoying her, even tonight. Jenny, Alex's girlfriend, was nearby, dancing jovially with her friends. Two guys who lived on Chloe's road leaned on the opposite bar, talking excitedly, gesticulating this way and that. But there was no one Chloe could see that she actually felt like talking to. Even her brother would do. She just felt like meeting someone. But there was no one to be seen. Until she saw him.

Andy and Kyle had just come out of the men's toilets, laughing about some private joke as they rejoined the masses, nudging one another with lively playfulness. Andy was looking great in his red polo shirt and jeans, his smile dazzling beneath the disco lights which made the twinkle in his eye even more pronounced than usual. Chloe watched his every move, trying to figure out what it was that she was feeling. Girls in all directions watched him too, wanting him, trying to catch his eye. But Chloe wasn't one of those girls. Finally she realised that there never was and never was going to be anything between them. She didn't like him – not really, not in a way that actually meant anything. Plus, Andy signified the old her – the past, the awful summer she longed to learn from but forget. She gazed at him one last time, but then turned away. In that moment, Chloe felt closure, and it felt good. It was time to move forward, to new things, to better things.

Chloe spotted another familiar face in the crowd. It was Hugh – the boy from her drama class. He was too far away to call over, but

310

despite her embarrassment from earlier on, Chloe found she wanted to talk to him. Her neck tingled.

She crossed the room and joined the girls in doing some shots before hitting the dance floor. The night was going amazingly. But then she saw Hugh again, and butterflies in her stomach danced. What was going on? Why had seeing him here, amidst hundreds of other people, made her entire body feel drawn to him? Maybe she was drunk. She must be. But it was a pleasant sensation nonetheless, and Chloe felt herself blushing beneath the flashing lights.

Suddenly, as if he could feel the intensity of Chloe's stares from the other side of the club, Hugh turned and looked straight at her. Her heart leaped, startled by the precision of his gaze as he caught her focusing right on him. Chloe blushed even more, not sure whether to look away or to hold the stare of those eyes, as he began to approach.

"Psst, Chloe . . . who's that guy coming over?" Ella asked under her breath, having her friend's back and ensuring that she wasn't caught off-guard by any unwanted visitors.

But Hugh was wanted, and as Chloe walked towards him, seeking for their paths to meet away from her friends – to have him to herself – she threw her shoulders back, sucked her stomach in and strutted as perfectly as she could, until they were face to face.

"Hey," Hugh greeted, giving her a kiss on the cheek.

"Hey," she returned, feeling unusually coy.

"Having a good night?"

"Yeah, it's savage. What about you?"

"Yeah, so far so good." Hugh answered with a grin in his gorgeous Galway accent.

"Listen, Hugh, about earlier–"

"Don't worry about it," Hugh interjected, not wanting her to feel she had to explain.

"No, it's just I was upset . . . and it made me think about my ex, and . . ."

"Seriously, Chloe. Don't worry about it – as long as you're all right now?" Hugh asked, seemingly genuinely concerned.

"Yeah, I'm fine!" Chloe replied with a grin, glad that they'd got over that topic of conversation so swiftly.

"Great. So can I buy you a drink then?" Chloe willingly accepted.

So they continued talking, easing into one another's company, and Chloe slowly found herself beginning to flirt, her instincts telling her not to, but her reason reminding her that she was single now. And she was here with such a cool guy. Not only was he cool, but he represented something new – an unfamiliar face, from an unfamiliar world, a foreigner to the Southside regularity in which she'd found herself confined for so long. Chloe realised that if she was going to move on from her murky past, her messy summer, then Hugh was the perfect start. She wanted to take it slowly, though – it was still far too soon after Sam, and her heart needed time to heal before she got involved in anything even vaguely serious. But as it was, getting to know this seemingly lovely guy, Chloe felt on top of the world, taking baby steps into a better place, where she felt freer than she had in so long.

After almost an hour, the pair parted, heading their separate ways and wishing each other a pleasant evening.

"Is it OK if I, like . . . you know . . . text you or whatever . . . I mean . . ." Hugh tried nervously.

"Yeah, of course," Chloe said, delighted. "I'd love you too."

"OK, cool, well have a good night."

"You too," she returned, brimming with happiness as she turned away. She wouldn't rush into anything, she promised, but the tiny beginnings – the vague potential which had glistened tonight – could only bring good things. Chloe didn't stop smiling once all night.

*

Her smile didn't show any sign of leaving any time soon either. It flickered, but it never fully went away. Days passed, autumn faded but Chloe could already feel herself growing stronger. It was still hard to eat a proper dinner. It was still hard to think of Sam and realise just how far away he was. But Chloe was trying to focus on the positive things – how much she enjoyed her course, how amazing her mum was being – because those were the things that mattered. For the first time in so long, Chloe was able to look at life and see a brighter place, where gradually she could be herself – her happy self. There were still moments of weakness, when the old her came crawling back. More than once this week, she had found herself kneeling before the toilet bowl, her fingers poised, ready to do the awful deed. But somehow she had looked within herself and said "no". Just one mistake and she would erase the temporary glimmer of hope to which she was clinging – its glow was feeble, but with time, she knew it would grow. Her mother had arranged for her to see a food counsellor next week, and though the idea made Chloe nervous, if that was what had to be done, then she was prepared to give it a shot.

But there was one thing that was still left unresolved – one person with whom she still needed to put things right, especially if there was any hope of making it through these turbulent times. As she hopped off the bus and walked through the chilly evening air to Heather's house, the grey outdoors nipped at her soul. The breeze tickled passers-by, carrying on it the fading scent of shiny conkers, which sat beneath the trees, awaiting collection by juvenile warlords. Chloe was nervous, and although things were picking up for her, this was the one area where the outcome seemed uncertain – things really had been rocky between the pair, and maybe the future would decree that these two girls were going to go their separate ways. But despite their fading closeness this summer, that was a reality which Chloe prayed would not occur – she needed her friend more than ever, and she hoped it wasn't too late.

"Hey," Heather greeted her, opening the door to her friend and letting her in, "thanks for coming."

"Oh . . . no problem." Chloe replied, stepping into the sitting room and realising just how long it felt since she'd been there.

The girls stared at the ground, avoiding one another's eyes.

"Do you want, like, a cup of tea or something?" Heather offered, the awkwardness between them painfully palpable.

But Chloe didn't want tea. She just wanted things not to feel like this, and there was only one way of doing that. She dug deep within herself, longing to put things right.

"Heather, please – can we just talk about this? This is horrible," she began, exasperated by the throbbing silence.

"I know it is, Chloe . . . but what do you want me to do about it?" Heather snapped.

Chloe was shocked. "What?"

Heather was silent, looking as if she too was having to dig very deep to say the things which lurked within. Her eyes were tired.

"Look, I'm sorry . . . I just . . ." Heather sighed, her frustration evident, "I just feel like I know how this conversation is going to go, and it just pisses me off, OK?"

Chloe said nothing. Her friend was so much more angry than she had anticipated, and it was throwing her off completely. She was scared.

"What . . . what do you mean?" she finally asked.

Heather paused, collecting her thoughts as she stared away from her friend.

"I just . . . I knew you'd come here, and you'd tell me you've been messed up all summer, and you had an eating disorder but you're getting better now, and that we can be OK again, blah blah blah . . ." Heather's voice was bitter.

Again, Chloe was taken aback. Her friend really did seem annoyed, and what was worse, maybe that was how Chloe had imagined things would pan out. Had she got it wrong? Her mind raced with panic, her body freezing in nervous fear. Luckily, Heather continued.

"But, I mean . . . firstly – how am I supposed to believe you? Why should I take your word for it that you're better? All bloody summer you've lied and lied to me over and over again, and every fucking time I fell for it, Chloe . . ." she spat, fiddling with her necklace agitatedly.

"I'm sorry–"

"But that's not all," Heather said, clearly not finished, "not only do I feel like a gullible idiot, not only do I feel like it is going to be a long, long time before I can trust you again . . . not only that, Chloe . . . but I also feel hurt . . . like, so much." Heather stopped, her voice losing strength. "You just kept pushing me away . . . like you didn't want to know . . . like you just didn't care any more . . ."

"Heather–"

"And I know I shouldn't have brought Andy to the debs – I know that – but I was just so angry, Chloe . . . I was just so sick of you making me feel like shit . . . and I know that's pathetic of me, but I couldn't help it . . . you were my best friend," she finished, her voice a mere whisper.

Chloe was shocked. Her friend was nearly in tears, and Chloe couldn't believe what she'd just heard. She had never thought about it like that – never looked at it from Heather's perspective. She realised just how bad things were. Everything had changed.

"Heather, I don't know what to say . . . I knew things were shit, but not this shit. I never realised just how much I've been hurting you . . ."

Chloe struggled to find the words. Her confidence receded into the darkness from which it had been creeping this past week. She had been a fool to think it would be easy. She'd created much more of a mess than that.

"I guess all I can ask is that you give me a chance . . . I know I don't deserve it but . . ." Chloe tried to find a reason, to justify what she was asking. But she couldn't. It was a wonder Heather was still talking to her at all. How disgusting she had been to think Heather had been the one in the wrong all along. This was Chloe's fault, all of it. Her tears began to spill. She'd ruined everything.

But somehow, her friend wasn't giving up on her; not yet.

"Maybe you don't deserve another chance, Chloe . . . Maybe things are better this way . . ." Heather began, her eyes too welling up. Chloe prayed she'd continue. Finally she did. "But you were sick, Chloe, that much I know. And maybe you are getting better – I'm not sure . . . but if you are, then I want to help you . . ."

Chloe couldn't believe it. She stared into her friend's eyes for the first time and saw that she really meant it. Her heart leapt – it was too good to be true. Throwing her arms around Heather, Chloe squeezed her as tightly as she could, her tears pouring down in joyous relief. She felt her friend squeeze back – an embrace which felt so long overdue.

"Heather, I don't–"

"Ssh." Her friend silenced her, for words could not do justice to the intense relief which filled them both.

They cried and cried, laughing at one another for their girlie dramatics but not caring for, in that instant, things were back on track – friendship had proven that it could withstand even the toughest of times, even the toughest of summers. Chloe and Heather had made it, and what was best of all, they had made it together – and that made it taste all the more sweet.

*

That night in bed, Chloe sank into her sheets, feeling completely drained but strangely content. The musky darkness fuzzed all around her as dreamland called her downwards. She longed to look back over it all – over her day, her week, her summer – but her mind was weak with pure exhaustion. The buzzing of her phone was the only thing to make her move.

HEY CHLOE ITS HUGH. JUS WONDERIN IF U WANA GRAB A DRINK R SUMTIN AFTER COLLEGE 2MO? XX

Chloe grinned. There was nothing she would enjoy more. Quickly she replied.

SOUNDS SAVAGE. CANT W8 XX

And she really couldn't. Everything was looking up for Chloe Walsh and, despite her wounds still not having quite healed, the future promised that, in time, they would. Scars would remain, but they would only make her stronger. The moon cast a silvery light down upon the slumbering world, as sleep crept up on Chloe, this young woman on the cusp of her adult existence. For a while she hadn't known which way she would fall – headfirst into the promising future or backwards into the sinking darkness, where merciless shadows lurked and growled. But somehow, she had finally taken that plunge into a land of possibilities, where anything could occur – it was scary, but it was new, and right now, that was all Chloe needed. Her eyes shut gently, leaving her only a moment more to think. Growing up was hard, she conceded. But for Chloe, at last, life had begun. Truly begun.

18

The phone call had arrived on Thursday afternoon. It had been Barry's father. Alex had answered the phone. They had exchanged very few words, neither knowing what to say. It had been awful. It still was.

*

It was now Saturday morning, and the funeral was starting in just over an hour. Alex was in his room trying to do his tie, but for some reason was having trouble tying the knot correctly. Every morning for school, for as long as he could remember, he had carried out this simple task, yet here he was, fumbling like a clumsy fool. He hadn't been able to think straight since the moment he'd put down the phone and felt his whole world come crashing down around him. Alex was numb. His body refused to comprehend what had occurred and, strangely, the only thought which filled his mind was that he, Alex Walsh, had been the last person to see Barry alive – his last visitor. It felt like some strange privilege he didn't deserve. It didn't make sense. None of it did.

Last night, Alex had just lain in bed, staring at the ceiling, as the most bizarre mixture of thoughts rushed through his exhausted mind. He and Barry, aged twelve, throwing water bombs from the top floor of their school building onto the headmaster's head and never being caught for it. Sheer genius! Barry phoning Alex after the first time he'd had sex – a strange moment of proud bonding which they had bashfully enjoyed. And then there it was again, that single image of Barry putting the key into the ignition, and starting the engine, and pulling away, and zooming down the road, and the music, and the air, and the speed, and the traffic light . . .

"Fuck," Alex snarled, messing up his tie again. Why was he being such an idiot? He wanted to look perfect – to pay his respects in his black suit and tie and give Barry the goodbye he deserved. Not that he deserved any goodbye at all. That was the worst bit of all – that this entire event was the most unfair ordeal into which Alex had ever faced, and more than ever in his whole life, he felt truly alone. Jenny had called him a couple of times since the news had got out, but he had cancelled her calls. Andy had phoned too – to say that the Carter parents wanted the two of them to do a reading at the funeral. Alex hadn't known what to say. Surely the fact that Barry's parents hadn't even been able to ask him themselves reflected perfectly clearly what they thought of him. So how could he stand up there, in front of what was sure to be an overflowing congregation, and read God's word, when all he'd be able to hear would be the whispering mumbles of the entire church, nudging one another and informing their friends, "that's the boy who was in the car with him", "he's the one who survived"? They would look at him with sympathetic eyes, but unable to prevent the sense of injustice which would surely fill them as they thought of Barry Carter and his heartbreaking tragedy. Alex loathed the idea.

But for once in his life, Alex realised that this wasn't about him – this was about Barry Carter. And if his parents were offering Alex the honour of contributing to the send-off of his greatest friend, then he would take the glares and stares and murmuring audience and read those words as best he could. Because no matter what they thought – no matter how much they hated him – at least he was alive. Never again could Alex complain or feel anything other than eternally privileged for all that lay before him, for a simple truth had settled upon him over the preceding days: anything was better than nothing, than Barry's nothing.

Alex's parents had been brilliant – offering their support, but knowing that it was too soon, knowing that all they could do was wait for Alex to be ready, and pray and pour their hearts out in thanksgiving that they still had their son. Alex knew his father was especially cut up by it all, the accident never having left his mind, as he called on God more and more for any help he could possibly give. At least all Alex's school friends were going to be there today – a group of teenage boys now transformed into men, as the first of life's tragedies provided them with a new, frightening wisdom: forever didn't exist anymore, and youth was but a sweet memory.

Alex stared at himself in the mirror. Just as things had started to fall into place for him, this had come along and shattered everything. He was repeating school, he had a girlfriend for whom he cared so much and finally he'd woken up to the reality that he needed to change – he needed to realise just how lucky he was and start appreciating life. He got it – he'd learned his lesson. So why on earth had this happened? How had he lost one of his best friends just when life was actually going well – just when the stormy future was finally making sense? He couldn't understand and he realised he probably never would. For once, that would have to do.

"Do you want a hand with that?" A timid voice crept in as Chloe poked her head through the slightly ajar door.

"What?"

"The tie," she replied gently, stepping into the room in her black jeans and jacket, her hair tied back into a tidy ponytail.

Alex didn't reply, but watched as she crossed the room to him and gingerly began to undo the mess he'd made of the tie. She worked in silence, occasionally catching her brother's eye as she slowly carried out her task. She looked well, Alex noted, her face still thin and withdrawn but a vague vitality creeping back in where it had been lacking for so long now. It felt strange to have her so close – they never hugged or kissed or displayed any sort of sibling affection – yet here she was, tying his tie, and for a reason which Alex couldn't quite work out, he appreciated it more than he had ever appreciated anything before.

"There. All done," Chloe triumphed, smoothing down her handiwork and taking a step back from her brother, wanting to say a million things but not knowing quite how.

"Thanks," Alex answered, meaning it with all his heart.

They stood for a few seconds, not sure what to do, having never been in a situation even vaguely close to this before, until Chloe just gave an awkward but sincere smile and turned to leave the room.

But Alex wasn't finished.

"Chloe," he called after her, stopping her in her tracks.

"Yeah?" she replied, sounding surprised.

"Look, Chloe, I just wanted to check that you're, like . . . you know . . . that you're . . . OK? I mean . . . I know this summer hasn't been that great for you, and that you've been a bit . . . well . . . you know . . ." Alex tried, finding it hard to set his thoughts to words. Luckily Chloe seemed to have caught on.

"Yeah, Alex – I'm fine. Not there yet, but I'll get there, you know?"

"OK . . . good . . . well, good . . . I just, I know it hasn't been easy, yeah? I just hope . . . I just wanted to check you're all right again," he mumbled, tiptoeing further into his sister's personal life than he had ever dared to and realising just how separate they'd always kept from one another. In that moment, it felt like such a shame.

"And what about you?" Chloe asked in return. "Today's not going to be easy . . ."

"No."

"But, like, I'm here for you . . . you know?" she offered softly.

"Yeah . . . yeah, I know . . . thanks."

Chloe smiled. They stood once more in unfamiliar territory, yet somehow closer than ever before. Chloe began to laugh. Alex was confused.

"What's so funny?" he enquired gingerly, slightly put off.

"Just look at us," Chloe remarked, still chuckling nervously. "What are we like?"

"Yeah, I know," he affirmed with a smile.

A silent moment of reflection passed between them, as their minds raced through a barrage of thoughts, so many of them the same.

"What a summer," Chloe summarised, her laughter steadying as her face eased back into seriousness.

"Tell me about it." Alex sighed.

Silence hung once more.

"But we made it," Chloe reminded him, brighter again.

Tentatively, she placed her hand on Alex's arm, her slender fingers softly squeezing him in a rare moment of affection. Alex looked at her.

"Yeah . . . yeah, we did," he assured her, casting his eyes down upon the gesture and acknowledging it with a smile. It was only the simplest of touches, but it meant so much. For it was true – somehow, they had made it.

*

Chloe left her brother's room, heading downstairs to get some tissues for her handbag, dreading the coming hours. She didn't know how Alex was being so strong. Then again, there was something about him which told her he wasn't, that he was hurting, and Chloe found a strange comfort in this, knowing that at least he was human and that, after all this time, he still cared. She caught a glimpse of herself in the hall mirror as she made for the kitchen. She paused. Time had changed her, there was no doubt about that. But finally, Chloe was in a place in which she could begin to smile, in which she could look to the future and realise that things could only get better and that the past few months would soon be erased into an insignificant memory, when life was dark and gloomy but was now replaced with the glowing light of possibilities. Maybe Barry's death had finally put it all into perspective. But either way, Chloe had made it out the other end of a life-changing summer, and though it still wasn't easy, she knew that time would make it all better and that she, Chloe Walsh, would be better too.

*

September's dregs lurked outside the window panes, as a biting wind called forth a silent group of mourners. Alex and Chloe were just two of the hundreds coming to pay their respects. They sat beside one another in the back of the Walshs' car, where not a word was spoken all the way to the church. Alex stared out his window. Chloe stared out hers. The future stared back at both of them, smiling, knowing that life wasn't easy but promising the twins that, from now on, things were going to be OK. The time had come and, somehow, they had made it. This time, they really had.

Acknowledgements

I can't believe that I am here, writing the acknowledgements for my second novel – it feels surreal yet amazing, and there are a great number of incredible people to whom I owe this feeling:

Mum, my best friend, and Dad, my hero – I hope retirement brings you all the happiness that you deserve, and lots more trips to Cambridge for copious amounts of cocktails! Love always.

David, the world's best brother. I can't tell you how nice it is to be back in the same country as you – we should celebrate in this great little Italian place I know! And to Julie-Ann and Sophie – for making him smile so very much.

The Holohans, Gilligans, Fitzgeralds, Crosbies, Canavans, Cantrells, Powells, Duffs and all my extended family for their unfailing generosity and love. Thank you.

David Snower, for our time together – rescued into the past.

Patricia Scanlan, my 'book mother', for holding my hand and remaining one hundred per cent behind me.

Mrs. Quin and Alil, whom I will never forget for their continued support, and for helping me get to where I am today.

Ciara Considine, my editor, for making me feel like an actual writer, and helping me to improve, develop and create a book of which I am so proud.

Breda Purdue, Ciara Doorley, Ruth Shern and all at Hodder Headline Ireland – great publishers, and great friends – for all their hard work in helping *Forget* get to number one, along with Jennie Cotter at Plunkett Communications – a legend!

To my friends in Cambridge – everyone in Caius, the English crew and all the other wicked people who made my first year just so much fun, confirming that I definitely made the right choice. The Five, and all the other lovely ladies – here's to shisha, Prêt lunches and dancing the night away. The boys – my two amigos, the Six Nations posse, and all the other young gentlemen with good 'chat' and even better 'banter', for keeping a smile always on my face.

To my friends from home. Here we are, a year on, and nothing has changed – long may it continue. The Jay's Green Devil, JP '05, Pornstars and the rest of my stunning girls – here's to weekly emails, the best Inter-railing holiday ever, and knowing that Forever Young really does mean forever. The lads, for providing so much quality material for the book, and remaining just as hilariously carefree as always – especially all those who enjoy a spot of 'pirouetting' in the streets!

And finally, to everyone who survived Ayia Napa – this book is for you!